Walt Disney

# MICKEY MOUSE

## Dark Mines of the
## Phantom Metal

## Dark Mines of the Phantom Metal

From Italian *Topolino* #2880, 2011
Writer and Artist: Andrea "Casty" Castellan
Inker: Michele Mazzon
Colorists: Disney Italia with Nicole and Travis Seitler
Letterers: Nicole and Travis Seitler
Translation and Dialogue: Jonathan H. Gray

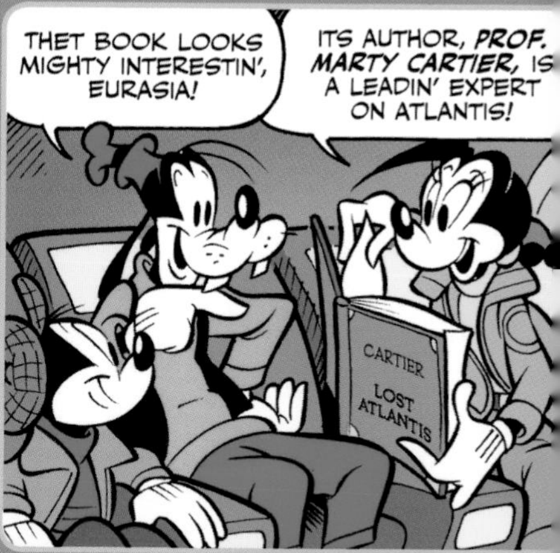
THET BOOK LOOKS MIGHTY INTERESTIN', EURASIA!
ITS AUTHOR, PROF. MARTY CARTIER, IS A LEADIN' EXPERT ON ATLANTIS!
CARTIER
LOST ATLANTIS

## Goofy Gift

From Australian *Mickey Mouse* #3, 1953
Artist and Letterer: Dick Moores
Colorist: Digikore Studios

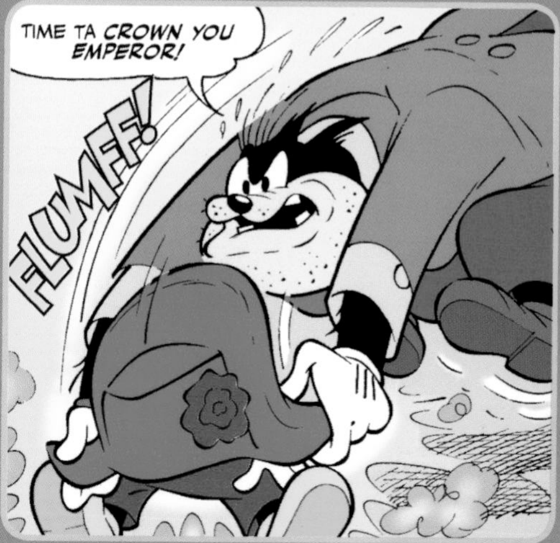
TIME TA CROWN YOU EMPEROR!
FLUMFF!

## The Twelve Buttons of Napoleon

From Italian *Topolino* #1073, 1976
Writer and Artist: Romano Scarpa
Inker: Sandro Zemolin
Colorists: Digikore Studios
Letterers: Nicole and Travis Seitler
Translation and Dialogue: Joe Torcivia

## Dogs of War

From Italian *Topolino* #2822, 2009
Writer and Artist: Marco Palazzi
Colorist: Disney Italia
Letterers: Nicole and Travis Seitler
Translation and Dialogue: David Gerstein

Special thanks to Daniel Saeva, Julie Dorris, Manny Mederos, Roberto Santillo, Chris Troise, Camilla Vedove, Stefano Ambrosio, and Carlotta Quattrocolo.

For international rights, contact **licensing@idwpublishing.com**

ISBN: 978-1-63140-857-1

20 19 18 17 1 2 3 4

IDW®
www.IDWPUBLISHING.com

**Ted Adams**, CEO & Publisher • **Greg Goldstein**, President & COO • **Robbie Robbins**, EVP/Sr. Graphic Artist • **Chris Ryall**, Chief Creative Officer • **David Hedgecock**, Editor-in-Chief • **Laurie Windrow**, Senior Vice President of Sales & Marketing • **Matthew Ruzicka**, CPA, Chief Financial Officer • **Dirk Wood**, VP of Marketing • **Lorelei Bunjes**, VP of Digital Services • **Jeff Webber**, VP of Licensing, Digital and Subsidiary Rights • **Jerry Bennington**, VP of New Product Development

Facebook: facebook.com/idwpublishing • Twitter: @idwpublishing • YouTube: youtube.com/idwpublishing
Tumblr: tumblr.idwpublishing.com • Instagram: instagram.com/idwpublishing



Originally published as MICKEY MOUSE issues #13–16 (Legacy #323–325).

## The Same Old Story

From *Mickey Mouse* Sunday comic strip, 1939
Writer: Merrill De Maris
Artist: Manuel Gonzales
Inker and Letterer: Ted Thwaites
Colorist: Digikore Studios

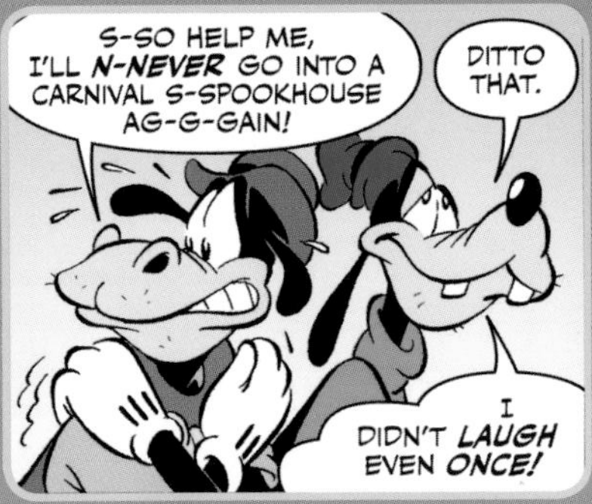
S-SO HELP ME, I'LL N-NEVER GO INTO A CARNIVAL S-SPOOKHOUSE AG-G-GAIN!
DITTO THAT.
I DIDN'T LAUGH EVEN ONCE!

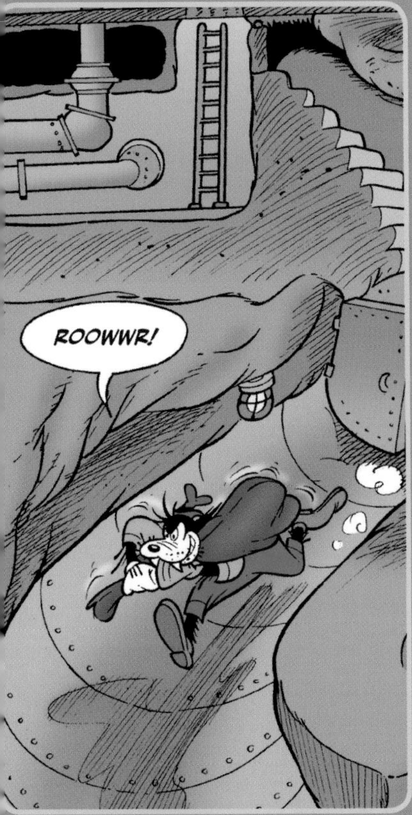
ROOWWR!

## A Goofy Look at Fear

From Dutch *Donald Duck* #44/2004
Writer: Jos Beekman
Artist: Michel Nadorp
Colorists: Sanoma with Nicole and Travis Seitler
Letterers: Nicole and Travis Seitler
Translation and Dialogue: Jonathan H. Gray

## The Weregoof's Curse

From Italian *Topolino* #1102, 1977
Writer and Artist: Romano Scarpa
Inker: Sandro Del Conte
Colorists: Digikore Studios with Erik Rosengarten
Letterers: Nicole and Travis Seitler
Translation and Dialogue: Thad Komorowski

## Egg-shell-ent

From British *Mickey Mouse Annual* #1, 1930
Writer, Artist, and Letterer: Wilfred Haughton
Colorist: Digikore Studios

Series Editor: Sarah Gaydos
Archival Editor: David Gerstein

Cover Artist: Andrea "Casty" Castellan and Michele Mazzon
Cover Colorist: Andrea "Casty" Castellan
Collection Editors: Justin Eisinger
& Alonzo Simon
Collection Designer: Clyde Grapa
Publisher: Ted Adams

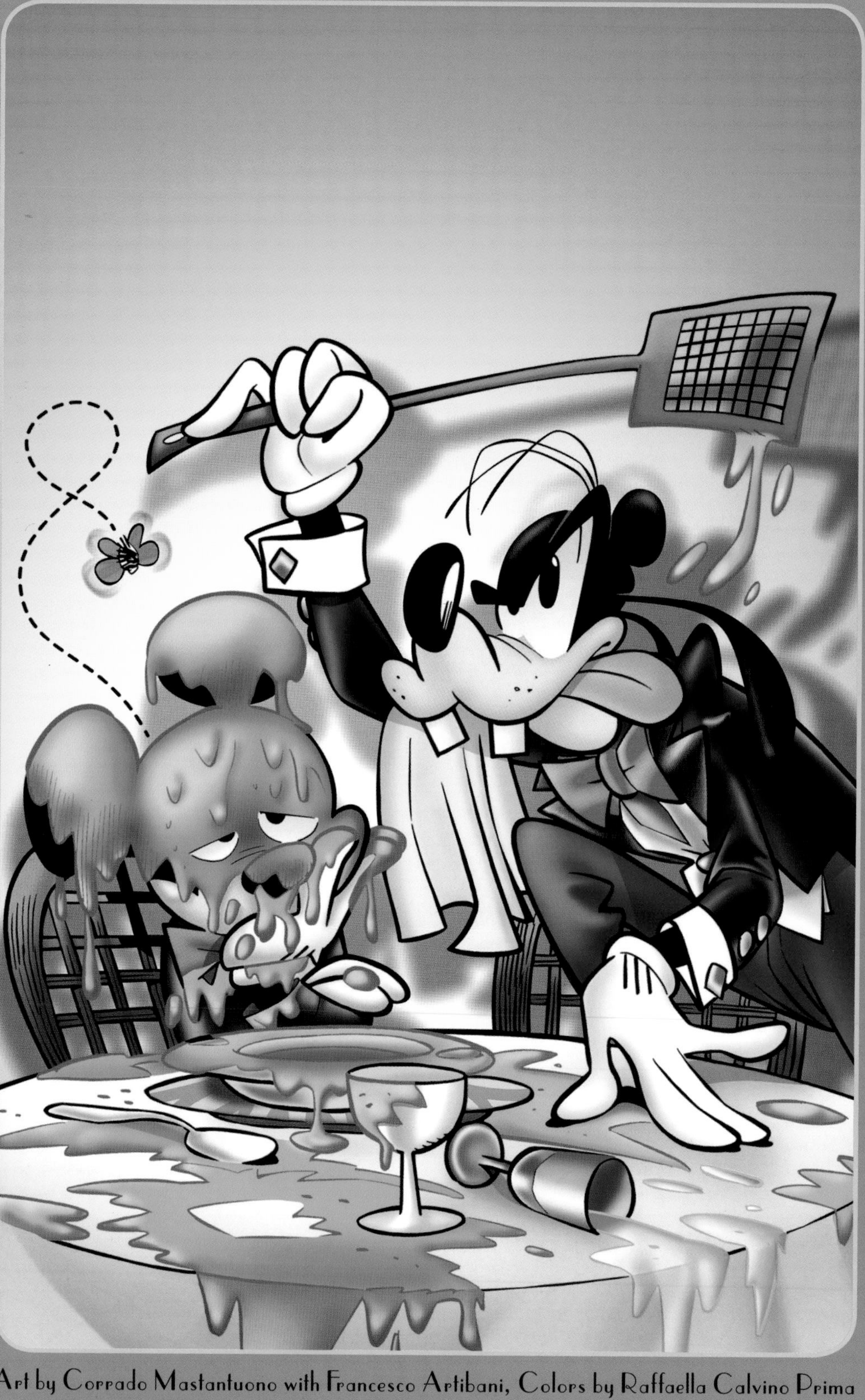

Art by Corrado Mastantuono with Francesco Artibani, Colors by Raffaella Calvino Prima

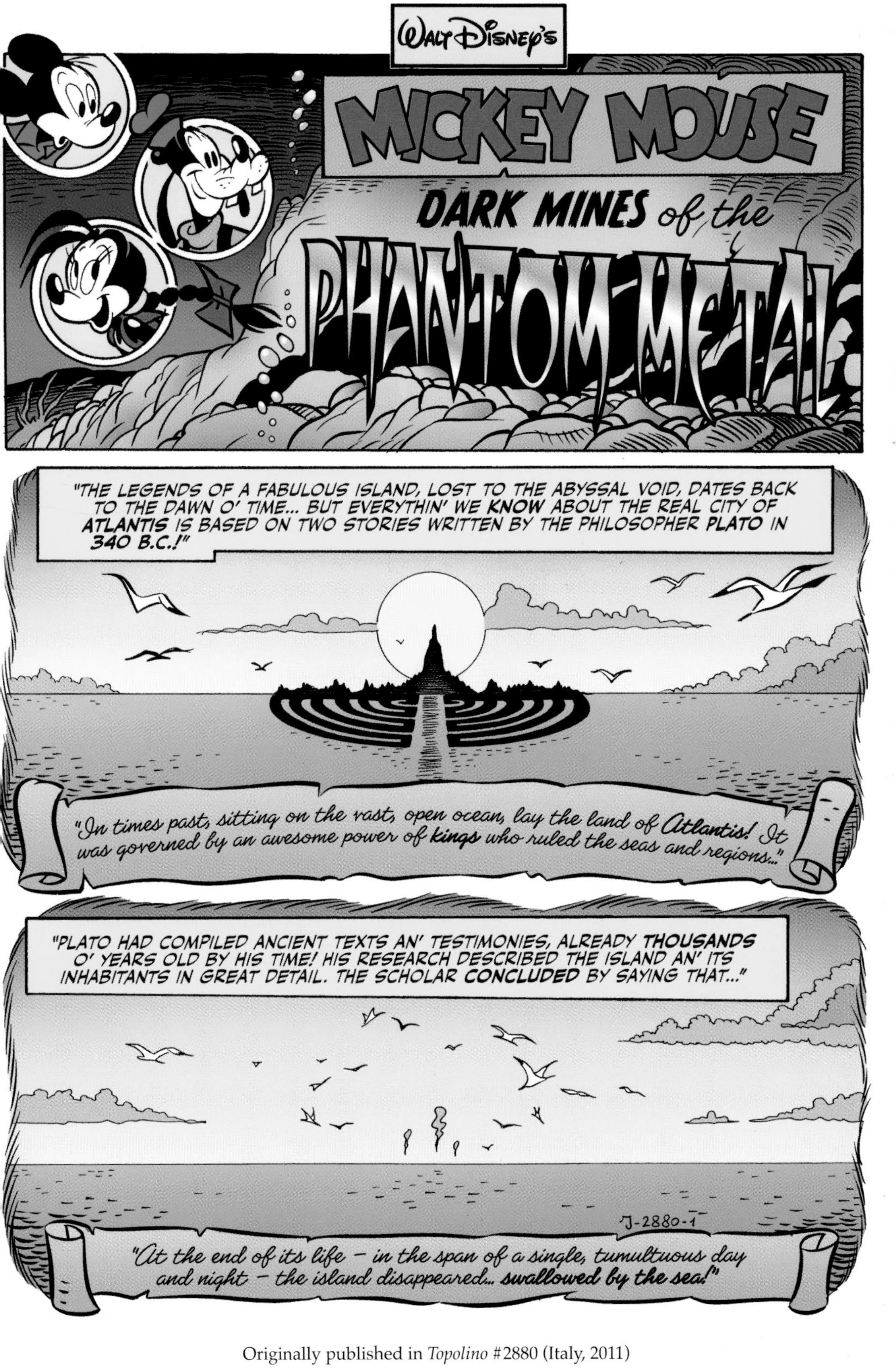
WALT DISNEY'S
MICKEY MOUSE
DARK MINES of the PHANTOM METAL
"THE LEGENDS OF A FABULOUS ISLAND, LOST TO THE ABYSSAL VOID, DATES BACK TO THE DAWN O' TIME... BUT EVERYTHIN' WE **KNOW** ABOUT THE REAL CITY OF **ATLANTIS** IS BASED ON TWO STORIES WRITTEN BY THE PHILOSOPHER **PLATO** IN 340 B.C.!"
"In times past, sitting on the vast, open ocean, lay the land of Atlantis! It was governed by an awesome power of **kings** who ruled the seas and regions..."
"PLATO HAD COMPILED ANCIENT TEXTS AN' TESTIMONIES, ALREADY **THOUSANDS** O' YEARS OLD BY HIS TIME! HIS RESEARCH DESCRIBED THE ISLAND AN' ITS INHABITANTS IN GREAT DETAIL. THE SCHOLAR **CONCLUDED** BY SAYING THAT..."
J-2880-1
"At the end of its life – in the span of a single, tumultuous day and night – the island disappeared... **swallowed by the sea!**"

Originally published in *Topolino* #2880 (Italy, 2011)

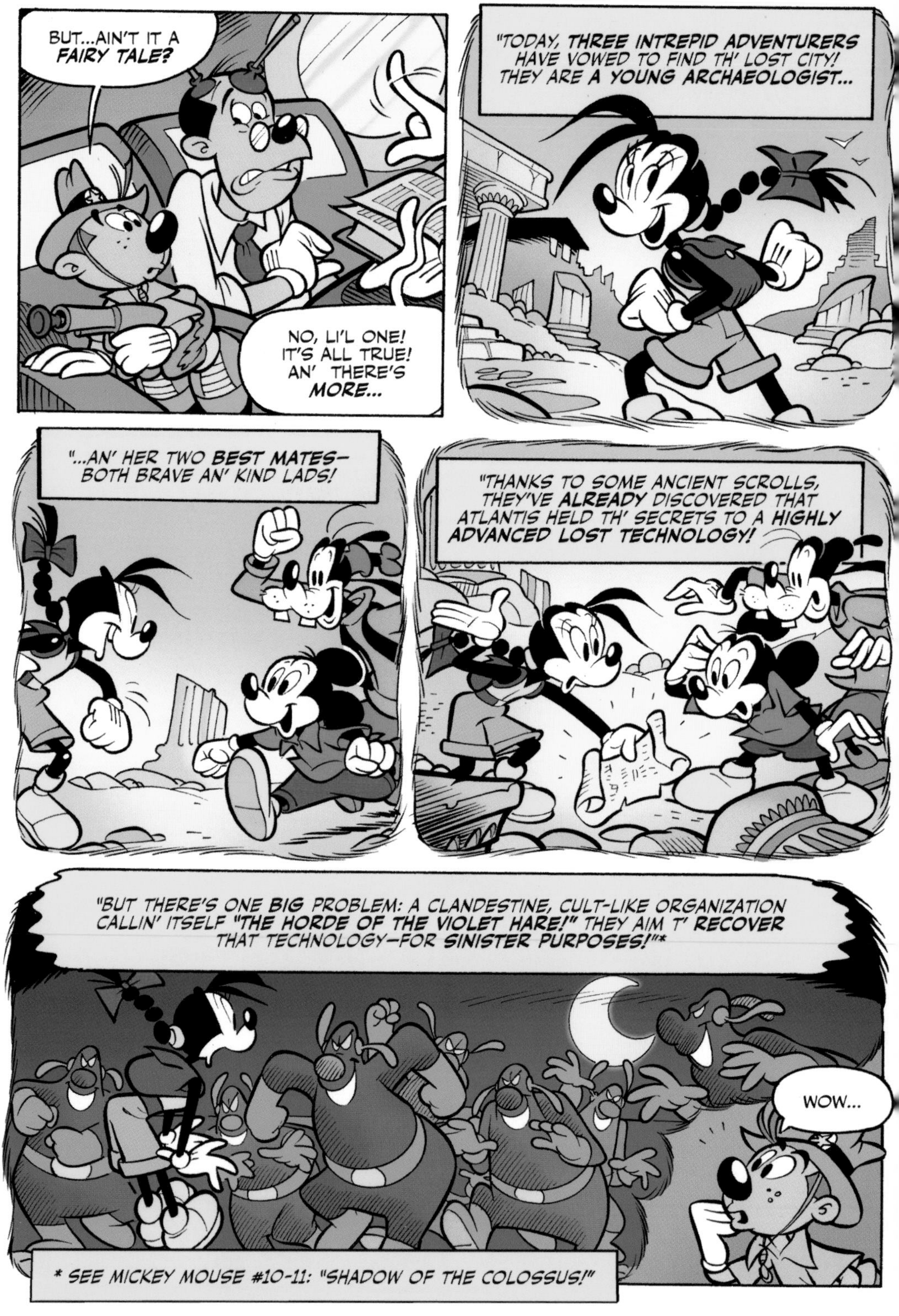
BUT...AIN'T IT A FAIRY TALE?
NO, LI'L ONE! IT'S ALL TRUE! AN' THERE'S MORE...
"TODAY, THREE INTREPID ADVENTURERS HAVE VOWED TO FIND TH' LOST CITY! THEY ARE A YOUNG ARCHAEOLOGIST...
"...AN' HER TWO BEST MATES— BOTH BRAVE AN' KIND LADS!
"THANKS TO SOME ANCIENT SCROLLS, THEY'VE ALREADY DISCOVERED THAT ATLANTIS HELD TH' SECRETS TO A HIGHLY ADVANCED LOST TECHNOLOGY!
"BUT THERE'S ONE BIG PROBLEM: A CLANDESTINE, CULT-LIKE ORGANIZATION CALLIN' ITSELF "THE HORDE OF THE VIOLET HARE!" THEY AIM T' RECOVER THAT TECHNOLOGY—FOR SINISTER PURPOSES!"*
WOW...
* SEE MICKEY MOUSE #10-11: "SHADOW OF THE COLOSSUS!"

THASSA GREAT STORY... EH, POP?

YES, SON!

I CAN'T *BELIEVE* YOU KEPT MY LI'L TIMMY *OCCUPIED!* I CAN'T THANK YOU ENOUGH, MISS...

TOFT! *EURASIA TOFT!*

A ROUND OF APPLAUSE FOR OUR *SAVIOR,* EURASIA TOFT!

*CLAP* CLAP *CLAP* CLAP CLAP *CLAP*

OH, BLIMEY! THANKS!

THET BOOK LOOKS MIGHTY INTERESTIN', EURASIA!

ITS AUTHOR, *PROF. MARTY CARTIER,* IS A LEADIN' EXPERT ON ATLANTIS!

CARTIER
LOST ATLANTIS

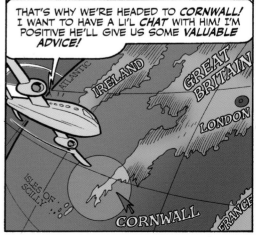

THAT'S WHY WE'RE HEADED TO *CORNWALL!* I WANT TO HAVE A LI'L *CHAT* WITH HIM! I'M POSITIVE HE'LL GIVE US SOME *VALUABLE ADVICE!*

ATLANTIC

IRELAND

GREAT BRITAIN

LONDON

ISLES OF SCILLY

CORNWALL

FRANCE

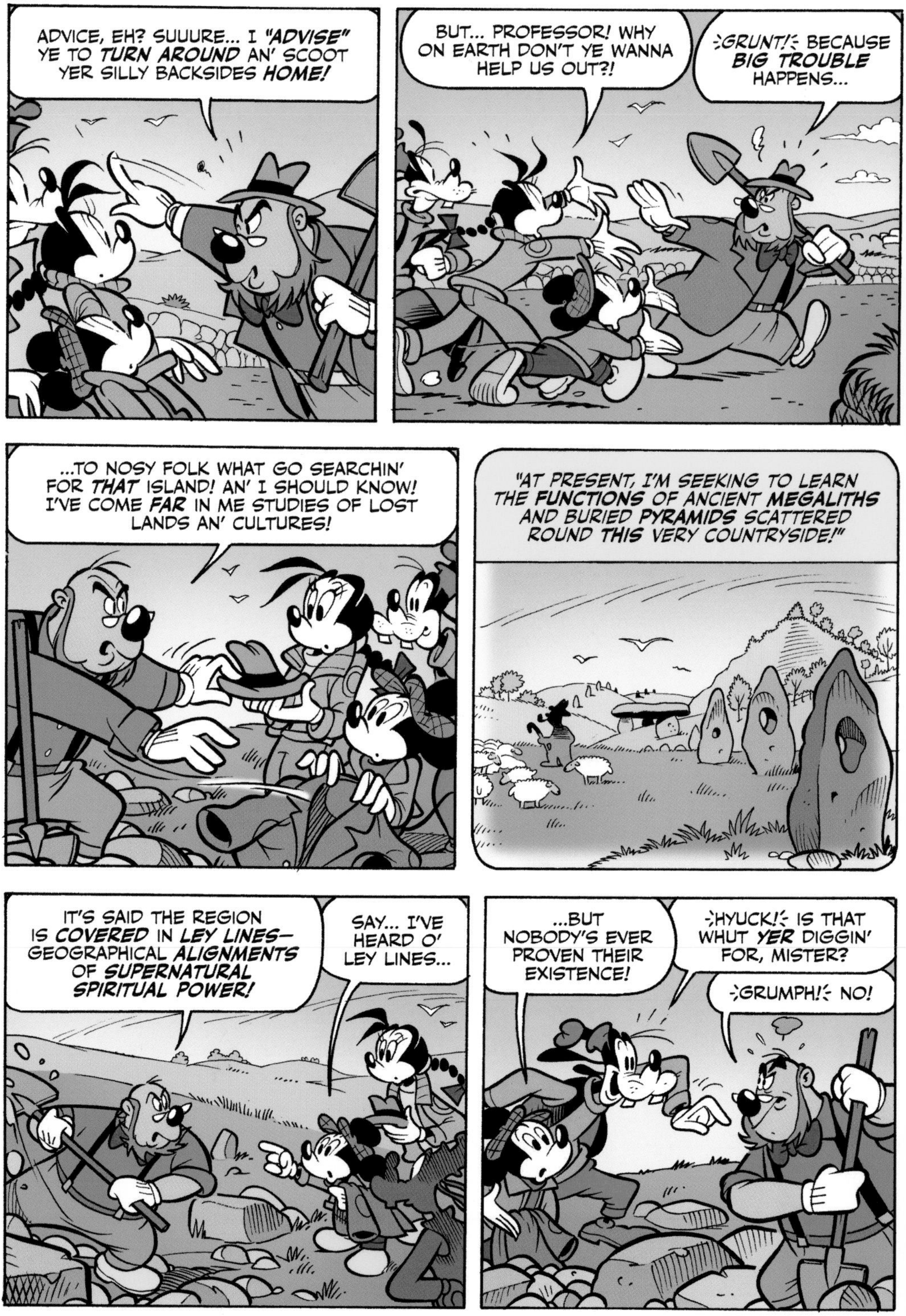
ADVICE, EH? SUUURE... I "ADVISE" YE TO TURN AROUND AN' SCOOT YER SILLY BACKSIDES HOME!
BUT... PROFESSOR! WHY ON EARTH DON'T YE WANNA HELP US OUT?!
GRUNT! BECAUSE BIG TROUBLE HAPPENS...
...TO NOSY FOLK WHAT GO SEARCHIN' FOR THAT ISLAND! AN' I SHOULD KNOW! I'VE COME FAR IN ME STUDIES OF LOST LANDS AN' CULTURES!
"AT PRESENT, I'M SEEKING TO LEARN THE FUNCTIONS OF ANCIENT MEGALITHS AND BURIED PYRAMIDS SCATTERED ROUND THIS VERY COUNTRYSIDE!"
IT'S SAID THE REGION IS COVERED IN LEY LINES— GEOGRAPHICAL ALIGNMENTS OF SUPERNATURAL SPIRITUAL POWER!
SAY... I'VE HEARD O' LEY LINES...
...BUT NOBODY'S EVER PROVEN THEIR EXISTENCE!
HYUCK! IS THAT WHUT YER DIGGIN' FOR, MISTER?
GRUMPH! NO!

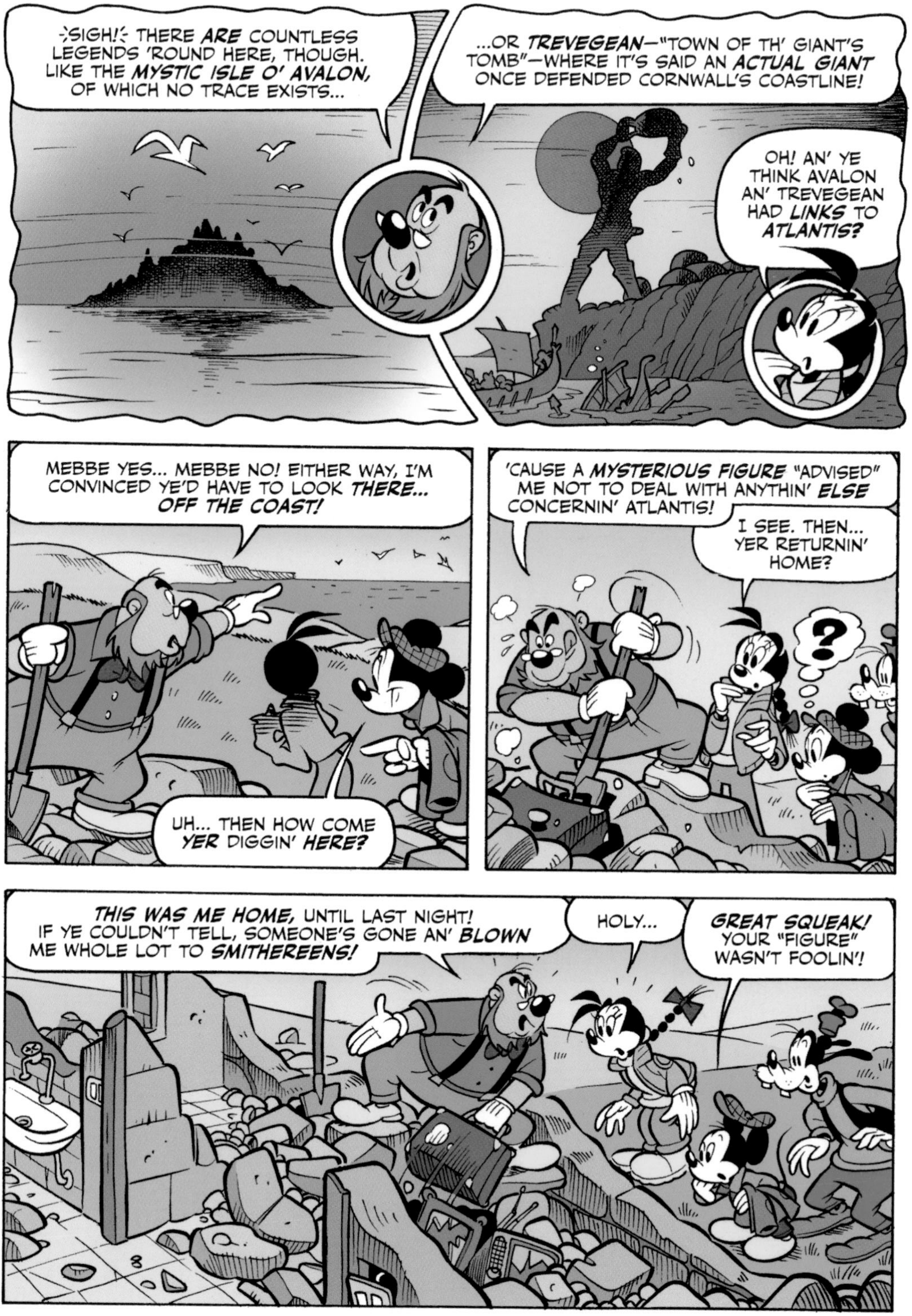
-SIGH!- THERE ARE COUNTLESS LEGENDS 'ROUND HERE, THOUGH. LIKE THE MYSTIC ISLE O' AVALON, OF WHICH NO TRACE EXISTS...
...OR TREVEGEAN—"TOWN OF TH' GIANT'S TOMB"—WHERE IT'S SAID AN ACTUAL GIANT ONCE DEFENDED CORNWALL'S COASTLINE!
OH! AN' YE THINK AVALON AN' TREVEGEAN HAD LINKS TO ATLANTIS?
MEBBE YES... MEBBE NO! EITHER WAY, I'M CONVINCED YE'D HAVE TO LOOK THERE... OFF THE COAST!
UH... THEN HOW COME YER DIGGIN' HERE?
'CAUSE A MYSTERIOUS FIGURE "ADVISED" ME NOT TO DEAL WITH ANYTHIN' ELSE CONCERNIN' ATLANTIS!
I SEE. THEN... YER RETURNIN' HOME?
?
THIS WAS ME HOME, UNTIL LAST NIGHT! IF YE COULDN'T TELL, SOMEONE'S GONE AN' BLOWN ME WHOLE LOT TO SMITHEREENS!
HOLY...
GREAT SQUEAK! YOUR "FIGURE" WASN'T FOOLIN'!

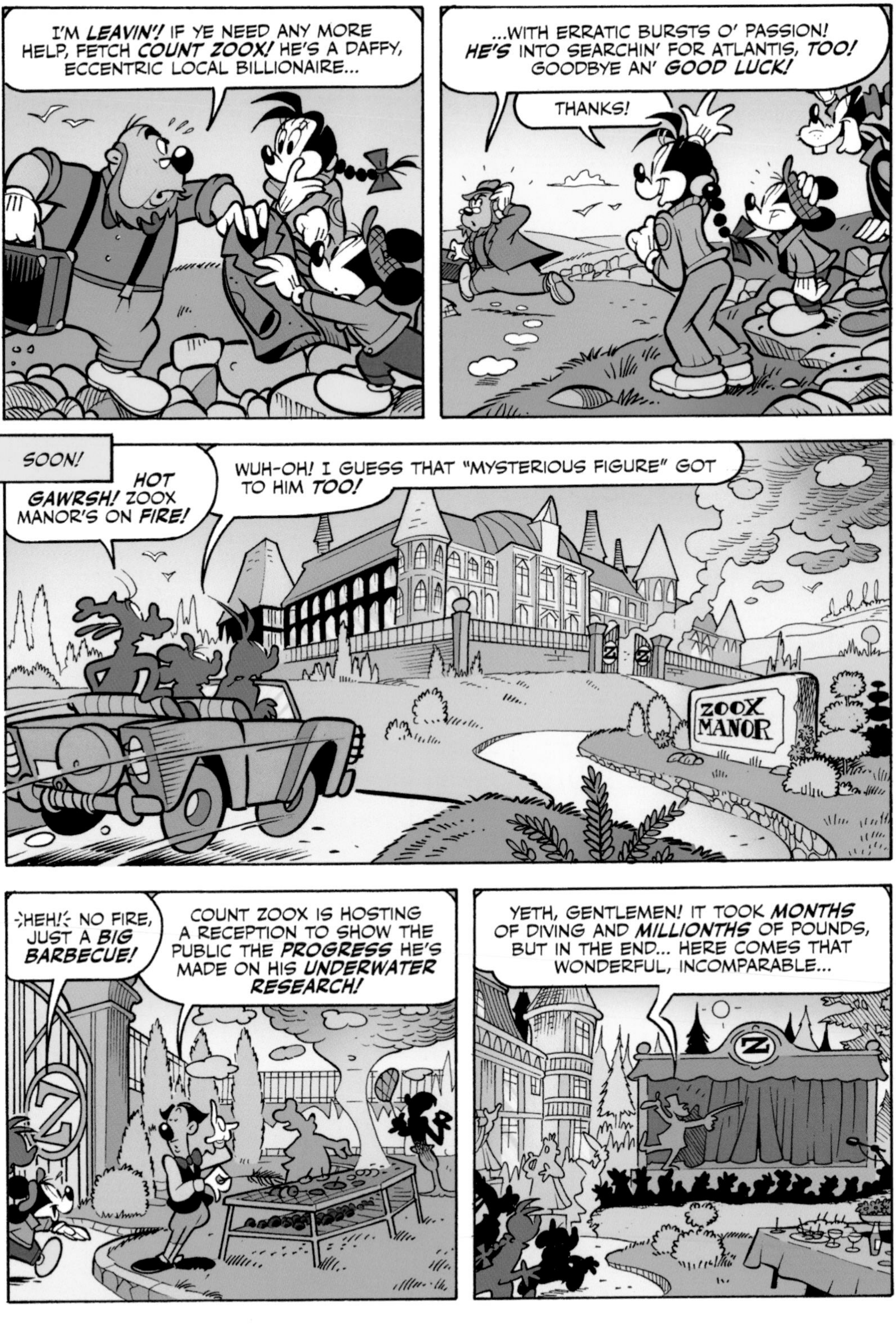
I'M LEAVIN'! IF YE NEED ANY MORE HELP, FETCH COUNT ZOOX! HE'S A DAFFY, ECCENTRIC LOCAL BILLIONAIRE...
...WITH ERRATIC BURSTS O' PASSION! HE'S INTO SEARCHIN' FOR ATLANTIS, TOO! GOODBYE AN' GOOD LUCK!
THANKS!
SOON!
HOT GAWRSH! ZOOX MANOR'S ON FIRE!
WUH-OH! I GUESS THAT "MYSTERIOUS FIGURE" GOT TO HIM TOO!
ZOOX MANOR
HEH! NO FIRE, JUST A BIG BARBECUE!
COUNT ZOOX IS HOSTING A RECEPTION TO SHOW THE PUBLIC THE PROGRESS HE'S MADE ON HIS UNDERWATER RESEARCH!
YETH, GENTLEMEN! IT TOOK MONTHS OF DIVING AND MILLIONTHS OF POUNDS, BUT IN THE END... HERE COMES THAT WONDERFUL, INCOMPARABLE...

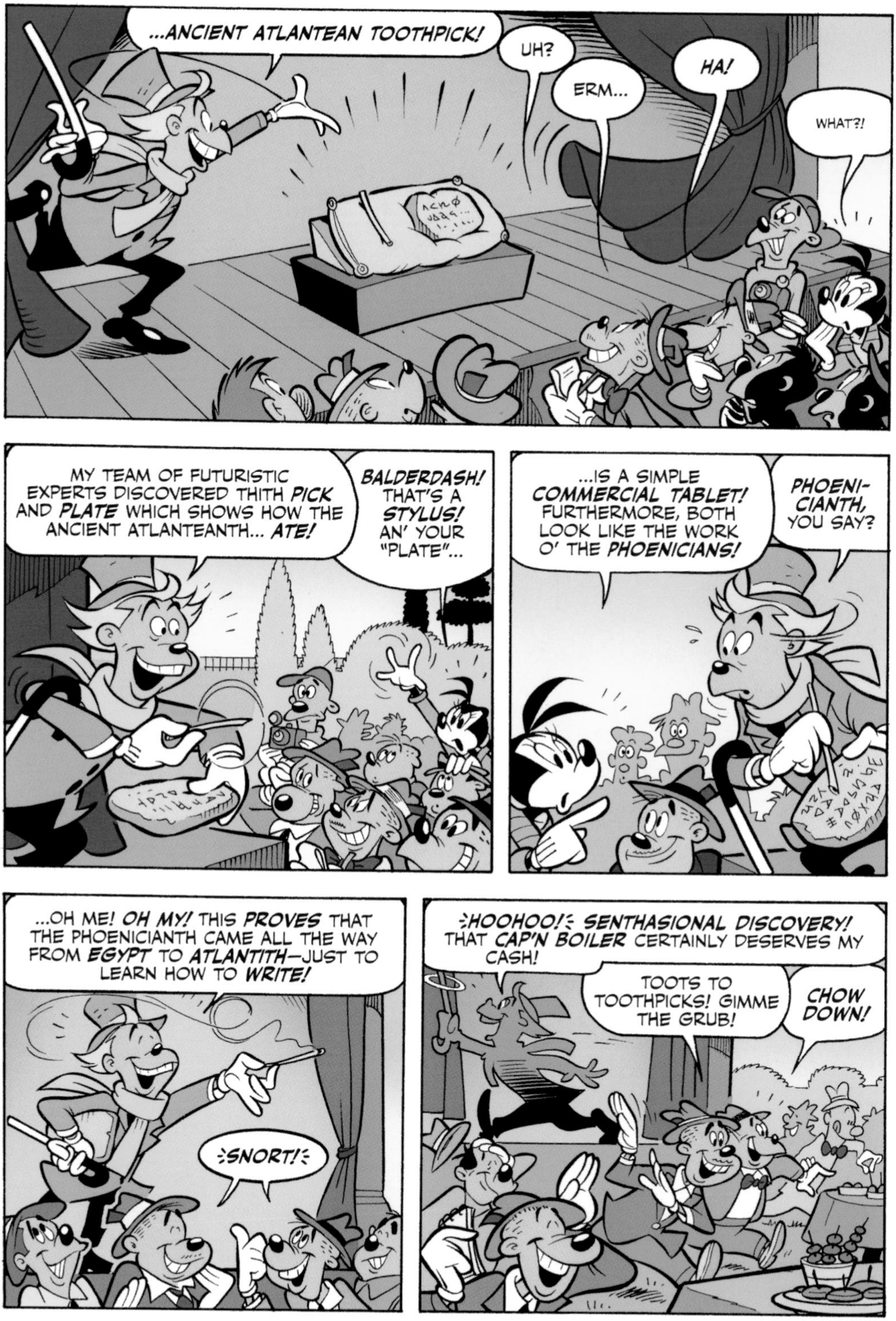
...ANCIENT ATLANTEAN TOOTHPICK!
UH?
ERM...
HA!
WHAT?!
MY TEAM OF FUTURISTIC EXPERTS DISCOVERED THITH PICK AND PLATE WHICH SHOWS HOW THE ANCIENT ATLANTEANTH... ATE!
BALDERDASH! THAT'S A STYLUS! AN' YOUR "PLATE"...
...IS A SIMPLE COMMERCIAL TABLET! FURTHERMORE, BOTH LOOK LIKE THE WORK O' THE PHOENICIANS!
PHOENICIANTH, YOU SAY?
...OH ME! OH MY! THIS PROVES THAT THE PHOENICIANTH CAME ALL THE WAY FROM EGYPT TO ATLANTITH—JUST TO LEARN HOW TO WRITE!
SNORT!
HOOHOO! SENTHASIONAL DISCOVERY! THAT CAP'N BOILER CERTAINLY DESERVES MY CASH!
TOOTS TO TOOTHPICKS! GIMME THE GRUB!
CHOW DOWN!

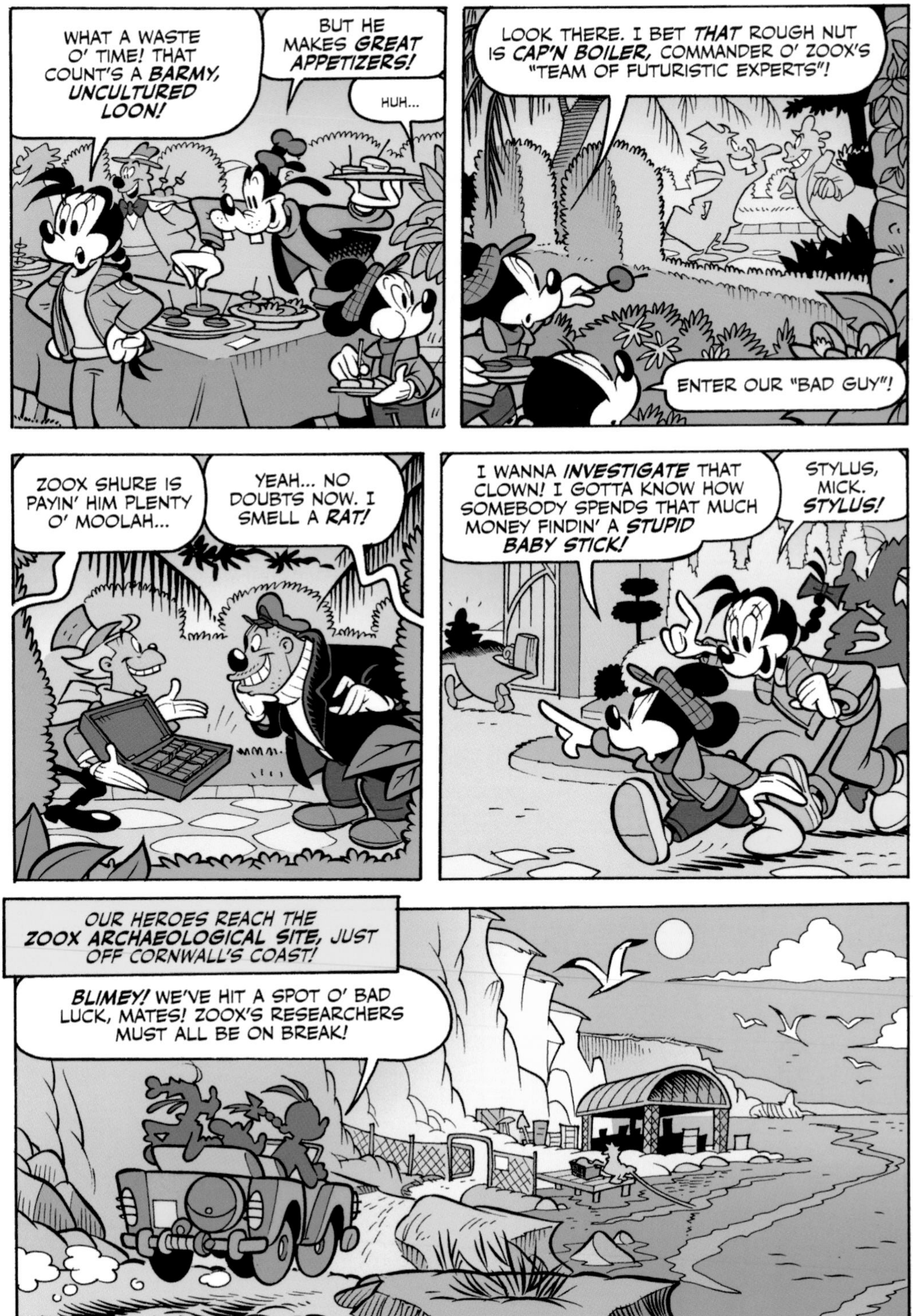
WHAT A WASTE O' TIME! THAT COUNT'S A BARMY, UNCULTURED LOON!
BUT HE MAKES GREAT APPETIZERS!
HUH...
LOOK THERE. I BET THAT ROUGH NUT IS CAP'N BOILER, COMMANDER O' ZOOX'S "TEAM OF FUTURISTIC EXPERTS"!
ENTER OUR "BAD GUY"!
ZOOX SHURE IS PAYIN' HIM PLENTY O' MOOLAH...
YEAH... NO DOUBTS NOW. I SMELL A RAT!
I WANNA INVESTIGATE THAT CLOWN! I GOTTA KNOW HOW SOMEBODY SPENDS THAT MUCH MONEY FINDIN' A STUPID BABY STICK!
STYLUS, MICK. STYLUS!
OUR HEROES REACH THE ZOOX ARCHAEOLOGICAL SITE, JUST OFF CORNWALL'S COAST!
BLIMEY! WE'VE HIT A SPOT O' BAD LUCK, MATES! ZOOX'S RESEARCHERS MUST ALL BE ON BREAK!

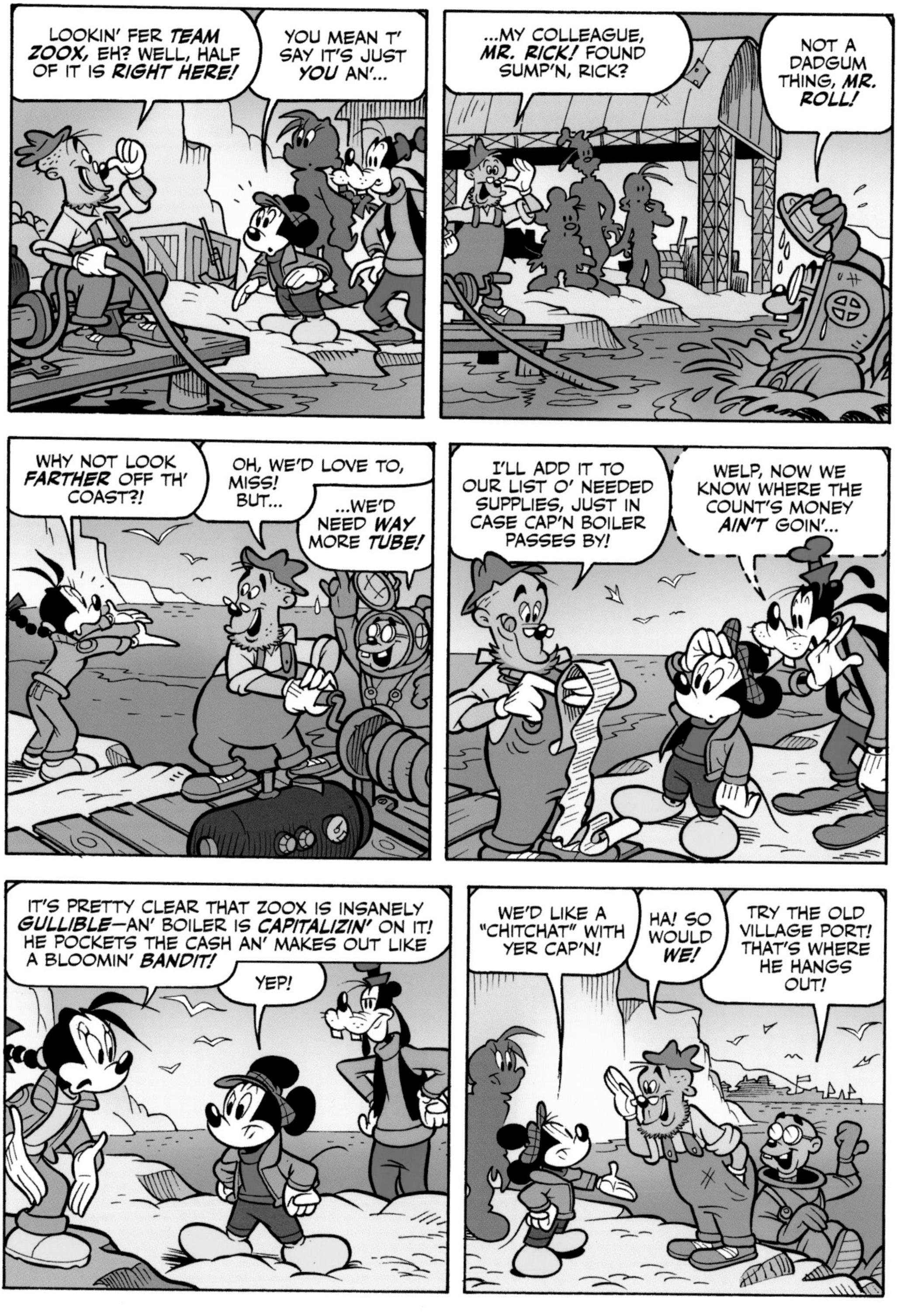
LOOKIN' FER TEAM ZOOX, EH? WELL, HALF OF IT IS RIGHT HERE!
YOU MEAN T' SAY IT'S JUST YOU AN'...
...MY COLLEAGUE, MR. RICK! FOUND SUMP'N, RICK?
NOT A DADGUM THING, MR. ROLL!
WHY NOT LOOK FARTHER OFF TH' COAST?!
OH, WE'D LOVE TO, MISS! BUT...
...WE'D NEED WAY MORE TUBE!
I'LL ADD IT TO OUR LIST O' NEEDED SUPPLIES, JUST IN CASE CAP'N BOILER PASSES BY!
WELP, NOW WE KNOW WHERE THE COUNT'S MONEY AIN'T GOIN'...
IT'S PRETTY CLEAR THAT ZOOX IS INSANELY GULLIBLE—AN' BOILER IS CAPITALIZIN' ON IT! HE POCKETS THE CASH AN' MAKES OUT LIKE A BLOOMIN' BANDIT!
YEP!
WE'D LIKE A "CHITCHAT" WITH YER CAP'N!
HA! SO WOULD WE!
TRY THE OLD VILLAGE PORT! THAT'S WHERE HE HANGS OUT!

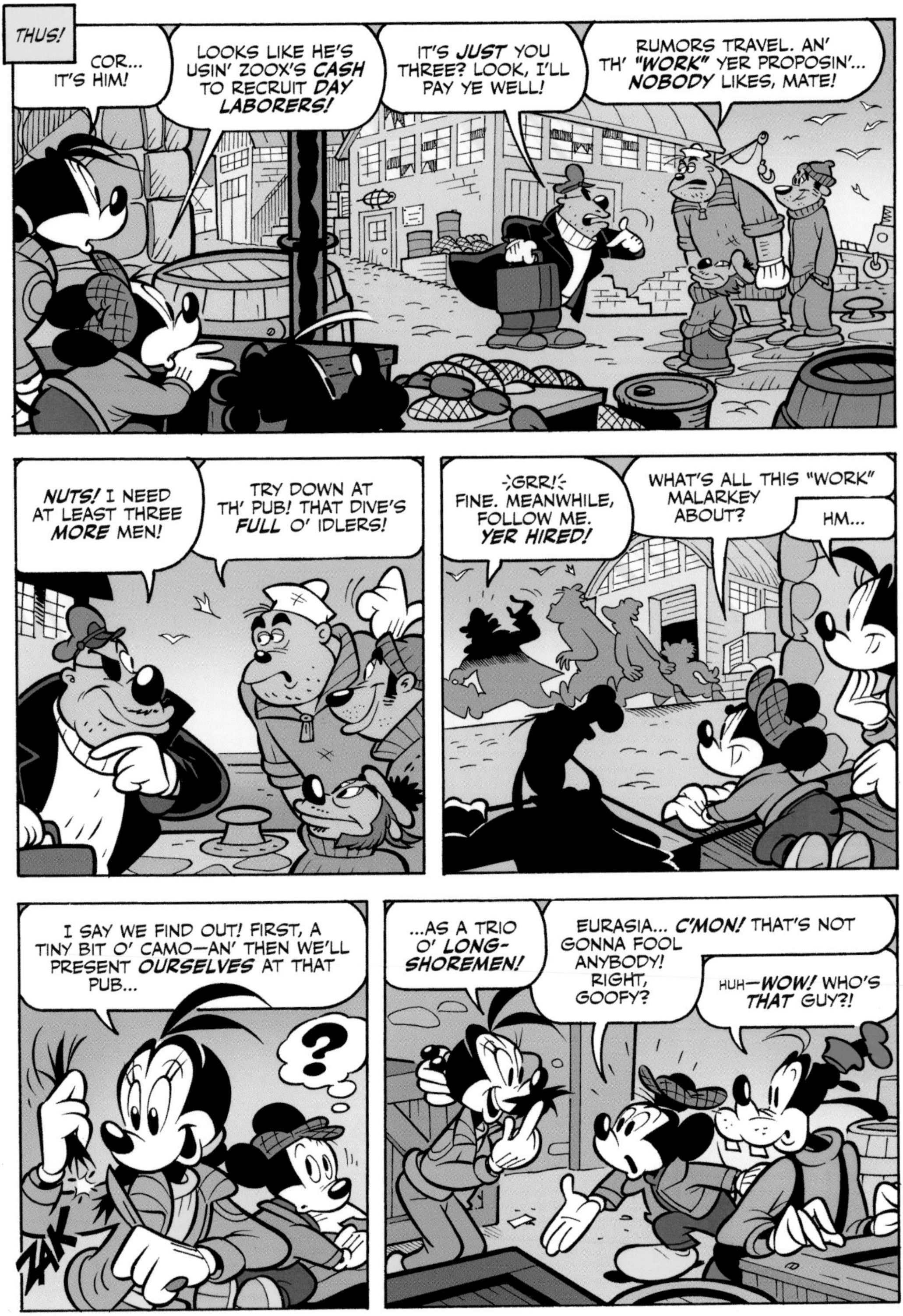
THUS!
COR... IT'S HIM!
LOOKS LIKE HE'S USIN' ZOOX'S CASH TO RECRUIT DAY LABORERS!
IT'S JUST YOU THREE? LOOK, I'LL PAY YE WELL!
RUMORS TRAVEL. AN' TH' "WORK" YER PROPOSIN'... NOBODY LIKES, MATE!
NUTS! I NEED AT LEAST THREE MORE MEN!
TRY DOWN AT TH' PUB! THAT DIVE'S FULL O' IDLERS!
GRR! FINE. MEANWHILE, FOLLOW ME. YER HIRED!
WHAT'S ALL THIS "WORK" MALARKEY ABOUT?
HM...
I SAY WE FIND OUT! FIRST, A TINY BIT O' CAMO—AN' THEN WE'LL PRESENT OURSELVES AT THAT PUB...
?
ZAK
...AS A TRIO O' LONG-SHOREMEN!
EURASIA... C'MON! THAT'S NOT GONNA FOOL ANYBODY! RIGHT, GOOFY?
HUH—WOW! WHO'S THAT GUY?!

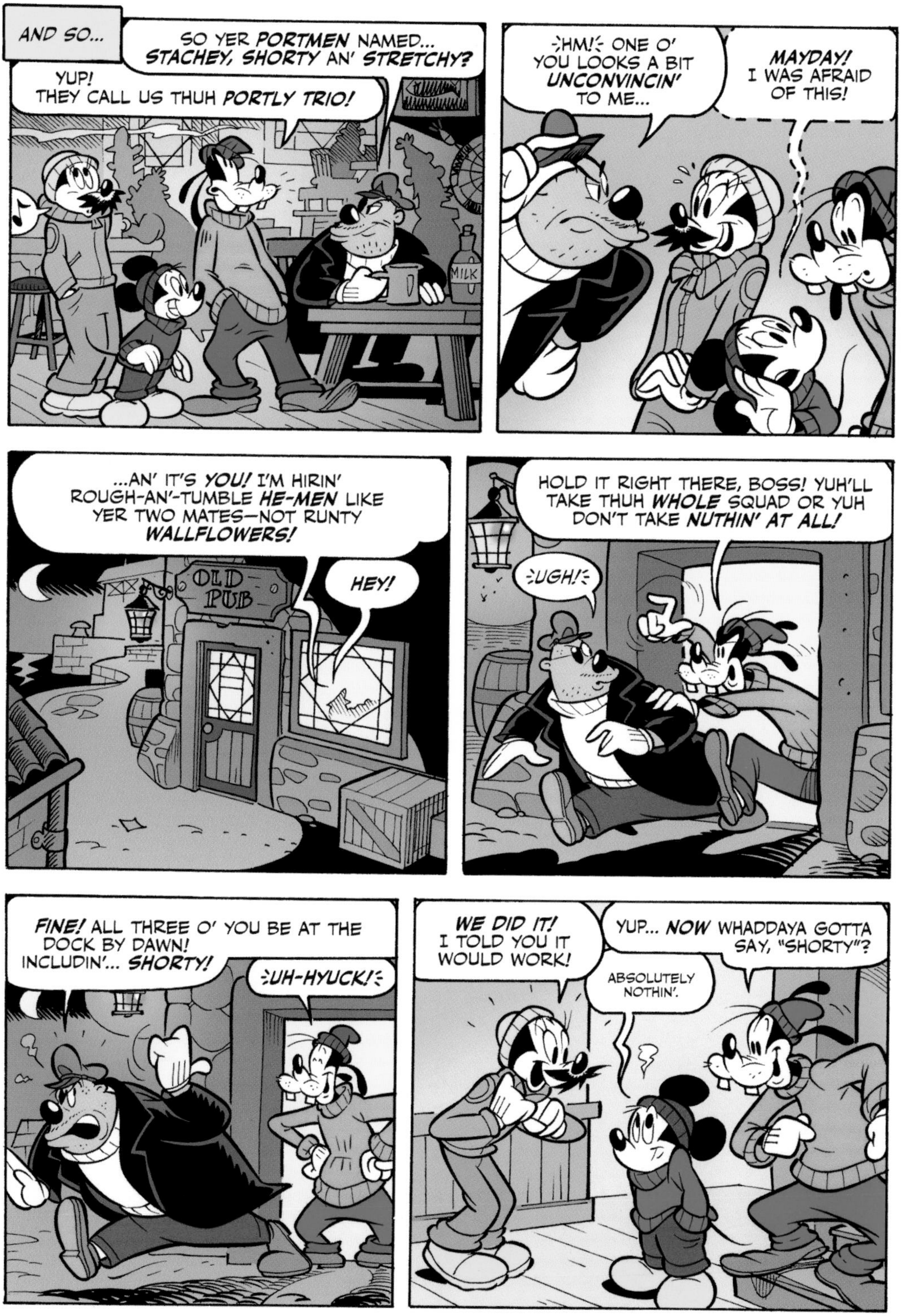
AND SO...
SO YER PORTMEN NAMED... STACHEY, SHORTY AN' STRETCHY?
YUP! THEY CALL US THUH PORTLY TRIO!
MILK
HM! ONE O' YOU LOOKS A BIT UNCONVINCIN' TO ME...
MAYDAY! I WAS AFRAID OF THIS!
...AN' IT'S YOU! I'M HIRIN' ROUGH-AN'-TUMBLE HE-MEN LIKE YER TWO MATES—NOT RUNTY WALLFLOWERS!
OLD PUB
HEY!
HOLD IT RIGHT THERE, BOSS! YUH'LL TAKE THUH WHOLE SQUAD OR YUH DON'T TAKE NUTHIN' AT ALL!
UGH!
FINE! ALL THREE O' YOU BE AT THE DOCK BY DAWN! INCLUDIN'... SHORTY!
UH-HYUCK!
WE DID IT! I TOLD YOU IT WOULD WORK!
YUP... NOW WHADDAYA GOTTA SAY, "SHORTY"?
ABSOLUTELY NOTHIN'.

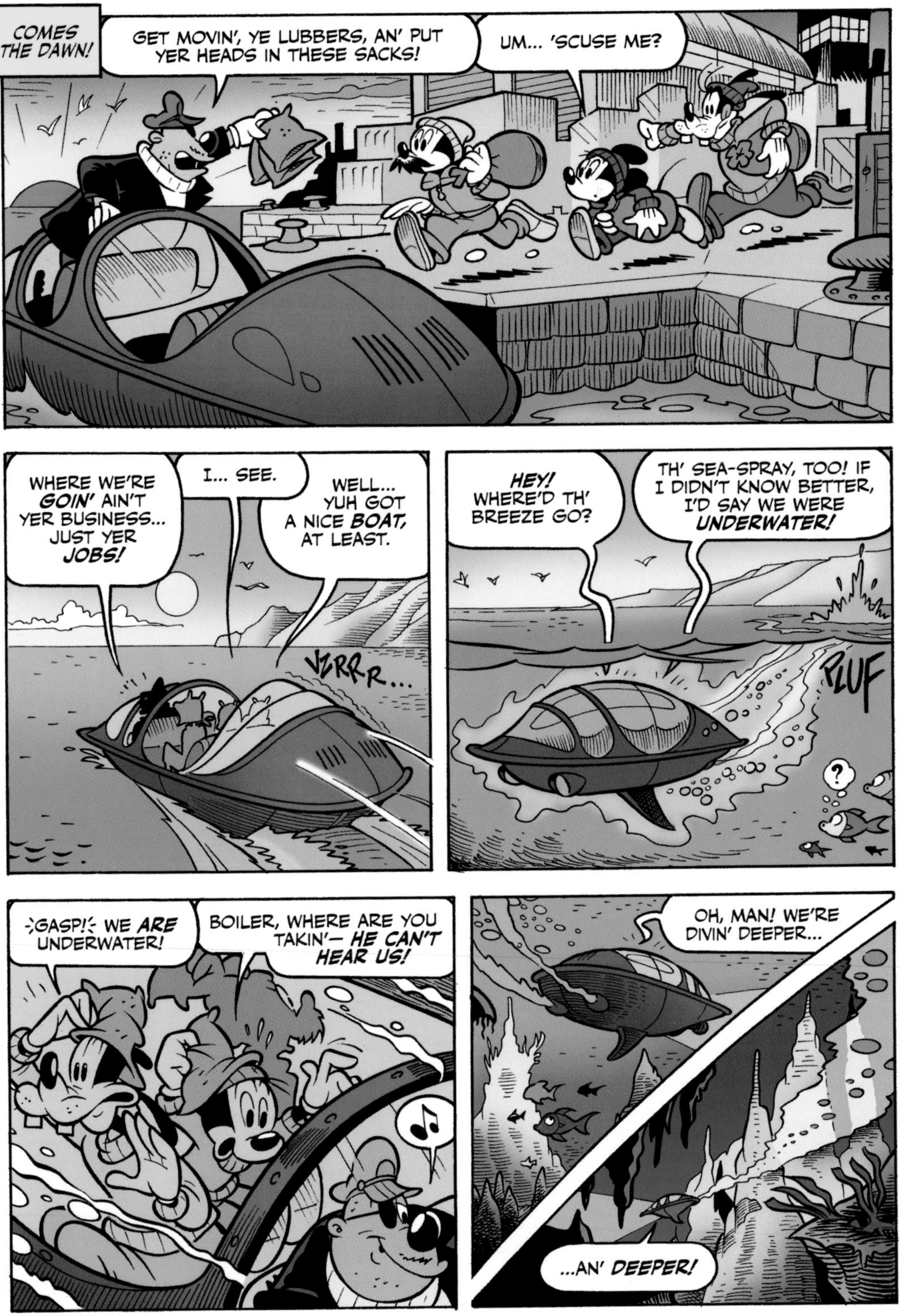
COMES THE DAWN!
GET MOVIN', YE LUBBERS, AN' PUT YER HEADS IN THESE SACKS!
UM... 'SCUSE ME?
WHERE WE'RE GOIN' AIN'T YER BUSINESS... JUST YER JOBS!
I... SEE.
WELL... YUH GOT A NICE BOAT, AT LEAST.
VZRRR...
HEY! WHERE'D TH' BREEZE GO?
TH' SEA-SPRAY, TOO! IF I DIDN'T KNOW BETTER, I'D SAY WE WERE UNDERWATER!
PLUF
?
GASP! WE ARE UNDERWATER!
BOILER, WHERE ARE YOU TAKIN'— HE CAN'T HEAR US!
♪
OH, MAN! WE'RE DIVIN' DEEPER...
...AN' DEEPER!

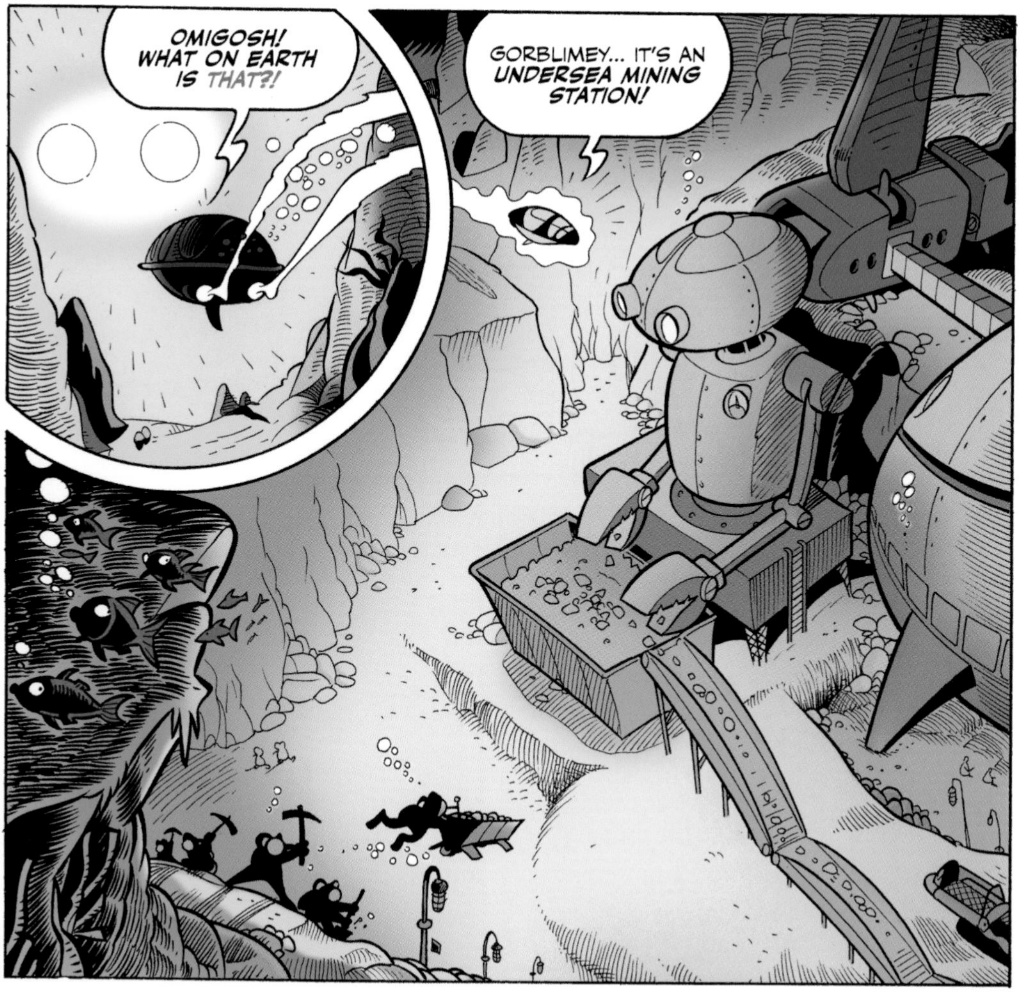
OMIGOSH! WHAT ON EARTH IS THAT?!
GORBLIMEY... IT'S AN UNDERSEA MINING STATION!
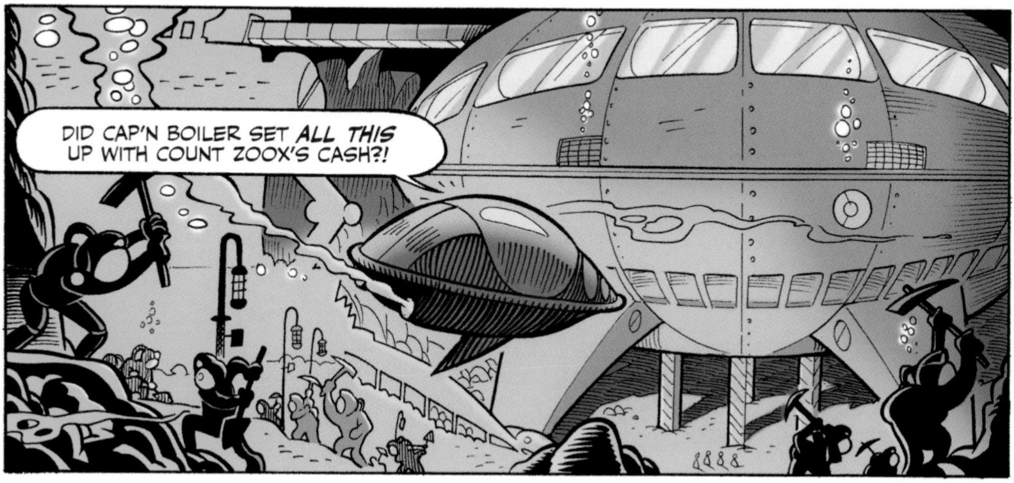
DID CAP'N BOILER SET ALL THIS UP WITH COUNT ZOOX'S CASH?!

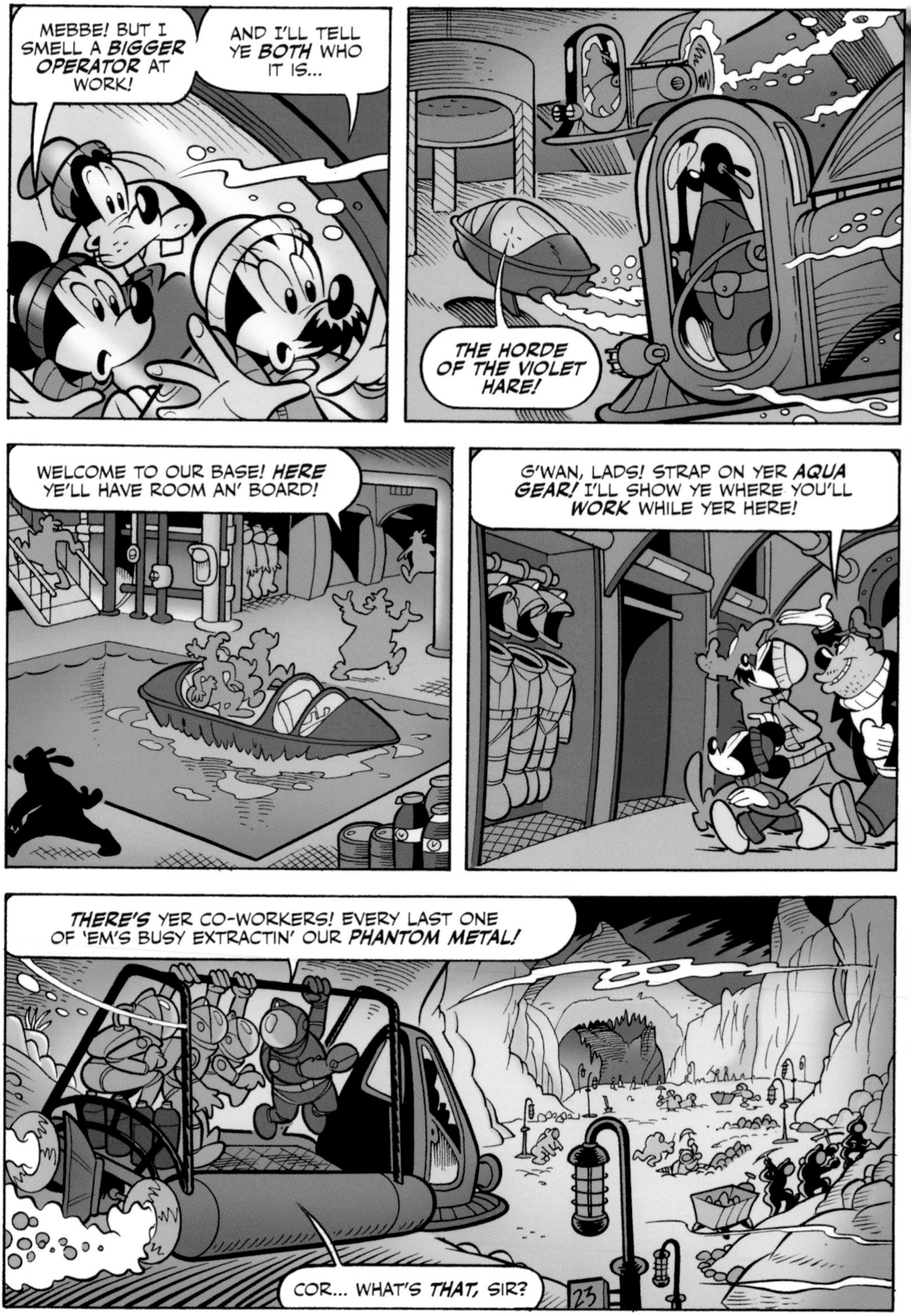
MEBBE! BUT I SMELL A BIGGER OPERATOR AT WORK!
AND I'LL TELL YE BOTH WHO IT IS...
THE HORDE OF THE VIOLET HARE!
WELCOME TO OUR BASE! HERE YE'LL HAVE ROOM AN' BOARD!
G'WAN, LADS! STRAP ON YER AQUA GEAR! I'LL SHOW YE WHERE YOU'LL WORK WHILE YER HERE!
THERE'S YER CO-WORKERS! EVERY LAST ONE OF 'EM'S BUSY EXTRACTIN' OUR PHANTOM METAL!
COR... WHAT'S THAT, SIR?
23

NONE O' YOUR CONCERN! ALL YE GOTTA DO IS RECOGNIZE IT... AN' TAKE IT OUT!
IT'S... GLOWING.
THE METAL'S BURIED IN VEINS! TO FIND IT, WE USE EXPLOSIVES TRIGGERED WITH TIMED DETONATORS... JUST LIKE THE ONES YER SITTIN' ON!
YIPE!
BOOM
YOU'LL WORK IN PAIRS O' THREE...
COLLECT THE SHARDS O' PHANTOM METAL, THEN LOAD 'EM INTO YER MINI CARGO-SUB THAT'LL TAKE 'EM TO...
...THE "DRAGONFLY!"

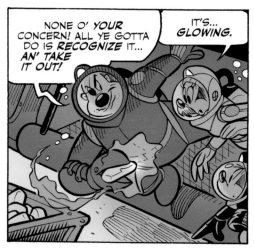

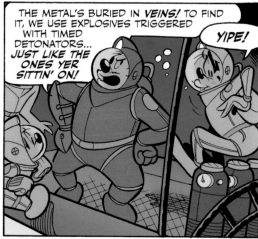

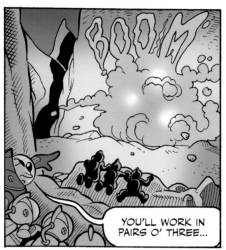

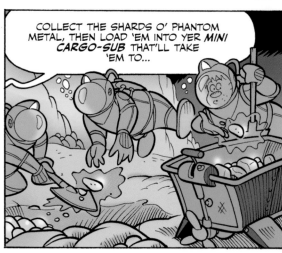

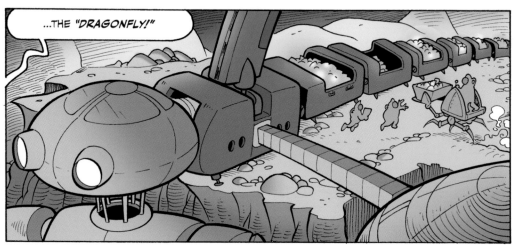

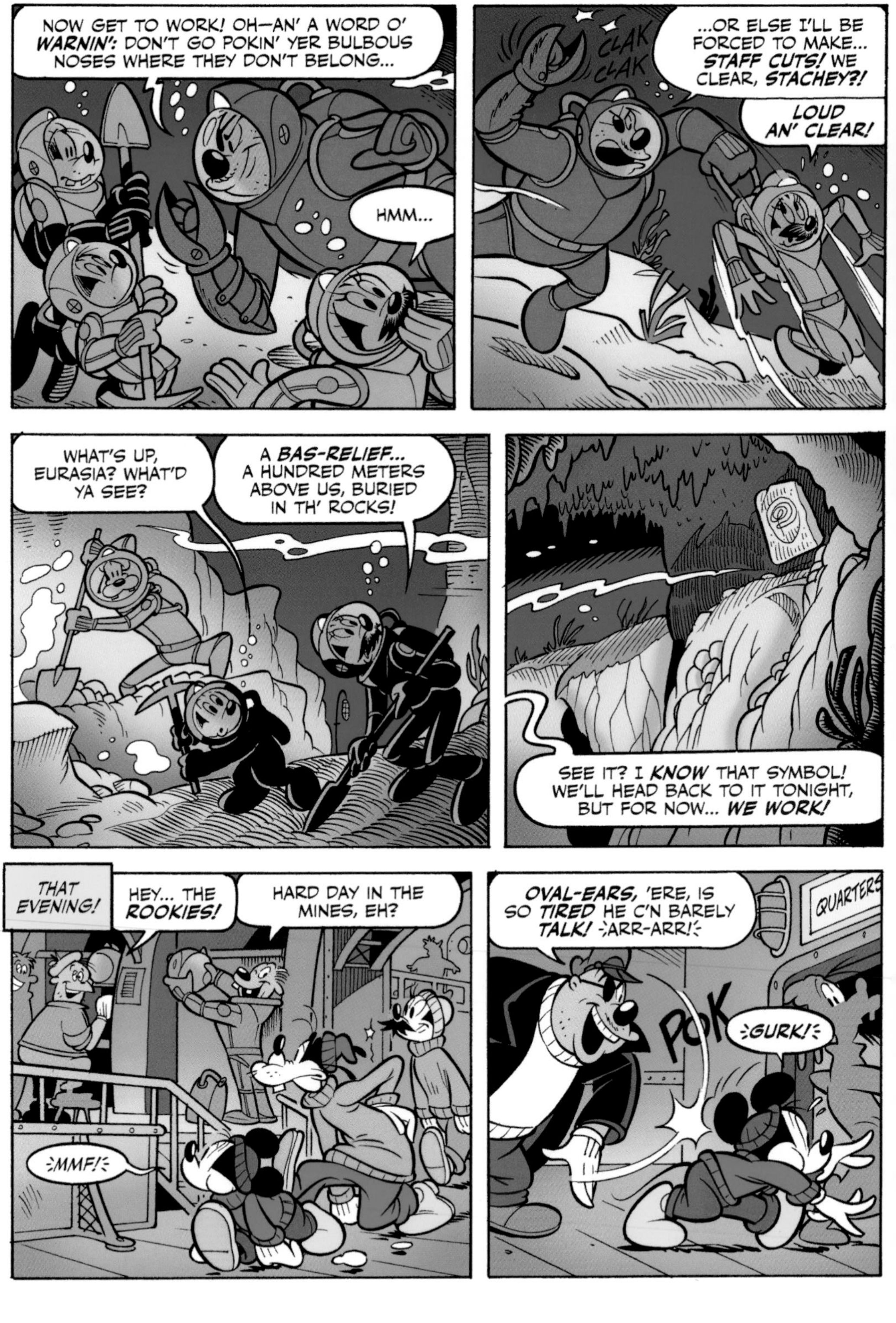
NOW GET TO WORK! OH—AN' A WORD O' WARNIN': DON'T GO POKIN' YER BULBOUS NOSES WHERE THEY DON'T BELONG...
HMM...
CLAK CLAK
...OR ELSE I'LL BE FORCED TO MAKE... STAFF CUTS! WE CLEAR, STACHEY?!
LOUD AN' CLEAR!
WHAT'S UP, EURASIA? WHAT'D YA SEE?
A BAS-RELIEF... A HUNDRED METERS ABOVE US, BURIED IN TH' ROCKS!
SEE IT? I KNOW THAT SYMBOL! WE'LL HEAD BACK TO IT TONIGHT, BUT FOR NOW... WE WORK!
THAT EVENING!
HEY... THE ROOKIES!
HARD DAY IN THE MINES, EH?
MMF!
OVAL-EARS, 'ERE, IS SO TIRED HE C'N BARELY TALK! ARR-ARR!
QUARTERS
POK
GURK!

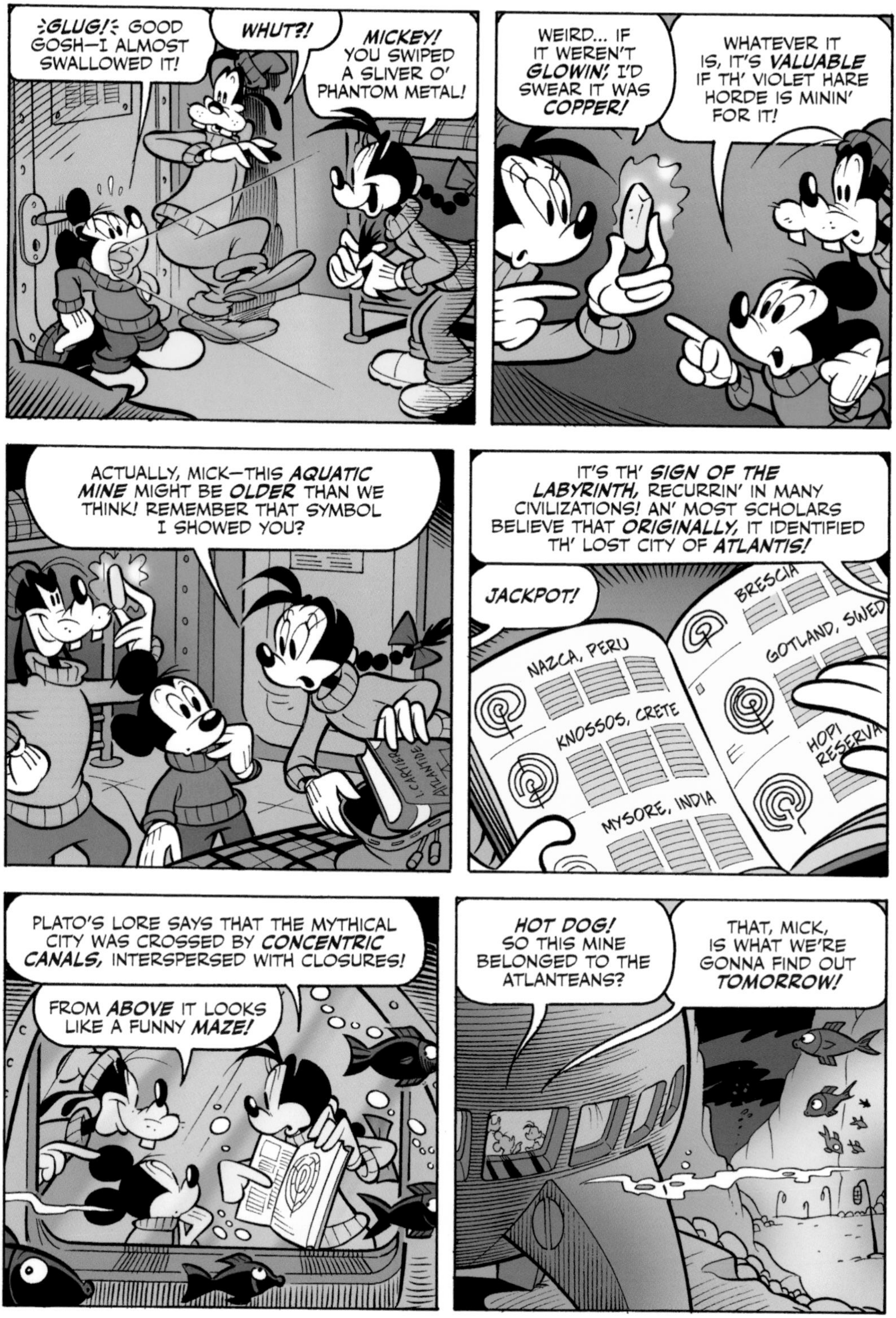

GLUG! GOOD GOSH—I ALMOST SWALLOWED IT!
WHUT?!
MICKEY! YOU SWIPED A SLIVER O' PHANTOM METAL!
WEIRD... IF IT WEREN'T GLOWIN', I'D SWEAR IT WAS COPPER!
WHATEVER IT IS, IT'S VALUABLE IF TH' VIOLET HARE HORDE IS MININ' FOR IT!
ACTUALLY, MICK—THIS AQUATIC MINE MIGHT BE OLDER THAN WE THINK! REMEMBER THAT SYMBOL I SHOWED YOU?
I. CARTIER ATLANTIDE
IT'S TH' SIGN OF THE LABYRINTH, RECURRIN' IN MANY CIVILIZATIONS! AN' MOST SCHOLARS BELIEVE THAT ORIGINALLY, IT IDENTIFIED TH' LOST CITY OF ATLANTIS!
JACKPOT!
NAZCA, PERU
KNOSSOS, CRETE
MYSORE, INDIA
BRESCIA
GOTLAND, SWED
HOPI RESERVA
PLATO'S LORE SAYS THAT THE MYTHICAL CITY WAS CROSSED BY CONCENTRIC CANALS, INTERSPERSED WITH CLOSURES!
FROM ABOVE IT LOOKS LIKE A FUNNY MAZE!
HOT DOG! SO THIS MINE BELONGED TO THE ATLANTEANS?
THAT, MICK, IS WHAT WE'RE GONNA FIND OUT TOMORROW!

AND SO—THE FOLLOWING DAY!

LUNCH BREAK! IT'S NOW OR NEVER, GANG!

HEY, A *HIDDEN PASSAGE!* THERE'S *STEPS* BACK HERE!

GET IN! *HURRY!*

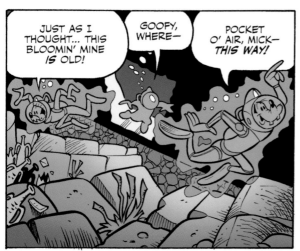

JUST AS I THOUGHT... THIS BLOOMIN' MINE *IS* OLD!

GOOFY, WHERE—

POCKET O' AIR, MICK— *THIS WAY!*

UH-OH... MICK! EURASIA! I THINK I FIGGERED OUT *WHERE* CAP'N BOILER GOT THAT *"TOOTHPICK"!*

?

SWEET SQUEAK... WHAT *IS* THIS PLACE?

THAT'S WOT I AIM TO *FIND OUT!*

I WAS RIGHT! THESE *ARE* PHOENICIAN TABLETS! WHICH MEANS... 2500 YEARS AGO, THIS CAVE WAS *STILL ON THE SURFACE!*

WHAT DO THEY SAY?

BELIEVE IT OR NOT—THEY'RE *BILLS OF SALE!* PHOENICIAN NAVIGATORS AN' TRADERS ONCE SAILED TO THIS SIDE OF THE POND...

...TO PURCHASE GREAT GOLLOPS OF TH' *PHANTOM METAL* THE ATLANTEANS CALLED... —SWEET BLESSED STARS ABOVE!— *IT'S ORICHALCUM!*

MICKEY! *MICKEY!* ACCORDING TO PLATO, ORICHALCUM WAS THE *MYSTERY METAL* THAT ONCE *COVERED THE WALLS OF ATLANTIS!*

SO BEFORE THE PHOENICIANS, THIS MINE WAS *ATLANTEAN!*

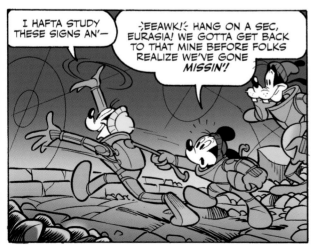

I HAFTA STUDY THESE SIGNS AN'—

⸙EEAWK!⸙ HANG ON A SEC, EURASIA! WE GOTTA GET BACK TO THAT MINE BEFORE FOLKS REALIZE WE'VE GONE *MISSIN'!*

*GAAAWRSH!* LOOKIT THUH *VIEW!* FROM UP HERE, THUH *VEINS* O' THUH MINE...

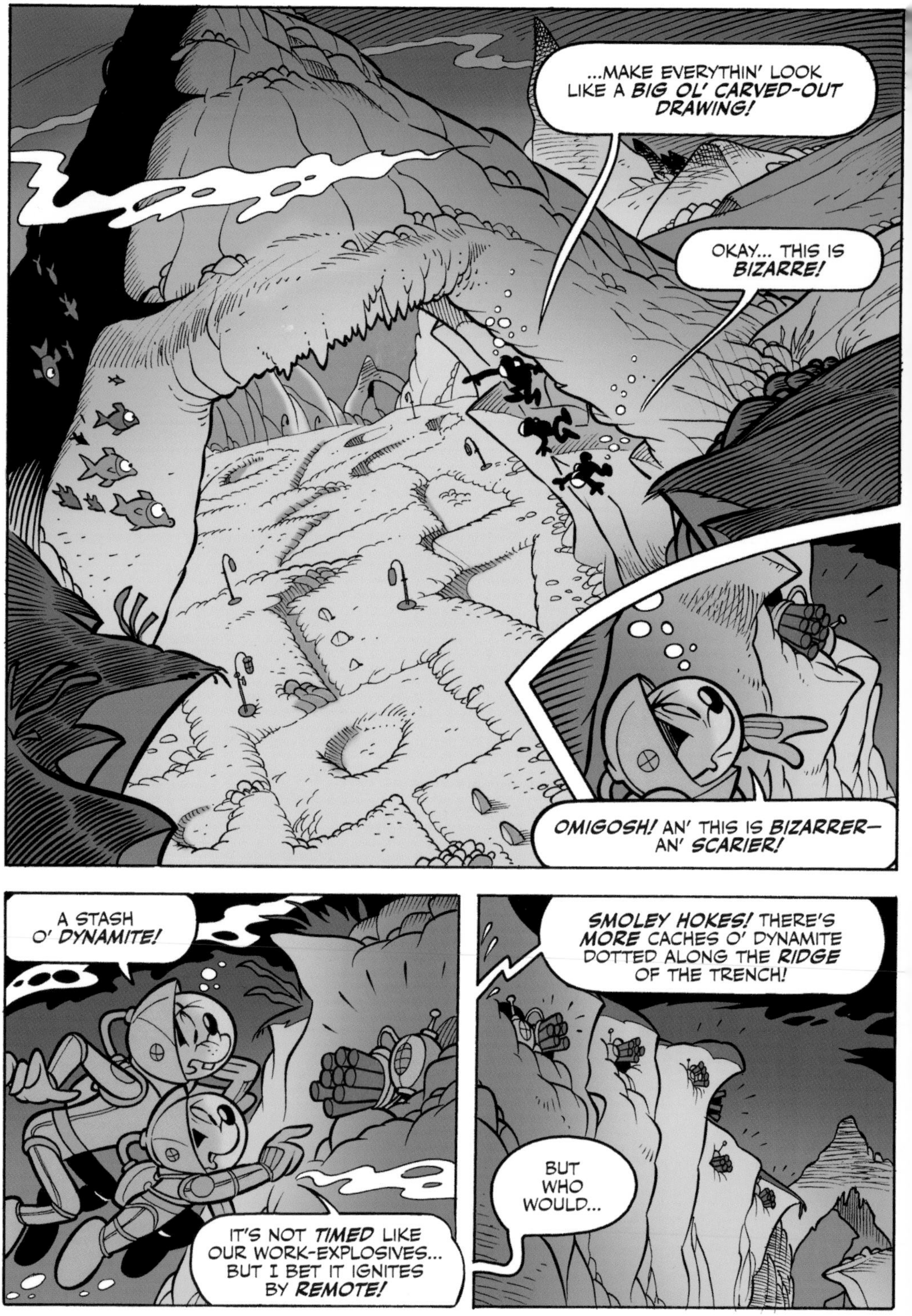
...MAKE EVERYTHIN' LOOK LIKE A BIG OL' CARVED-OUT DRAWING!
OKAY... THIS IS BIZARRE!
OMIGOSH! AN' THIS IS BIZARRER— AN' SCARIER!
A STASH O' DYNAMITE!
IT'S NOT TIMED LIKE OUR WORK-EXPLOSIVES... BUT I BET IT IGNITES BY REMOTE!
SMOLEY HOKES! THERE'S MORE CACHES O' DYNAMITE DOTTED ALONG THE RIDGE OF THE TRENCH!
BUT WHO WOULD...

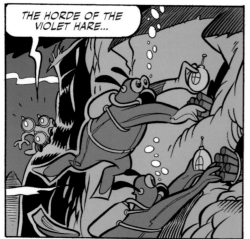

THE HORDE OF THE VIOLET HARE...

⸲GASP!⸳ ONCE THE WORKERS ARE DONE, TH' HORDE'S GONNA *COLLAPSE* TH' TRENCH—*LEAVIN'* NO WITNESSES!

! ! !

WE GOTTA WARN TH' WORKERS! *EVERYBODY'S* IN DANGER!

TUT-TUT, NOSY FISHIES! *CURIOSITY KILLS.*

⸲GAK!⸳

WAIT, BOSS... YER WRONG!

WE'VE BEEN BUSY... ER, PLACIN' MORE EXPLOSIVES! GET *WITH* IT, BEANPOLE!

HUP!

IZZAT SO... WELL, THEN—RIDDLE ME THIS, *"STACHEY"*...

WHERE'D YER *FACIAL FUZZ* GO, HMM?

UH... *OH!* I-I SHAVED IT?!

OH, NO!

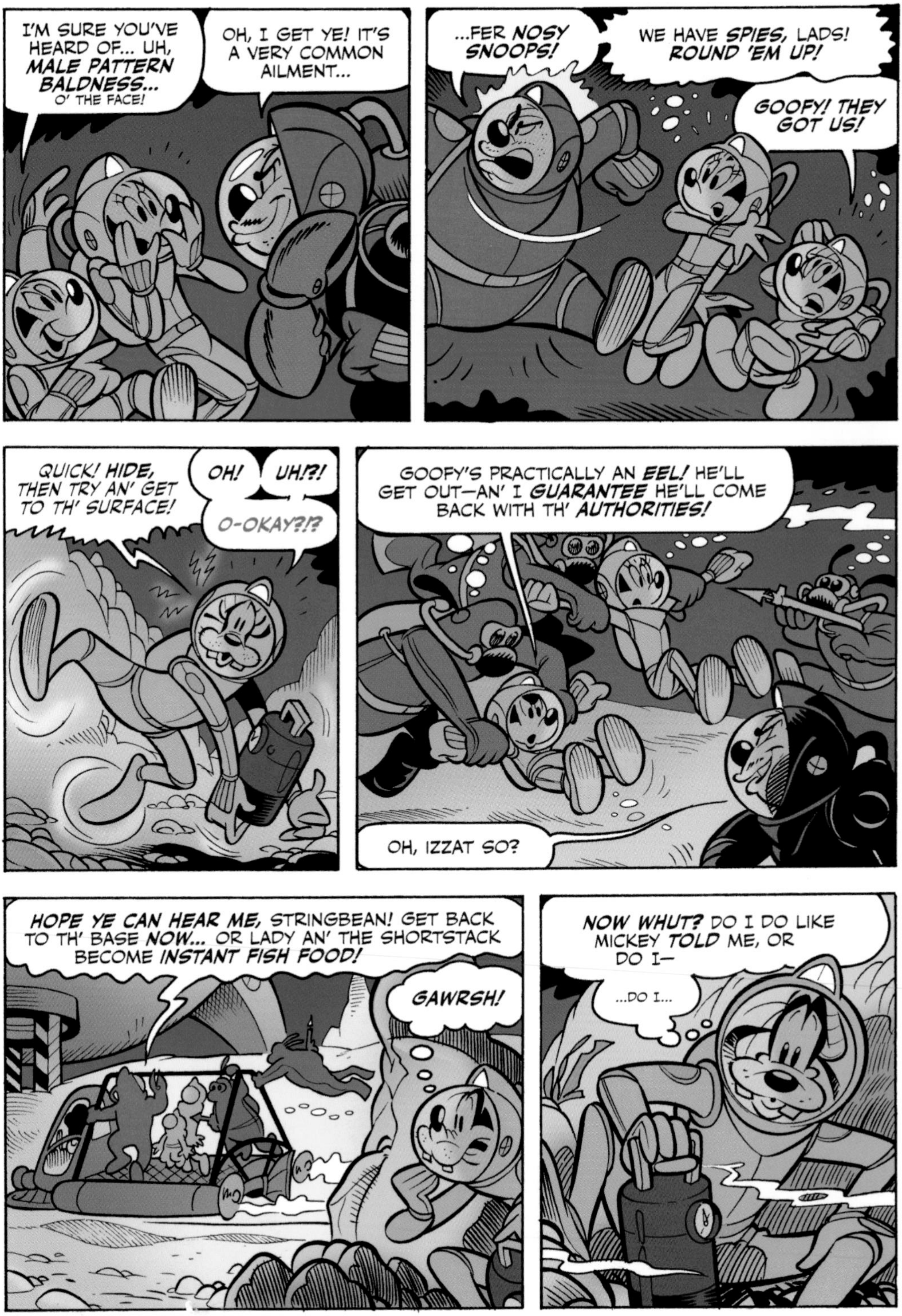

I'M SURE YOU'VE HEARD OF... UH, MALE PATTERN BALDNESS... O' THE FACE!
OH, I GET YE! IT'S A VERY COMMON AILMENT...
...FER NOSY SNOOPS!
WE HAVE SPIES, LADS! ROUND 'EM UP!
GOOFY! THEY GOT US!
QUICK! HIDE, THEN TRY AN' GET TO TH' SURFACE!
OH!
UH!?!
O-OKAY?!?
GOOFY'S PRACTICALLY AN EEL! HE'LL GET OUT—AN' I GUARANTEE HE'LL COME BACK WITH TH' AUTHORITIES!
OH, IZZAT SO?
HOPE YE CAN HEAR ME, STRINGBEAN! GET BACK TO TH' BASE NOW... OR LADY AN' THE SHORTSTACK BECOME INSTANT FISH FOOD!
GAWRSH!
NOW WHUT? DO I DO LIKE MICKEY TOLD ME, OR DO I—
...DO I...

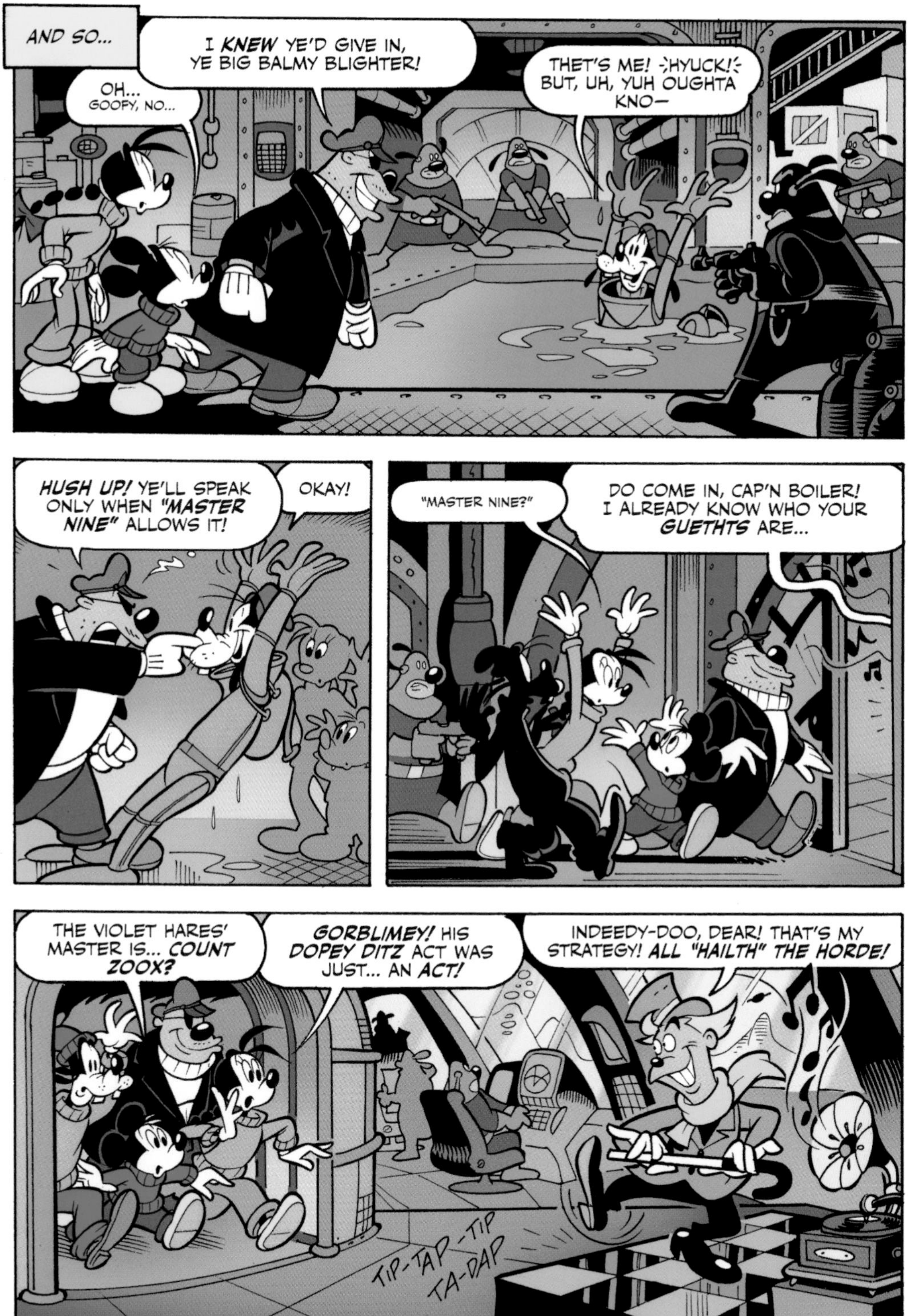
AND SO...
OH... GOOFY, NO...
I *KNEW* YE'D GIVE IN, YE BIG BALMY BLIGHTER!
THET'S ME! HYUCK! BUT, UH, YUH OUGHTA KNO—
*HUSH UP!* YE'LL SPEAK ONLY WHEN *"MASTER NINE"* ALLOWS IT!
OKAY!
"MASTER NINE?"
DO COME IN, CAP'N BOILER! I ALREADY KNOW WHO YOUR *GUETHTS* ARE...
THE VIOLET HARES' MASTER IS... *COUNT ZOOX?*
*GORBLIMEY!* HIS *DOPEY DITZ* ACT WAS JUST... AN *ACT!*
INDEEDY-DOO, DEAR! THAT'S MY STRATEGY! *ALL "HAILTH" THE HORDE!*
TIP-TAP-TIP TA-DAP

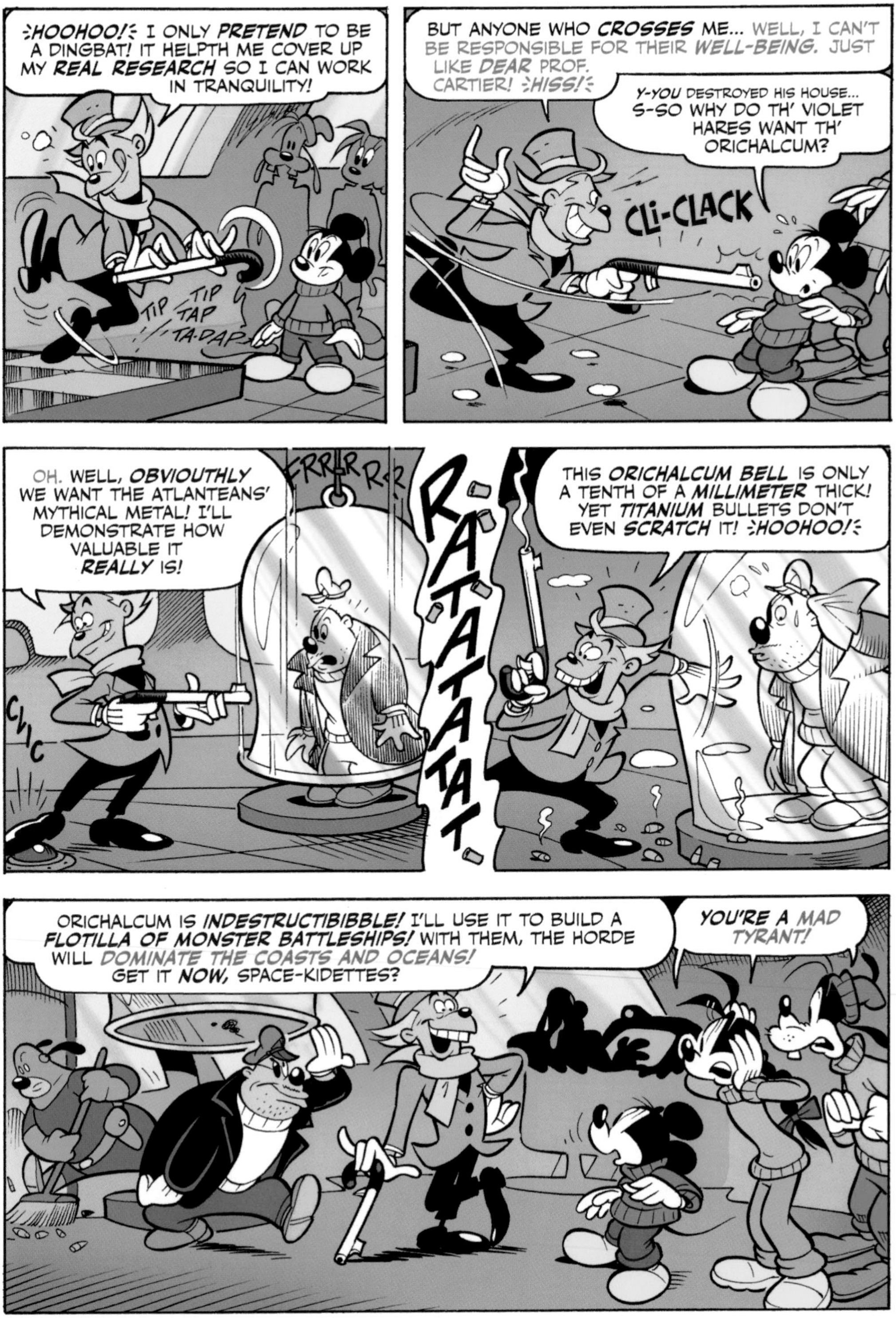

HOOHOO! I ONLY PRETEND TO BE A DINGBAT! IT HELPTH ME COVER UP MY REAL RESEARCH SO I CAN WORK IN TRANQUILITY!
TIP TIP TAP TA-DAP
BUT ANYONE WHO CROSSES ME... WELL, I CAN'T BE RESPONSIBLE FOR THEIR WELL-BEING. JUST LIKE DEAR PROF. CARTIER! HISS!
Y-YOU DESTROYED HIS HOUSE... S-SO WHY DO TH' VIOLET HARES WANT TH' ORICHALCUM?
CLI-CLACK
OH. WELL, OBVIOUTHLY WE WANT THE ATLANTEANS' MYTHICAL METAL! I'LL DEMONSTRATE HOW VALUABLE IT REALLY IS!
FRRRR R-R
CVIC
RATATATAT
THIS ORICHALCUM BELL IS ONLY A TENTH OF A MILLIMETER THICK! YET TITANIUM BULLETS DON'T EVEN SCRATCH IT! HOOHOO!
ORICHALCUM IS INDESTRUCTIBIBBLE! I'LL USE IT TO BUILD A FLOTILLA OF MONSTER BATTLESHIPS! WITH THEM, THE HORDE WILL DOMINATE THE COASTS AND OCEANS! GET IT NOW, SPACE-KIDETTES?
YOU'RE A MAD TYRANT!

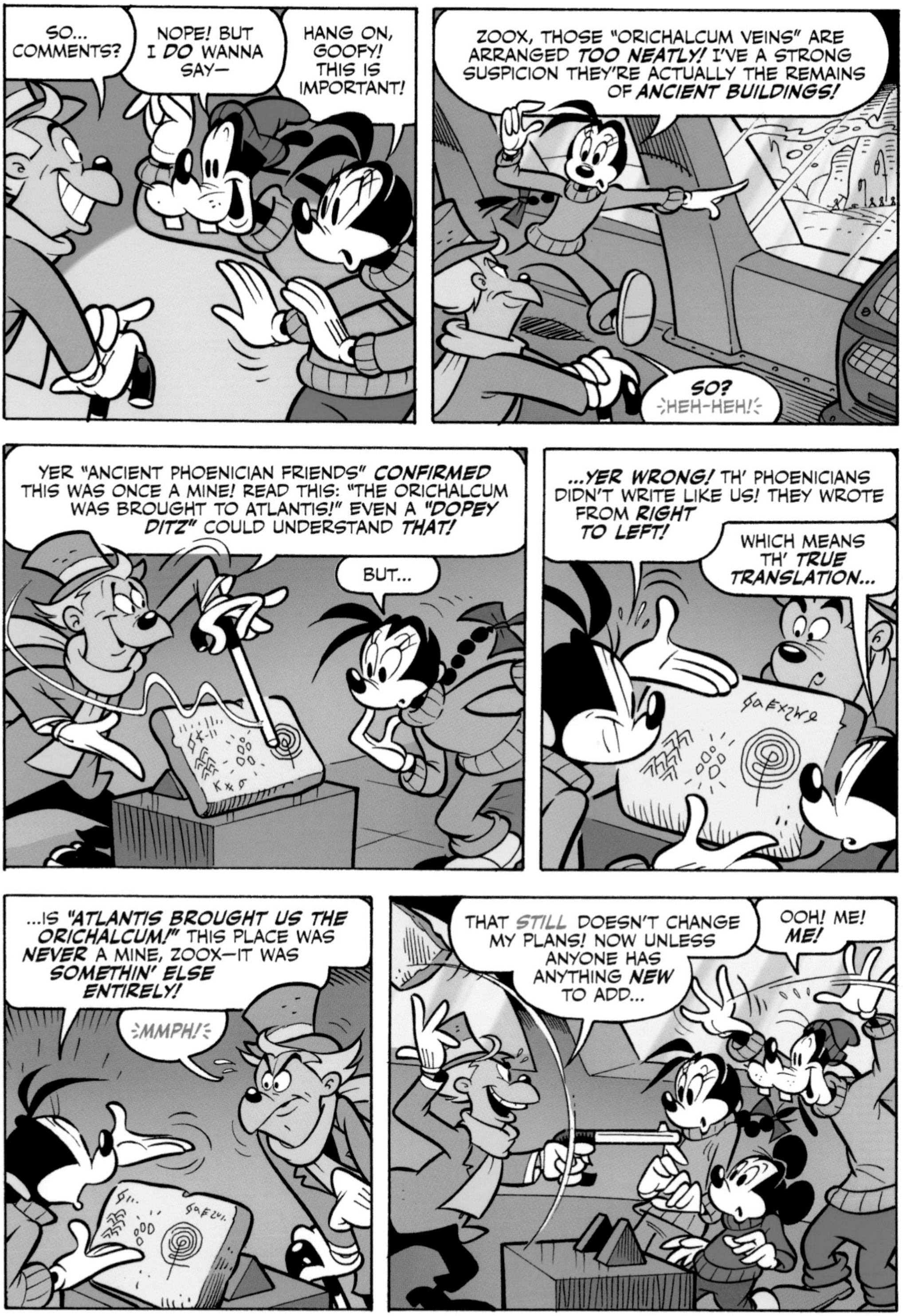
SO... COMMENTS?
NOPE! BUT I DO WANNA SAY—
HANG ON, GOOFY! THIS IS IMPORTANT!
ZOOX, THOSE "ORICHALCUM VEINS" ARE ARRANGED TOO NEATLY! I'VE A STRONG SUSPICION THEY'RE ACTUALLY THE REMAINS OF ANCIENT BUILDINGS!
SO? HEH-HEH!
YER "ANCIENT PHOENICIAN FRIENDS" CONFIRMED THIS WAS ONCE A MINE! READ THIS: "THE ORICHALCUM WAS BROUGHT TO ATLANTIS!" EVEN A "DOPEY DITZ" COULD UNDERSTAND THAT!
BUT...
...YER WRONG! TH' PHOENICIANS DIDN'T WRITE LIKE US! THEY WROTE FROM RIGHT TO LEFT!
WHICH MEANS TH' TRUE TRANSLATION...
...IS "ATLANTIS BROUGHT US THE ORICHALCUM!" THIS PLACE WAS NEVER A MINE, ZOOX—IT WAS SOMETHIN' ELSE ENTIRELY!
MMPH!
THAT STILL DOESN'T CHANGE MY PLANS! NOW UNLESS ANYONE HAS ANYTHING NEW TO ADD...
OOH! ME! ME!

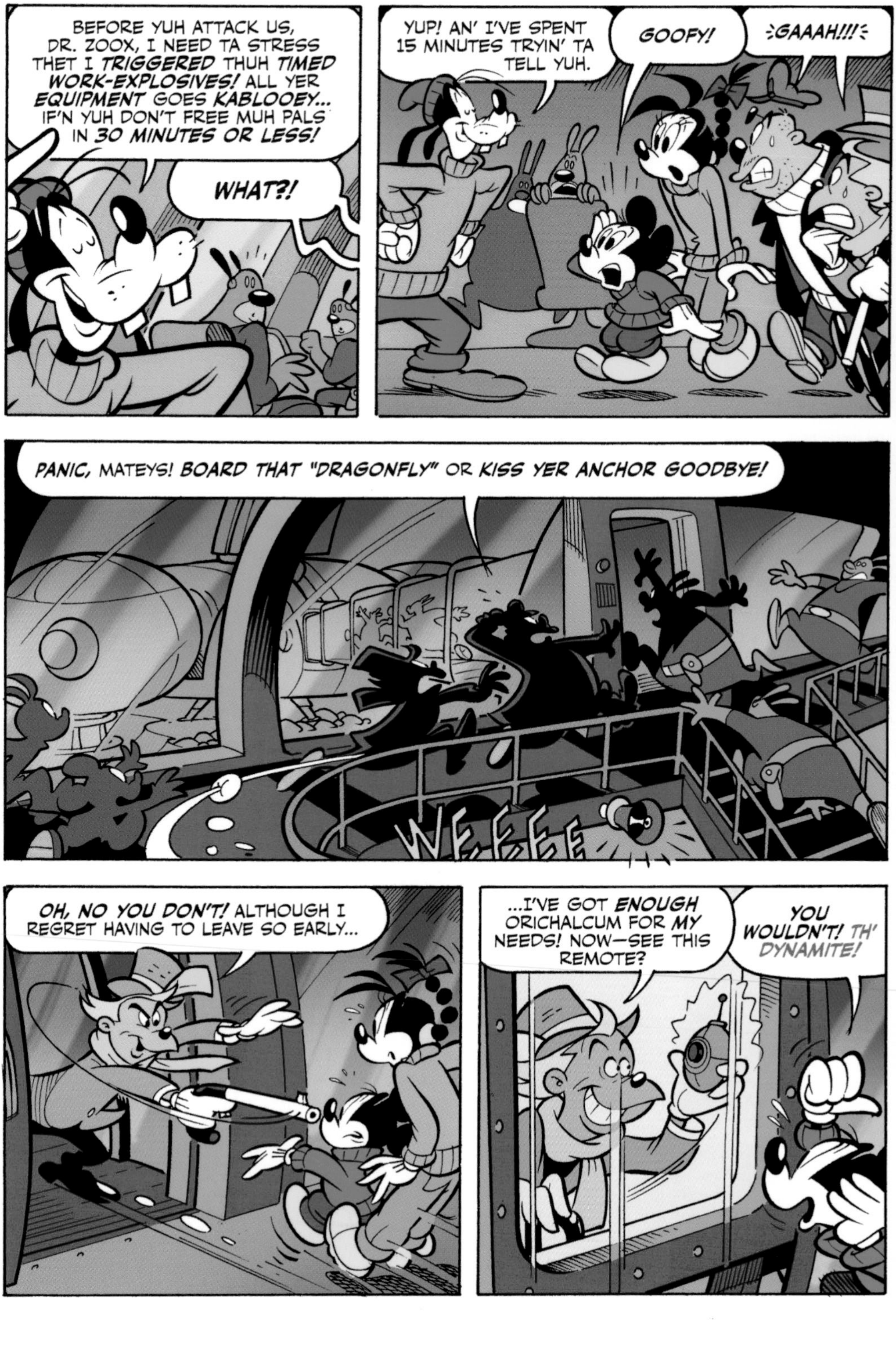
BEFORE YUH ATTACK US, DR. ZOOX, I NEED TA STRESS THET I TRIGGERED THUH TIMED WORK-EXPLOSIVES! ALL YER EQUIPMENT GOES KABLOOEY... IF'N YUH DON'T FREE MUH PALS IN 30 MINUTES OR LESS!
WHAT?!
YUP! AN' I'VE SPENT 15 MINUTES TRYIN' TA TELL YUH.
GOOFY!
GAAAH!!!
PANIC, MATEYS! BOARD THAT "DRAGONFLY" OR KISS YER ANCHOR GOODBYE!
WEEEE
OH, NO YOU DON'T! ALTHOUGH I REGRET HAVING TO LEAVE SO EARLY...
...I'VE GOT ENOUGH ORICHALCUM FOR MY NEEDS! NOW—SEE THIS REMOTE?
YOU WOULDN'T! TH' DYNAMITE!

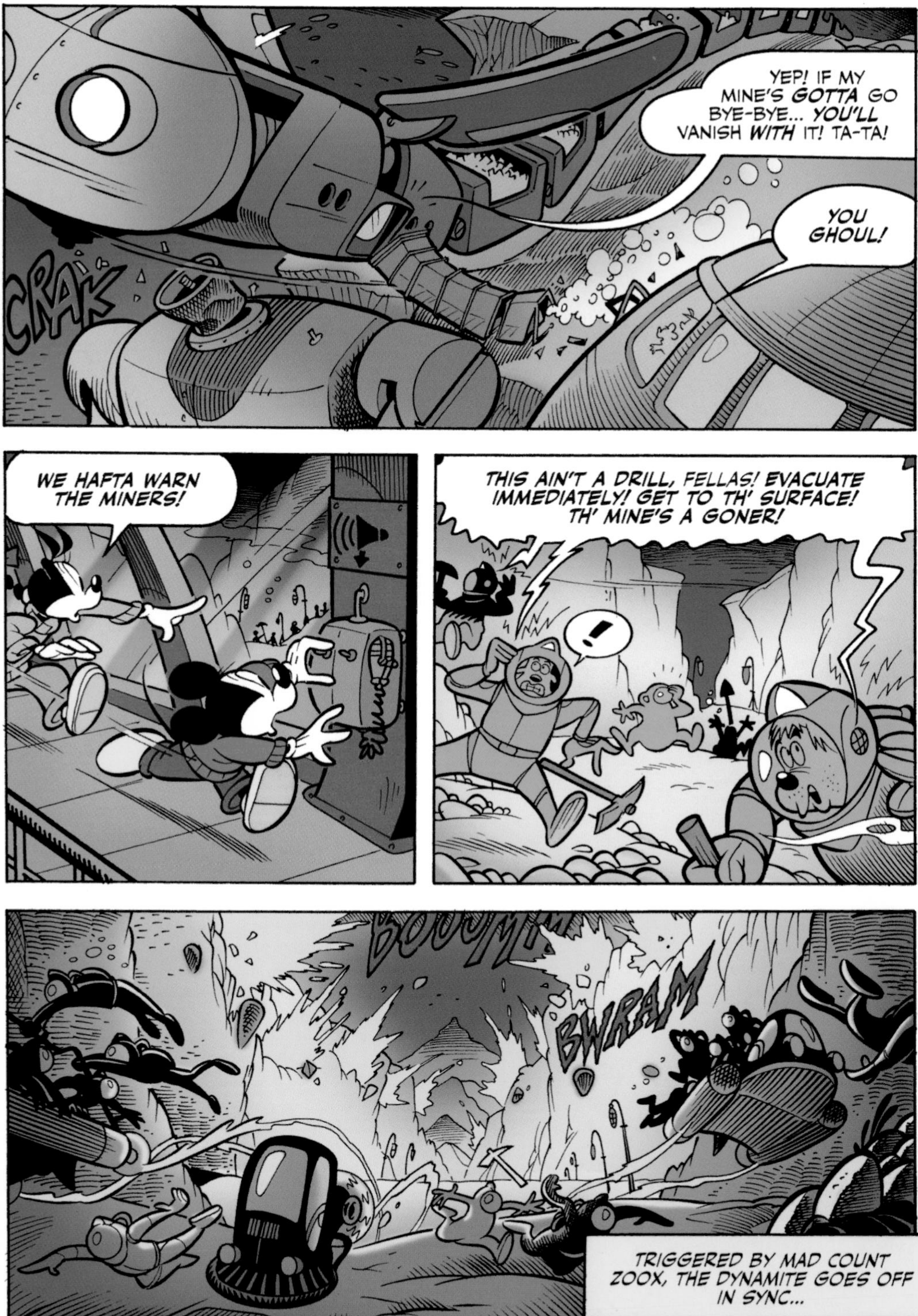
YEP! IF MY MINE'S GOTTA GO BYE-BYE... YOU'LL VANISH WITH IT! TA-TA!
YOU GHOUL!
CRAK
WE HAFTA WARN THE MINERS!
THIS AIN'T A DRILL, FELLAS! EVACUATE IMMEDIATELY! GET TO TH' SURFACE! TH' MINE'S A GONER!
!
BWRAM
TRIGGERED BY MAD COUNT ZOOX, THE DYNAMITE GOES OFF IN SYNC...

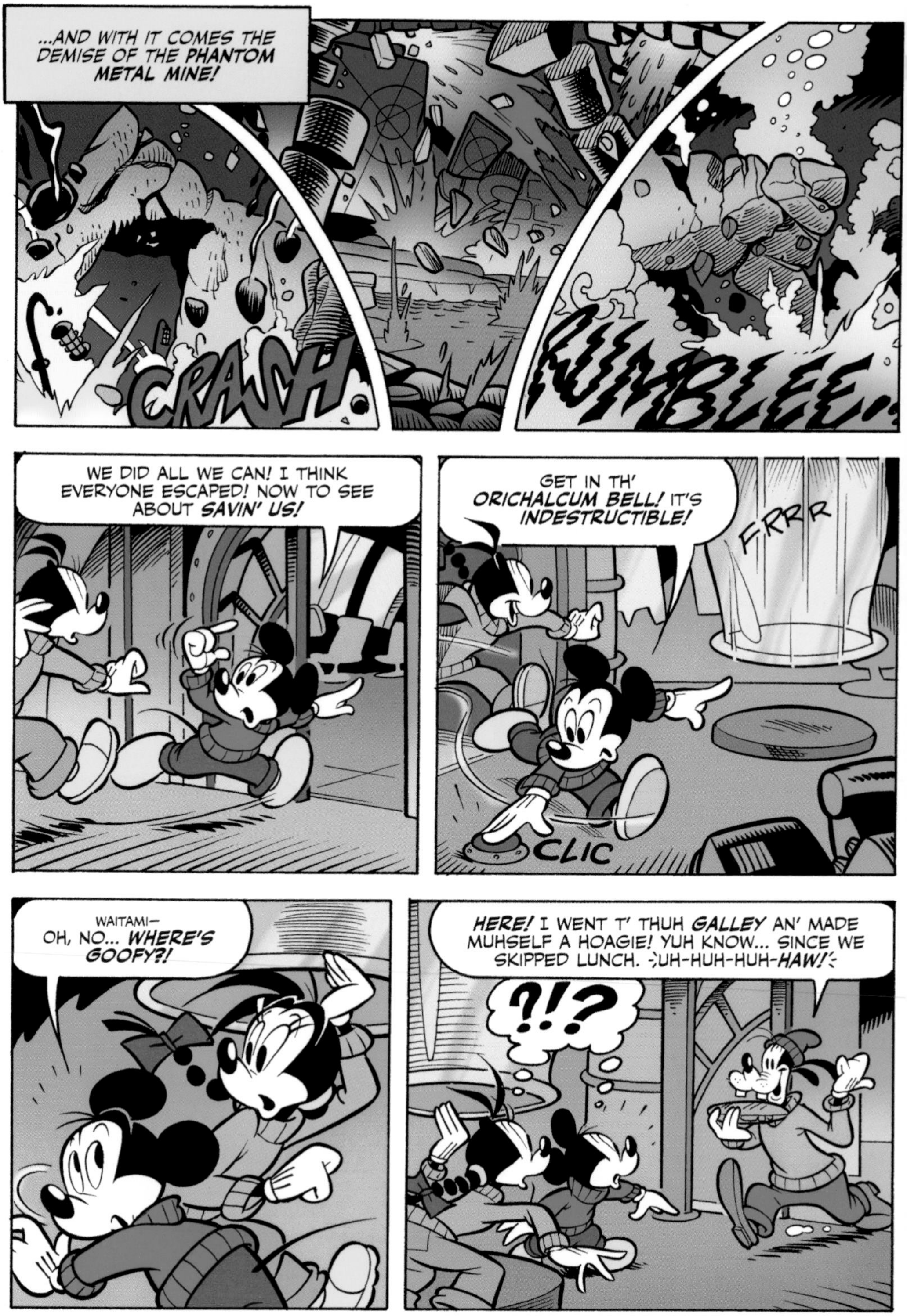
...AND WITH IT COMES THE DEMISE OF THE PHANTOM METAL MINE!
CRASH
RUMBLEEE...
WE DID ALL WE CAN! I THINK EVERYONE ESCAPED! NOW TO SEE ABOUT SAVIN' US!
GET IN TH' ORICHALCUM BELL! IT'S INDESTRUCTIBLE!
FRRR
CLIC
WAITAMI— OH, NO... WHERE'S GOOFY?!
HERE! I WENT T' THUH GALLEY AN' MADE MUHSELF A HOAGIE! YUH KNOW... SINCE WE SKIPPED LUNCH. UH-HUH-HUH-HAW!
?!?

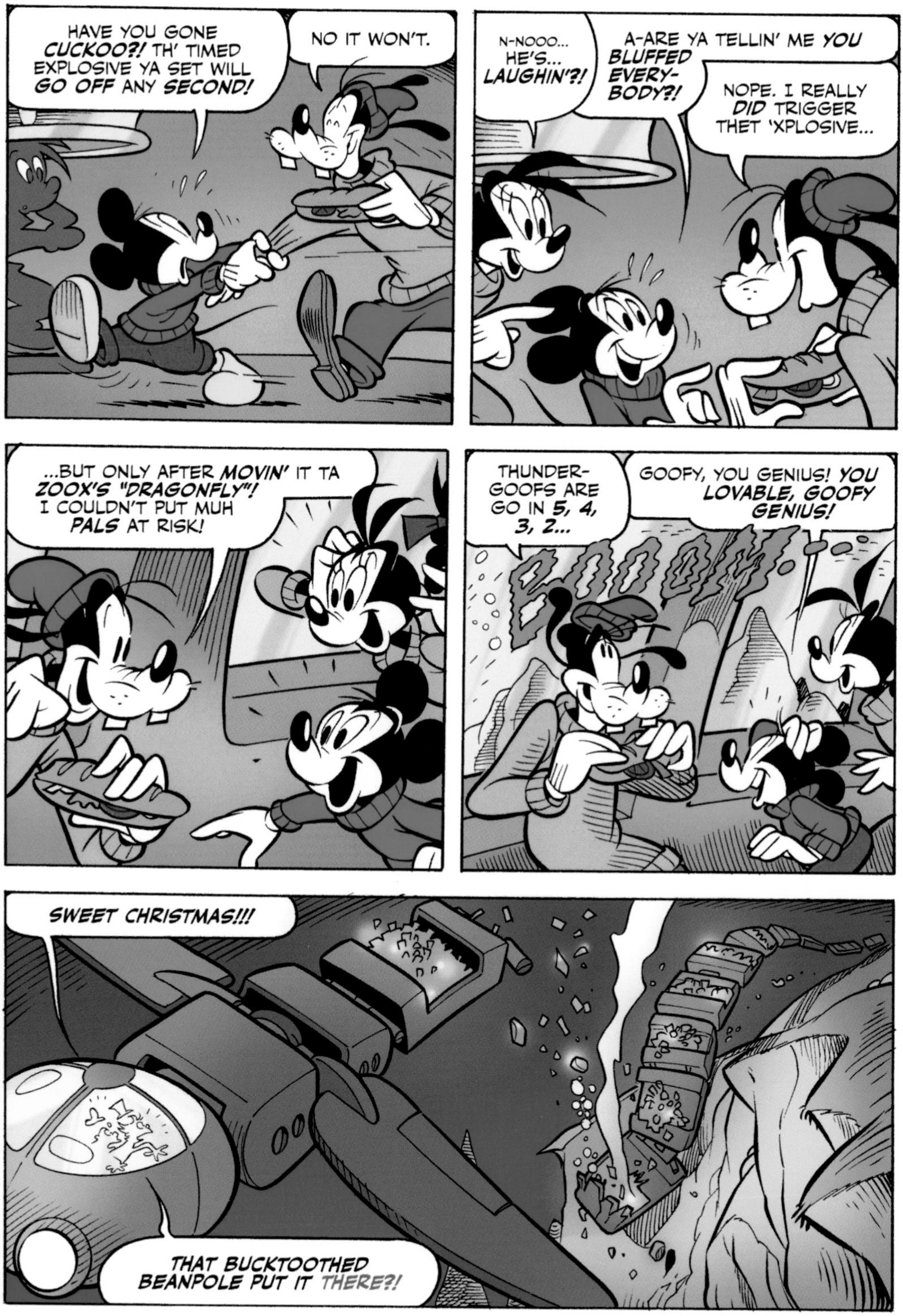
HAVE YOU GONE CUCKOO?! TH' TIMED EXPLOSIVE YA SET WILL GO OFF ANY SECOND!
NO IT WON'T.
N-NOOO... HE'S... LAUGHIN'?!
A-ARE YA TELLIN' ME YOU BLUFFED EVERY-BODY?!
NOPE. I REALLY DID TRIGGER THET 'XPLOSIVE...
...BUT ONLY AFTER MOVIN' IT TA ZOOX'S "DRAGONFLY"! I COULDN'T PUT MUH PALS AT RISK!
THUNDER-GOOFS ARE GO IN 5, 4, 3, 2...
GOOFY, YOU GENIUS! YOU LOVABLE, GOOFY GENIUS!
BOOOM!
SWEET CHRISTMAS!!!
THAT BUCKTOOTHED BEANPOLE PUT IT THERE?!

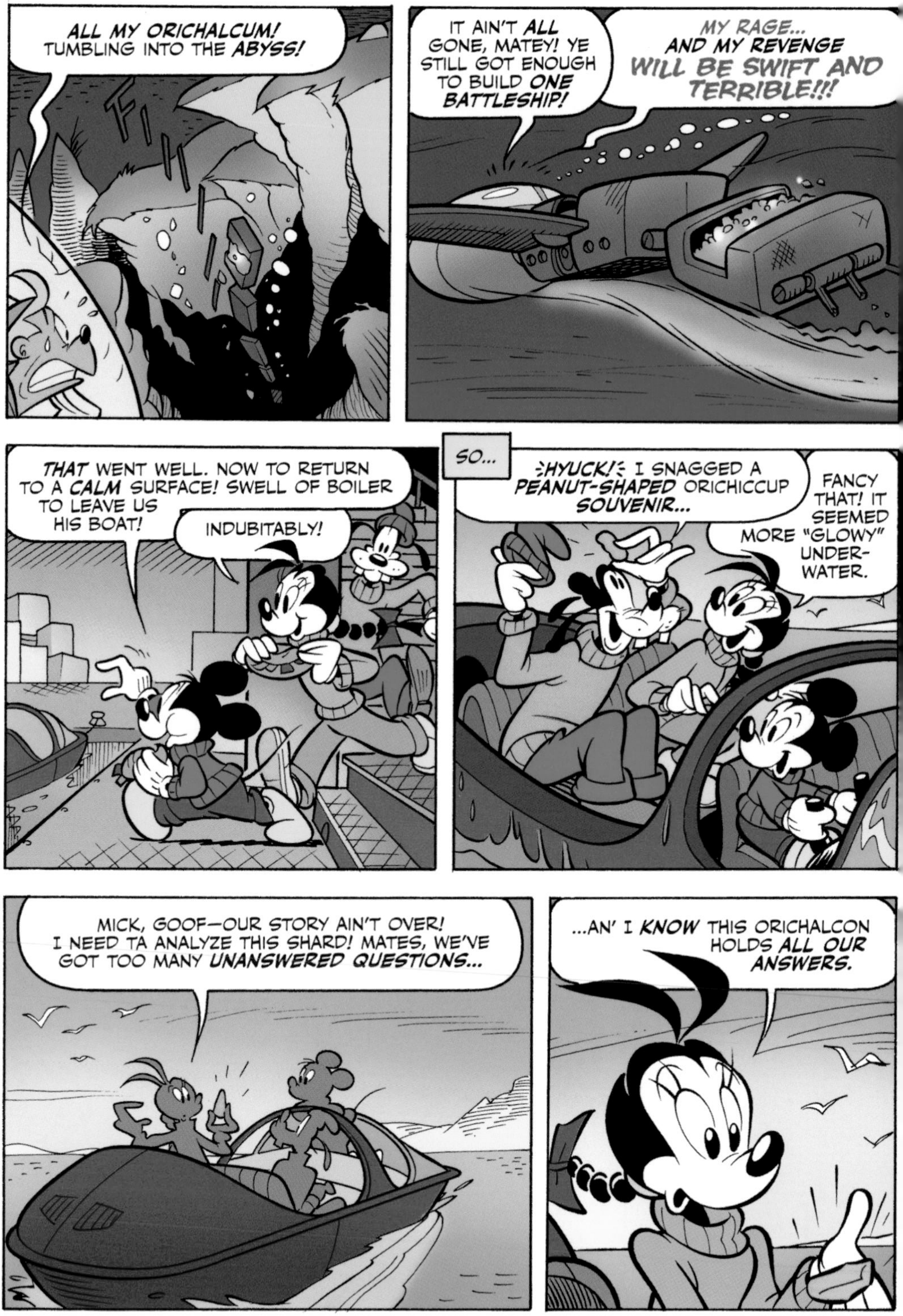
ALL MY ORICHALCUM! TUMBLING INTO THE ABYSS!
FFF
IT AIN'T ALL GONE, MATEY! YE STILL GOT ENOUGH TO BUILD ONE BATTLESHIP!
MY RAGE... AND MY REVENGE WILL BE SWIFT AND TERRIBLE!!!
THAT WENT WELL. NOW TO RETURN TO A CALM SURFACE! SWELL OF BOILER TO LEAVE US HIS BOAT!
INDUBITABLY!
SO...
HYUCK! I SNAGGED A PEANUT-SHAPED ORICHICCUP SOUVENIR...
FANCY THAT! IT SEEMED MORE "GLOWY" UNDER-WATER.
MICK, GOOF—OUR STORY AIN'T OVER! I NEED TA ANALYZE THIS SHARD! MATES, WE'VE GOT TOO MANY UNANSWERED QUESTIONS...
...AN' I KNOW THIS ORICHALCON HOLDS ALL OUR ANSWERS.

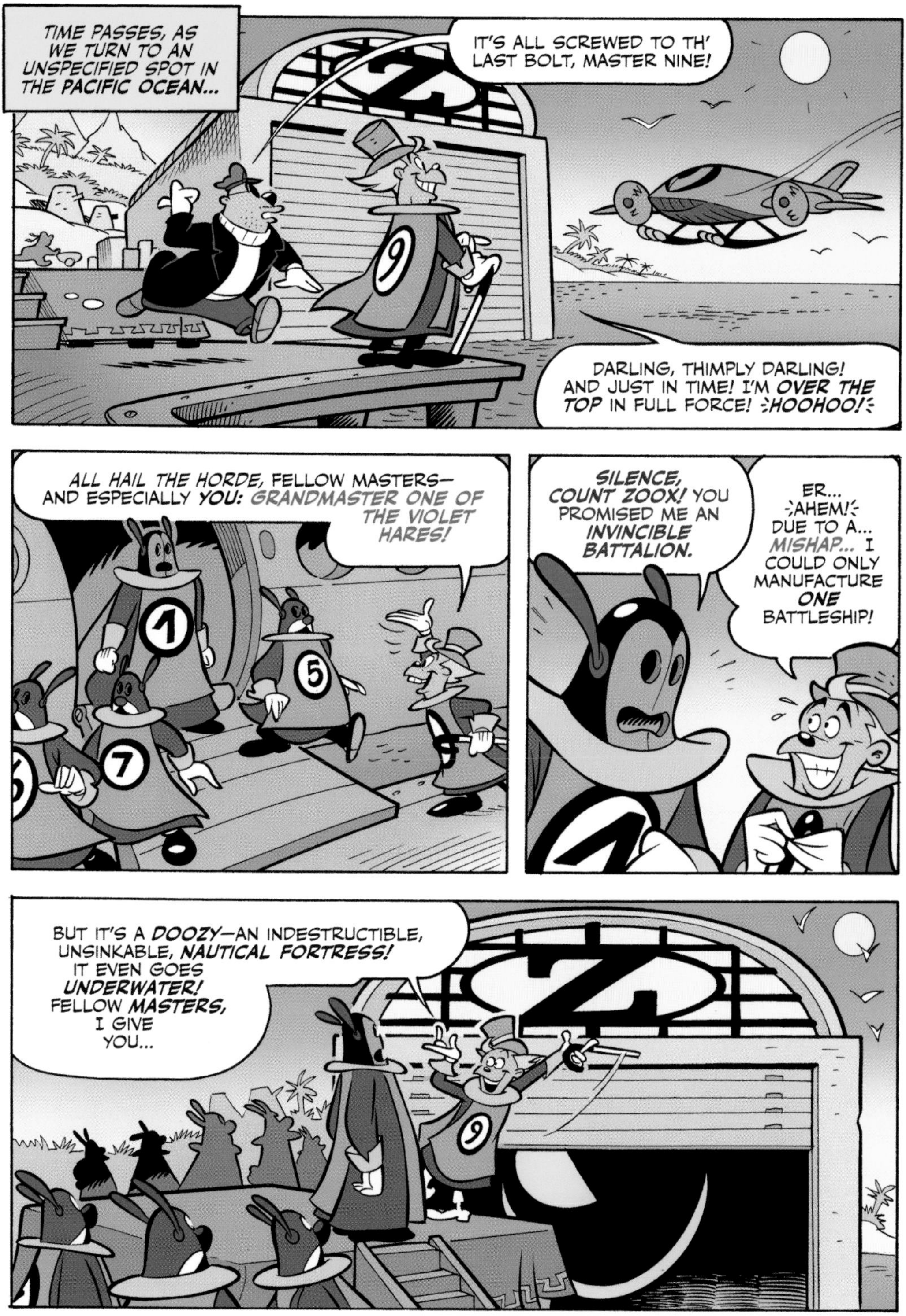
TIME PASSES, AS WE TURN TO AN UNSPECIFIED SPOT IN THE PACIFIC OCEAN...
IT'S ALL SCREWED TO TH' LAST BOLT, MASTER NINE!
DARLING, THIMPLY DARLING! AND JUST IN TIME! I'M OVER THE TOP IN FULL FORCE! HOOHOO!
ALL HAIL THE HORDE, FELLOW MASTERS—AND ESPECIALLY YOU: GRANDMASTER ONE OF THE VIOLET HARES!
SILENCE, COUNT ZOOX! YOU PROMISED ME AN INVINCIBLE BATTALION.
ER... AHEM! DUE TO A... MISHAP... I COULD ONLY MANUFACTURE ONE BATTLESHIP!
BUT IT'S A DOOZY—AN INDESTRUCTIBLE, UNSINKABLE, NAUTICAL FORTRESS! IT EVEN GOES UNDERWATER! FELLOW MASTERS, I GIVE YOU...

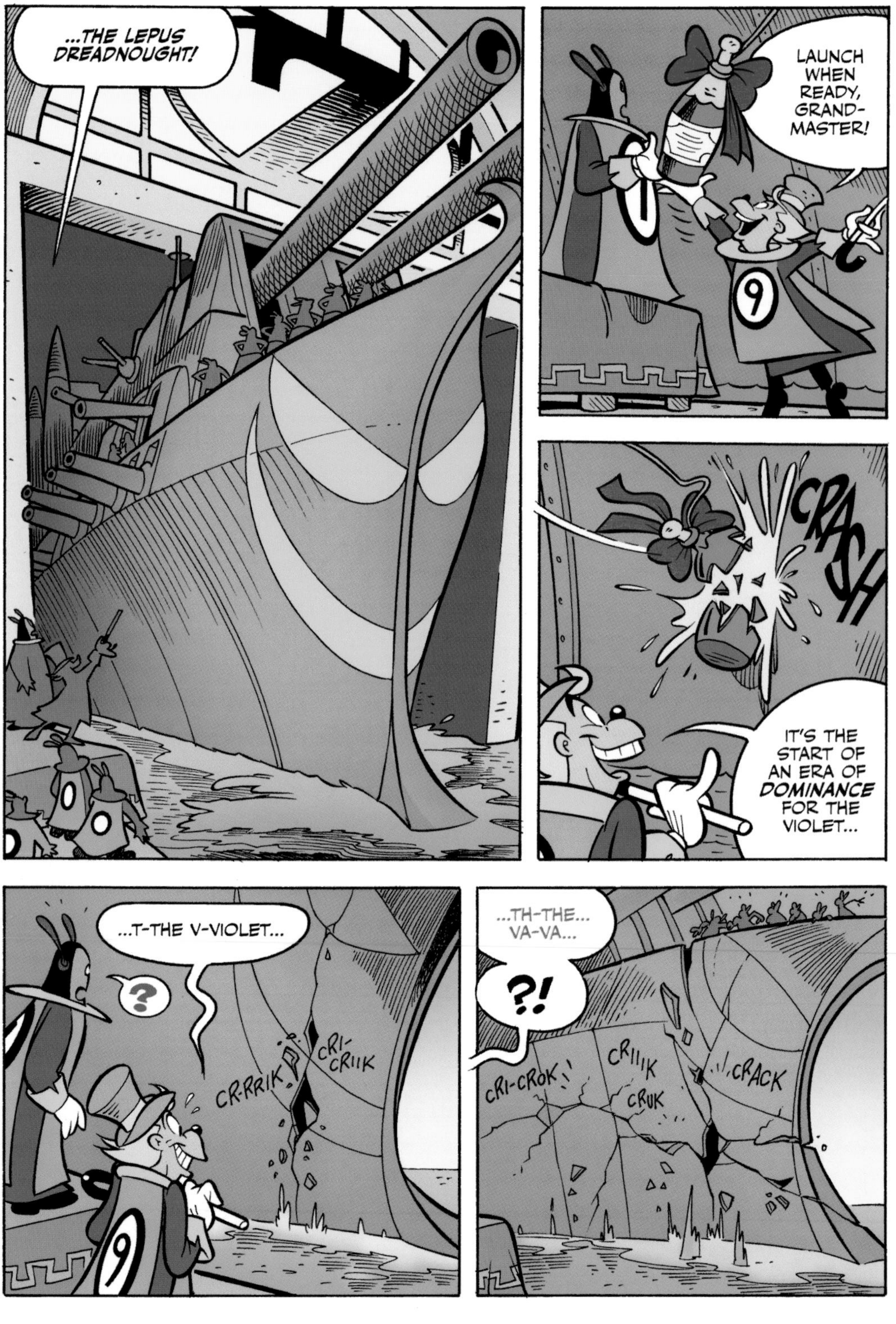
...THE LEPUS DREADNOUGHT!
LAUNCH WHEN READY, GRAND-MASTER!
CRASH
IT'S THE START OF AN ERA OF DOMINANCE FOR THE VIOLET...
...T-THE V-VIOLET...
?
CR-RRIK
CRI-CRIIK
...TH-THE... VA-VA...
?!
CRI-CROK
CRIIIK
CRUK
CRACK

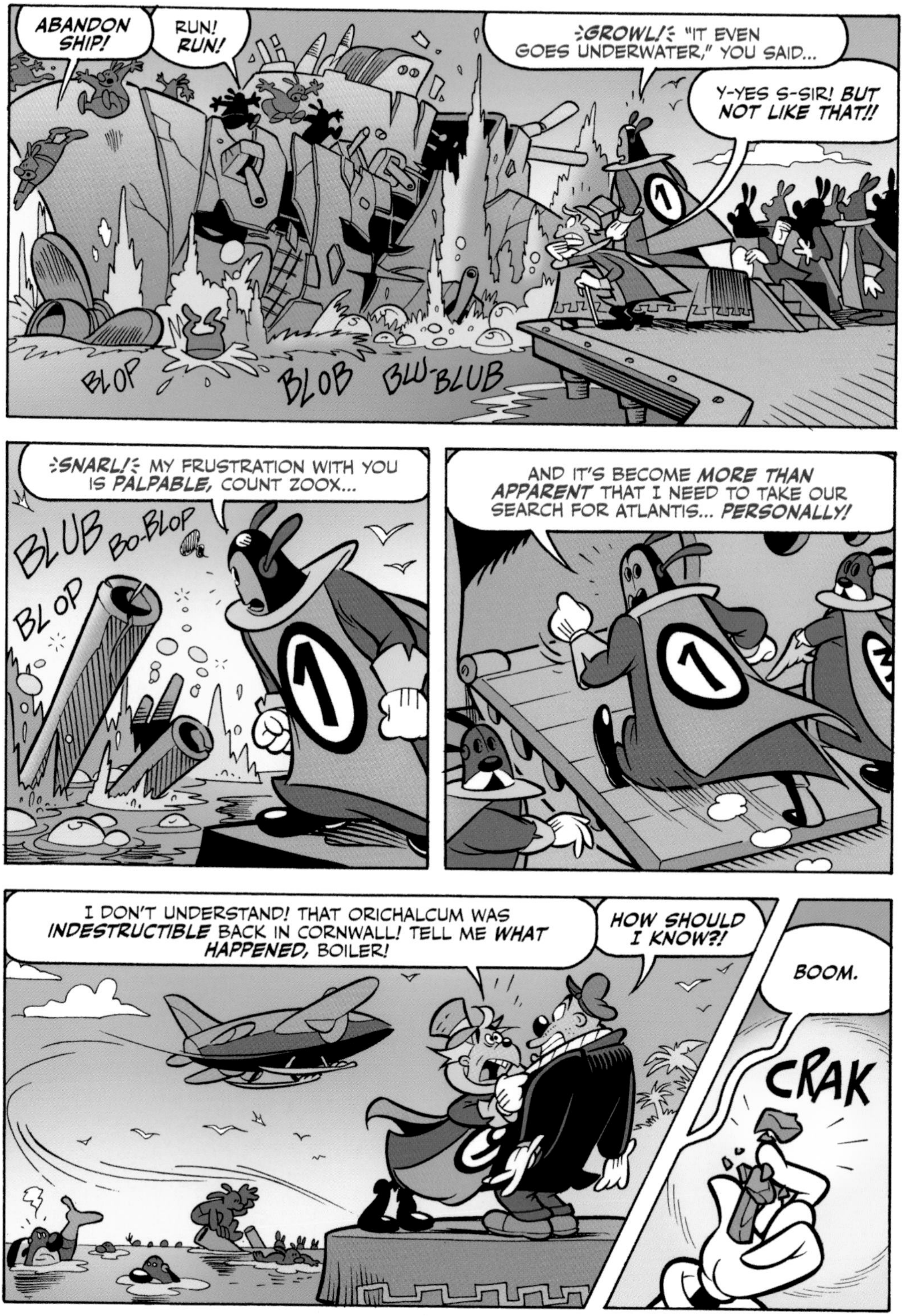
ABANDON SHIP!
RUN! RUN!
GROWL! "IT EVEN GOES UNDERWATER," YOU SAID...
Y-YES S-SIR! BUT NOT LIKE THAT!!
BLOP
BLOB
BLU-BLUB
SNARL! MY FRUSTRATION WITH YOU IS PALPABLE, COUNT ZOOX...
BLUB
BO-BLOP
BLOP
AND IT'S BECOME MORE THAN APPARENT THAT I NEED TO TAKE OUR SEARCH FOR ATLANTIS... PERSONALLY!
I DON'T UNDERSTAND! THAT ORICHALCUM WAS INDESTRUCTIBLE BACK IN CORNWALL! TELL ME WHAT HAPPENED, BOILER!
HOW SHOULD I KNOW?!
BOOM.
CRAK

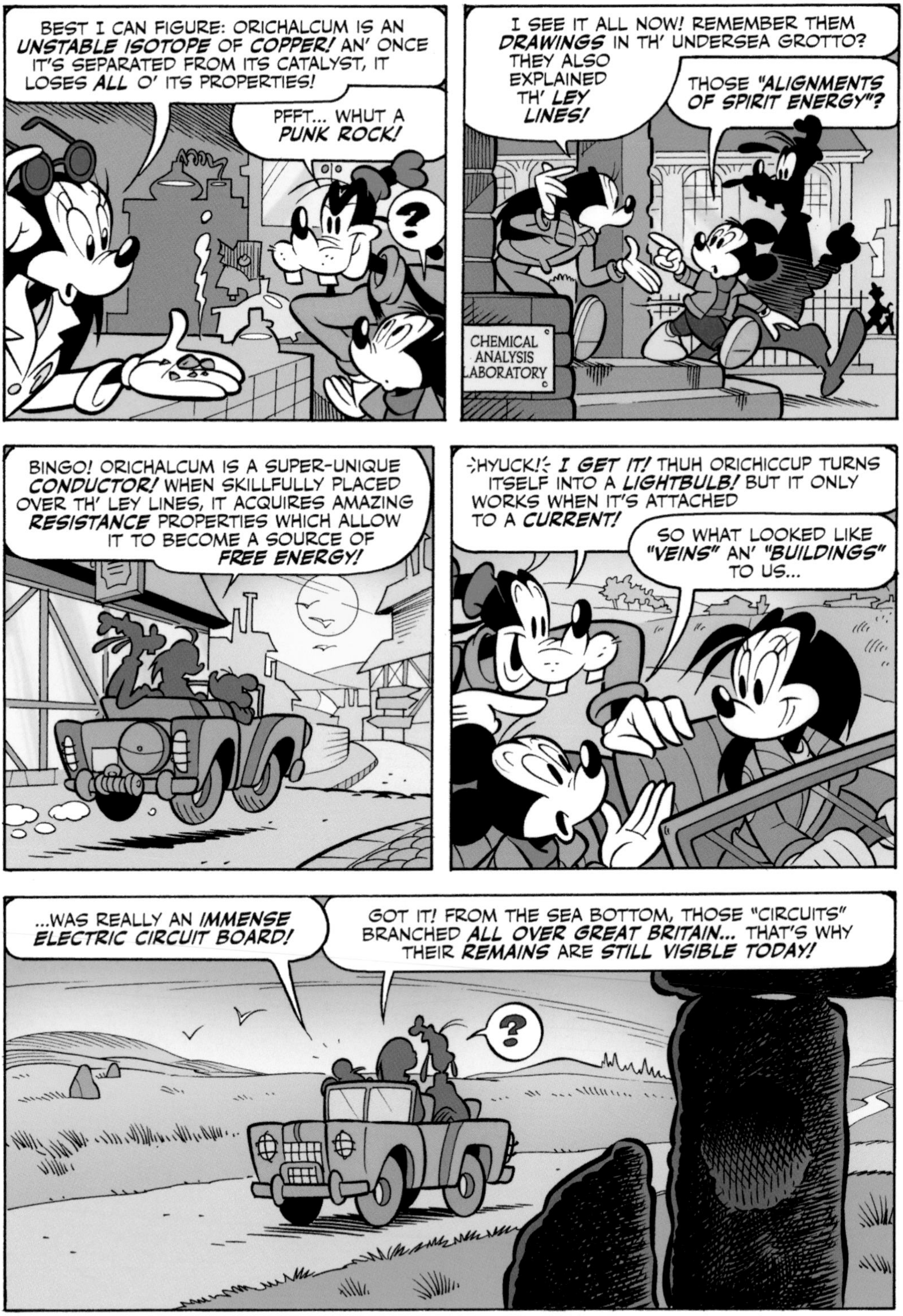
BEST I CAN FIGURE: ORICHALCUM IS AN *UNSTABLE ISOTOPE* OF *COPPER!* AN' ONCE IT'S SEPARATED FROM ITS CATALYST, IT LOSES *ALL* O' ITS PROPERTIES!
PFFT... WHUT A *PUNK ROCK!*
?
I SEE IT ALL NOW! REMEMBER THEM *DRAWINGS* IN TH' UNDERSEA GROTTO? THEY ALSO EXPLAINED TH' *LEY LINES!*
THOSE *"ALIGNMENTS OF SPIRIT ENERGY"?*
CHEMICAL ANALYSIS LABORATORY
BINGO! ORICHALCUM IS A SUPER-UNIQUE *CONDUCTOR!* WHEN SKILLFULLY PLACED OVER TH' LEY LINES, IT ACQUIRES AMAZING *RESISTANCE* PROPERTIES WHICH ALLOW IT TO BECOME A SOURCE OF *FREE ENERGY!*
HYUCK! *I GET IT!* THUH ORICHICCUP TURNS ITSELF INTO A *LIGHTBULB!* BUT IT ONLY WORKS WHEN IT'S ATTACHED TO A *CURRENT!*
SO WHAT LOOKED LIKE *"VEINS"* AN' *"BUILDINGS"* TO US...
...WAS REALLY AN *IMMENSE ELECTRIC CIRCUIT BOARD!*
GOT IT! FROM THE SEA BOTTOM, THOSE "CIRCUITS" BRANCHED *ALL OVER GREAT BRITAIN...* THAT'S WHY THEIR *REMAINS* ARE *STILL VISIBLE TODAY!*
?

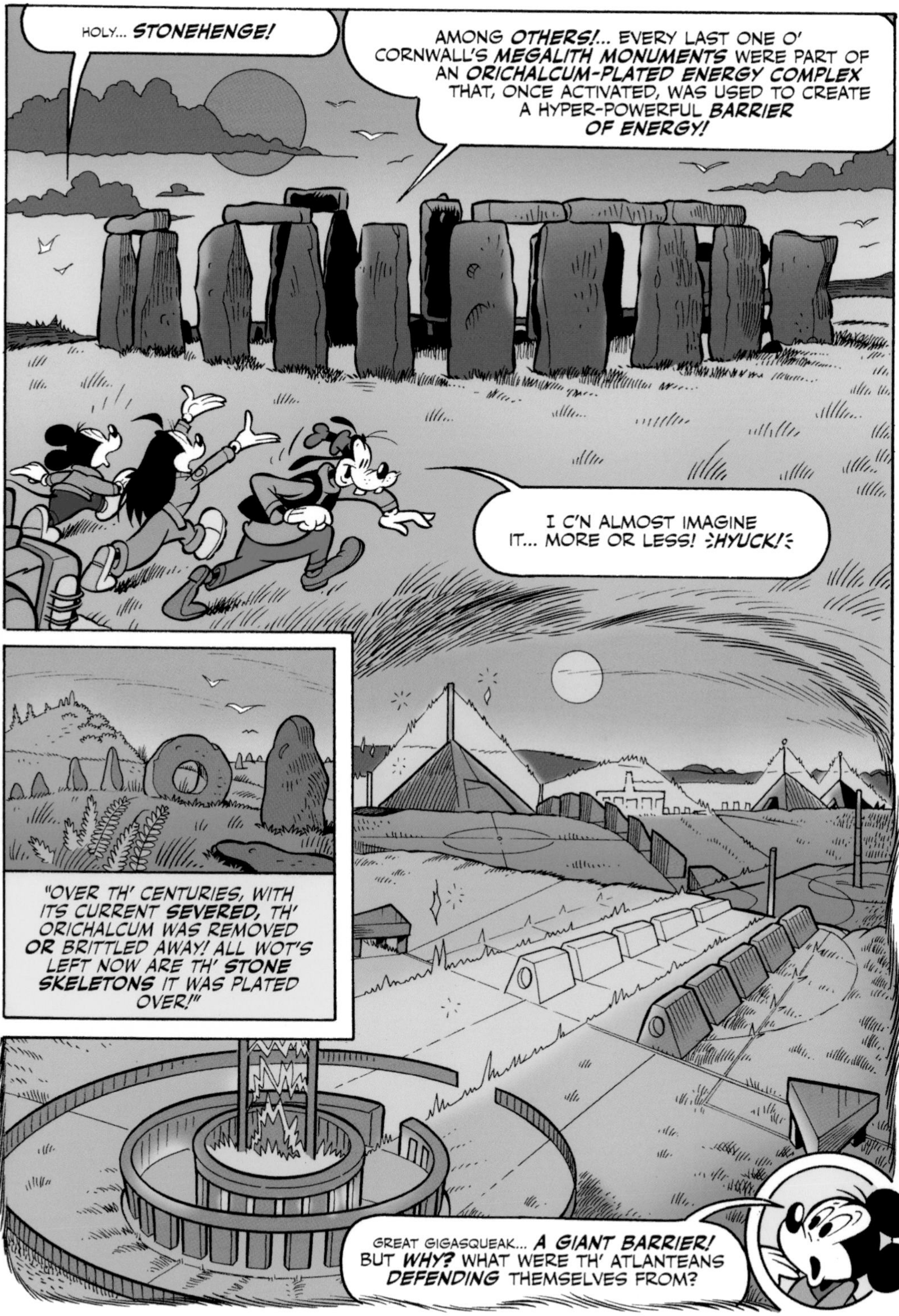
HOLY... STONEHENGE!
AMONG OTHERS!... EVERY LAST ONE O' CORNWALL'S MEGALITH MONUMENTS WERE PART OF AN ORICHALCUM-PLATED ENERGY COMPLEX THAT, ONCE ACTIVATED, WAS USED TO CREATE A HYPER-POWERFUL BARRIER OF ENERGY!
I C'N ALMOST IMAGINE IT... MORE OR LESS! HYUCK!
"OVER TH' CENTURIES, WITH ITS CURRENT SEVERED, TH' ORICHALCUM WAS REMOVED OR BRITTLED AWAY! ALL WOT'S LEFT NOW ARE TH' STONE SKELETONS IT WAS PLATED OVER!"
GREAT GIGASQUEAK... A GIANT BARRIER! BUT WHY? WHAT WERE TH' ATLANTEANS DEFENDING THEMSELVES FROM?

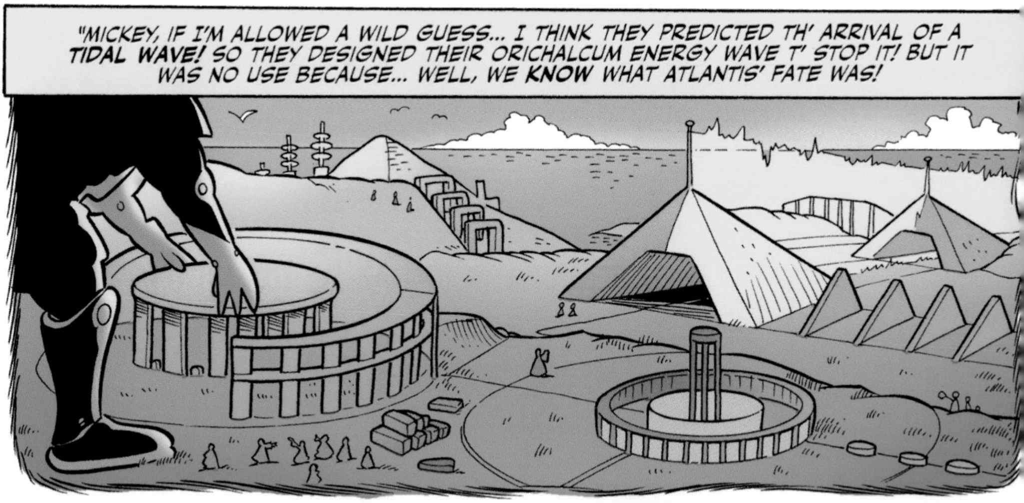
"MICKEY, IF I'M ALLOWED A WILD GUESS... I THINK THEY PREDICTED TH' ARRIVAL OF A TIDAL WAVE! SO THEY DESIGNED THEIR ORICHALCUM ENERGY WAVE T' STOP IT! BUT IT WAS NO USE BECAUSE... WELL, WE KNOW WHAT ATLANTIS' FATE WAS!

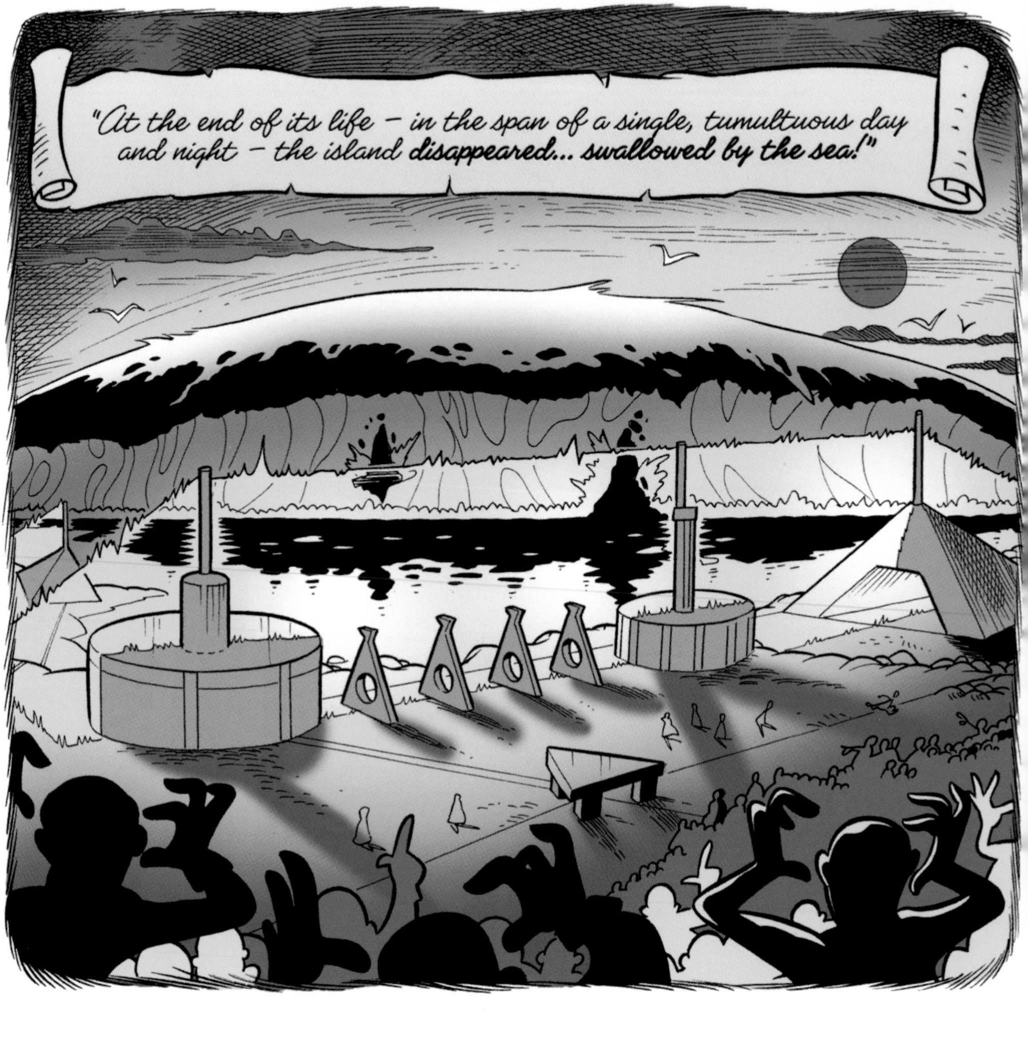
"At the end of its life – in the span of a single, tumultuous day and night – the island disappeared... swallowed by the sea!"

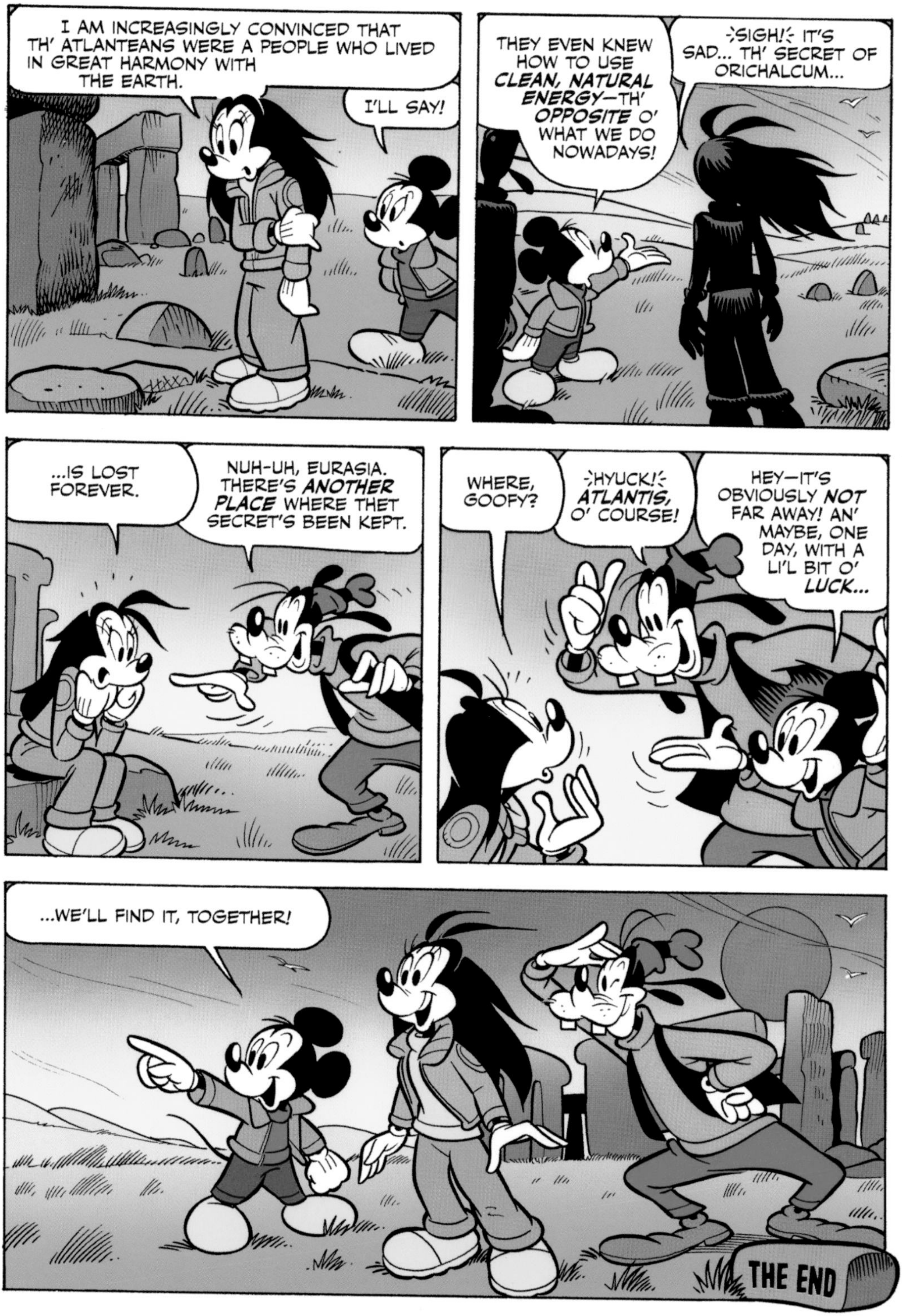
I AM INCREASINGLY CONVINCED THAT TH' ATLANTEANS WERE A PEOPLE WHO LIVED IN GREAT HARMONY WITH THE EARTH.
I'LL SAY!
THEY EVEN KNEW HOW TO USE **CLEAN, NATURAL ENERGY**—TH' **OPPOSITE** O' WHAT WE DO NOWADAYS!
*SIGH!* IT'S SAD... TH' SECRET OF ORICHALCUM...
...IS LOST FOREVER.
NUH-UH, EURASIA. THERE'S **ANOTHER PLACE** WHERE THET SECRET'S BEEN KEPT.
WHERE, GOOFY?
*HYUCK!* **ATLANTIS,** O' COURSE!
HEY—IT'S OBVIOUSLY **NOT** FAR AWAY! AN' MAYBE, ONE DAY, WITH A LI'L BIT O' **LUCK...**
...WE'LL FIND IT, TOGETHER!
THE END

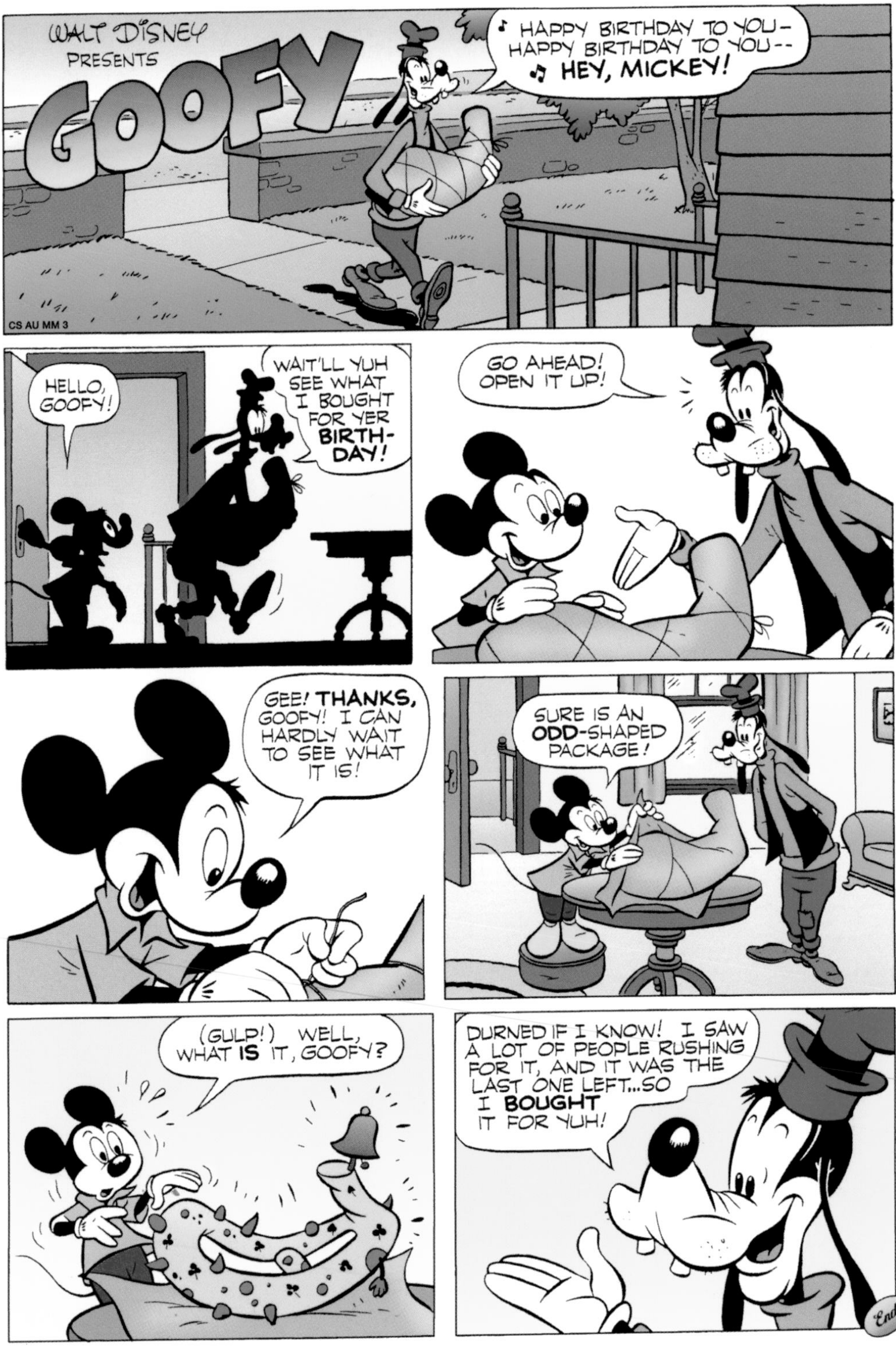
WALT DISNEY PRESENTS
GOOFY
♪ HAPPY BIRTHDAY TO YOU– HAPPY BIRTHDAY TO YOU-- ♫ HEY, MICKEY!
CS AU MM 3
HELLO, GOOFY!
WAIT'LL YUH SEE WHAT I BOUGHT FOR YER BIRTH-DAY!
GO AHEAD! OPEN IT UP!
GEE! THANKS, GOOFY! I CAN HARDLY WAIT TO SEE WHAT IT IS!
SURE IS AN ODD-SHAPED PACKAGE!
(GULP!) WELL, WHAT IS IT, GOOFY?
DURNED IF I KNOW! I SAW A LOT OF PEOPLE RUSHING FOR IT, AND IT WAS THE LAST ONE LEFT...SO I BOUGHT IT FOR YUH!
End

Originally published in *Mickey Mouse* #3 (Australia, 1953)

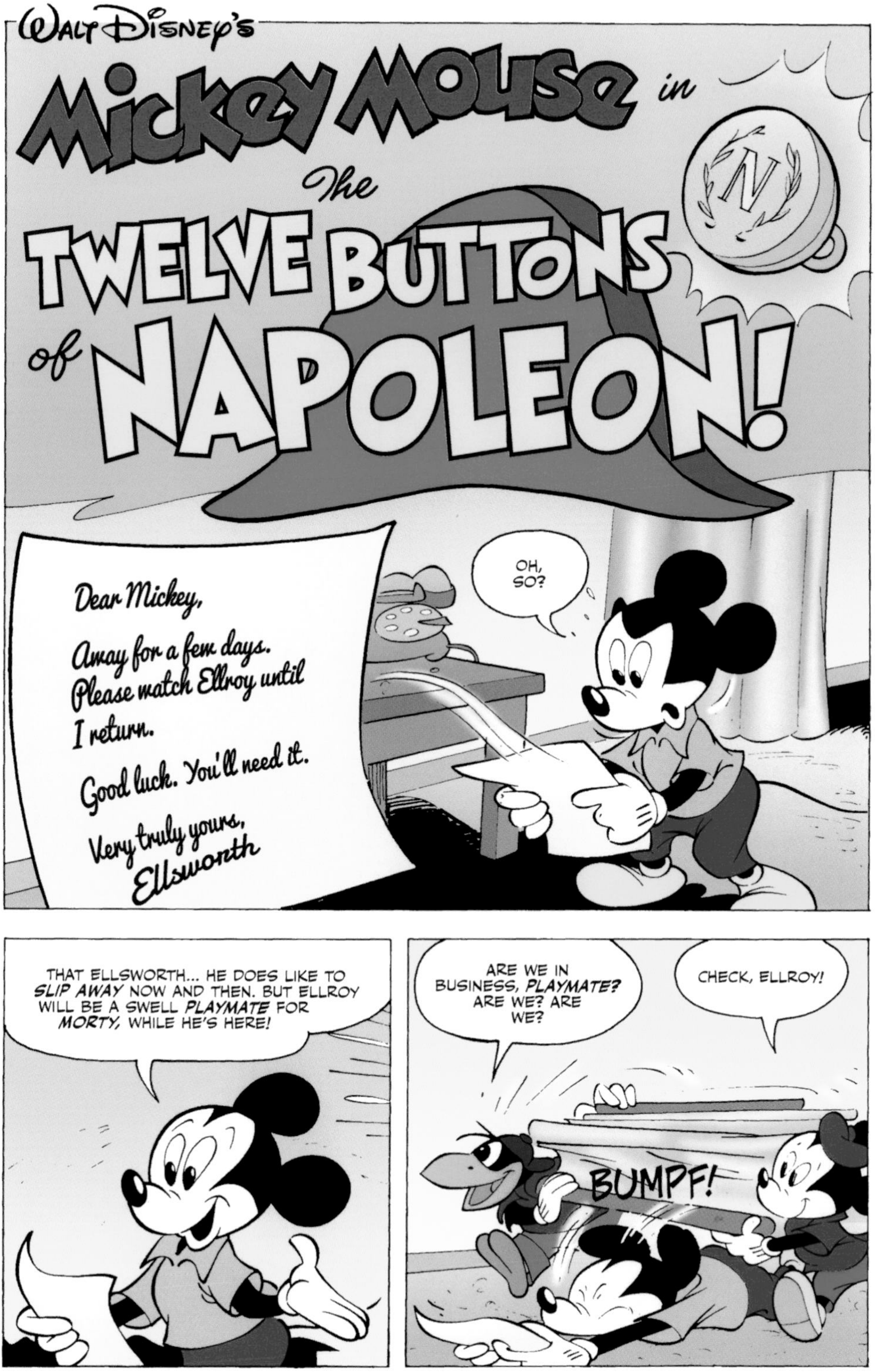
Walt Disney's
Mickey Mouse in
The Twelve Buttons of Napoleon!
N
Dear Mickey,
Away for a few days. Please watch Ellroy until I return.
Good luck. You'll need it.
Very truly yours, Ellsworth
OH, SO?
THAT ELLSWORTH... HE DOES LIKE TO SLIP AWAY NOW AND THEN. BUT ELLROY WILL BE A SWELL PLAYMATE FOR MORTY, WHILE HE'S HERE!
ARE WE IN BUSINESS, PLAYMATE? ARE WE? ARE WE?
CHECK, ELLROY!
BUMPF!

Originally published in *Topolino* #1073 (Italy, 1976)

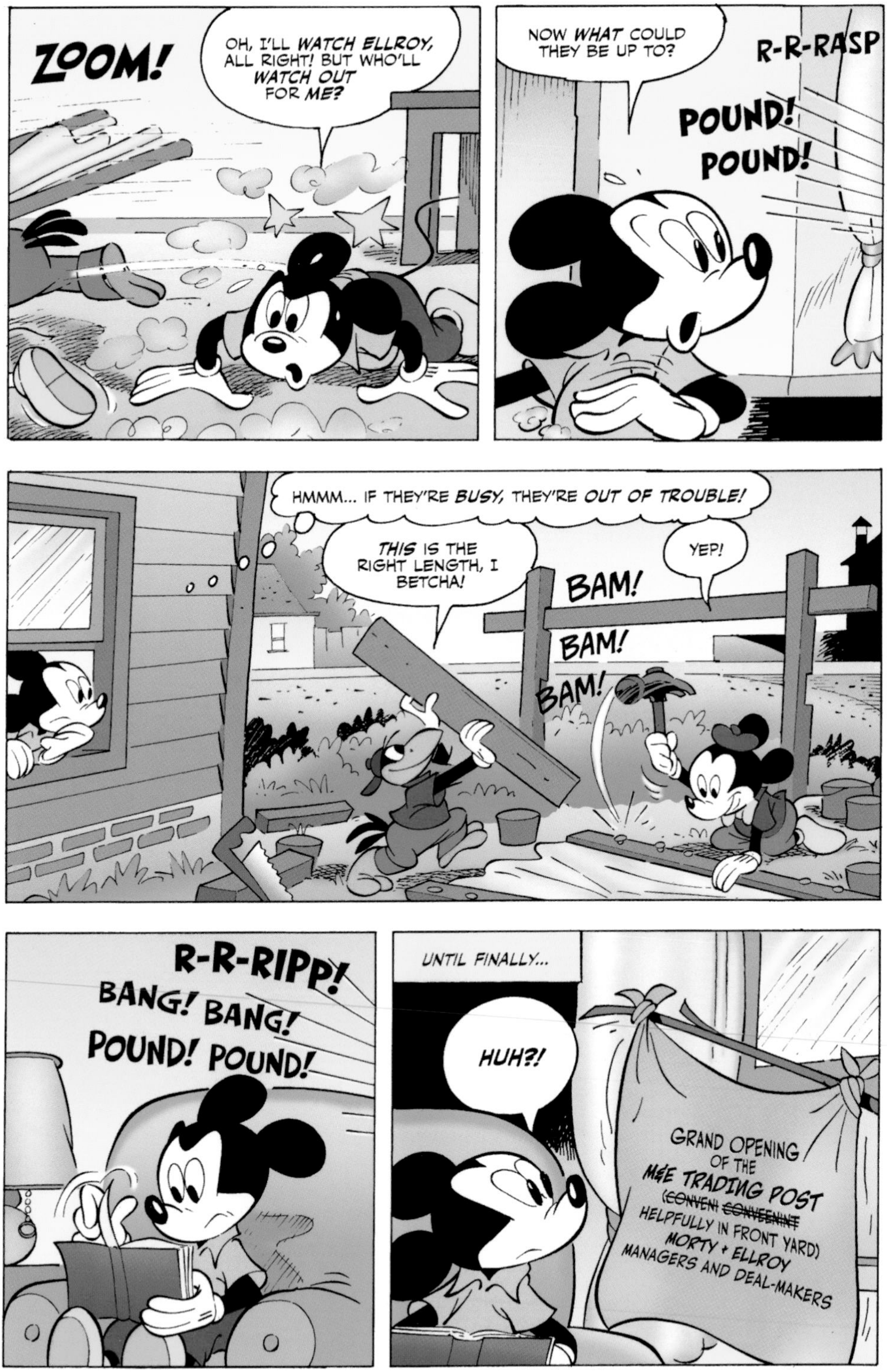
ZOOM!
OH, I'LL WATCH ELLROY, ALL RIGHT! BUT WHO'LL WATCH OUT FOR ME?
NOW WHAT COULD THEY BE UP TO?
R-R-RASP
POUND! POUND!
HMMM... IF THEY'RE BUSY, THEY'RE OUT OF TROUBLE!
THIS IS THE RIGHT LENGTH, I BETCHA!
YEP!
BAM! BAM! BAM!
R-R-RIPP!
BANG! BANG!
POUND! POUND!
UNTIL FINALLY...
HUH?!
GRAND OPENING OF THE M&E TRADING POST (CONVEN! CONVEENINT HELPFULLY IN FRONT YARD) MORTY + ELLROY MANAGERS AND DEAL-MAKERS

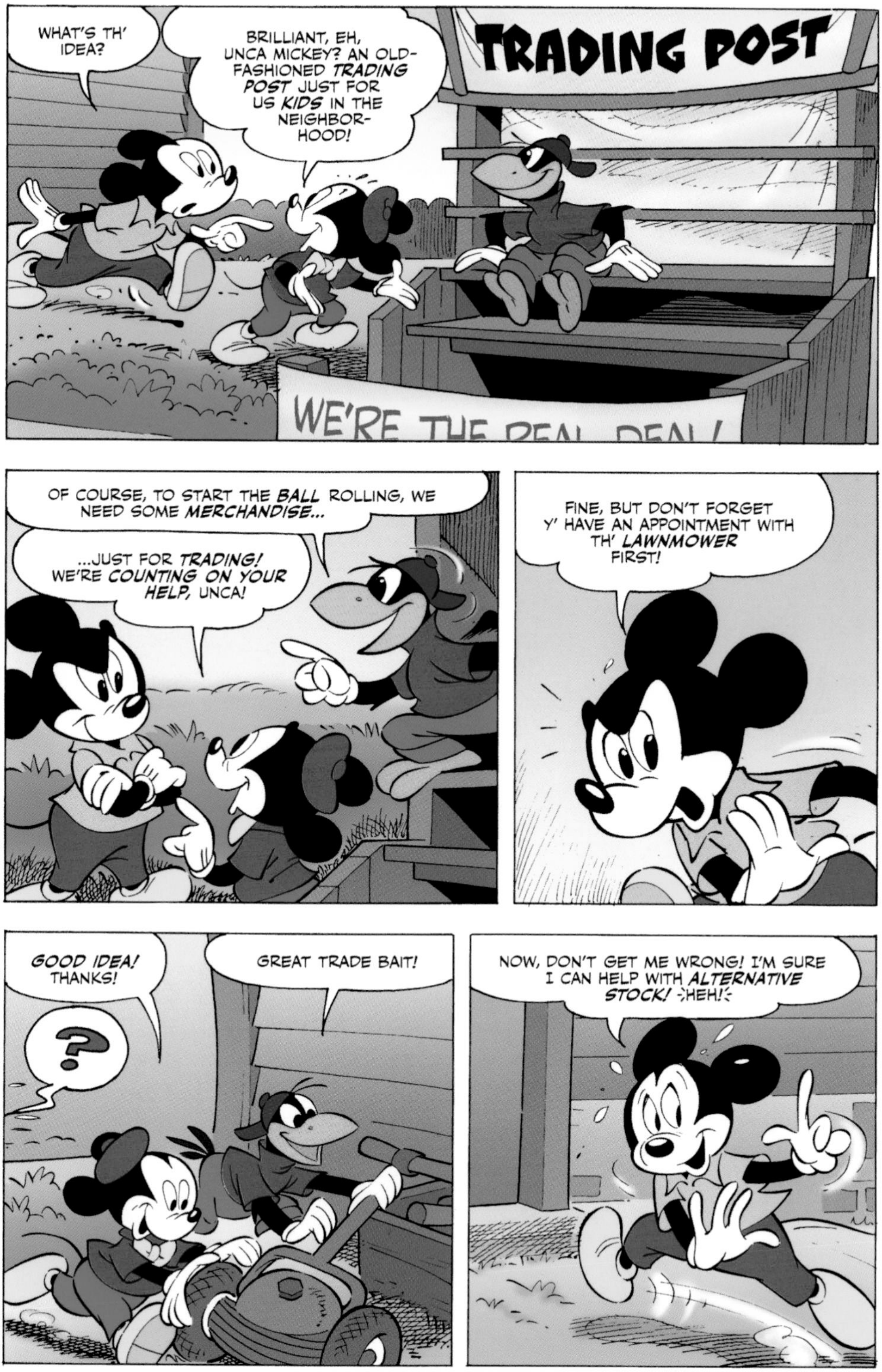
WHAT'S TH' IDEA?
BRILLIANT, EH, UNCA MICKEY? AN OLD-FASHIONED *TRADING POST* JUST FOR US *KIDS* IN THE NEIGHBOR-HOOD!
TRADING POST
WE'RE THE REAL DEAL!
OF COURSE, TO START THE *BALL* ROLLING, WE NEED SOME *MERCHANDISE*...
...JUST FOR *TRADING!* WE'RE *COUNTING ON YOUR HELP*, UNCA!
FINE, BUT DON'T FORGET Y' HAVE AN APPOINTMENT WITH TH' *LAWNMOWER* FIRST!
*GOOD IDEA!* THANKS!
?
GREAT TRADE BAIT!
NOW, DON'T GET ME WRONG! I'M SURE I CAN HELP WITH *ALTERNATIVE STOCK!* HEH!

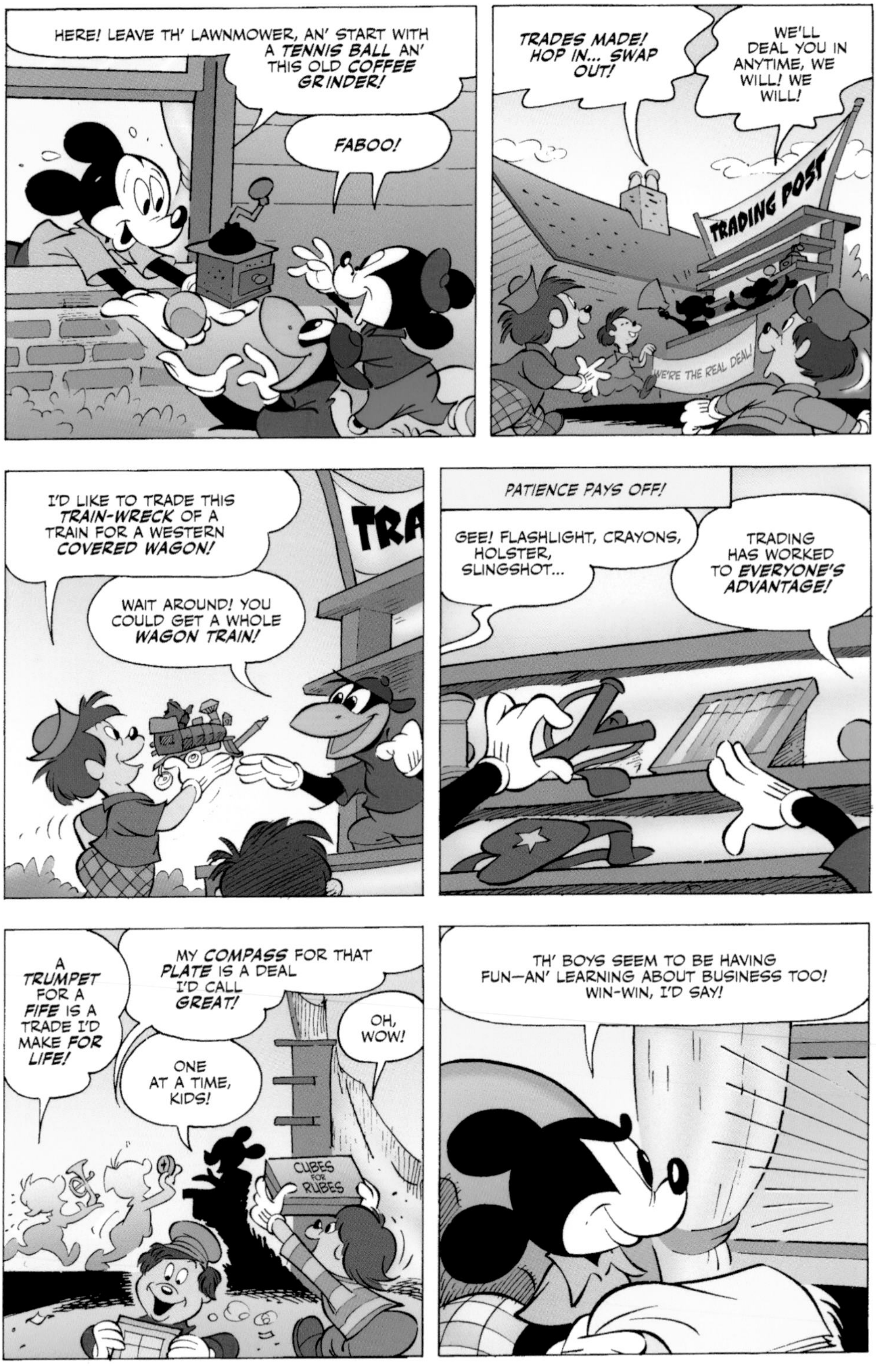
HERE! LEAVE TH' LAWNMOWER, AN' START WITH A TENNIS BALL AN' THIS OLD COFFEE GRINDER!
FABOO!
TRADES MADE! HOP IN... SWAP OUT!
WE'LL DEAL YOU IN ANYTIME, WE WILL! WE WILL!
TRADING POST
WE'RE THE REAL DEAL!
I'D LIKE TO TRADE THIS TRAIN-WRECK OF A TRAIN FOR A WESTERN COVERED WAGON!
WAIT AROUND! YOU COULD GET A WHOLE WAGON TRAIN!
PATIENCE PAYS OFF!
GEE! FLASHLIGHT, CRAYONS, HOLSTER, SLINGSHOT...
TRADING HAS WORKED TO EVERYONE'S ADVANTAGE!
A TRUMPET FOR A FIFE IS A TRADE I'D MAKE FOR LIFE!
MY COMPASS FOR THAT PLATE IS A DEAL I'D CALL GREAT!
ONE AT A TIME, KIDS!
OH, WOW!
CUBES FOR RUBES
TH' BOYS SEEM TO BE HAVING FUN—AN' LEARNING ABOUT BUSINESS TOO! WIN-WIN, I'D SAY!

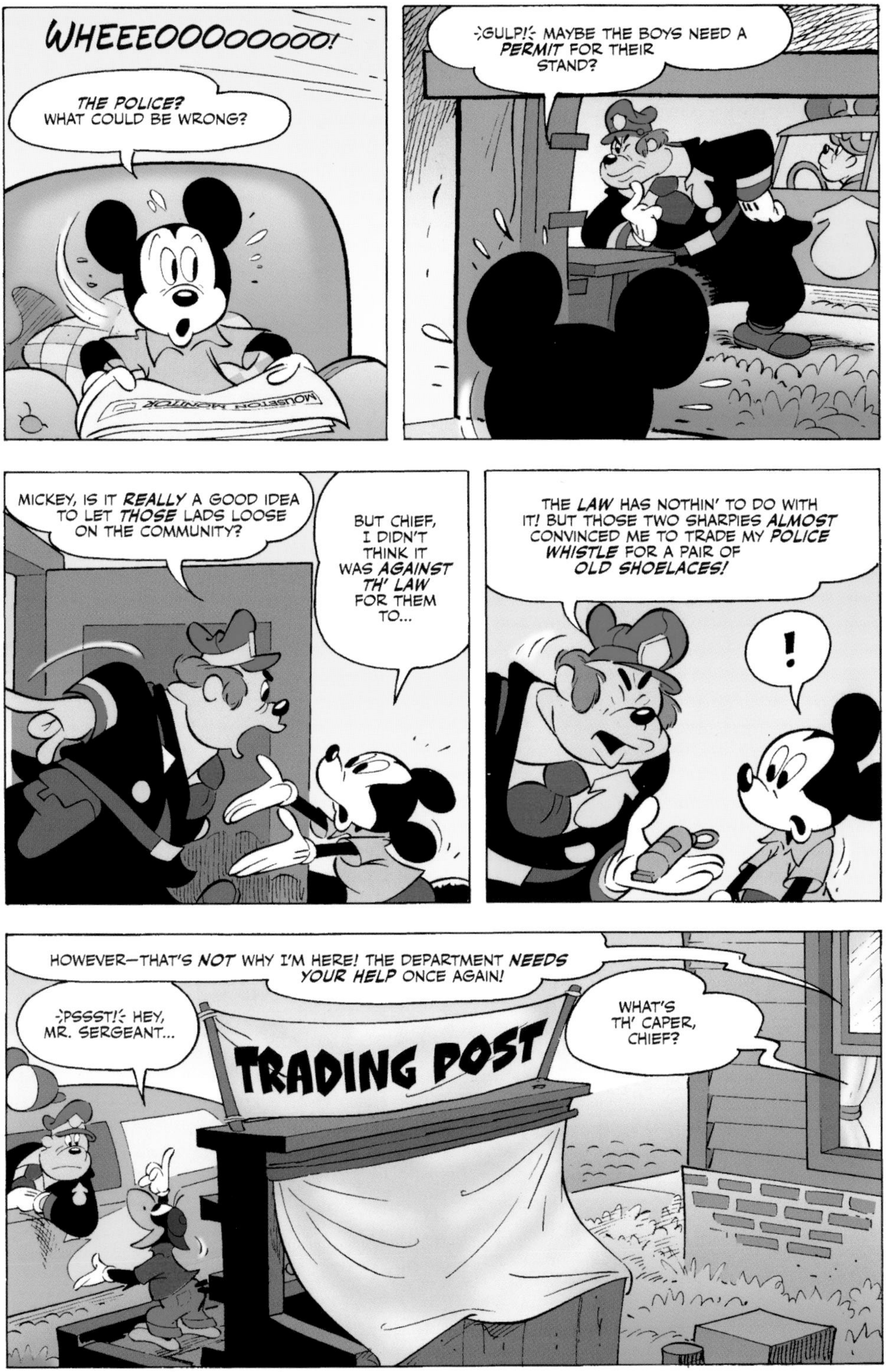
WHEEEOOOOOOOOO!
THE POLICE? WHAT COULD BE WRONG?
MOUSETON MONITOR
-GULP!- MAYBE THE BOYS NEED A PERMIT FOR THEIR STAND?
MICKEY, IS IT REALLY A GOOD IDEA TO LET THOSE LADS LOOSE ON THE COMMUNITY?
BUT CHIEF, I DIDN'T THINK IT WAS AGAINST TH' LAW FOR THEM TO...
THE LAW HAS NOTHIN' TO DO WITH IT! BUT THOSE TWO SHARPIES ALMOST CONVINCED ME TO TRADE MY POLICE WHISTLE FOR A PAIR OF OLD SHOELACES!
!
HOWEVER—THAT'S NOT WHY I'M HERE! THE DEPARTMENT NEEDS YOUR HELP ONCE AGAIN!
-PSSST!- HEY, MR. SERGEANT...
TRADING POST
WHAT'S TH' CAPER, CHIEF?

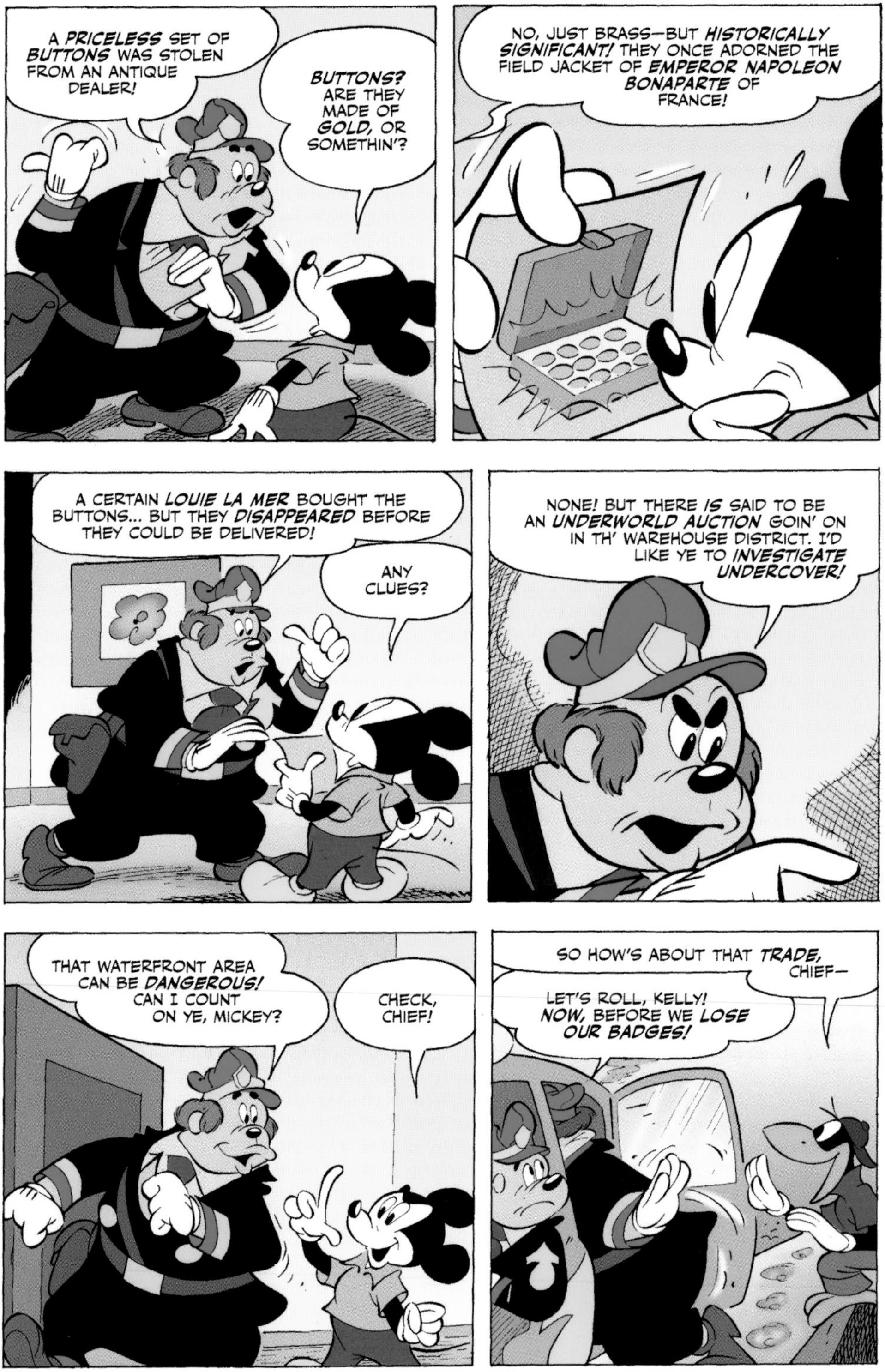
A PRICELESS SET OF BUTTONS WAS STOLEN FROM AN ANTIQUE DEALER!
BUTTONS? ARE THEY MADE OF GOLD, OR SOMETHIN'?
NO, JUST BRASS—BUT HISTORICALLY SIGNIFICANT! THEY ONCE ADORNED THE FIELD JACKET OF EMPEROR NAPOLEON BONAPARTE OF FRANCE!
A CERTAIN LOUIE LA MER BOUGHT THE BUTTONS... BUT THEY DISAPPEARED BEFORE THEY COULD BE DELIVERED!
ANY CLUES?
NONE! BUT THERE IS SAID TO BE AN UNDERWORLD AUCTION GOIN' ON IN TH' WAREHOUSE DISTRICT. I'D LIKE YE TO INVESTIGATE UNDERCOVER!
THAT WATERFRONT AREA CAN BE DANGEROUS! CAN I COUNT ON YE, MICKEY?
CHECK, CHIEF!
SO HOW'S ABOUT THAT TRADE, CHIEF—
LET'S ROLL, KELLY! NOW, BEFORE WE LOSE OUR BADGES!

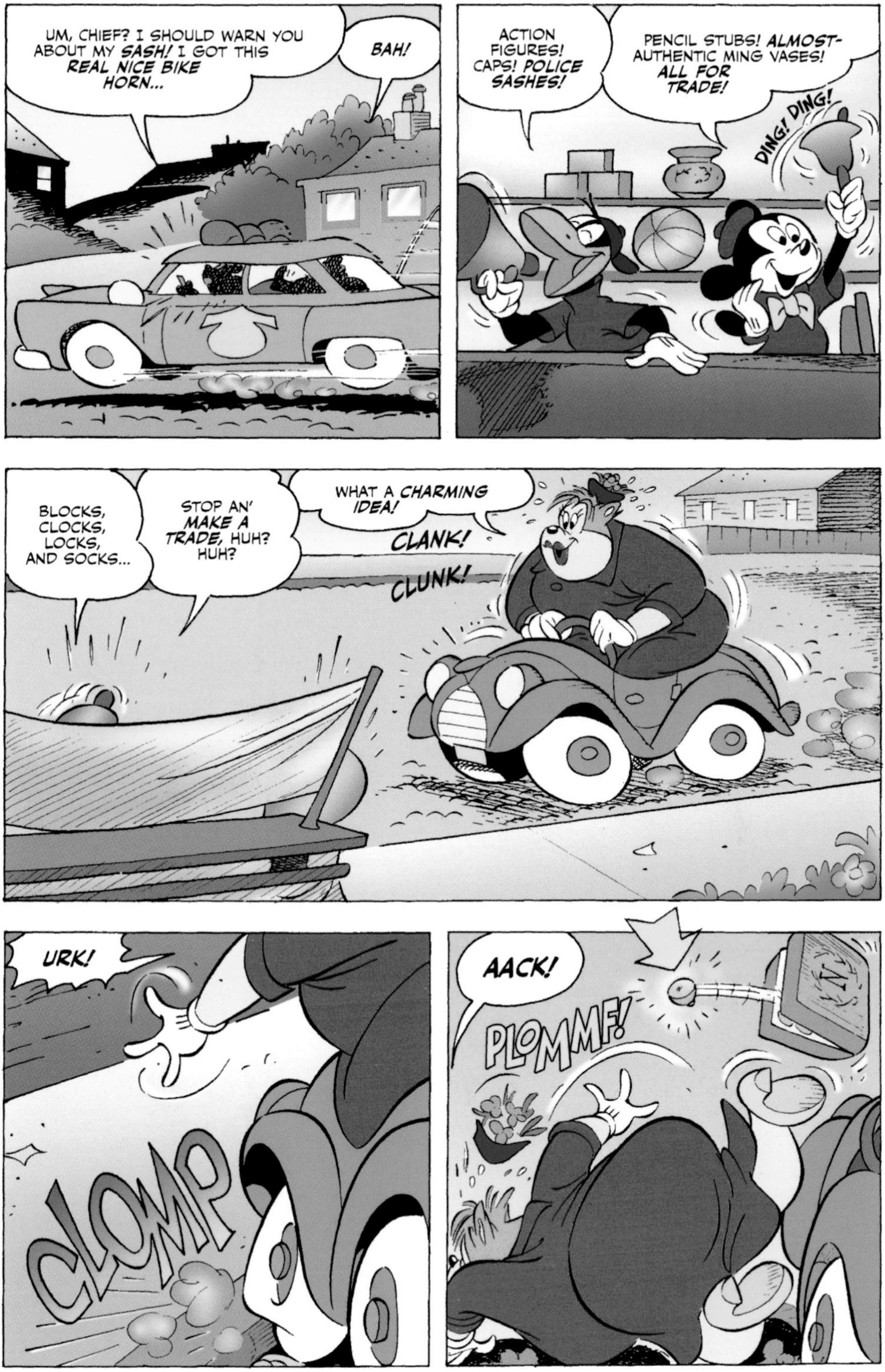
UM, CHIEF? I SHOULD WARN YOU ABOUT MY SASH! I GOT THIS REAL NICE BIKE HORN...
BAH!
ACTION FIGURES! CAPS! POLICE SASHES!
PENCIL STUBS! ALMOST-AUTHENTIC MING VASES! ALL FOR TRADE!
DING! DING!
BLOCKS, CLOCKS, LOCKS, AND SOCKS...
STOP AN' MAKE A TRADE, HUH? HUH?
WHAT A CHARMING IDEA!
CLANK!
CLUNK!
URK!
CLOMP
AACK!
PLOMMF!

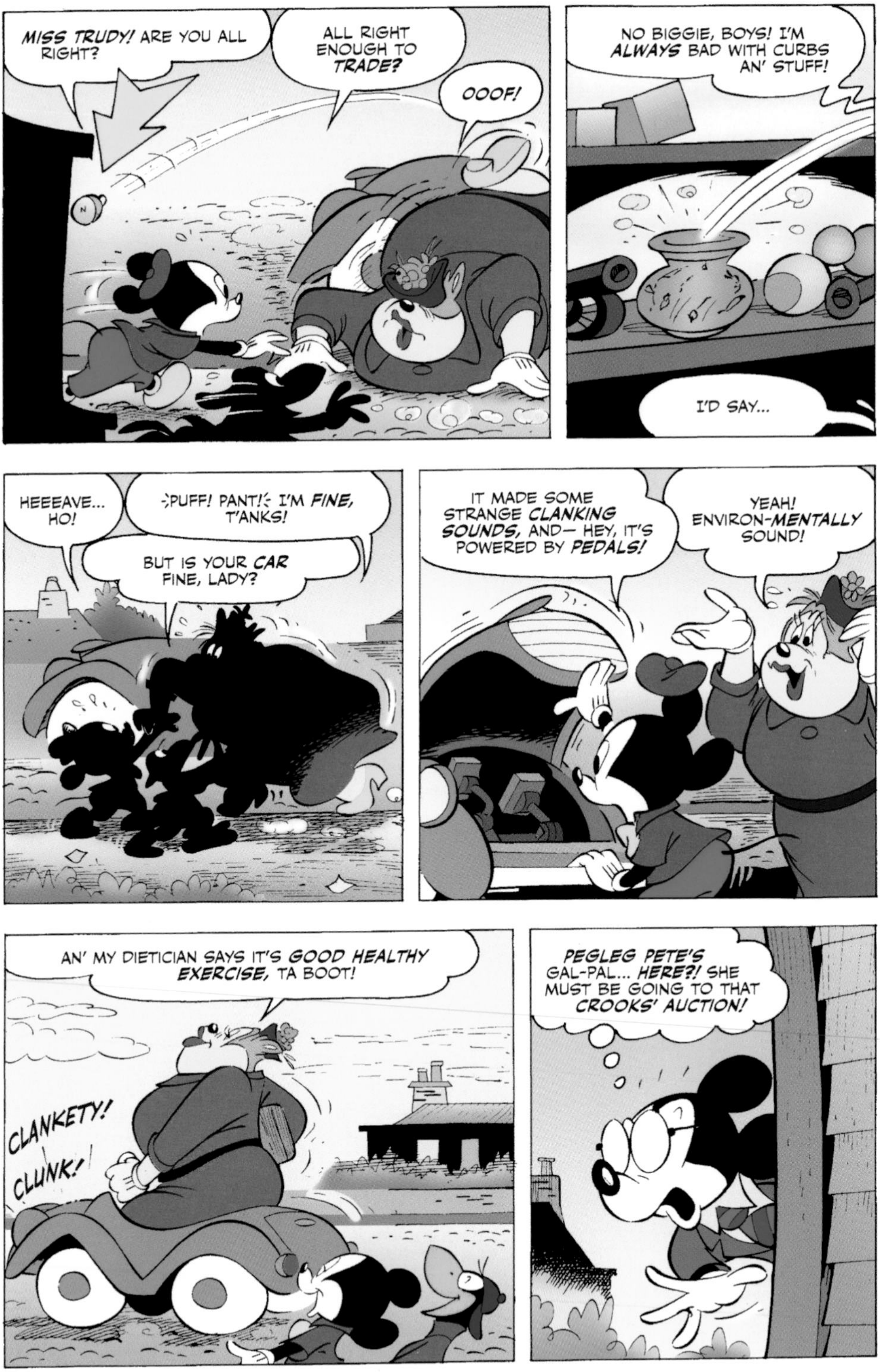
MISS TRUDY! ARE YOU ALL RIGHT?
ALL RIGHT ENOUGH TO TRADE?
OOOF!
NO BIGGIE, BOYS! I'M ALWAYS BAD WITH CURBS AN' STUFF!
I'D SAY...
HEEEAVE... HO!
PUFF! PANT! I'M FINE, T'ANKS!
BUT IS YOUR CAR FINE, LADY?
IT MADE SOME STRANGE CLANKING SOUNDS, AND— HEY, IT'S POWERED BY PEDALS!
YEAH! ENVIRON-MENTALLY SOUND!
AN' MY DIETICIAN SAYS IT'S GOOD HEALTHY EXERCISE, TA BOOT!
CLANKETY! CLUNK!
PEGLEG PETE'S GAL-PAL... HERE?! SHE MUST BE GOING TO THAT CROOKS' AUCTION!

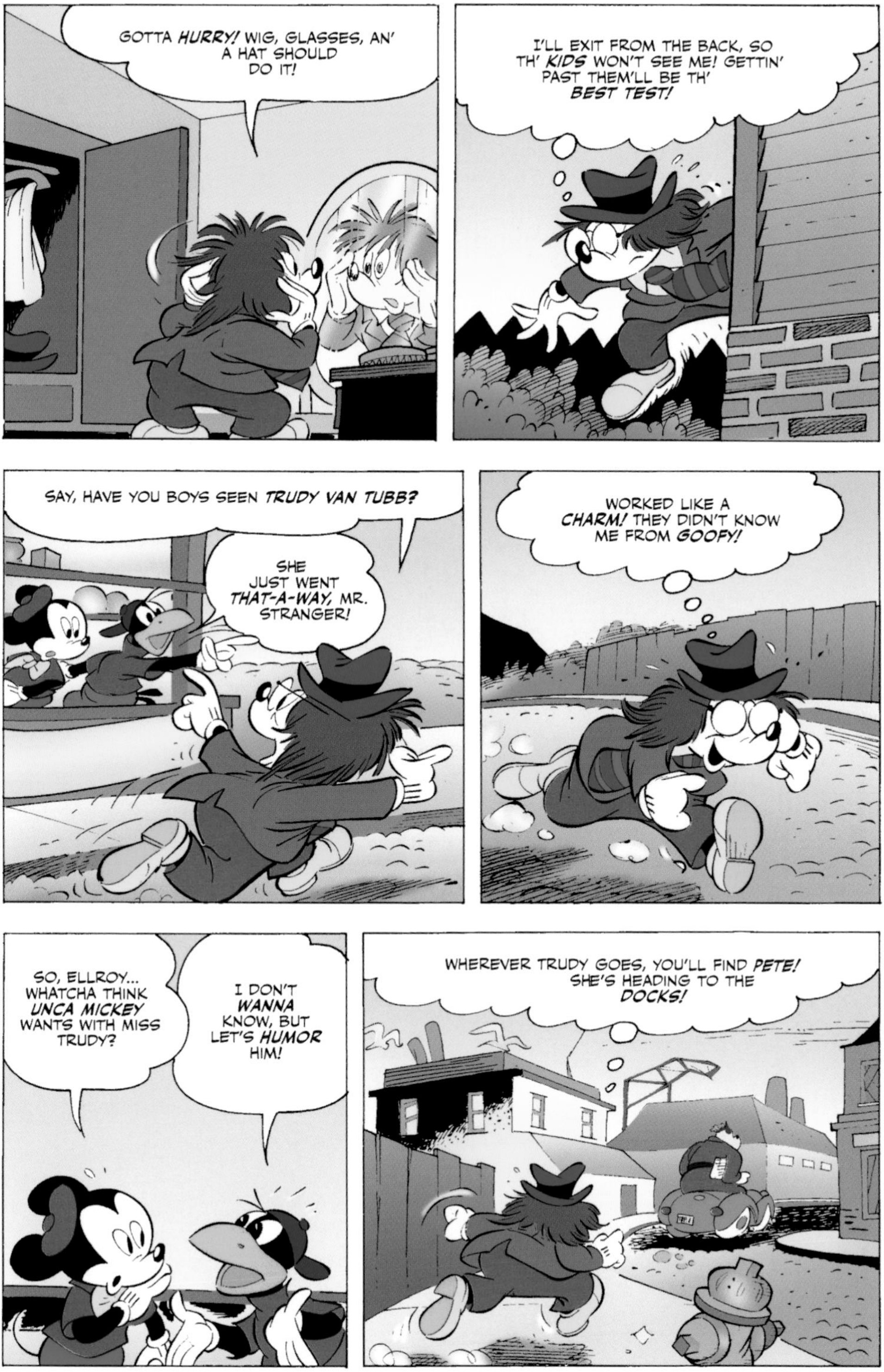
GOTTA HURRY! WIG, GLASSES, AN' A HAT SHOULD DO IT!
I'LL EXIT FROM THE BACK, SO TH' KIDS WON'T SEE ME! GETTIN' PAST THEM'LL BE TH' BEST TEST!
SAY, HAVE YOU BOYS SEEN TRUDY VAN TUBB?
SHE JUST WENT THAT-A-WAY, MR. STRANGER!
WORKED LIKE A CHARM! THEY DIDN'T KNOW ME FROM GOOFY!
SO, ELLROY... WHATCHA THINK UNCA MICKEY WANTS WITH MISS TRUDY?
I DON'T WANNA KNOW, BUT LET'S HUMOR HIM!
WHEREVER TRUDY GOES, YOU'LL FIND PETE! SHE'S HEADING TO THE DOCKS!

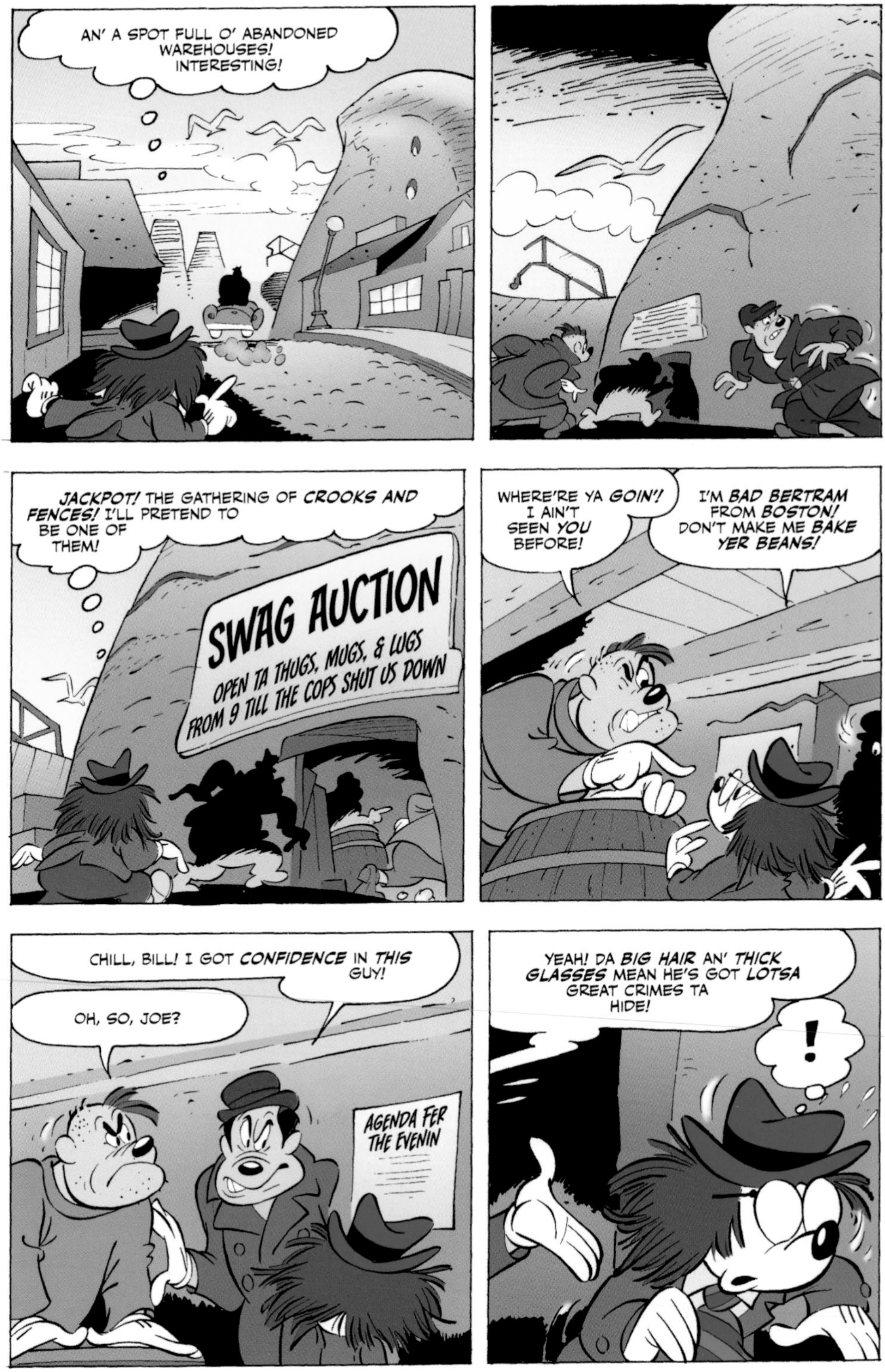
AN' A SPOT FULL O' ABANDONED WAREHOUSES! INTERESTING!
JACKPOT! THE GATHERING OF CROOKS AND FENCES! I'LL PRETEND TO BE ONE OF THEM!
SWAG AUCTION
OPEN TA THUGS, MUGS, & LUGS FROM 9 TILL THE COPS SHUT US DOWN
WHERE'RE YA GOIN'! I AIN'T SEEN YOU BEFORE!
I'M BAD BERTRAM FROM BOSTON! DON'T MAKE ME BAKE YER BEANS!
CHILL, BILL! I GOT CONFIDENCE IN THIS GUY!
OH, SO, JOE?
AGENDA FER THE EVENIN
YEAH! DA BIG HAIR AN' THICK GLASSES MEAN HE'S GOT LOTSA GREAT CRIMES TA HIDE!
!

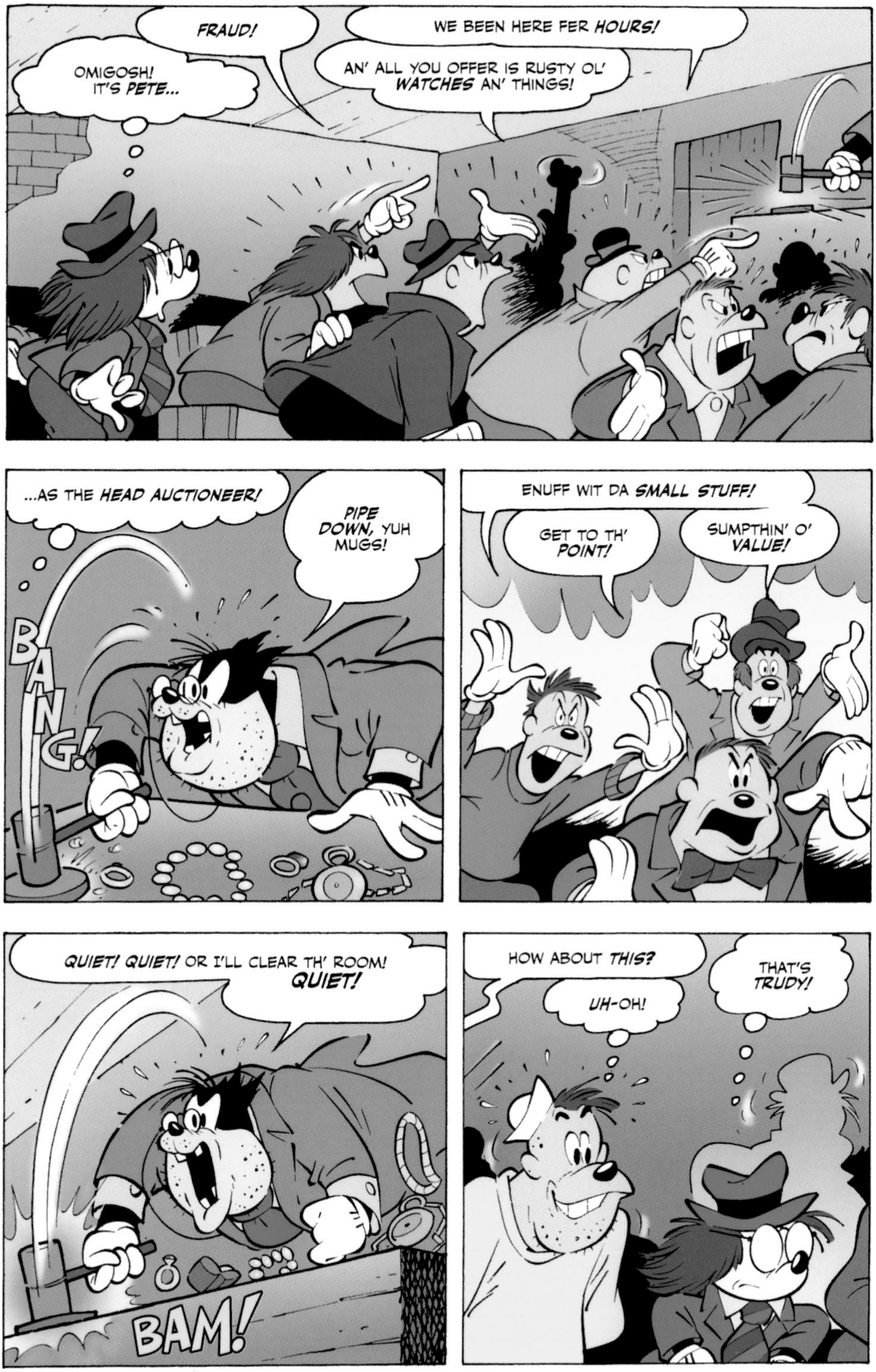
OMIGOSH! IT'S PETE...
FRAUD!
WE BEEN HERE FER HOURS!
AN' ALL YOU OFFER IS RUSTY OL' WATCHES AN' THINGS!
...AS THE HEAD AUCTIONEER!
PIPE DOWN, YUH MUGS!
BANG!
ENUFF WIT DA SMALL STUFF!
GET TO TH' POINT!
SUMPTHIN' O' VALUE!
QUIET! QUIET! OR I'LL CLEAR TH' ROOM! QUIET!
BAM!
HOW ABOUT THIS?
UH-OH!
THAT'S TRUDY!

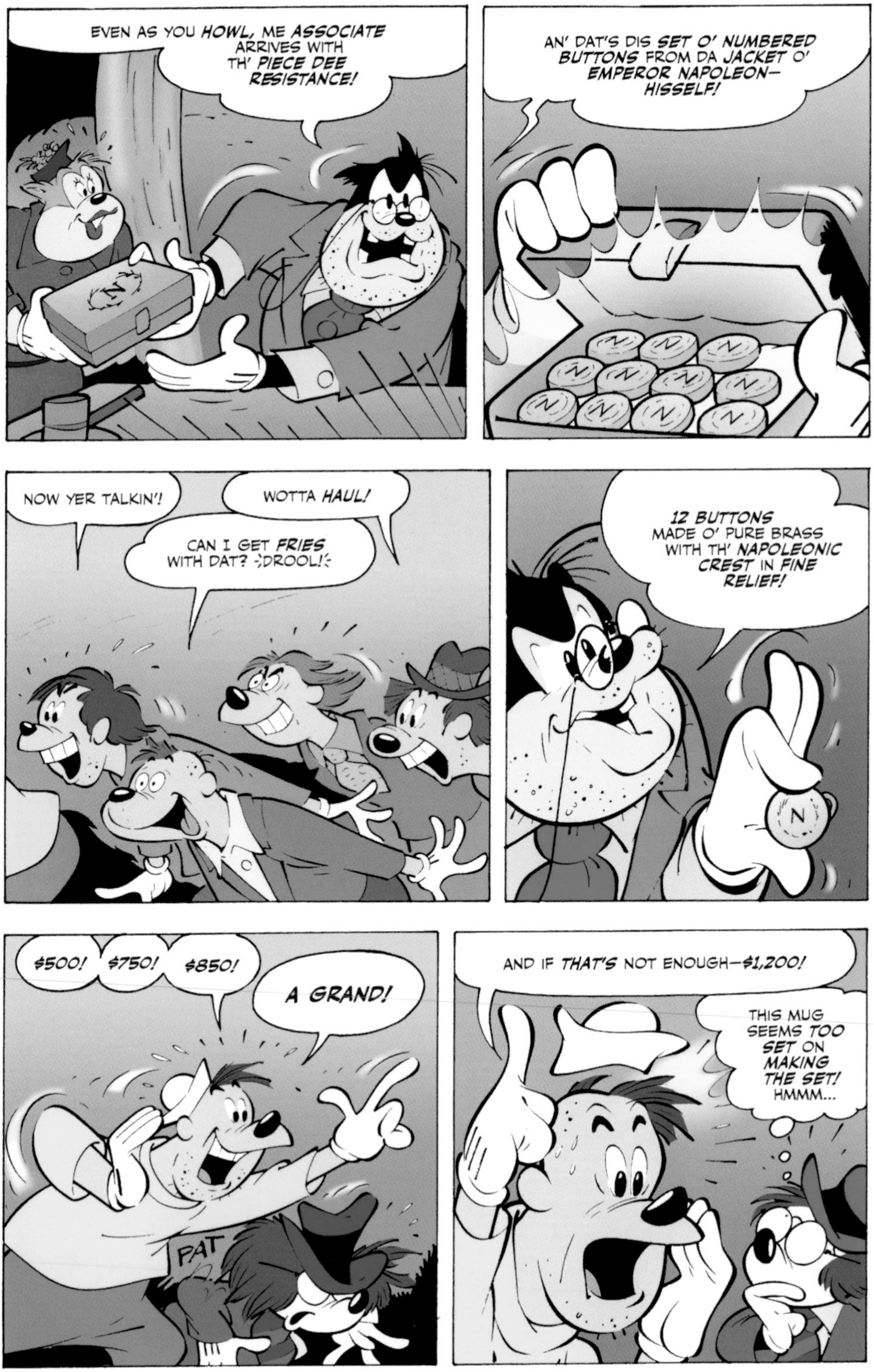

EVEN AS YOU *HOWL*, ME *ASSOCIATE* ARRIVES WITH TH' *PIECE DEE RESISTANCE!*
AN' DAT'S DIS *SET O' NUMBERED BUTTONS* FROM DA *JACKET* O' *EMPEROR NAPOLEON—HISSELF!*
NOW YER TALKIN'!
WOTTA *HAUL!*
CAN I GET *FRIES* WITH DAT? *DROOL!*
*12 BUTTONS* MADE O' PURE BRASS WITH TH' *NAPOLEONIC CREST* IN *FINE RELIEF!*
*$500!*
*$750!*
*$850!*
*A GRAND!*
PAT
AND IF *THAT'S* NOT ENOUGH—*$1,200!*
THIS MUG SEEMS *TOO SET* ON *MAKING THE SET!* HMMM...

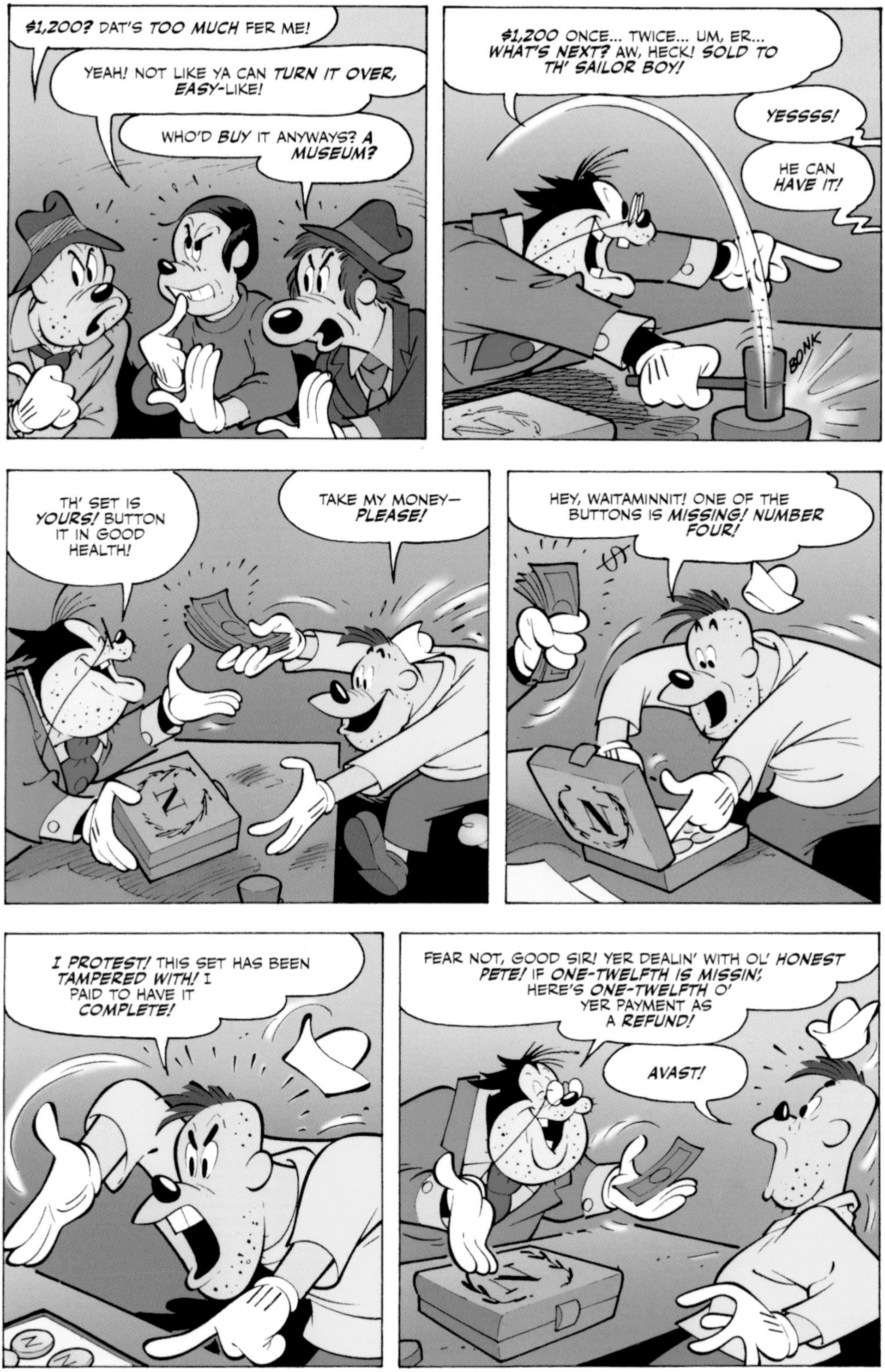
$1,200? DAT'S TOO MUCH FER ME!
YEAH! NOT LIKE YA CAN TURN IT OVER, EASY-LIKE!
WHO'D BUY IT ANYWAYS? A MUSEUM?
$1,200 ONCE... TWICE... UM, ER... WHAT'S NEXT? AW, HECK! SOLD TO TH' SAILOR BOY!
YESSSS!
HE CAN HAVE IT!
BONK
TH' SET IS YOURS! BUTTON IT IN GOOD HEALTH!
TAKE MY MONEY— PLEASE!
HEY, WAITAMINNIT! ONE OF THE BUTTONS IS MISSING! NUMBER FOUR!
I PROTEST! THIS SET HAS BEEN TAMPERED WITH! I PAID TO HAVE IT COMPLETE!
FEAR NOT, GOOD SIR! YER DEALIN' WITH OL' HONEST PETE! IF ONE-TWELFTH IS MISSIN', HERE'S ONE-TWELFTH O' YER PAYMENT AS A REFUND!
AVAST!

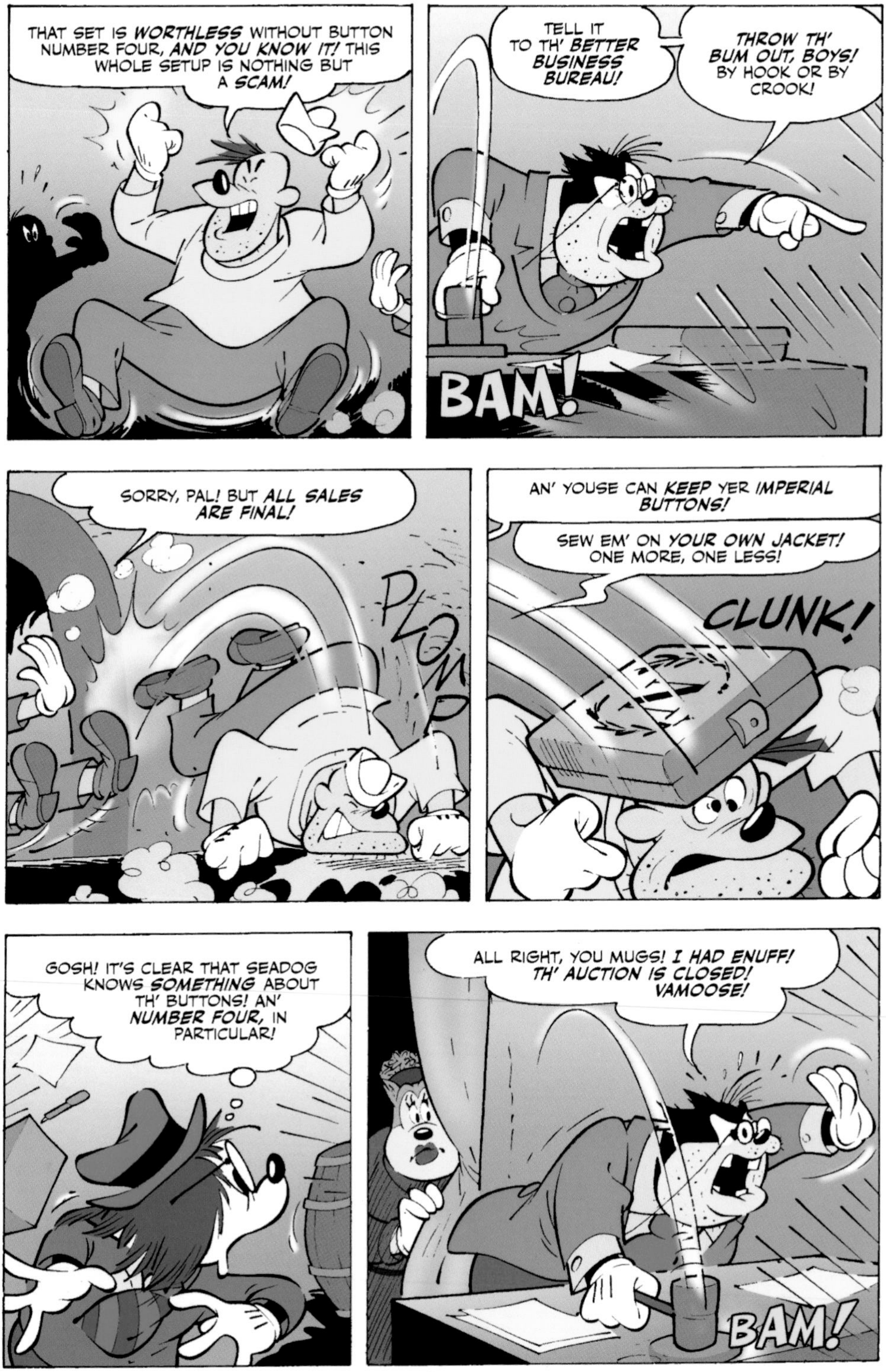
THAT SET IS WORTHLESS WITHOUT BUTTON NUMBER FOUR, AND YOU KNOW IT! THIS WHOLE SETUP IS NOTHING BUT A SCAM!
TELL IT TO TH' BETTER BUSINESS BUREAU!
THROW TH' BUM OUT, BOYS! BY HOOK OR BY CROOK!
BAM!
SORRY, PAL! BUT ALL SALES ARE FINAL!
PLOMP
AN' YOUSE CAN KEEP YER IMPERIAL BUTTONS!
SEW EM' ON YOUR OWN JACKET! ONE MORE, ONE LESS!
CLUNK!
GOSH! IT'S CLEAR THAT SEADOG KNOWS SOMETHING ABOUT TH' BUTTONS! AN' NUMBER FOUR, IN PARTICULAR!
ALL RIGHT, YOU MUGS! I HAD ENUFF! TH' AUCTION IS CLOSED! VAMOOSE!
BAM!

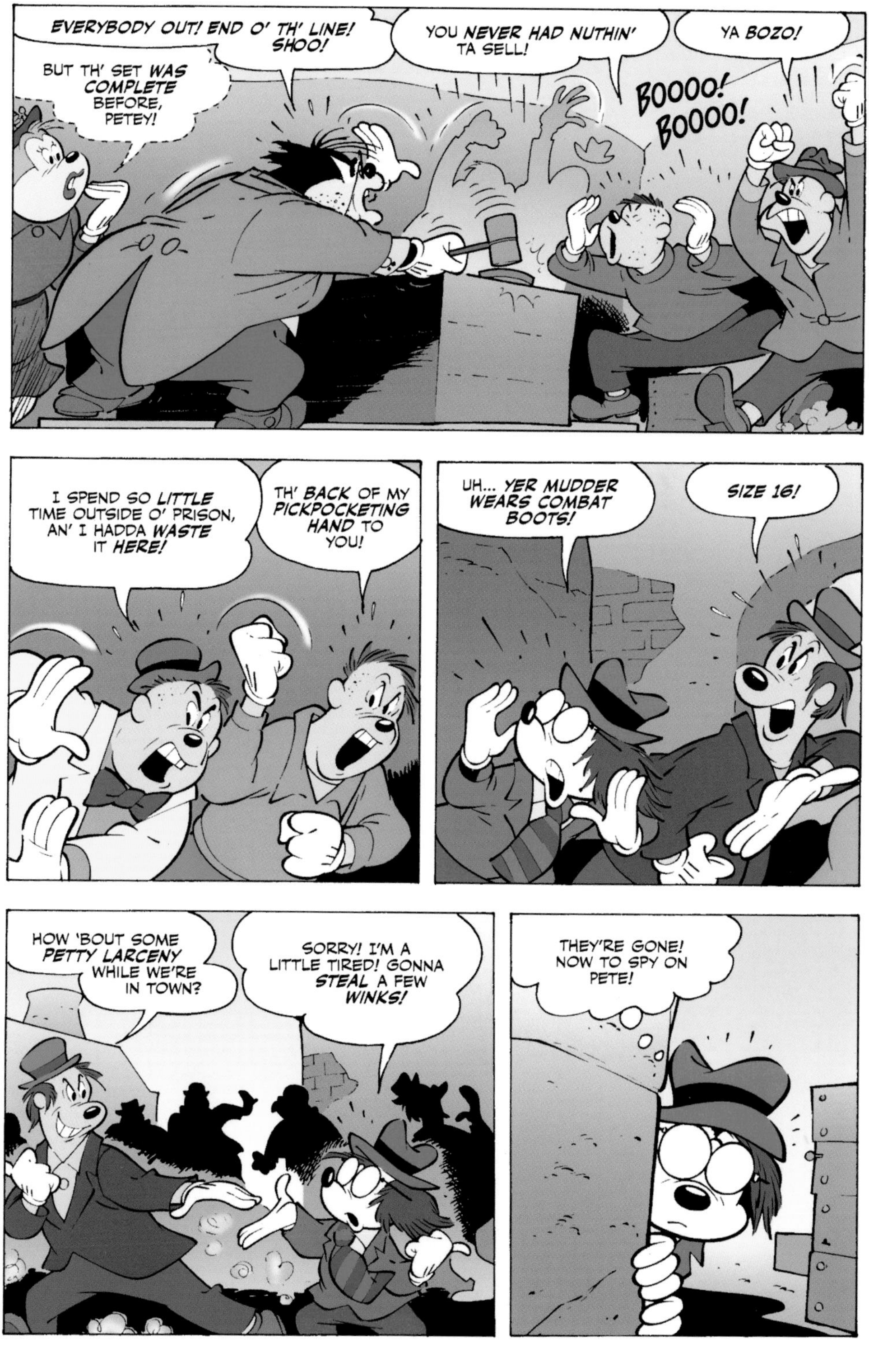
EVERYBODY OUT! END O' TH' LINE! SHOO!
BUT TH' SET WAS COMPLETE BEFORE, PETEY!
YOU NEVER HAD NUTHIN' TA SELL!
BOOOO! BOOOO!
YA BOZO!
I SPEND SO LITTLE TIME OUTSIDE O' PRISON, AN' I HADDA WASTE IT HERE!
TH' BACK OF MY PICKPOCKETING HAND TO YOU!
UH... YER MUDDER WEARS COMBAT BOOTS!
SIZE 16!
HOW 'BOUT SOME PETTY LARCENY WHILE WE'RE IN TOWN?
SORRY! I'M A LITTLE TIRED! GONNA STEAL A FEW WINKS!
THEY'RE GONE! NOW TO SPY ON PETE!

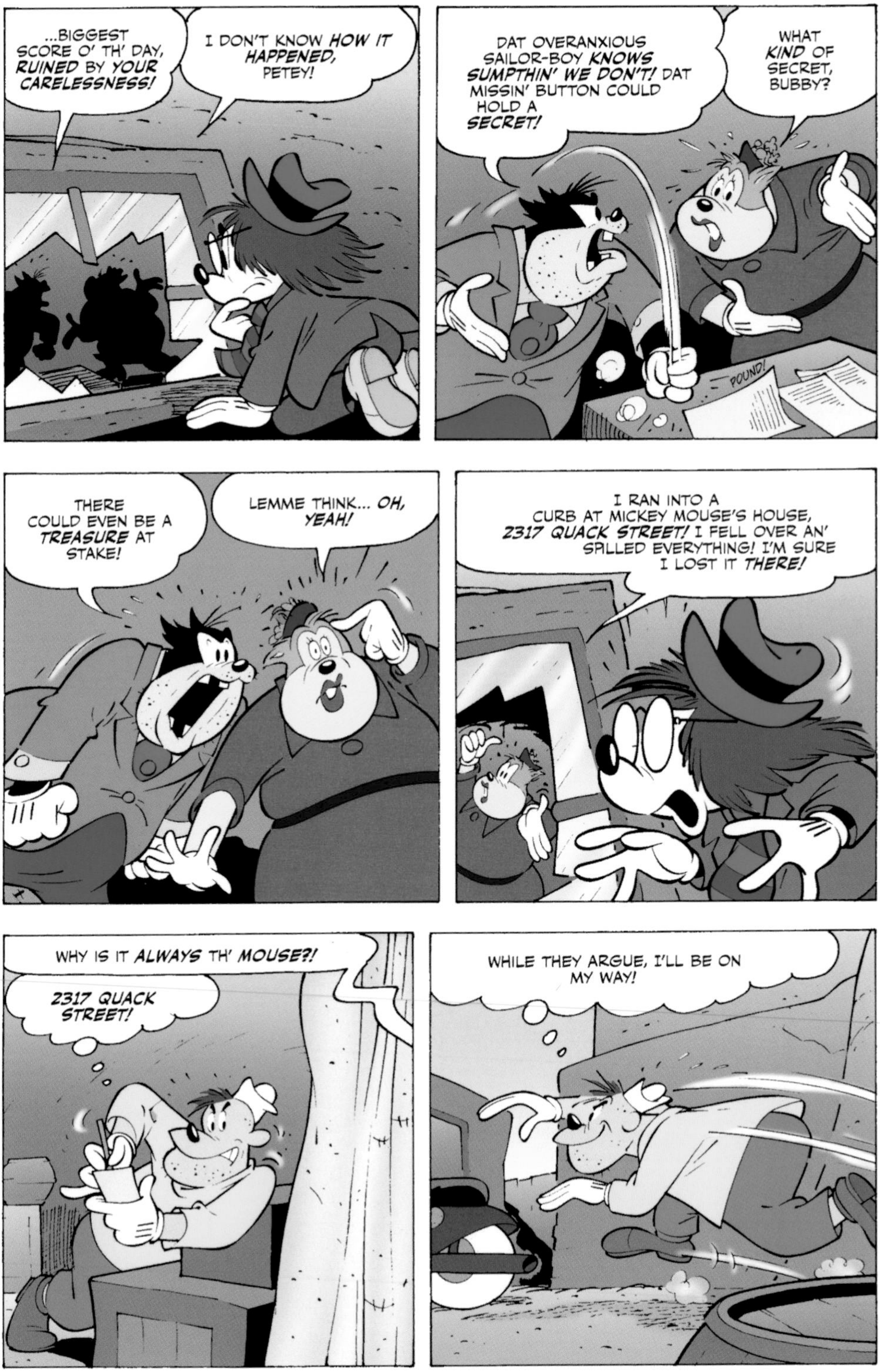
...BIGGEST SCORE O' TH' DAY, RUINED BY YOUR CARELESSNESS!
I DON'T KNOW HOW IT HAPPENED, PETEY!
DAT OVERANXIOUS SAILOR-BOY KNOWS SUMPTHIN' WE DON'T! DAT MISSIN' BUTTON COULD HOLD A SECRET!
WHAT KIND OF SECRET, BUBBY?
POUND!
THERE COULD EVEN BE A TREASURE AT STAKE!
LEMME THINK... OH, YEAH!
I RAN INTO A CURB AT MICKEY MOUSE'S HOUSE, 2317 QUACK STREET! I FELL OVER AN' SPILLED EVERYTHING! I'M SURE I LOST IT THERE!
WHY IS IT ALWAYS TH' MOUSE?!
2317 QUACK STREET!
WHILE THEY ARGUE, I'LL BE ON MY WAY!

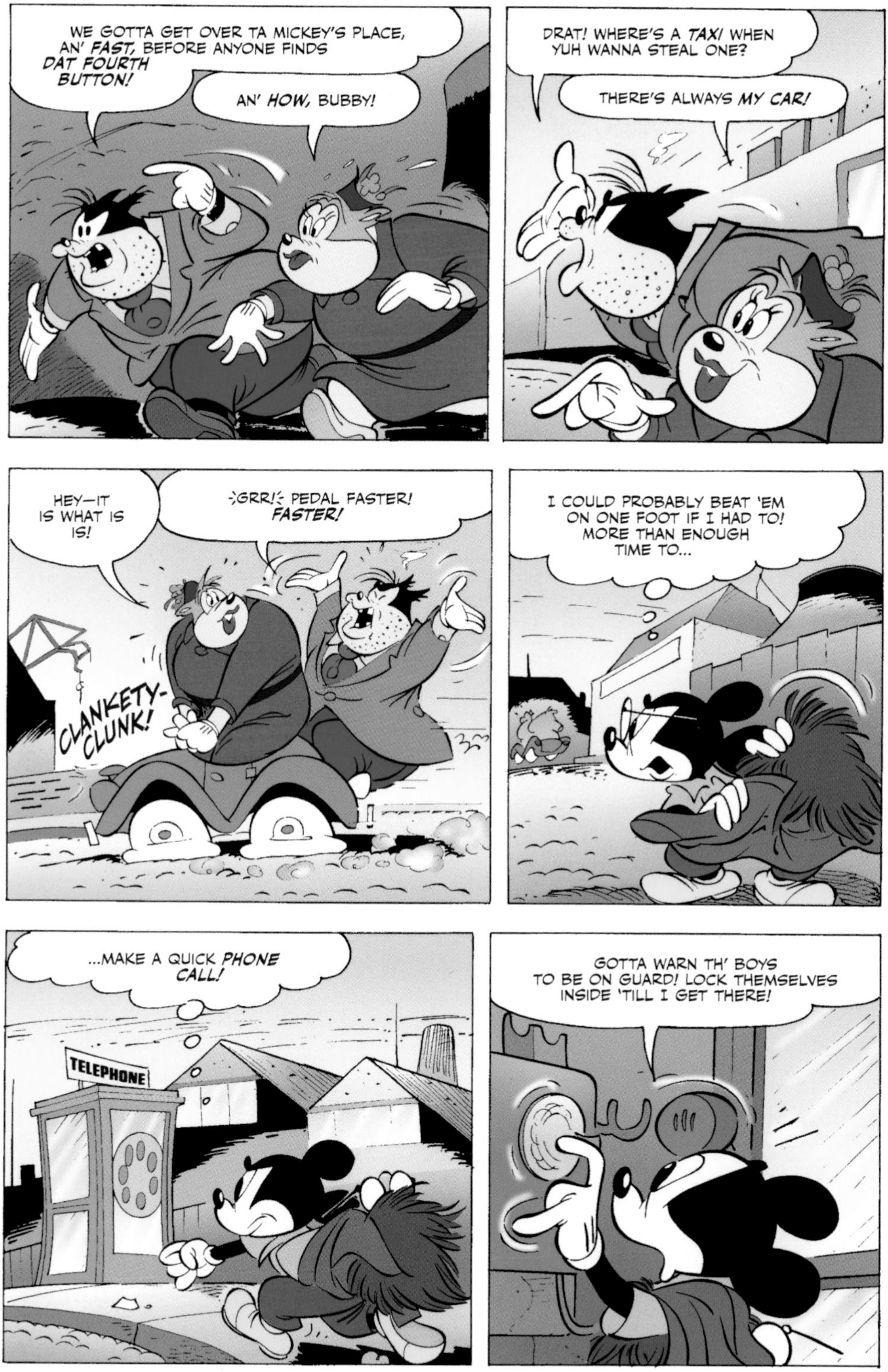
WE GOTTA GET OVER TA MICKEY'S PLACE, AN' FAST, BEFORE ANYONE FINDS DAT FOURTH BUTTON!
AN' HOW, BUBBY!
DRAT! WHERE'S A TAXI WHEN YUH WANNA STEAL ONE?
THERE'S ALWAYS MY CAR!
HEY—IT IS WHAT IS IS!
-GRR!- PEDAL FASTER! FASTER!
CLANKETY-CLUNK!
I COULD PROBABLY BEAT 'EM ON ONE FOOT IF I HAD TO! MORE THAN ENOUGH TIME TO...
...MAKE A QUICK PHONE CALL!
TELEPHONE
GOTTA WARN TH' BOYS TO BE ON GUARD! LOCK THEMSELVES INSIDE 'TILL I GET THERE!

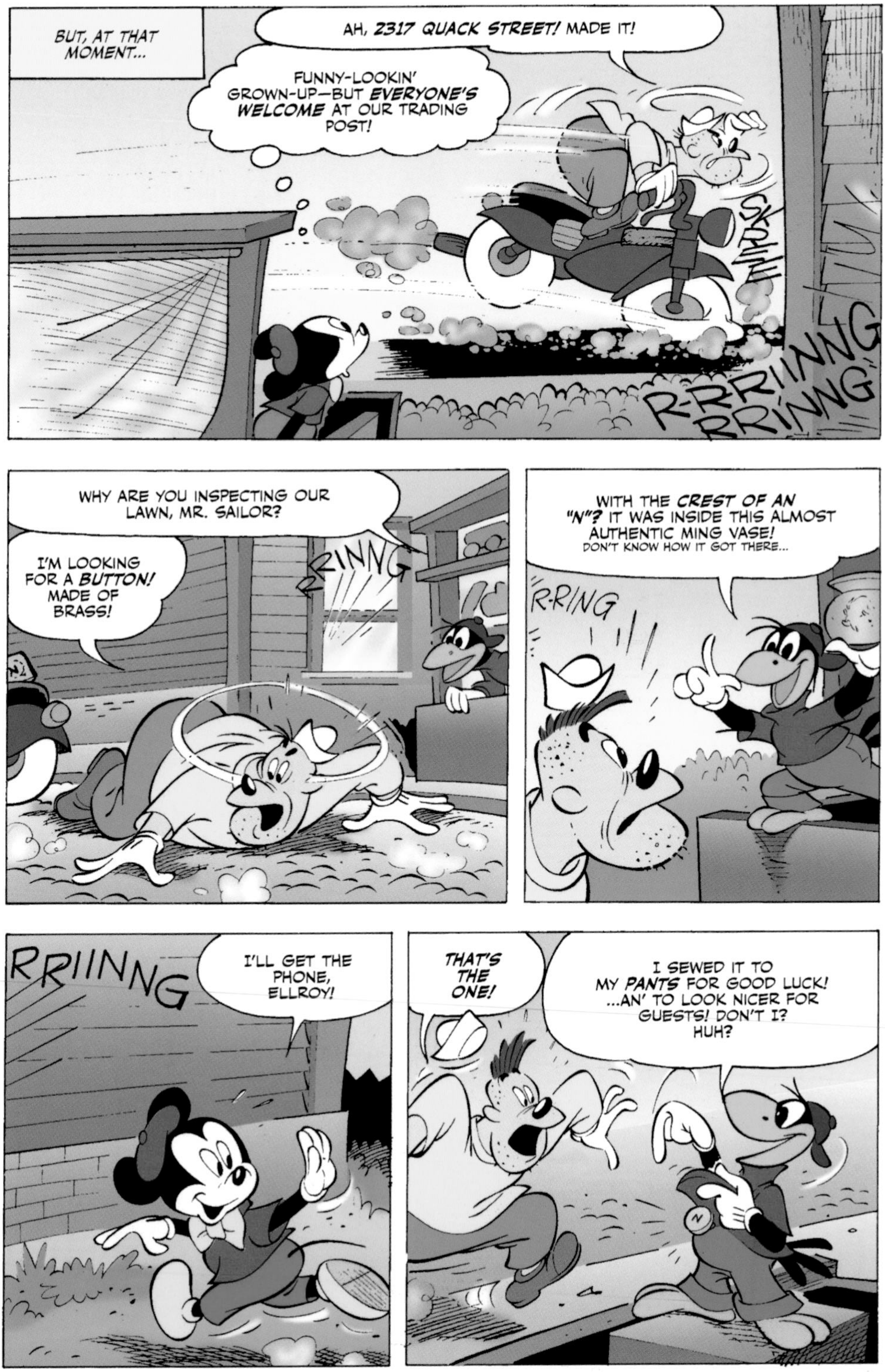
BUT, AT THAT MOMENT...
AH, 2317 QUACK STREET! MADE IT!
FUNNY-LOOKIN' GROWN-UP—BUT EVERYONE'S WELCOME AT OUR TRADING POST!
SKRRIIII
R-RRIINNG RRINNG
WHY ARE YOU INSPECTING OUR LAWN, MR. SAILOR?
I'M LOOKING FOR A BUTTON! MADE OF BRASS!
RRINNG
WITH THE CREST OF AN "N"? IT WAS INSIDE THIS ALMOST AUTHENTIC MING VASE! DON'T KNOW HOW IT GOT THERE...
R-RING
RRIINNG
I'LL GET THE PHONE, ELLROY!
THAT'S THE ONE!
I SEWED IT TO MY PANTS FOR GOOD LUCK! ...AN' TO LOOK NICER FOR GUESTS! DON'T I? HUH?

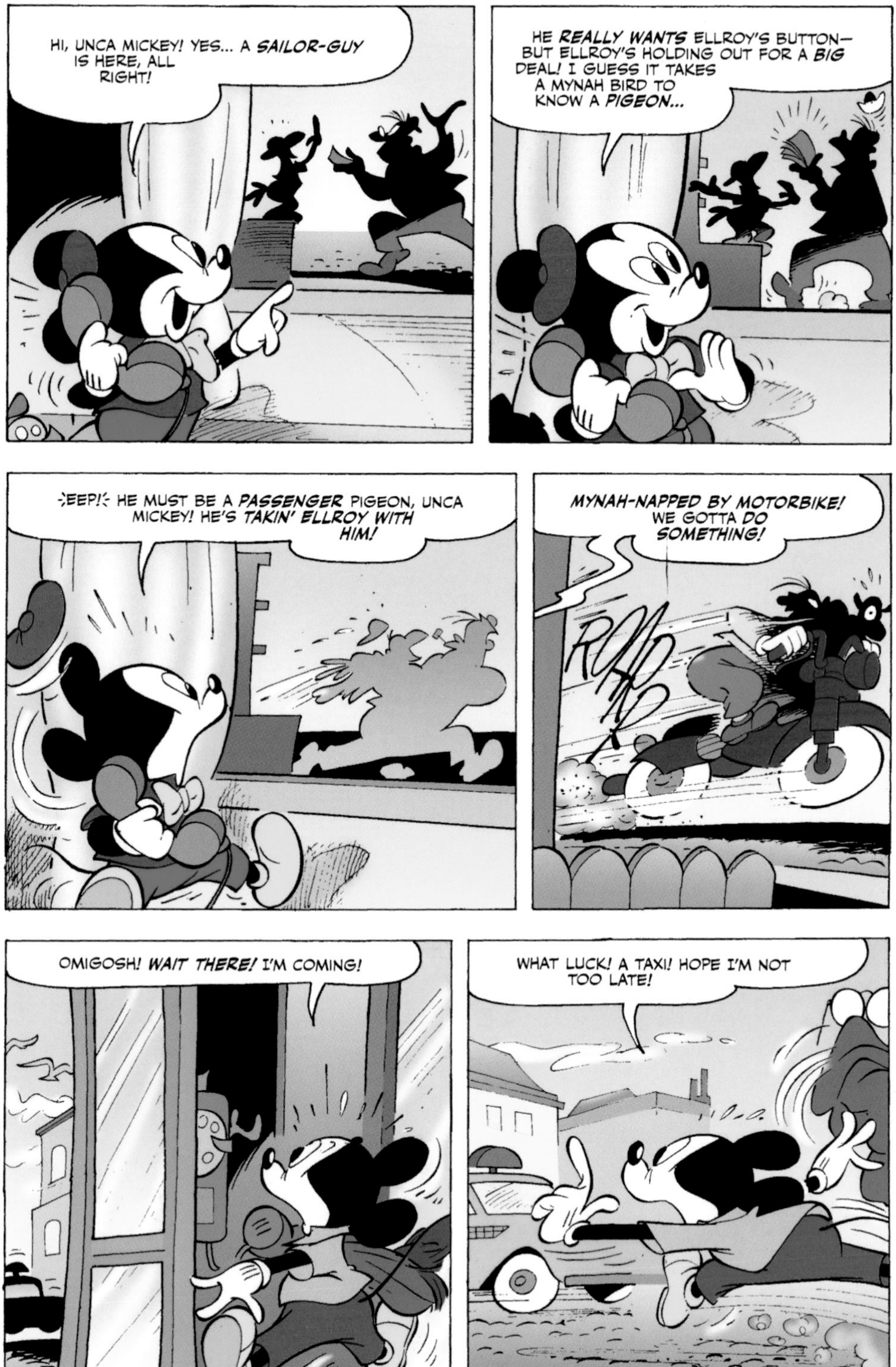
HI, UNCA MICKEY! YES... A SAILOR-GUY IS HERE, ALL RIGHT!
HE REALLY WANTS ELLROY'S BUTTON— BUT ELLROY'S HOLDING OUT FOR A BIG DEAL! I GUESS IT TAKES A MYNAH BIRD TO KNOW A PIGEON...
EEP! HE MUST BE A PASSENGER PIGEON, UNCA MICKEY! HE'S TAKIN' ELLROY WITH HIM!
MYNAH-NAPPED BY MOTORBIKE! WE GOTTA DO SOMETHING!
ROAR
OMIGOSH! WAIT THERE! I'M COMING!
WHAT LUCK! A TAXI! HOPE I'M NOT TOO LATE!

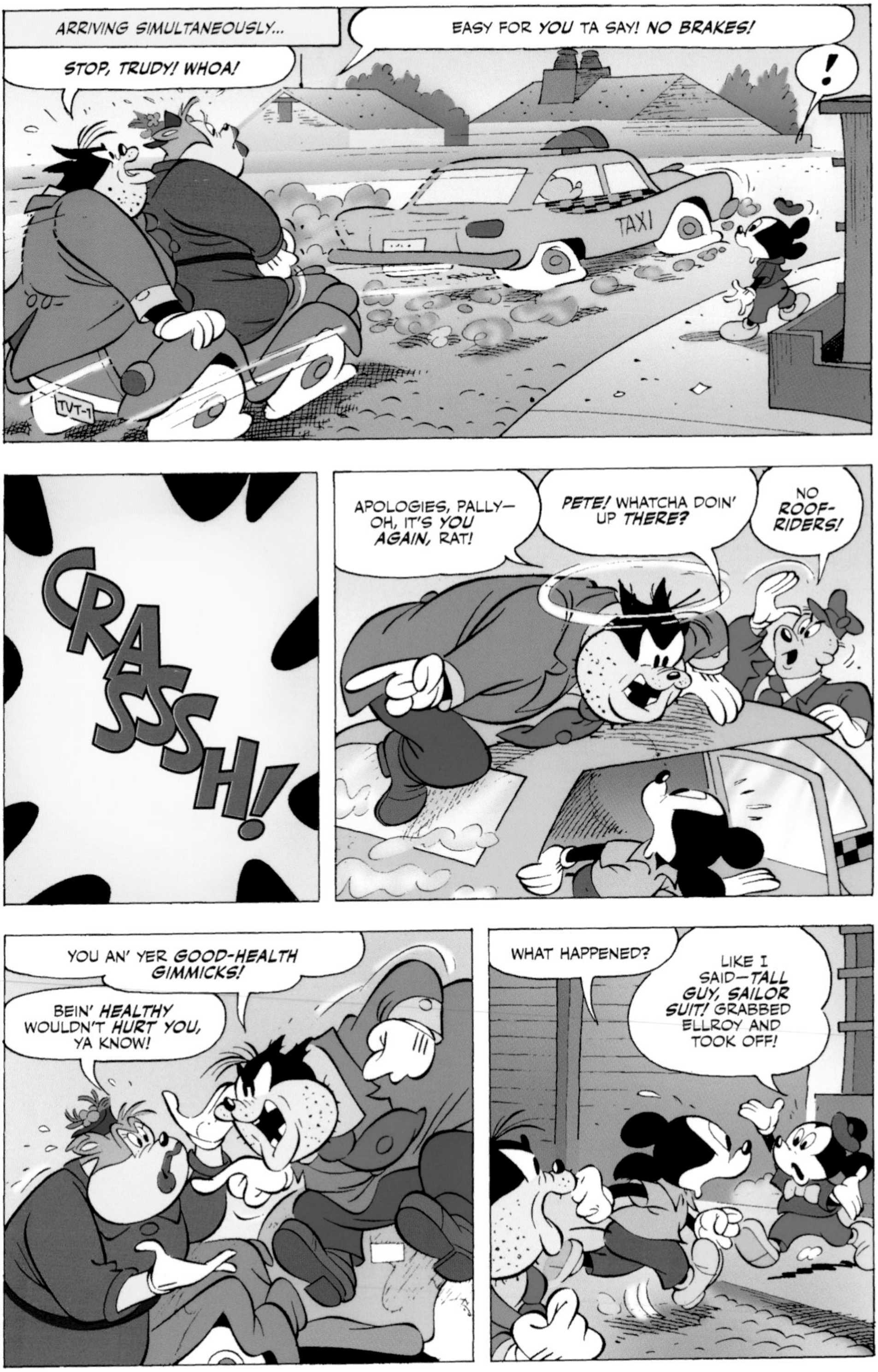

ARRIVING SIMULTANEOUSLY...
STOP, TRUDY! WHOA!
EASY FOR YOU TA SAY! NO BRAKES!
!
TAXI
TVT-1
CRASSSH!
APOLOGIES, PALLY— OH, IT'S YOU AGAIN, RAT!
PETE! WHATCHA DOIN' UP THERE?
NO ROOF-RIDERS!
YOU AN' YER GOOD-HEALTH GIMMICKS!
BEIN' HEALTHY WOULDN'T HURT YOU, YA KNOW!
WHAT HAPPENED?
LIKE I SAID—TALL GUY, SAILOR SUIT! GRABBED ELLROY AND TOOK OFF!

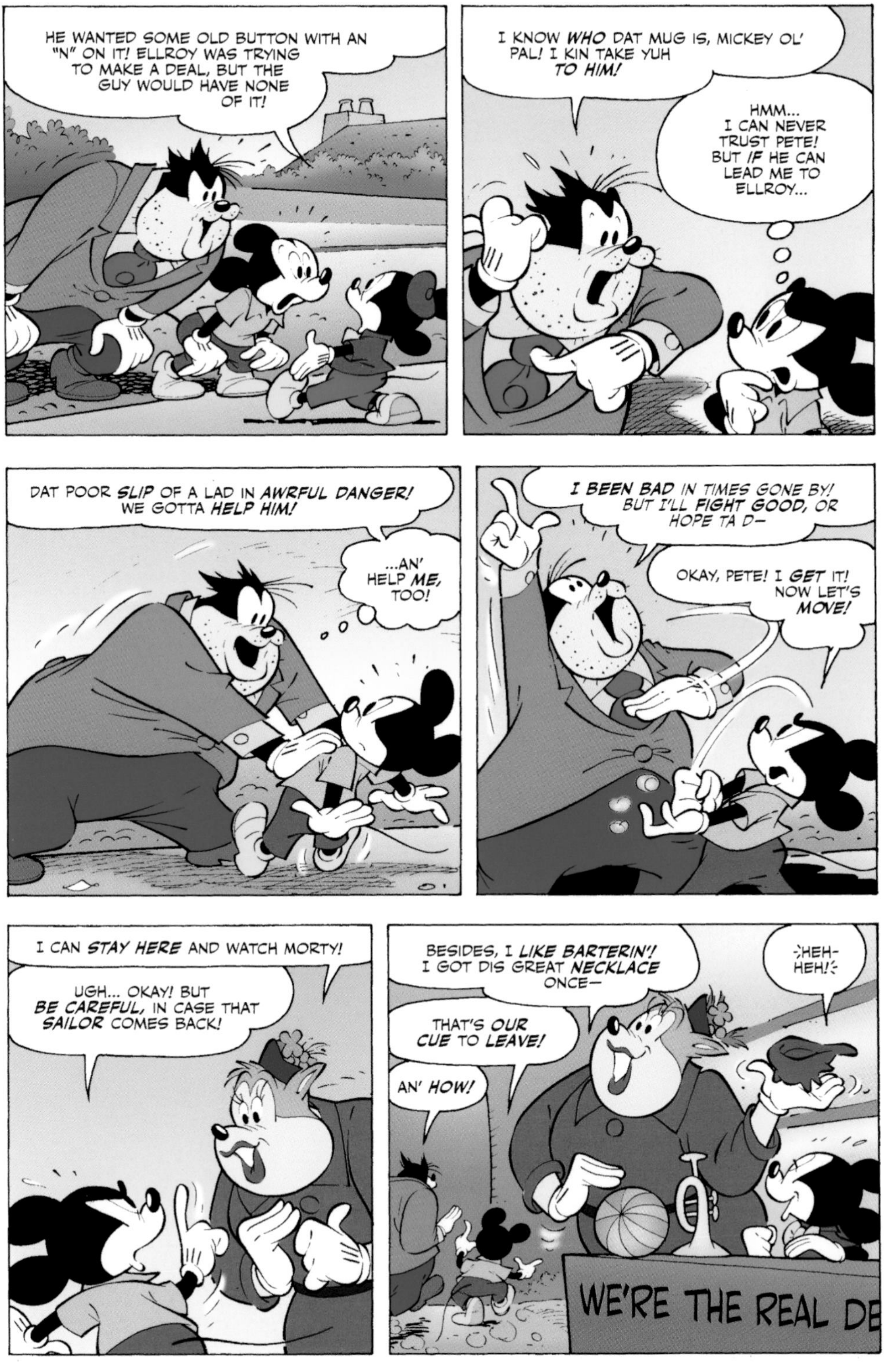
HE WANTED SOME OLD BUTTON WITH AN "N" ON IT! ELLROY WAS TRYING TO MAKE A DEAL, BUT THE GUY WOULD HAVE NONE OF IT!
I KNOW WHO DAT MUG IS, MICKEY OL' PAL! I KIN TAKE YUH TO HIM!
HMM... I CAN NEVER TRUST PETE! BUT IF HE CAN LEAD ME TO ELLROY...
DAT POOR SLIP OF A LAD IN AWRFUL DANGER! WE GOTTA HELP HIM!
...AN' HELP ME, TOO!
I BEEN BAD IN TIMES GONE BY! BUT I'LL FIGHT GOOD, OR HOPE TA D—
OKAY, PETE! I GET IT! NOW LET'S MOVE!
I CAN STAY HERE AND WATCH MORTY!
UGH... OKAY! BUT BE CAREFUL, IN CASE THAT SAILOR COMES BACK!
BESIDES, I LIKE BARTERIN'! I GOT DIS GREAT NECKLACE ONCE—
HEH-HEH!
THAT'S OUR CUE TO LEAVE!
AN' HOW!
WE'RE THE REAL DE

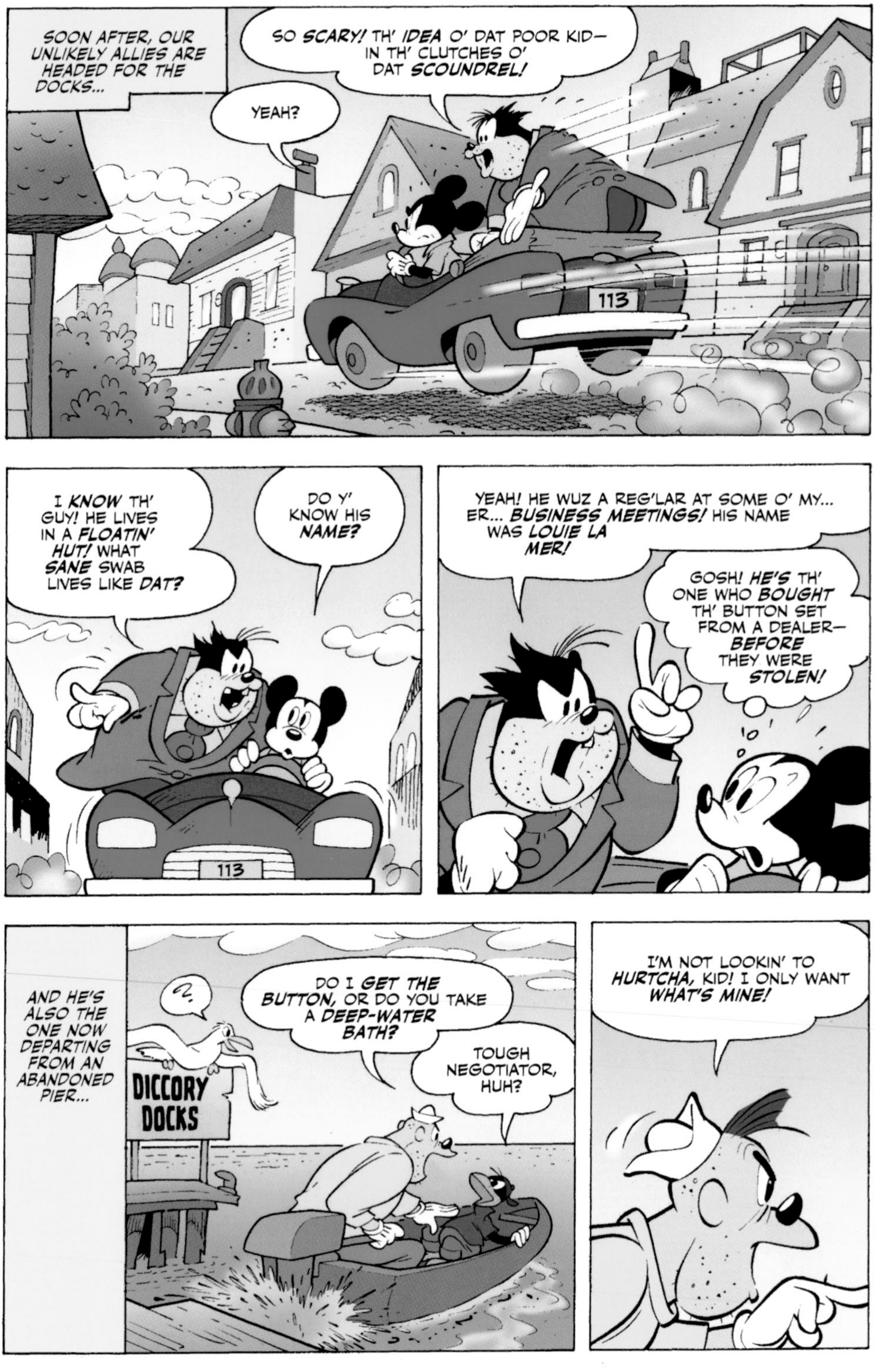
SOON AFTER, OUR UNLIKELY ALLIES ARE HEADED FOR THE DOCKS...
SO SCARY! TH' IDEA O' DAT POOR KID— IN TH' CLUTCHES O' DAT SCOUNDREL!
YEAH?
113
I KNOW TH' GUY! HE LIVES IN A FLOATIN' HUT! WHAT SANE SWAB LIVES LIKE DAT?
DO Y' KNOW HIS NAME?
113
YEAH! HE WUZ A REG'LAR AT SOME O' MY... ER... BUSINESS MEETINGS! HIS NAME WAS LOUIE LA MER!
GOSH! HE'S TH' ONE WHO BOUGHT TH' BUTTON SET FROM A DEALER— BEFORE THEY WERE STOLEN!
AND HE'S ALSO THE ONE NOW DEPARTING FROM AN ABANDONED PIER...
DO I GET THE BUTTON, OR DO YOU TAKE A DEEP-WATER BATH?
TOUGH NEGOTIATOR, HUH?
DICCORY DOCKS
I'M NOT LOOKIN' TO HURTCHA, KID! I ONLY WANT WHAT'S MINE!

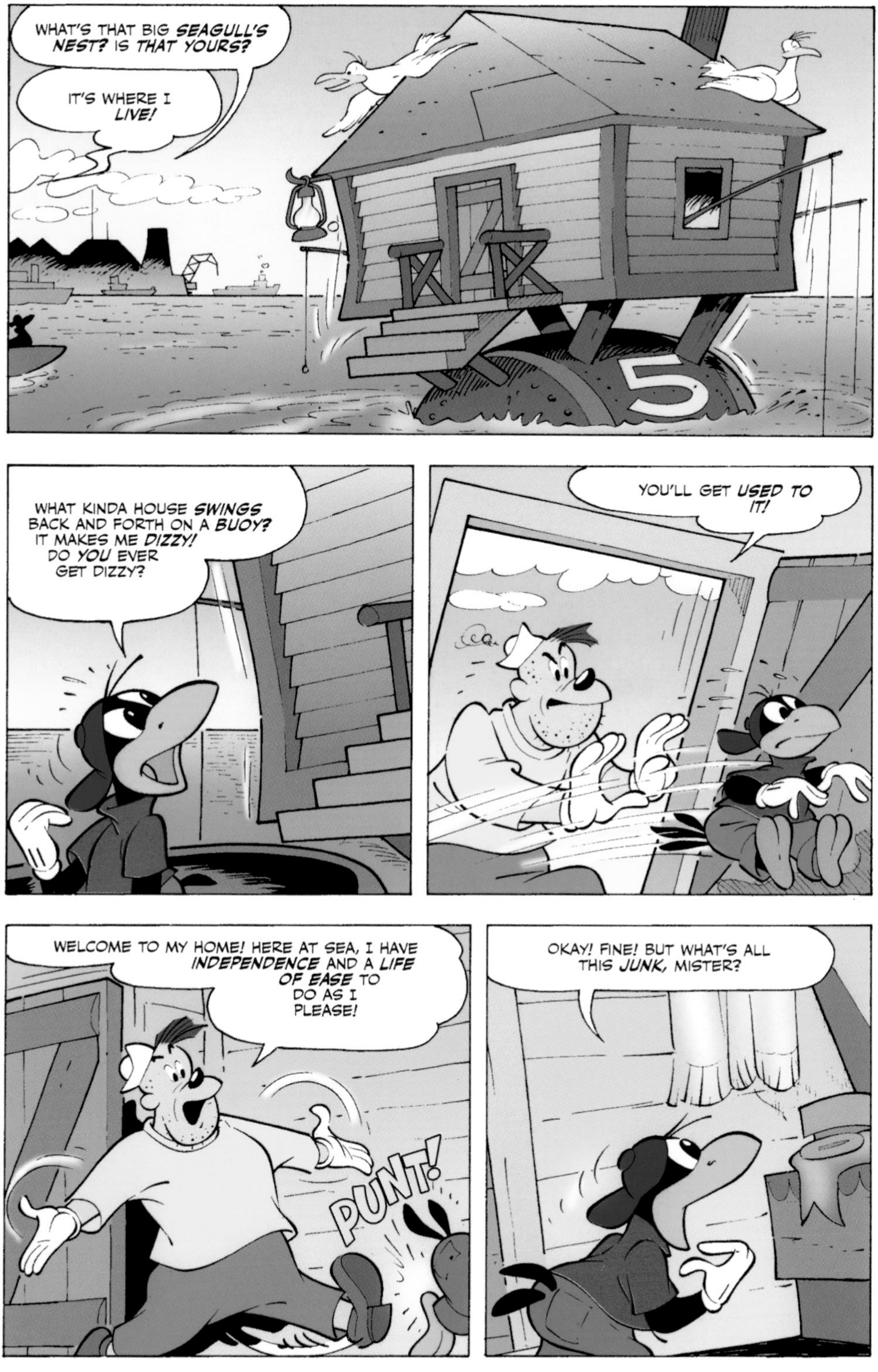
WHAT'S THAT BIG SEAGULL'S NEST? IS THAT YOURS?
IT'S WHERE I LIVE!
5
WHAT KINDA HOUSE SWINGS BACK AND FORTH ON A BUOY? IT MAKES ME DIZZY! DO YOU EVER GET DIZZY?
YOU'LL GET USED TO IT!
WELCOME TO MY HOME! HERE AT SEA, I HAVE INDEPENDENCE AND A LIFE OF EASE TO DO AS I PLEASE!
PUNT!
OKAY! FINE! BUT WHAT'S ALL THIS JUNK, MISTER?

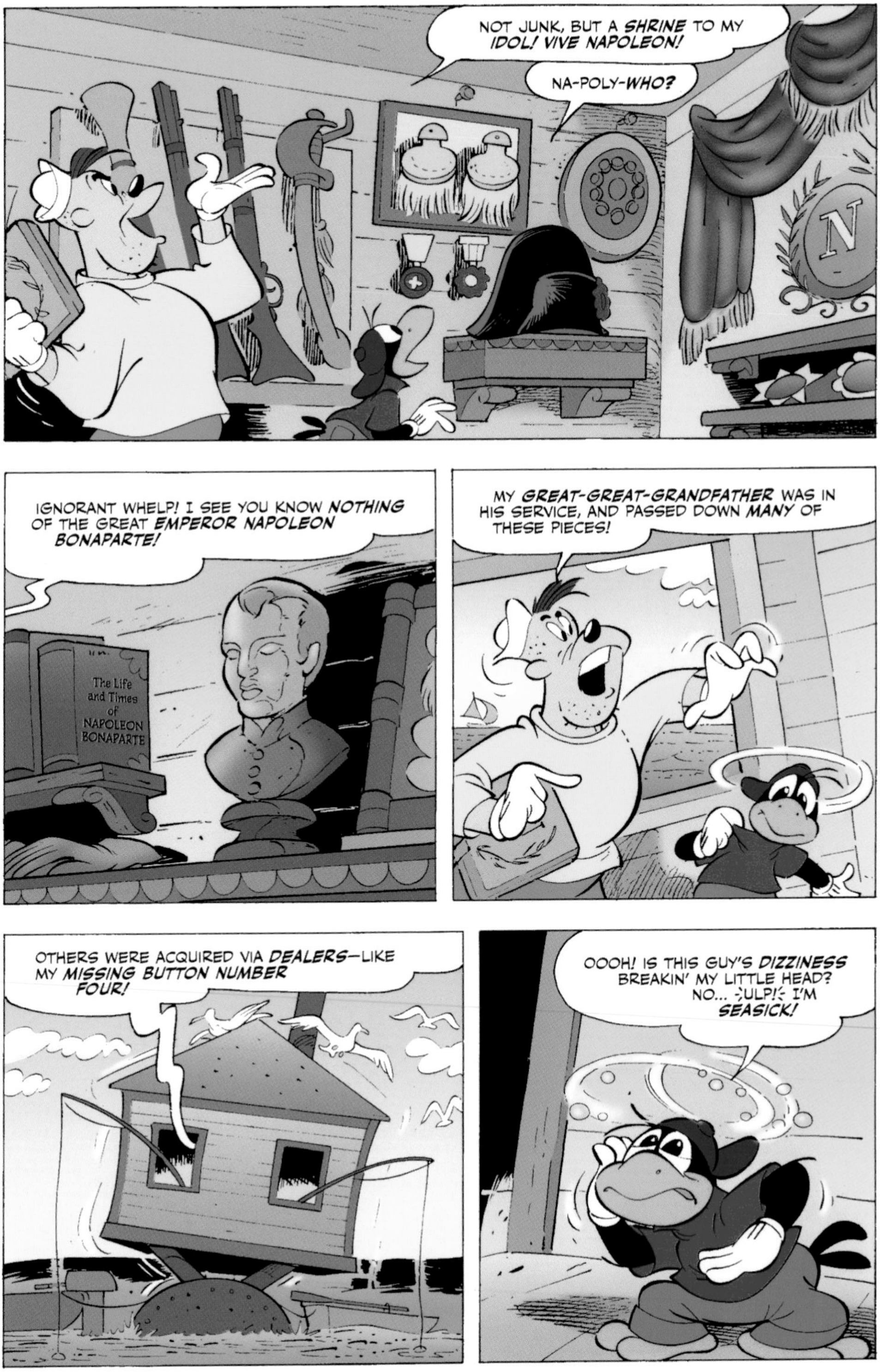
NOT JUNK, BUT A SHRINE TO MY IDOL! VIVE NAPOLEON!
NA-POLY-WHO?
IGNORANT WHELP! I SEE YOU KNOW NOTHING OF THE GREAT EMPEROR NAPOLEON BONAPARTE!
The Life and Times of NAPOLEON BONAPARTE
MY GREAT-GREAT-GRANDFATHER WAS IN HIS SERVICE, AND PASSED DOWN MANY OF THESE PIECES!
OTHERS WERE ACQUIRED VIA DEALERS—LIKE MY MISSING BUTTON NUMBER FOUR!
OOOH! IS THIS GUY'S DIZZINESS BREAKIN' MY LITTLE HEAD? NO... GULP! I'M SEASICK!

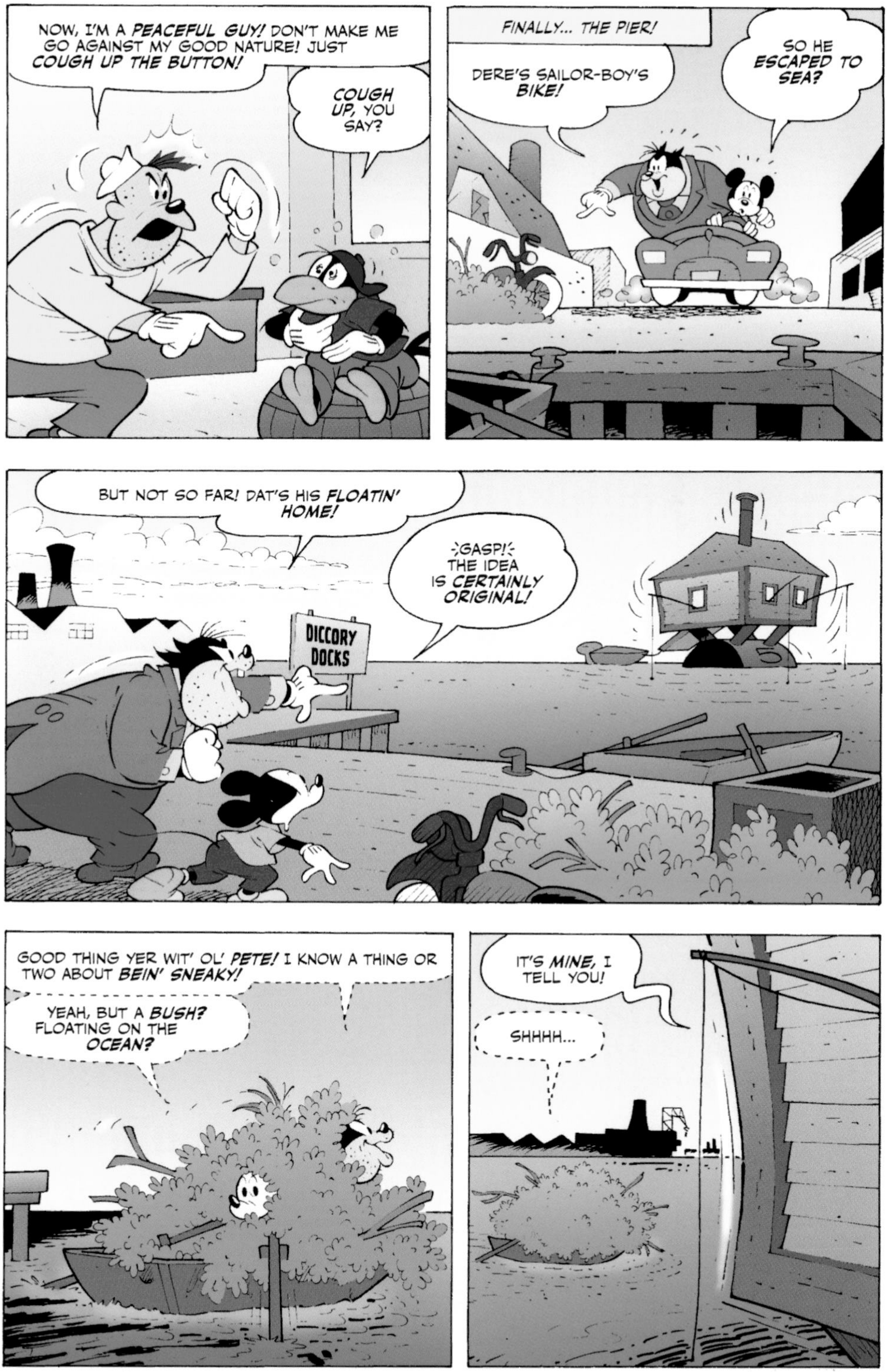
NOW, I'M A PEACEFUL GUY! DON'T MAKE ME GO AGAINST MY GOOD NATURE! JUST COUGH UP THE BUTTON!
COUGH UP, YOU SAY?
FINALLY... THE PIER!
DERE'S SAILOR-BOY'S BIKE!
SO HE ESCAPED TO SEA?
BUT NOT SO FAR! DAT'S HIS FLOATIN' HOME!
-GASP!- THE IDEA IS CERTAINLY ORIGINAL!
DICCORY DOCKS
GOOD THING YER WIT' OL' PETE! I KNOW A THING OR TWO ABOUT BEIN' SNEAKY!
YEAH, BUT A BUSH? FLOATING ON THE OCEAN?
IT'S MINE, I TELL YOU!
SHHHH...

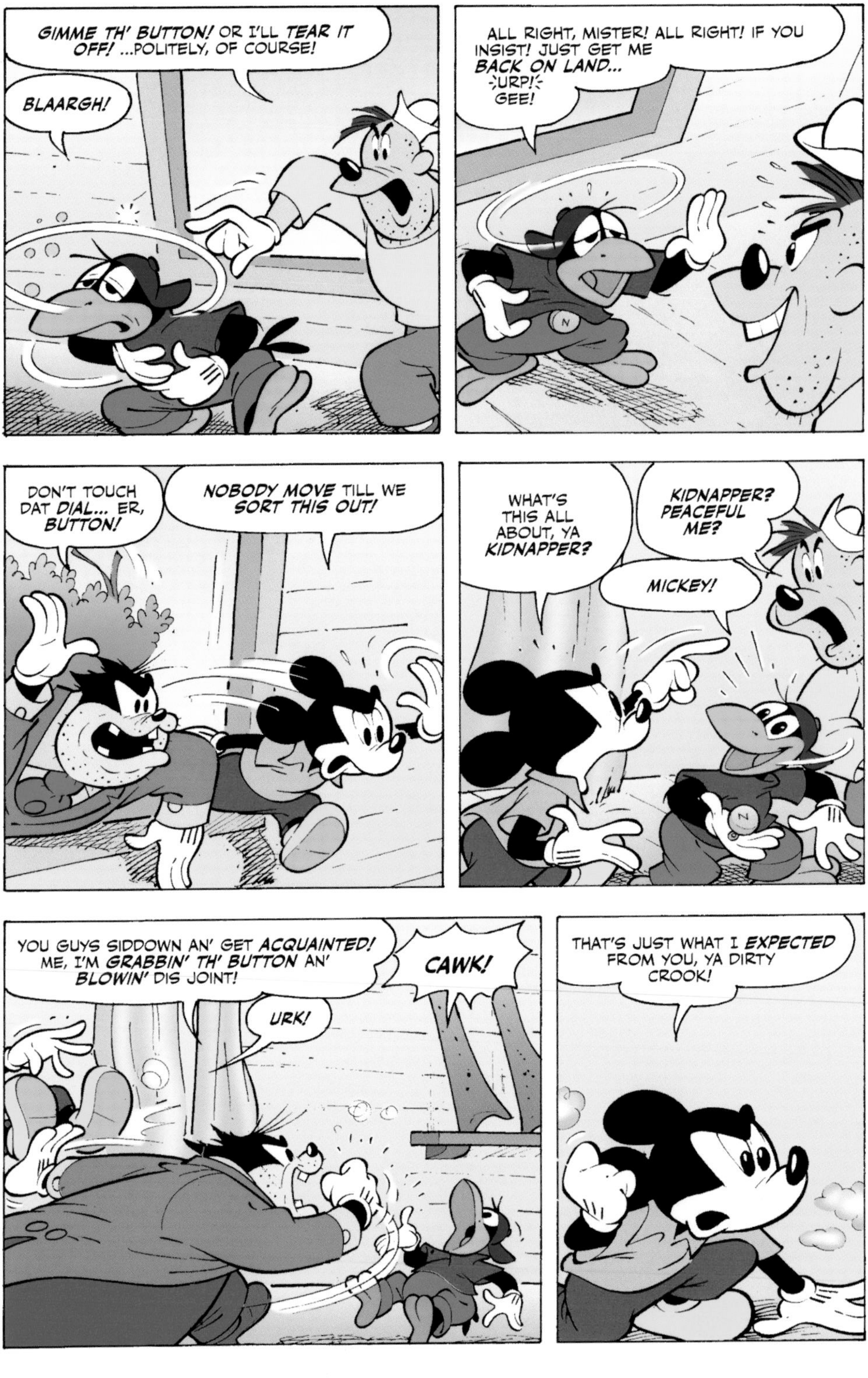
GIMME TH' BUTTON! OR I'LL TEAR IT OFF! ...POLITELY, OF COURSE!
BLAARGH!
ALL RIGHT, MISTER! ALL RIGHT! IF YOU INSIST! JUST GET ME BACK ON LAND... URP! GEE!
DON'T TOUCH DAT DIAL... ER, BUTTON!
NOBODY MOVE TILL WE SORT THIS OUT!
WHAT'S THIS ALL ABOUT, YA KIDNAPPER?
KIDNAPPER? PEACEFUL ME?
MICKEY!
YOU GUYS SIDDOWN AN' GET ACQUAINTED! ME, I'M GRABBIN' TH' BUTTON AN' BLOWIN' DIS JOINT!
CAWK!
URK!
THAT'S JUST WHAT I EXPECTED FROM YOU, YA DIRTY CROOK!

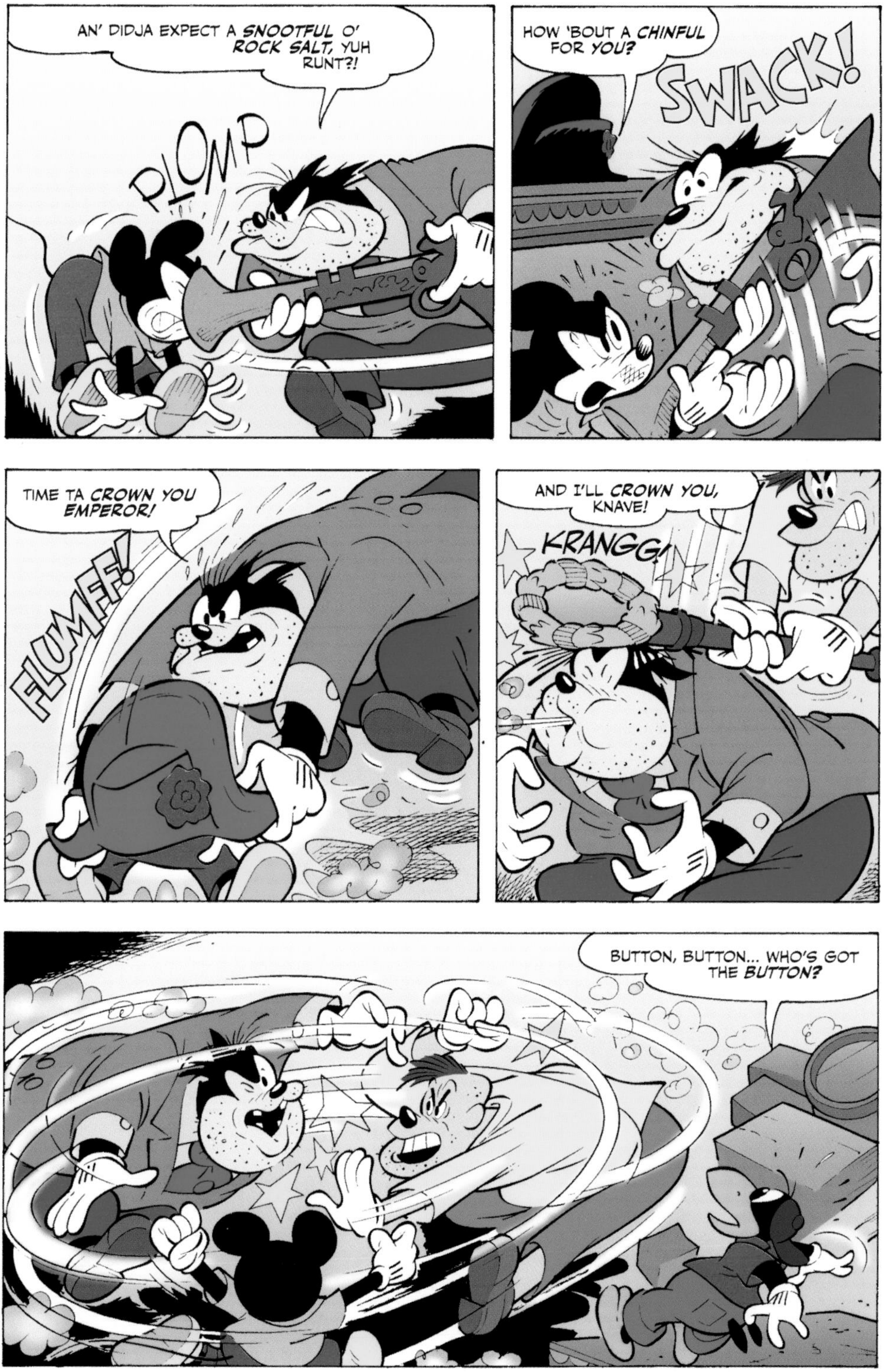
AN' DIDJA EXPECT A SNOOTFUL O' ROCK SALT, YUH RUNT?!
PLOMP
HOW 'BOUT A CHINFUL FOR YOU?
SWACK!
TIME TA CROWN YOU EMPEROR!
FLUMFF!
AND I'LL CROWN YOU, KNAVE!
KRANGG!
BUTTON, BUTTON... WHO'S GOT THE BUTTON?

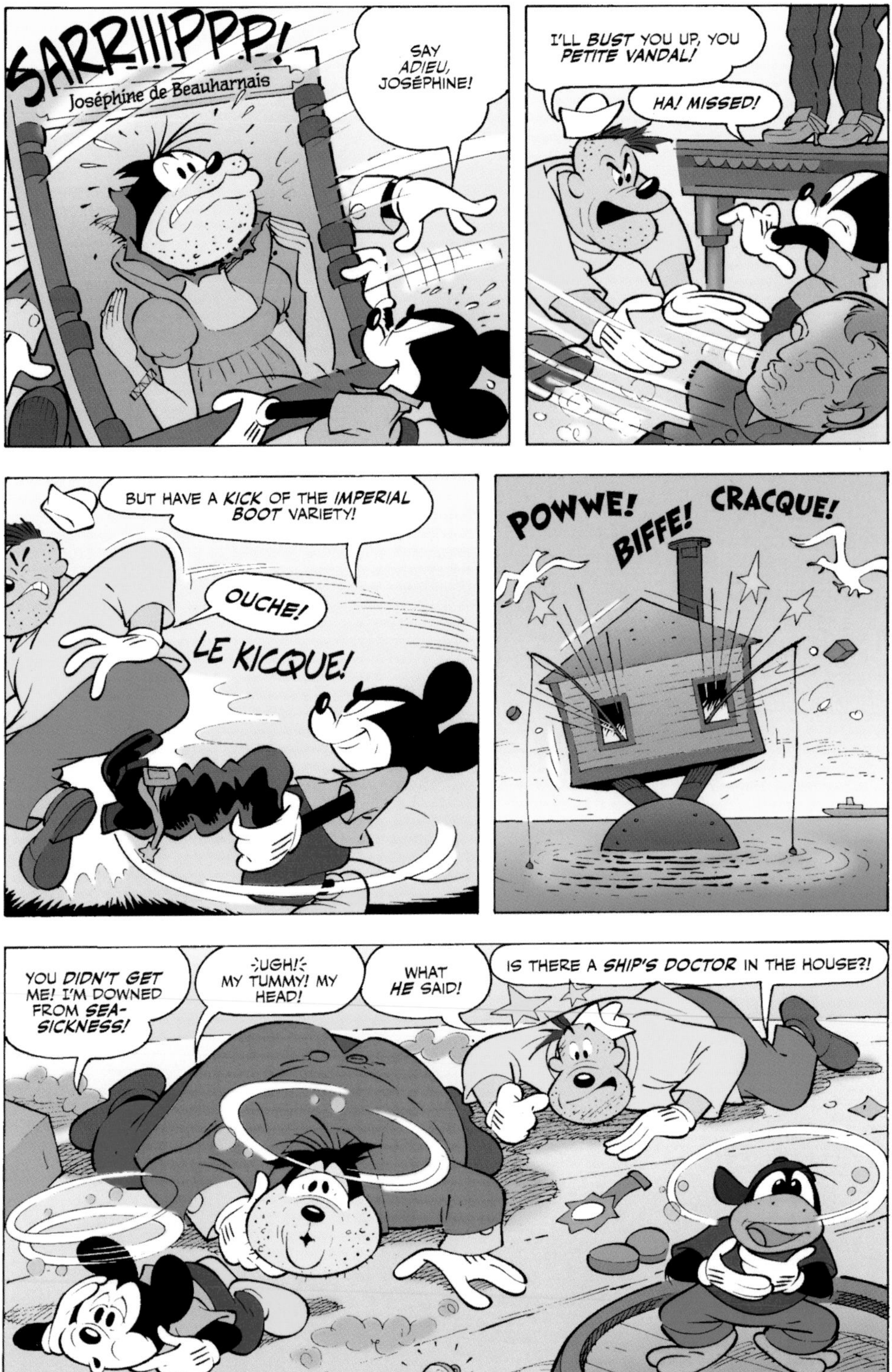
SARRIIIPPPP!
Joséphine de Beauharnais
SAY ADIEU, JOSÉPHINE!
I'LL BUST YOU UP, YOU PETITE VANDAL!
HA! MISSED!
BUT HAVE A KICK OF THE IMPERIAL BOOT VARIETY!
OUCHE!
LE KICQUE!
POWWE!
BIFFE!
CRACQUE!
YOU DIDN'T GET ME! I'M DOWNED FROM SEA-SICKNESS!
UGH! MY TUMMY! MY HEAD!
WHAT HE SAID!
IS THERE A SHIP'S DOCTOR IN THE HOUSE?!

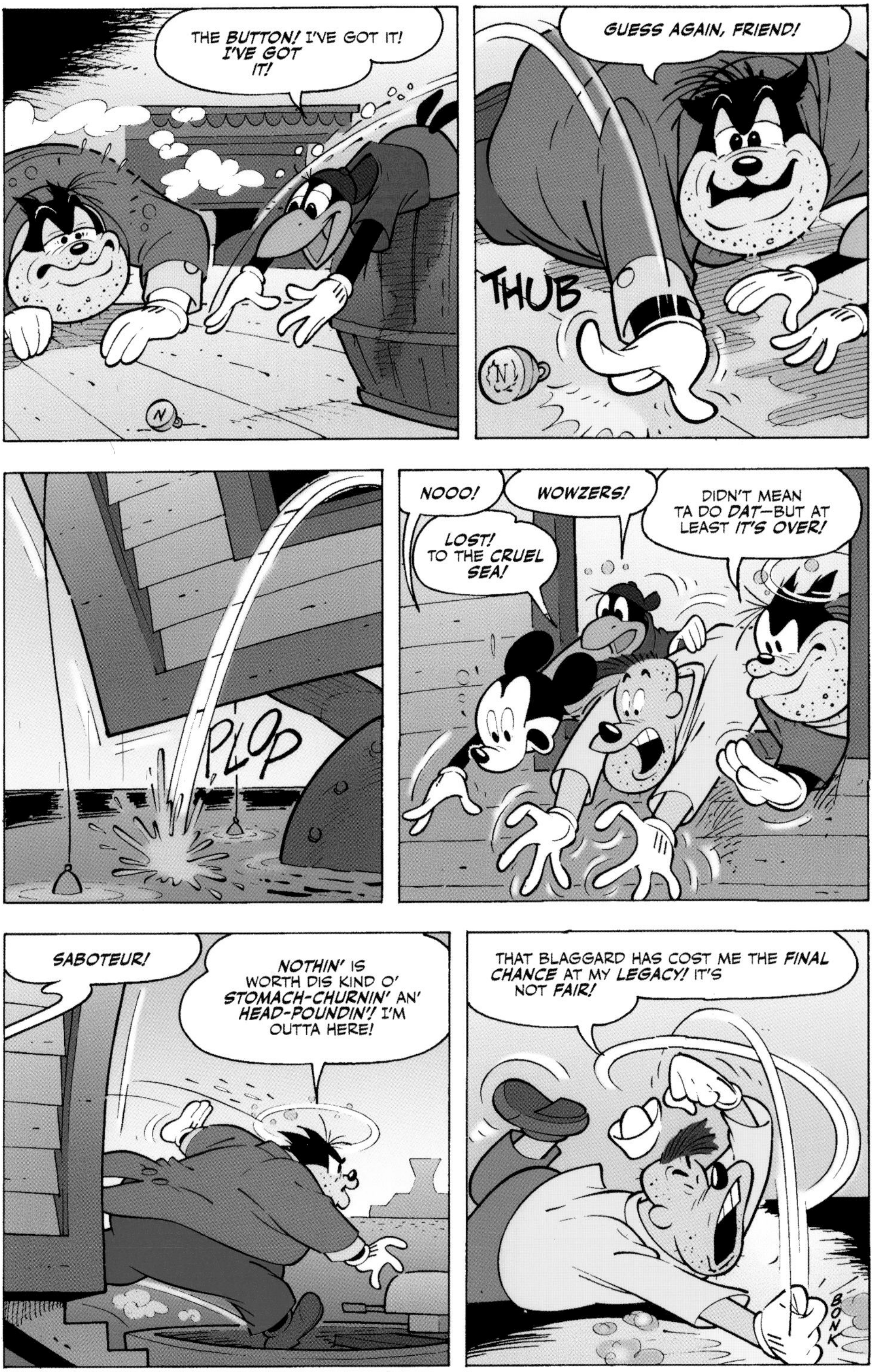
THE BUTTON! I'VE GOT IT! I'VE GOT IT!
GUESS AGAIN, FRIEND!
THUB
PLOP
NOOO!
LOST! TO THE CRUEL SEA!
WOWZERS!
DIDN'T MEAN TA DO DAT—BUT AT LEAST IT'S OVER!
SABOTEUR!
NOTHIN' IS WORTH DIS KIND O' STOMACH-CHURNIN' AN' HEAD-POUNDIN'! I'M OUTTA HERE!
THAT BLAGGARD HAS COST ME THE FINAL CHANCE AT MY LEGACY! IT'S NOT FAIR!
BONK

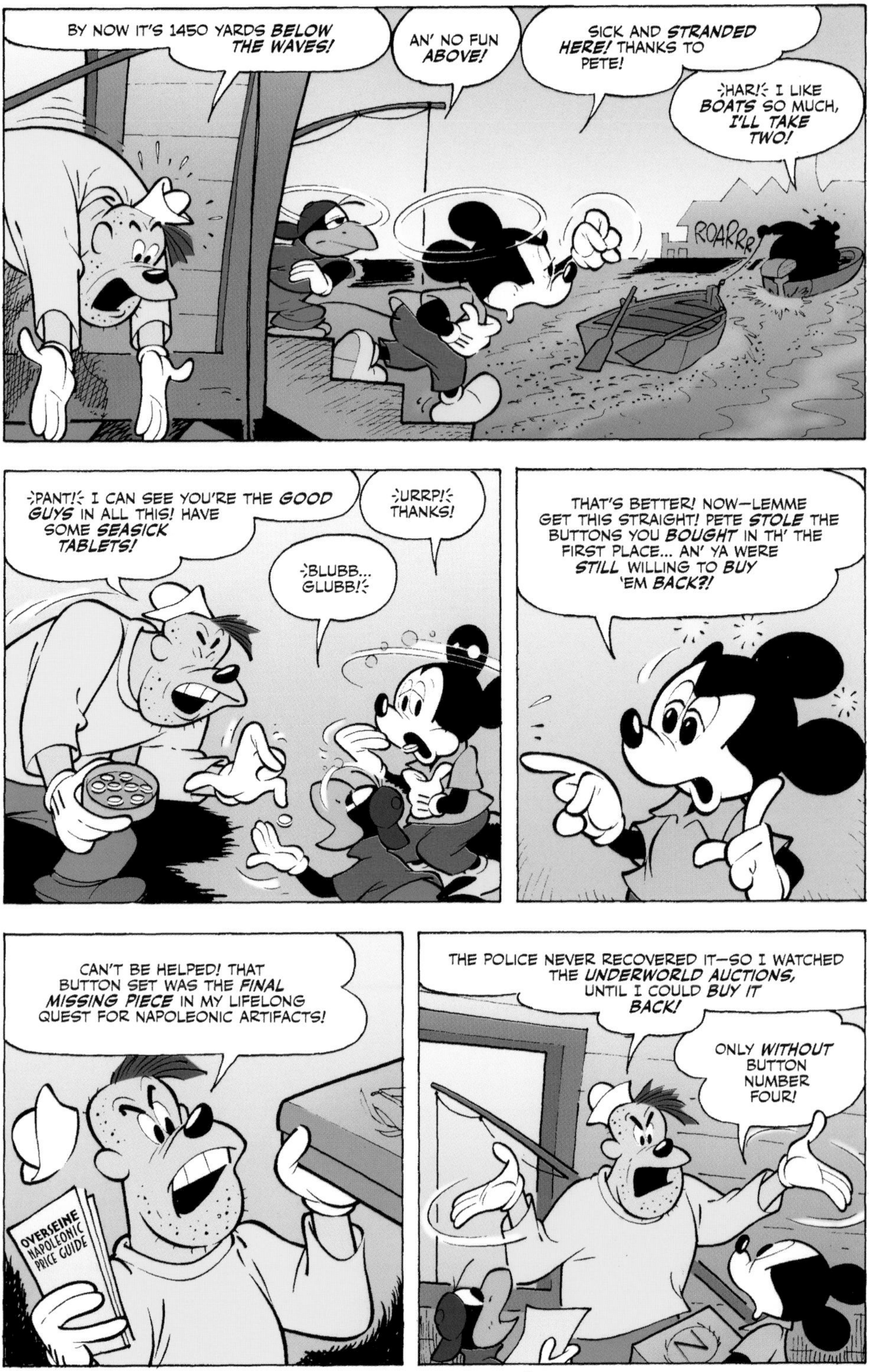
BY NOW IT'S 1450 YARDS BELOW THE WAVES!
AN' NO FUN ABOVE!
SICK AND STRANDED HERE! THANKS TO PETE!
HAR! I LIKE BOATS SO MUCH, I'LL TAKE TWO!
ROARRR
PANT! I CAN SEE YOU'RE THE GOOD GUYS IN ALL THIS! HAVE SOME SEASICK TABLETS!
URRP! THANKS!
BLUBB... GLUBB!
THAT'S BETTER! NOW—LEMME GET THIS STRAIGHT! PETE STOLE THE BUTTONS YOU BOUGHT IN TH' THE FIRST PLACE... AN' YA WERE STILL WILLING TO BUY 'EM BACK?!
CAN'T BE HELPED! THAT BUTTON SET WAS THE FINAL MISSING PIECE IN MY LIFELONG QUEST FOR NAPOLEONIC ARTIFACTS!
OVERSEINE NAPOLEONIC PRICE GUIDE
THE POLICE NEVER RECOVERED IT—SO I WATCHED THE UNDERWORLD AUCTIONS, UNTIL I COULD BUY IT BACK!
ONLY WITHOUT BUTTON NUMBER FOUR!

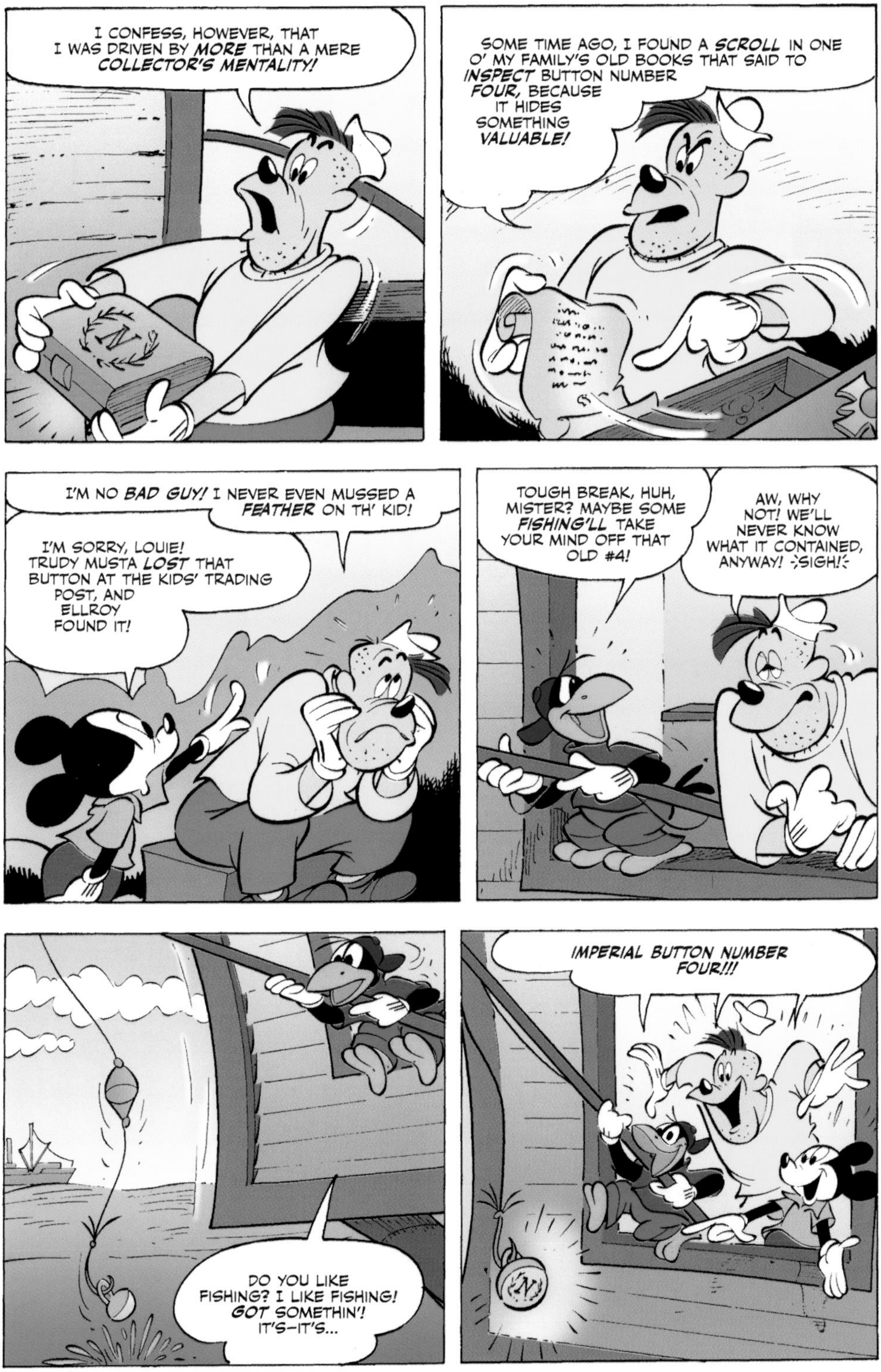
I CONFESS, HOWEVER, THAT I WAS DRIVEN BY MORE THAN A MERE COLLECTOR'S MENTALITY!
SOME TIME AGO, I FOUND A SCROLL IN ONE O' MY FAMILY'S OLD BOOKS THAT SAID TO INSPECT BUTTON NUMBER FOUR, BECAUSE IT HIDES SOMETHING VALUABLE!
I'M NO BAD GUY! I NEVER EVEN MUSSED A FEATHER ON TH' KID!
I'M SORRY, LOUIE! TRUDY MUSTA LOST THAT BUTTON AT THE KIDS' TRADING POST, AND ELLROY FOUND IT!
TOUGH BREAK, HUH, MISTER? MAYBE SOME FISHING'LL TAKE YOUR MIND OFF THAT OLD #4!
AW, WHY NOT! WE'LL NEVER KNOW WHAT IT CONTAINED, ANYWAY! SIGH!
DO YOU LIKE FISHING? I LIKE FISHING! GOT SOMETHIN'! IT'S—IT'S...
IMPERIAL BUTTON NUMBER FOUR!!!

THAT'S *REALLY* IT!

A *MYNAH* MIRACLE!

WHAT *LUCK*, LOUIE! IT MUSTA GOTTEN *HOOKED* WHEN PETE LOST IT! HIS LOSS IS OUR GAIN!

SO—THE SCROLL SAYS TO *INSPECT AND OPEN* THE NUMBER FOUR BUTTON!

IT COULD BE THE *KEY TO A REAL TREASURE...* IT COULD! IT COULD!

*YES!* THE TOP *UNSCREWS!*

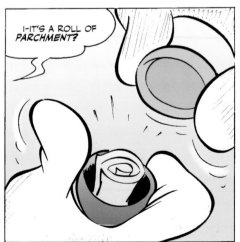

I-IT'S A ROLL OF *PARCHMENT?*

THERE'S SOMETHING *WRITTEN...* SO SMALL...

HOW *MUCH* COULD IT SAY?

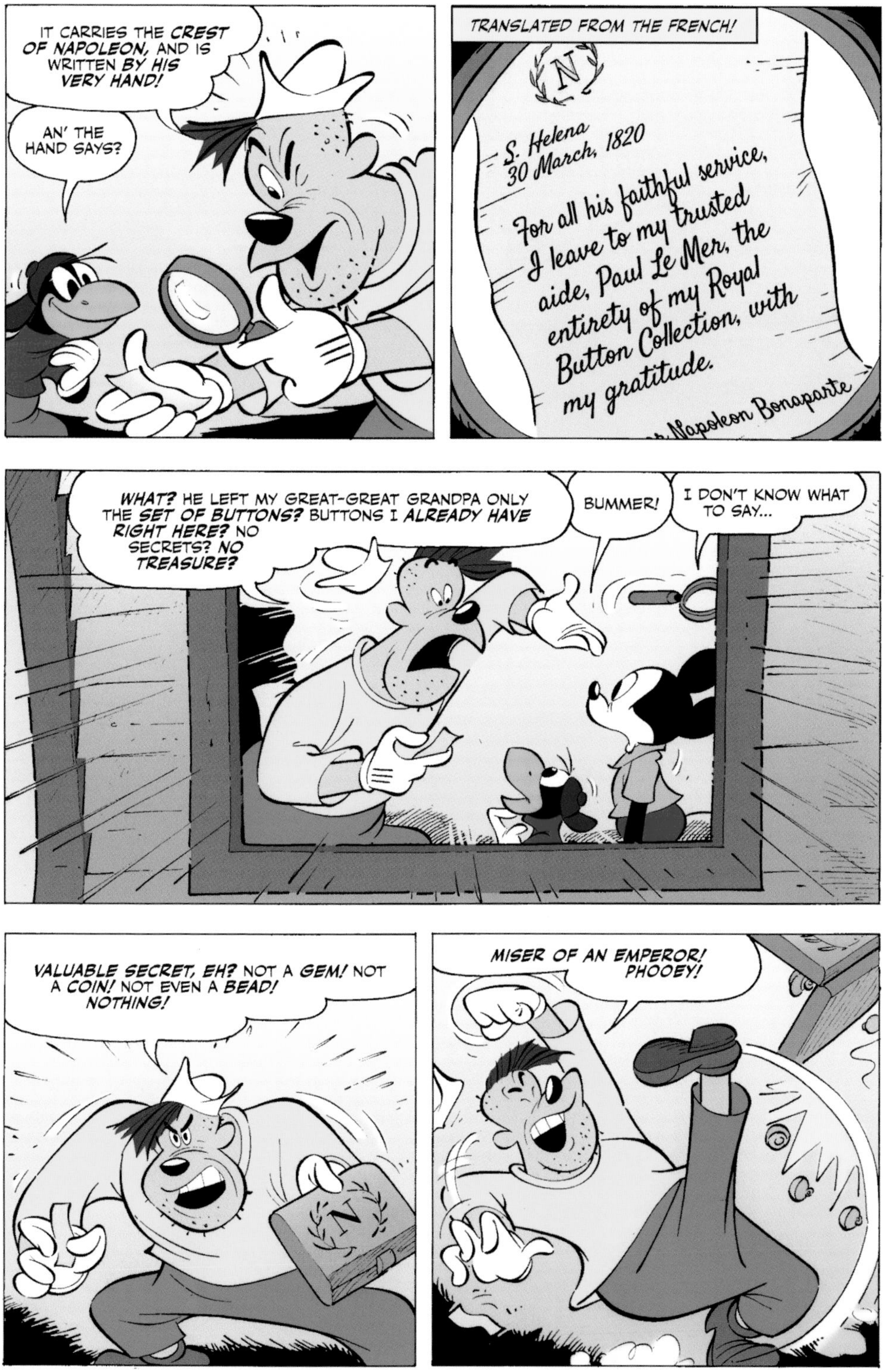
IT CARRIES THE CREST OF NAPOLEON, AND IS WRITTEN BY HIS VERY HAND!
AN' THE HAND SAYS?
TRANSLATED FROM THE FRENCH!
N
S. Helena
30 March, 1820
For all his faithful service, I leave to my trusted aide, Paul Le Mer, the entirety of my Royal Button Collection, with my gratitude.
Napoleon Bonaparte
WHAT? HE LEFT MY GREAT-GREAT GRANDPA ONLY THE SET OF BUTTONS? BUTTONS I ALREADY HAVE RIGHT HERE? NO SECRETS? NO TREASURE?
BUMMER!
I DON'T KNOW WHAT TO SAY...
VALUABLE SECRET, EH? NOT A GEM! NOT A COIN! NOT EVEN A BEAD! NOTHING!
N
MISER OF AN EMPEROR! PHOOEY!

CHEER UP, LOUIE! Y' *DO* HAVE AN AUTHENTIC *AUTOGRAPH* OF NAPOLEON! THAT'S GOTTA BE WORTH *SOMETHING!*

⨪SOB!⨪ BUT I'M *BROKE!* $1,200 TO PETE... EVEN *MORE* TO THE ORIGINAL ANTIQUE DEALER FOR THESE *BUTTONS!*

YOU'VE GOT *MORE* THAN JUST AN AUTOGRAPH, MISTER! *LOOK CLOSER* AT THIS *NAPOLEY-NOTE!*

SNAP

PARDON MY FRENCH, BUT IT SAYS... *"THE ENTIRETY OF MY ROYAL BUTTON COLLECTION,"* HUH, MISTER?

*I lea...
aide, P...
entirety...
Button Co...
m...*

THAT COULD MEAN THE *OTHERS* CONTAIN SOMETHING *TOO!*

LET'S GET 'EM *OPEN—NOW!*

?

DIAMONDS!

RUBIES!

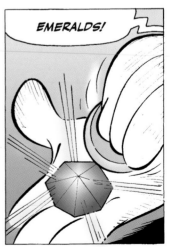

EMERALDS!

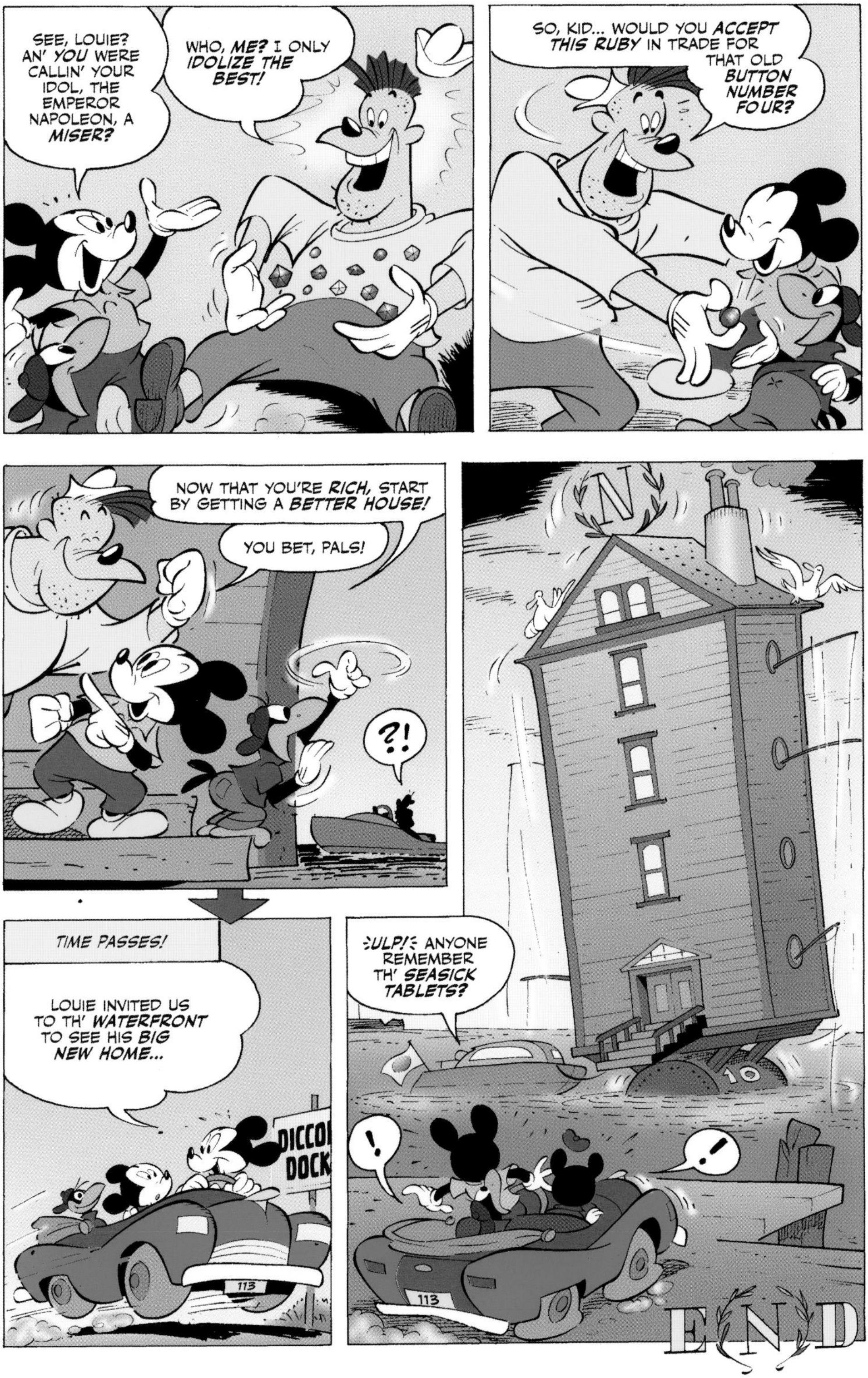
SEE, LOUIE? AN' YOU WERE CALLIN' YOUR IDOL, THE EMPEROR NAPOLEON, A MISER?
WHO, ME? I ONLY IDOLIZE THE BEST!
SO, KID... WOULD YOU ACCEPT THIS RUBY IN TRADE FOR THAT OLD BUTTON NUMBER FOUR?
NOW THAT YOU'RE RICH, START BY GETTING A BETTER HOUSE!
YOU BET, PALS!
?!
TIME PASSES!
LOUIE INVITED US TO TH' WATERFRONT TO SEE HIS BIG NEW HOME...
DICCOL DOCK
113
N
⫶ULP!⫶ ANYONE REMEMBER TH' SEASICK TABLETS?
!
!
10
113
END

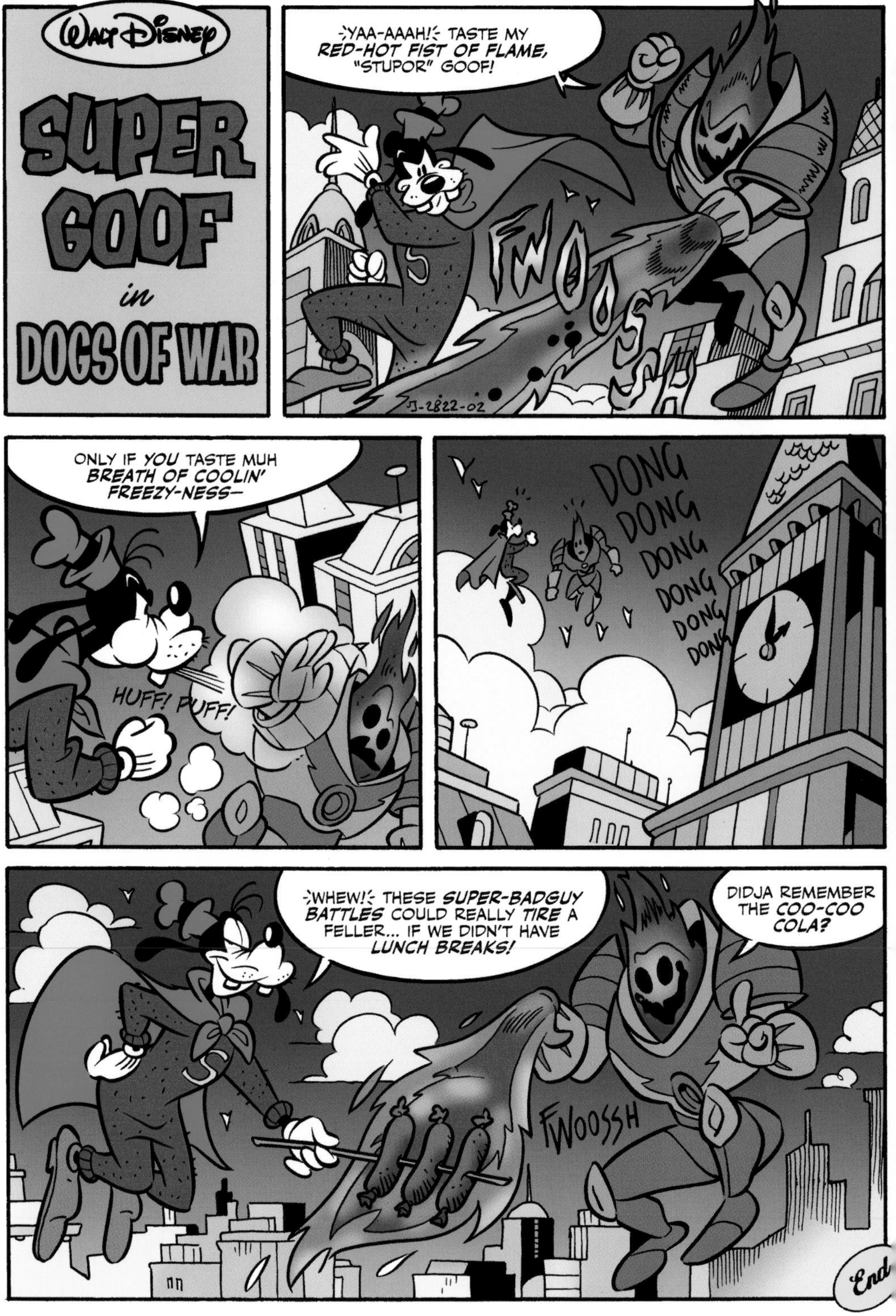
WALT DISNEY
SUPER GOOF
in
DOGS OF WAR
YAA-AAAH! TASTE MY RED-HOT FIST OF FLAME, "STUPOR" GOOF!
FWOOSSH
J-2822-02
ONLY IF YOU TASTE MUH BREATH OF COOLIN' FREEZY-NESS—
HUFF! PUFF!
DONG
DONG
DONG
DONG
DONG
DONG
WHEW! THESE SUPER-BADGUY BATTLES COULD REALLY TIRE A FELLER... IF WE DIDN'T HAVE LUNCH BREAKS!
DIDJA REMEMBER THE COO-COO COLA?
FWOOSSH
End

Originally published in *Topolino* #2822 (Italy, 2009)

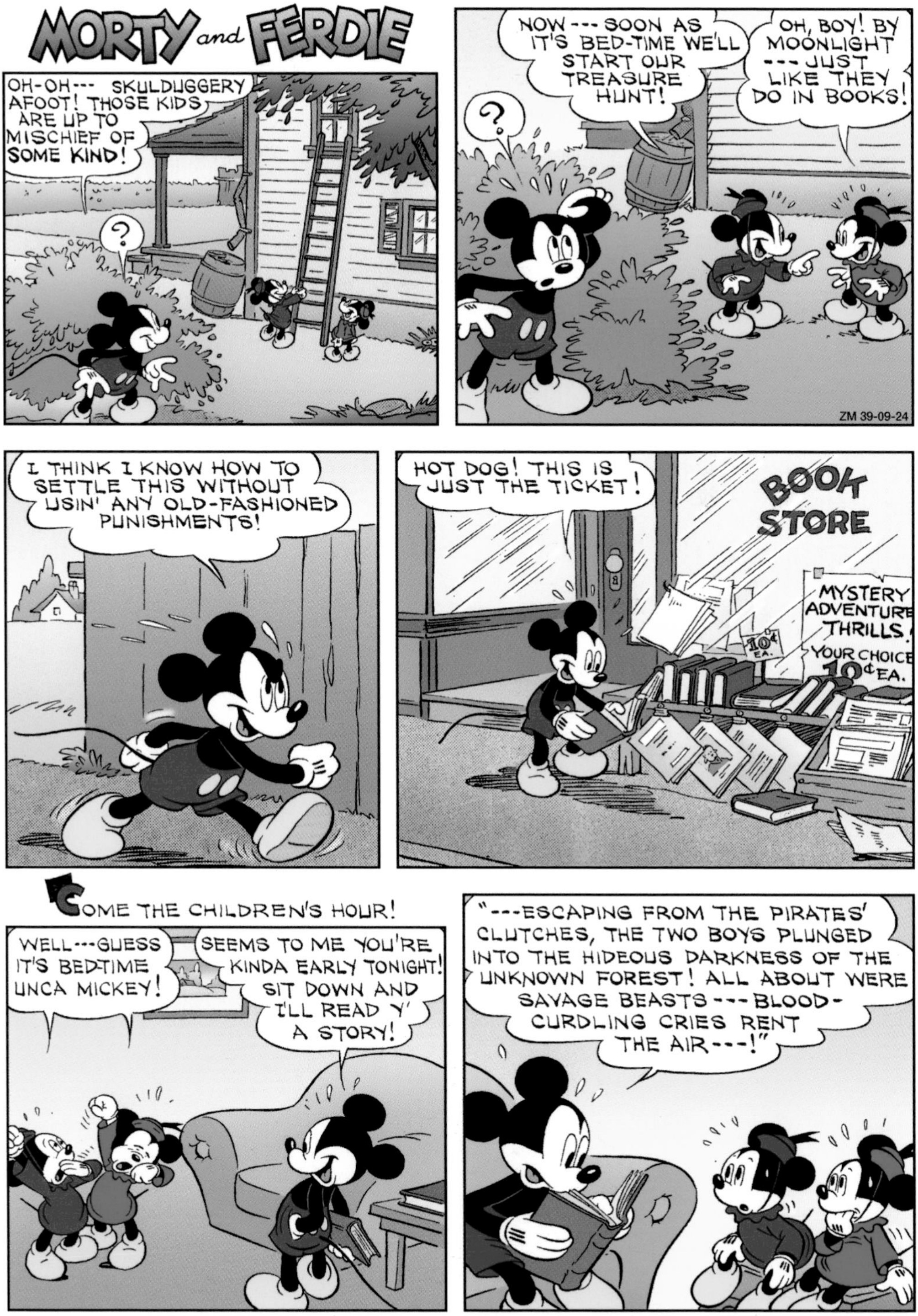
MORTY and FERDIE
OH-OH--- SKULDUGGERY AFOOT! THOSE KIDS ARE UP TO MISCHIEF OF SOME KIND!
?
?
NOW --- SOON AS IT'S BED-TIME WE'LL START OUR TREASURE HUNT!
OH, BOY! BY MOONLIGHT --- JUST LIKE THEY DO IN BOOKS!
ZM 39-09-24
I THINK I KNOW HOW TO SETTLE THIS WITHOUT USIN' ANY OLD-FASHIONED PUNISHMENTS!
HOT DOG! THIS IS JUST THE TICKET!
BOOK STORE
MYSTERY ADVENTURE THRILLS.
YOUR CHOICE 10¢ EA.
10¢ EA.
COME THE CHILDREN'S HOUR!
WELL---GUESS IT'S BED-TIME UNCA MICKEY!
SEEMS TO ME YOU'RE KINDA EARLY TONIGHT! SIT DOWN AND I'LL READ Y' A STORY!
"---ESCAPING FROM THE PIRATES' CLUTCHES, THE TWO BOYS PLUNGED INTO THE HIDEOUS DARKNESS OF THE UNKNOWN FOREST! ALL ABOUT WERE SAVAGE BEASTS --- BLOOD-CURDLING CRIES RENT THE AIR---!"

Originally published in *Mickey Mouse* Sunday comic strip (USA, 1939)

"---'THE TREASURE!' CRIED THE BOYS, 'WE'VE FOUND IT!' BUT EVEN AS THEY SPOKE, THE PIRATES CREPT SILENTLY UPON THEM WITH DRAWN CUTLASSES!" WELL, I GUESS WE BETTER GET TO BED, KIDS!

I BET THERE'LL BE NO TREASURE HUNT TONIGHT! THEY'RE PROB'LY BOTH HIDIN' UNDER THE COVERS!

GOSH, MAYBE I SCARED 'EM TOO MUCH! I'D BETTER SEE IF THEY'RE ALL RIGHT!

WELL, OF ALL TH' ---JUST WAIT 'TIL I FIND THOSE GUYS!

?

---RUNNIN' OUT IN THE MIDDLE OF THE NIGHT, IN SPITE OF --- HUH!!?

SLAM!

!

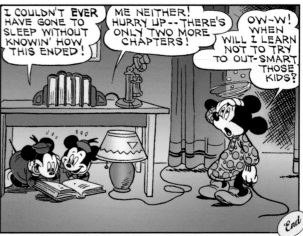

I COULDN'T EVER HAVE GONE TO SLEEP WITHOUT KNOWIN' HOW THIS ENDED!

ME NEITHER! HURRY UP-- THERE'S ONLY TWO MORE CHAPTERS!

OW-W! WHEN WILL I LEARN NOT TO TRY TO OUT-SMART THOSE KIDS?

End

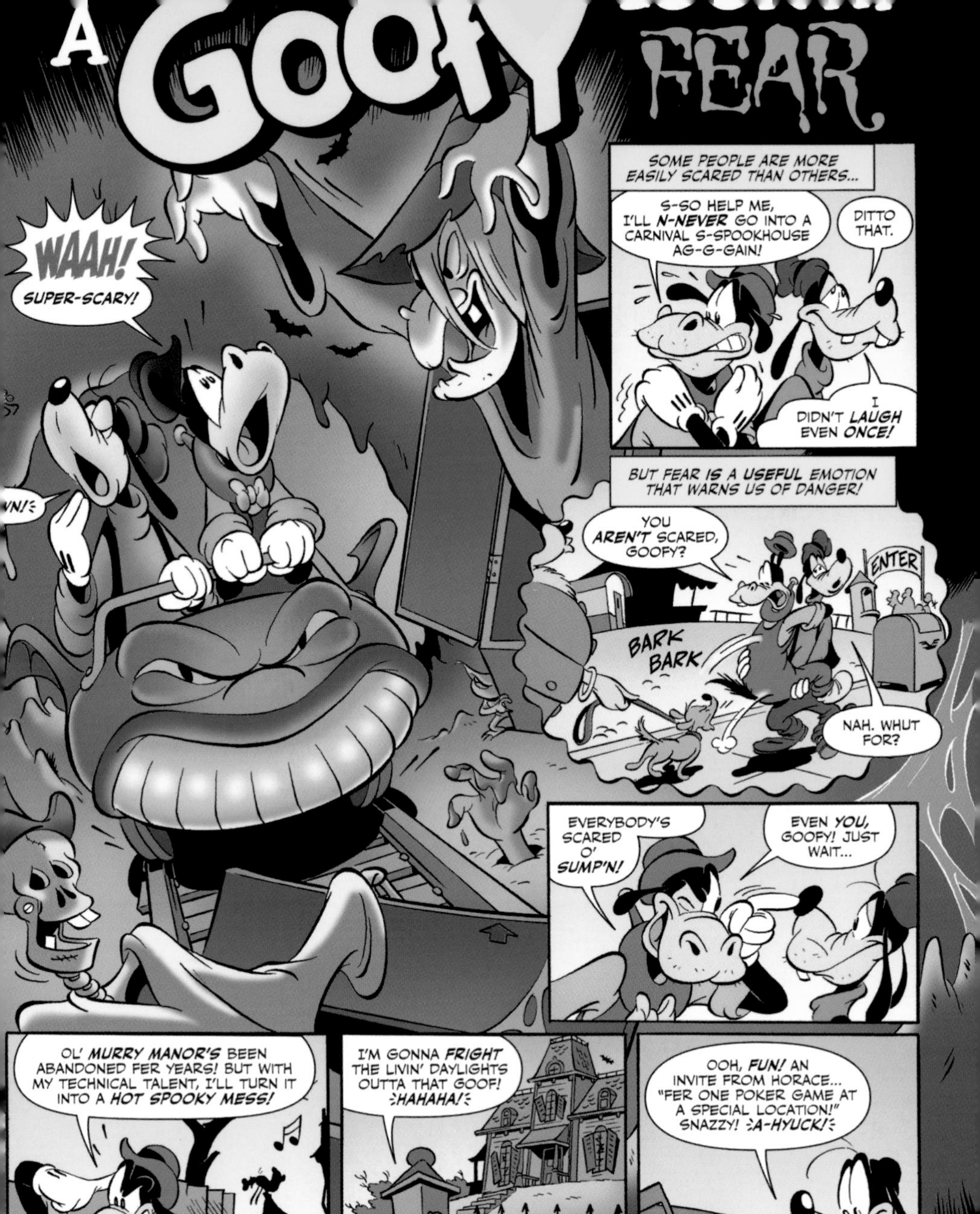
A GOOFY
FEAR
WAAH! SUPER-SCARY!
SOME PEOPLE ARE MORE EASILY SCARED THAN OTHERS...
S-SO HELP ME, I'LL N-NEVER GO INTO A CARNIVAL S-SPOOKHOUSE AG-G-GAIN!
DITTO THAT.
I DIDN'T LAUGH EVEN ONCE!
BUT FEAR IS A USEFUL EMOTION THAT WARNS US OF DANGER!
YOU AREN'T SCARED, GOOFY?
ENTER
BARK BARK
NAH. WHUT FOR?
EVERYBODY'S SCARED O' SUMP'N!
EVEN YOU, GOOFY! JUST WAIT...
OL' MURRY MANOR'S BEEN ABANDONED FER YEARS! BUT WITH MY TECHNICAL TALENT, I'LL TURN IT INTO A HOT SPOOKY MESS!
I'M GONNA FRIGHT THE LIVIN' DAYLIGHTS OUTTA THAT GOOF! HAHAHA!
OOH, FUN! AN INVITE FROM HORACE... "FER ONE POKER GAME AT A SPECIAL LOCATION!" SNAZZY! A-HYUCK!
GOOFY

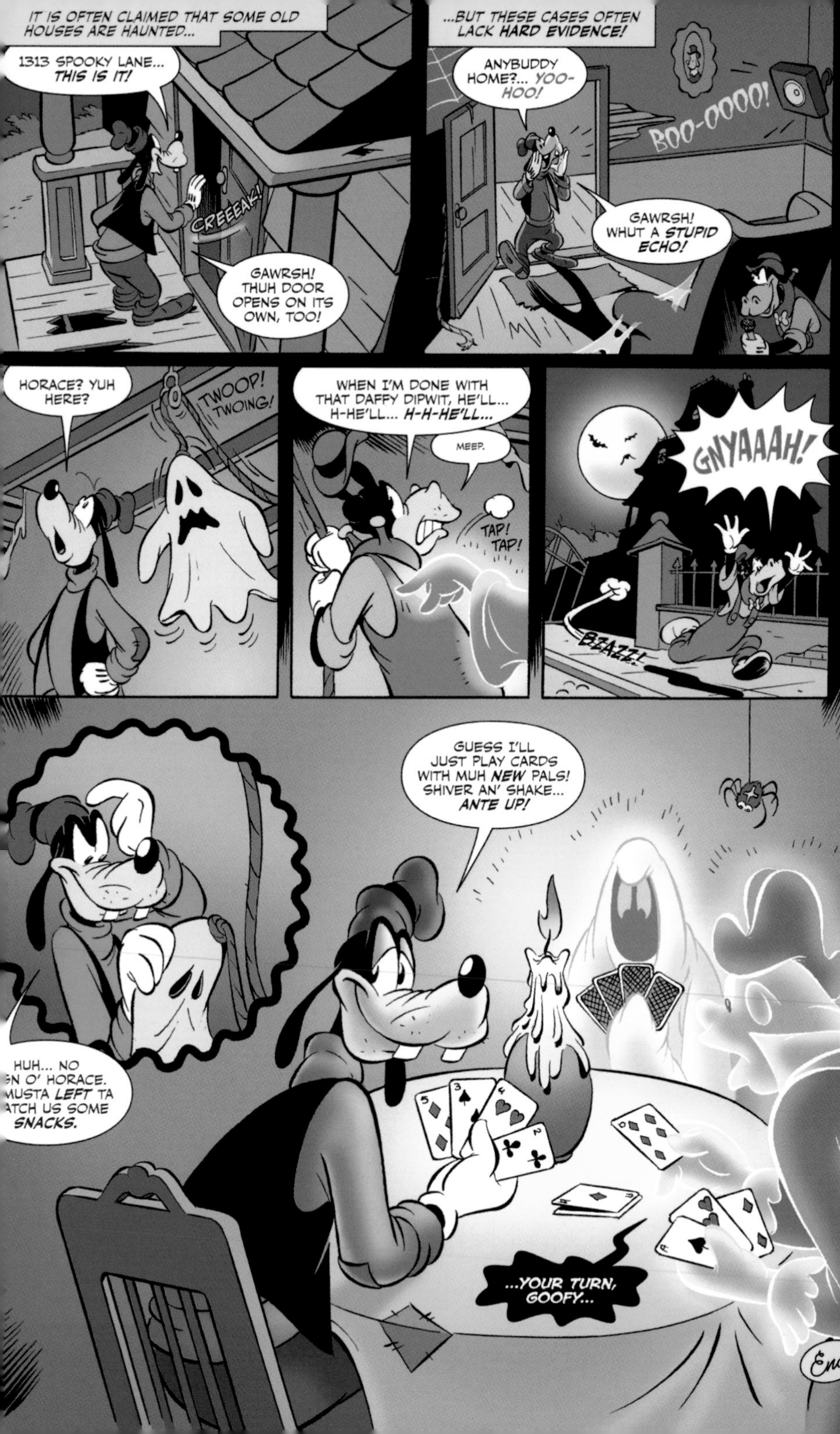

IT IS OFTEN CLAIMED THAT SOME OLD HOUSES ARE HAUNTED...
1313 SPOOKY LANE... THIS IS IT!
CREEEAK!
GAWRSH! THUH DOOR OPENS ON ITS OWN, TOO!
...BUT THESE CASES OFTEN LACK HARD EVIDENCE!
ANYBUDDY HOME?... YOO-HOO!
BOO-OOOO!
GAWRSH! WHUT A STUPID ECHO!
HORACE? YUH HERE?
TWOOP! TWOING!
WHEN I'M DONE WITH THAT DAFFY DIPWIT, HE'LL... H-HE'LL... H-H-HE'LL...
MEEP.
TAP! TAP!
GNYAAAH!
BZAZZ!
HUH... NO
GN O' HORACE.
MUSTA LEFT TA
ATCH US SOME
SNACKS.
GUESS I'LL JUST PLAY CARDS WITH MUH NEW PALS! SHIVER AN' SHAKE... ANTE UP!
...YOUR TURN, GOOFY...
End

# MICKEY MOUSE and THE WEREGOOF'S CURSE!

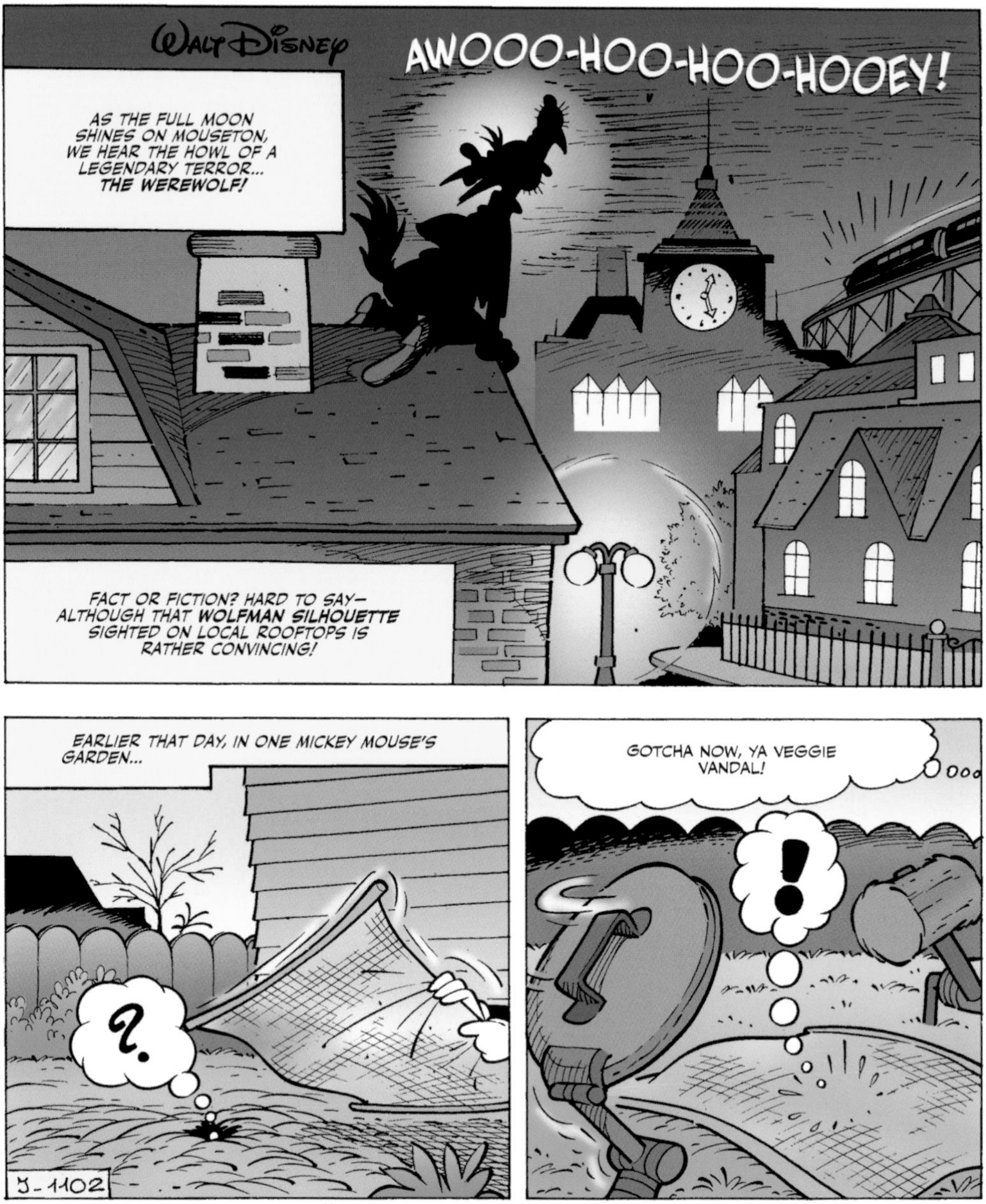
WALT DISNEY
AS THE FULL MOON SHINES ON MOUSETON, WE HEAR THE HOWL OF A LEGENDARY TERROR... THE WEREWOLF!
AWOOO-HOO-HOO-HOOEY!
FACT OR FICTION? HARD TO SAY— ALTHOUGH THAT WOLFMAN SILHOUETTE SIGHTED ON LOCAL ROOFTOPS IS RATHER CONVINCING!
EARLIER THAT DAY, IN ONE MICKEY MOUSE'S GARDEN...
?
I-1102
GOTCHA NOW, YA VEGGIE VANDAL!
!

Originally published in *Topolino* #1102 (Italy, 1977)

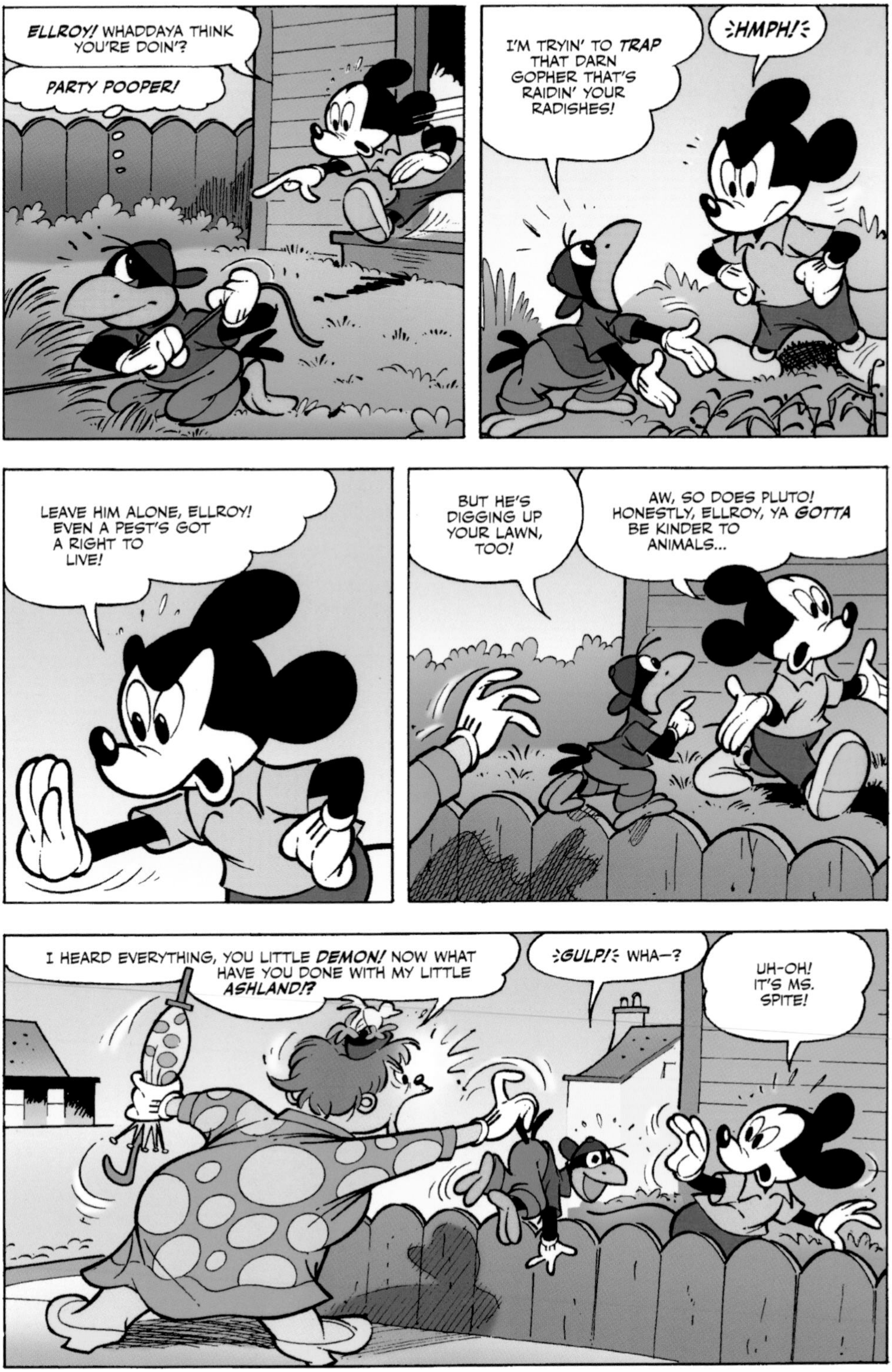
ELLROY! WHADDAYA THINK YOU'RE DOIN'?
PARTY POOPER!
I'M TRYIN' TO TRAP THAT DARN GOPHER THAT'S RAIDIN' YOUR RADISHES!
HMPH!
LEAVE HIM ALONE, ELLROY! EVEN A PEST'S GOT A RIGHT TO LIVE!
BUT HE'S DIGGING UP YOUR LAWN, TOO!
AW, SO DOES PLUTO! HONESTLY, ELLROY, YA GOTTA BE KINDER TO ANIMALS...
I HEARD EVERYTHING, YOU LITTLE DEMON! NOW WHAT HAVE YOU DONE WITH MY LITTLE ASHLAND!?
GULP! WHA—?
UH-OH! IT'S MS. SPITE!

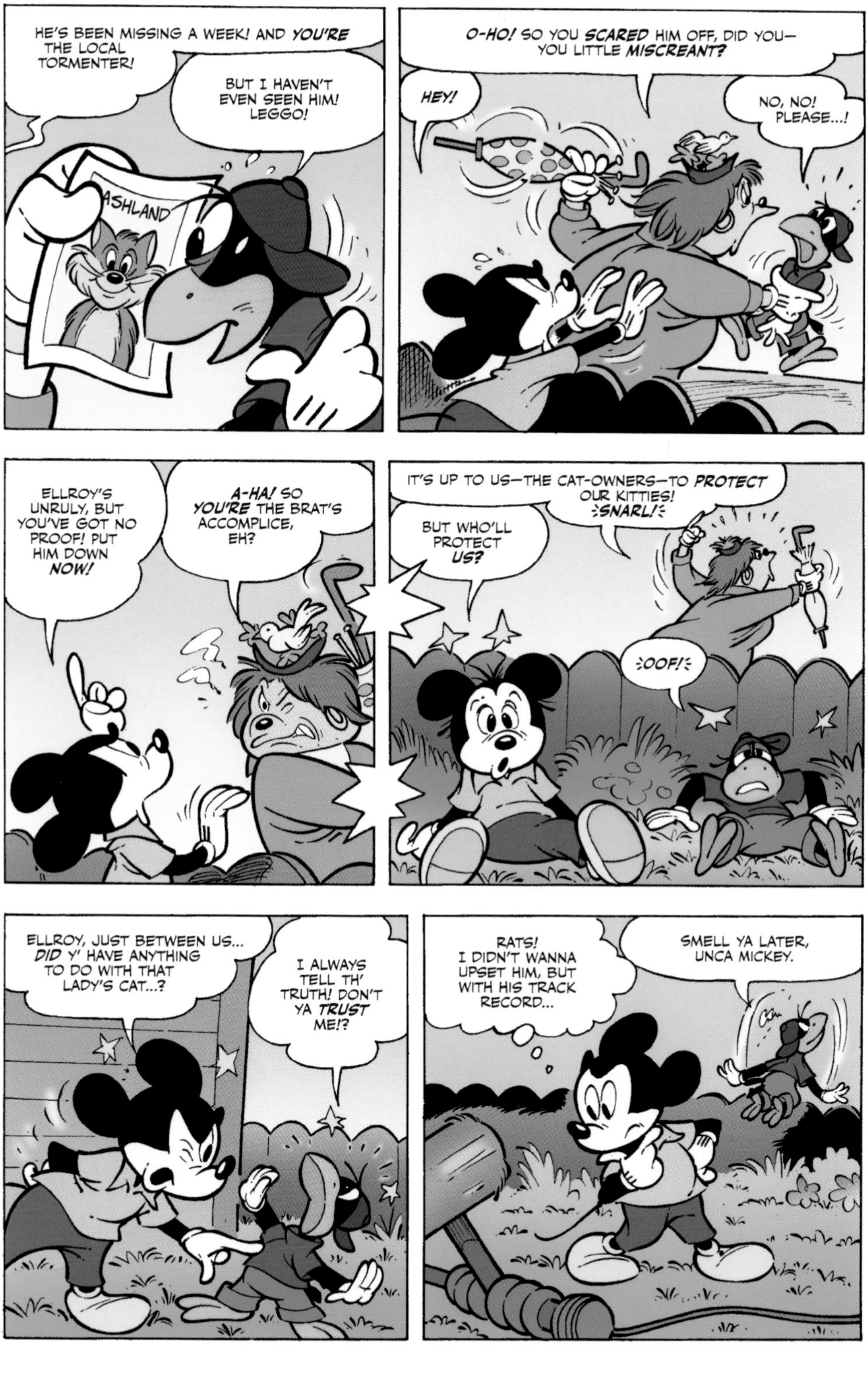
HE'S BEEN MISSING A WEEK! AND YOU'RE THE LOCAL TORMENTER!
BUT I HAVEN'T EVEN SEEN HIM! LEGGO!
ASHLAND
O-HO! SO YOU SCARED HIM OFF, DID YOU— YOU LITTLE MISCREANT?
HEY!
NO, NO! PLEASE...!
ELLROY'S UNRULY, BUT YOU'VE GOT NO PROOF! PUT HIM DOWN NOW!
A-HA! SO YOU'RE THE BRAT'S ACCOMPLICE, EH?
IT'S UP TO US—THE CAT-OWNERS—TO PROTECT OUR KITTIES! SNARL!
BUT WHO'LL PROTECT US?
OOF!
ELLROY, JUST BETWEEN US... DID Y' HAVE ANYTHING TO DO WITH THAT LADY'S CAT...?
I ALWAYS TELL TH' TRUTH! DON'T YA TRUST ME!?
RATS! I DIDN'T WANNA UPSET HIM, BUT WITH HIS TRACK RECORD...
SMELL YA LATER, UNCA MICKEY.

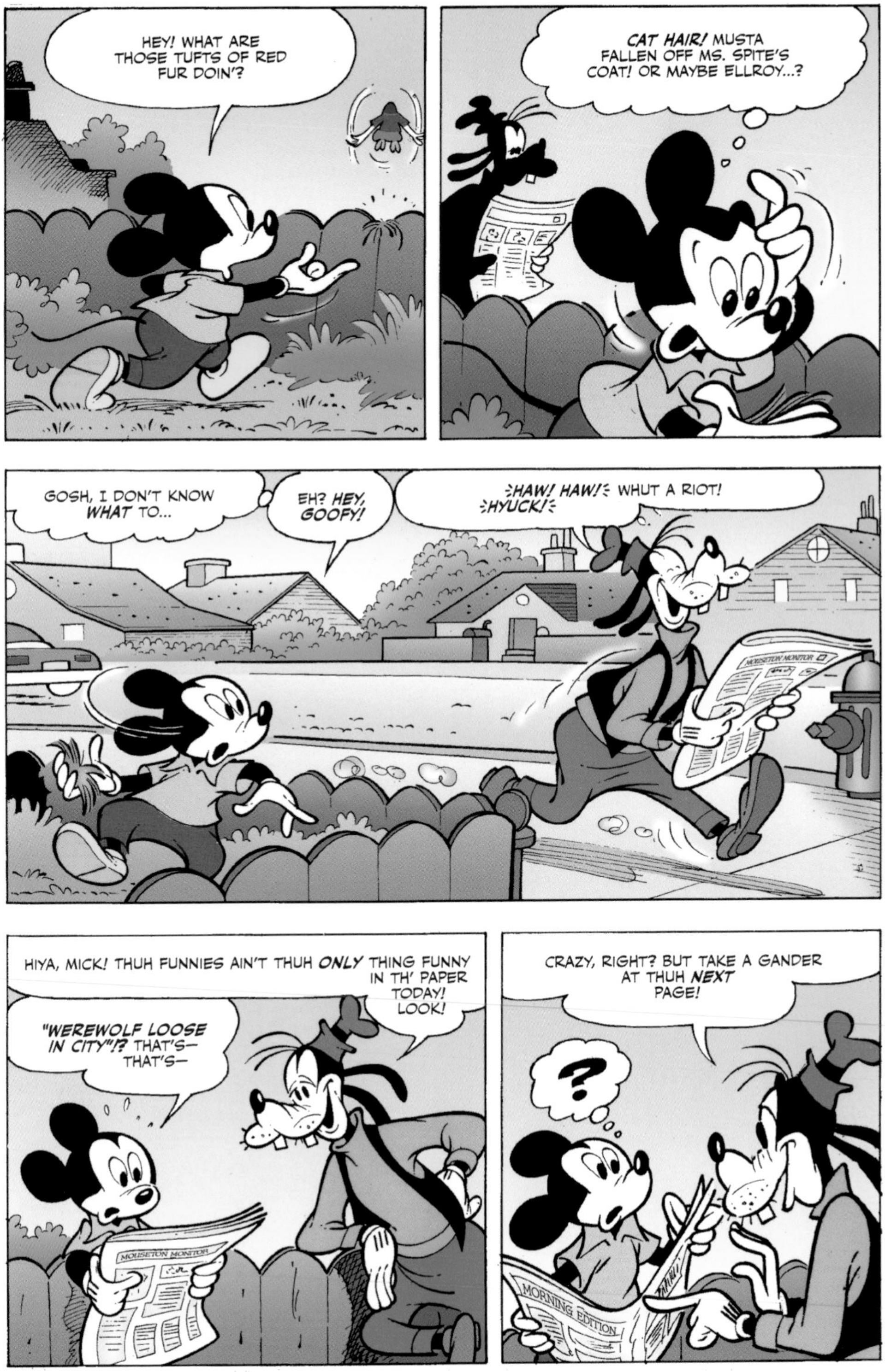
HEY! WHAT ARE THOSE TUFTS OF RED FUR DOIN'?
CAT HAIR! MUSTA FALLEN OFF MS. SPITE'S COAT! OR MAYBE ELLROY...?
GOSH, I DON'T KNOW WHAT TO...
EH? HEY, GOOFY!
HAW! HAW! WHUT A RIOT! HYUCK!
MOUSETON MONITOR
HIYA, MICK! THUH FUNNIES AIN'T THUH ONLY THING FUNNY IN TH' PAPER TODAY! LOOK!
"WEREWOLF LOOSE IN CITY"!? THAT'S— THAT'S—
MOUSETON MONITOR
CRAZY, RIGHT? BUT TAKE A GANDER AT THUH NEXT PAGE!
?
MORNING EDITION

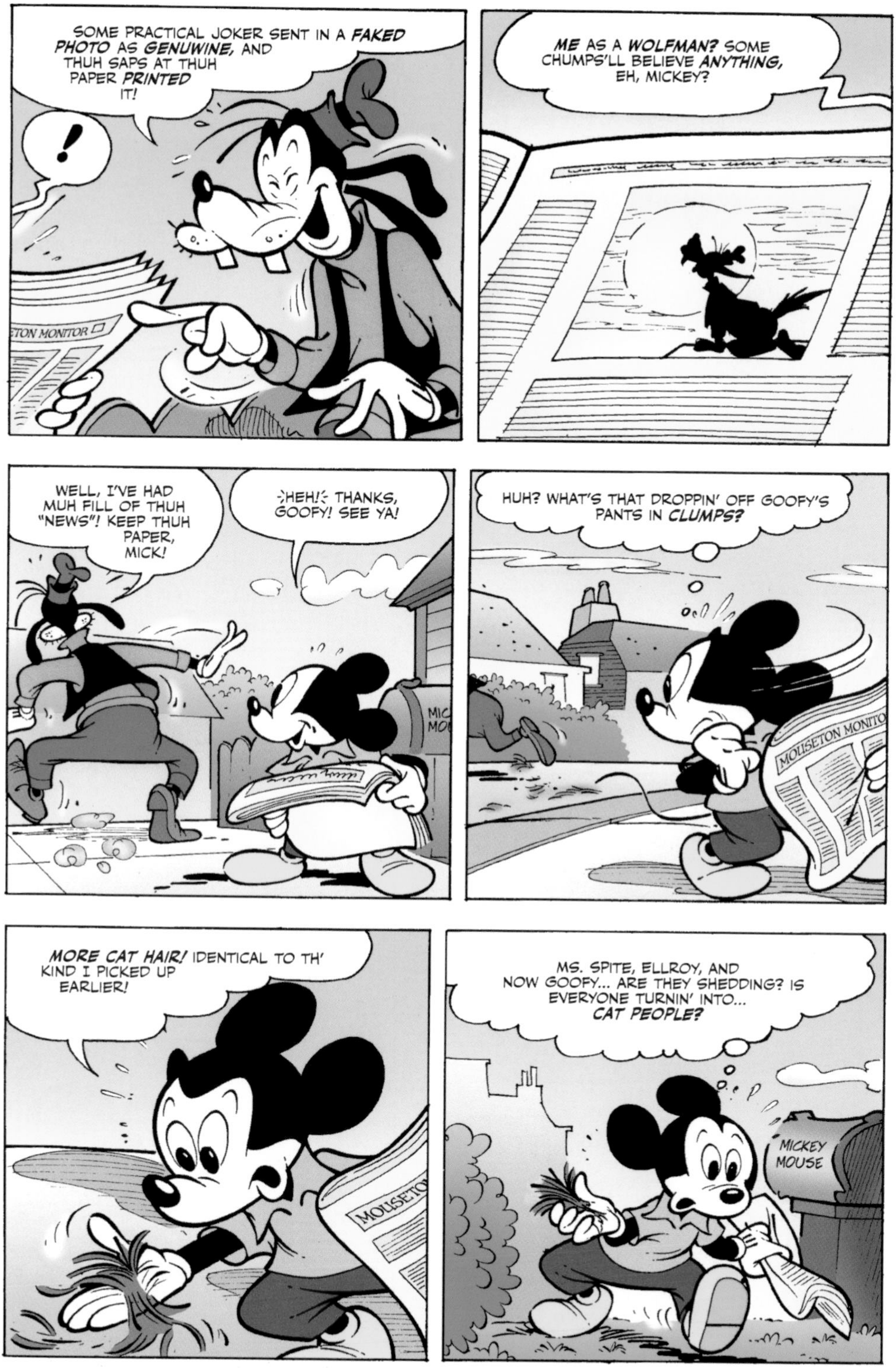
SOME PRACTICAL JOKER SENT IN A FAKED PHOTO AS GENUWINE, AND THUH SAPS AT THUH PAPER PRINTED IT!
!
ETON MONITOR
ME AS A WOLFMAN? SOME CHUMPS'LL BELIEVE ANYTHING, EH, MICKEY?
WELL, I'VE HAD MUH FILL OF THUH "NEWS"! KEEP THUH PAPER, MICK!
HEH! THANKS, GOOFY! SEE YA!
HUH? WHAT'S THAT DROPPIN' OFF GOOFY'S PANTS IN CLUMPS?
MOUSETON MONITO
MORE CAT HAIR! IDENTICAL TO TH' KIND I PICKED UP EARLIER!
MOUSETO
MS. SPITE, ELLROY, AND NOW GOOFY... ARE THEY SHEDDING? IS EVERYONE TURNIN' INTO... CAT PEOPLE?
MICKEY MOUSE

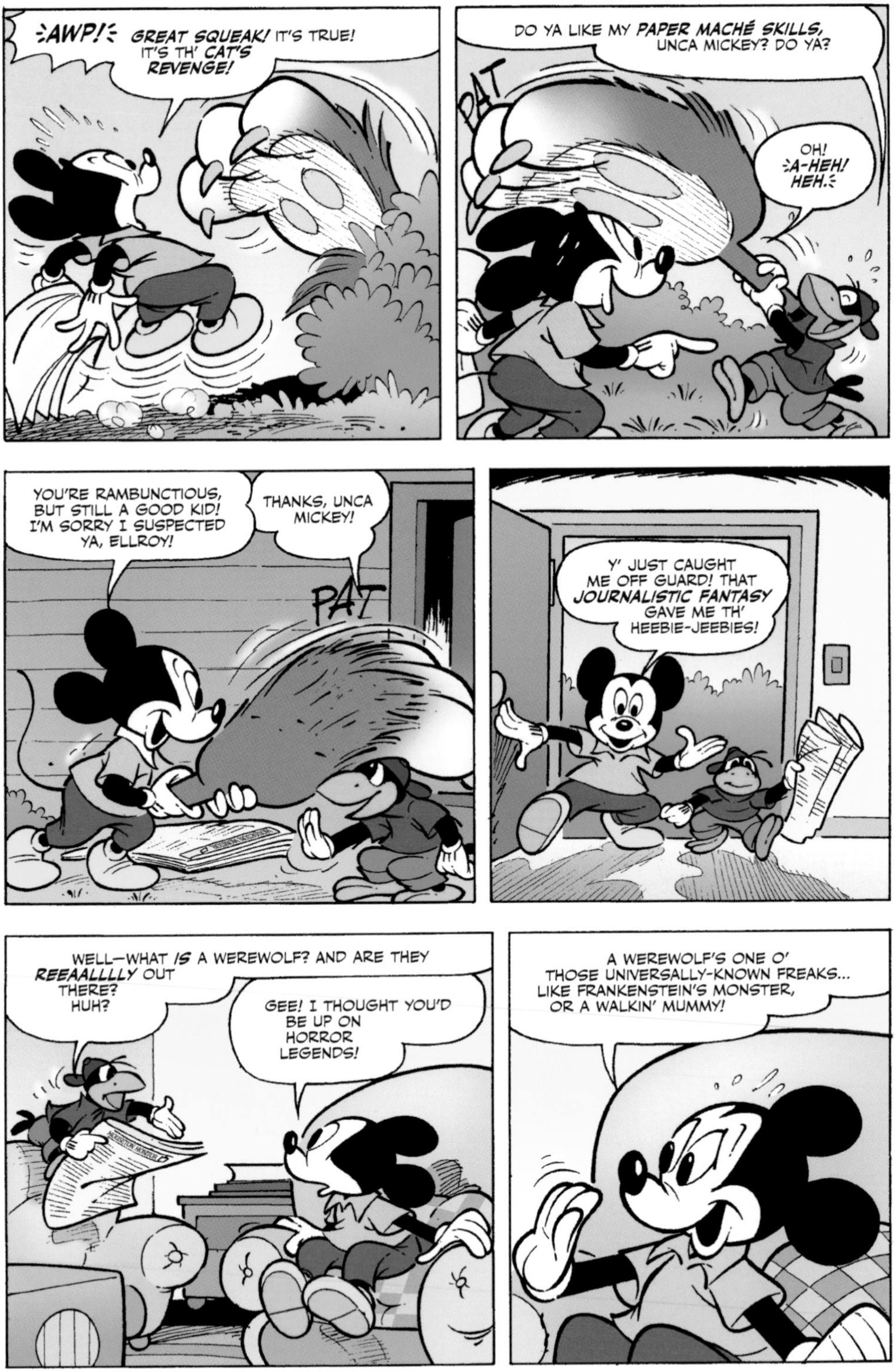
AWP!
GREAT SQUEAK! IT'S TRUE! IT'S TH' CAT'S REVENGE!
DO YA LIKE MY PAPER MACHÉ SKILLS, UNCA MICKEY? DO YA?
PAT
OH! A-HEH! HEH.
YOU'RE RAMBUNCTIOUS, BUT STILL A GOOD KID! I'M SORRY I SUSPECTED YA, ELLROY!
THANKS, UNCA MICKEY!
PAT
Y' JUST CAUGHT ME OFF GUARD! THAT JOURNALISTIC FANTASY GAVE ME TH' HEEBIE-JEEBIES!
WELL—WHAT IS A WEREWOLF? AND ARE THEY REEAALLLLY OUT THERE? HUH?
GEE! I THOUGHT YOU'D BE UP ON HORROR LEGENDS!
A WEREWOLF'S ONE O' THOSE UNIVERSALLY-KNOWN FREAKS... LIKE FRANKENSTEIN'S MONSTER, OR A WALKIN' MUMMY!

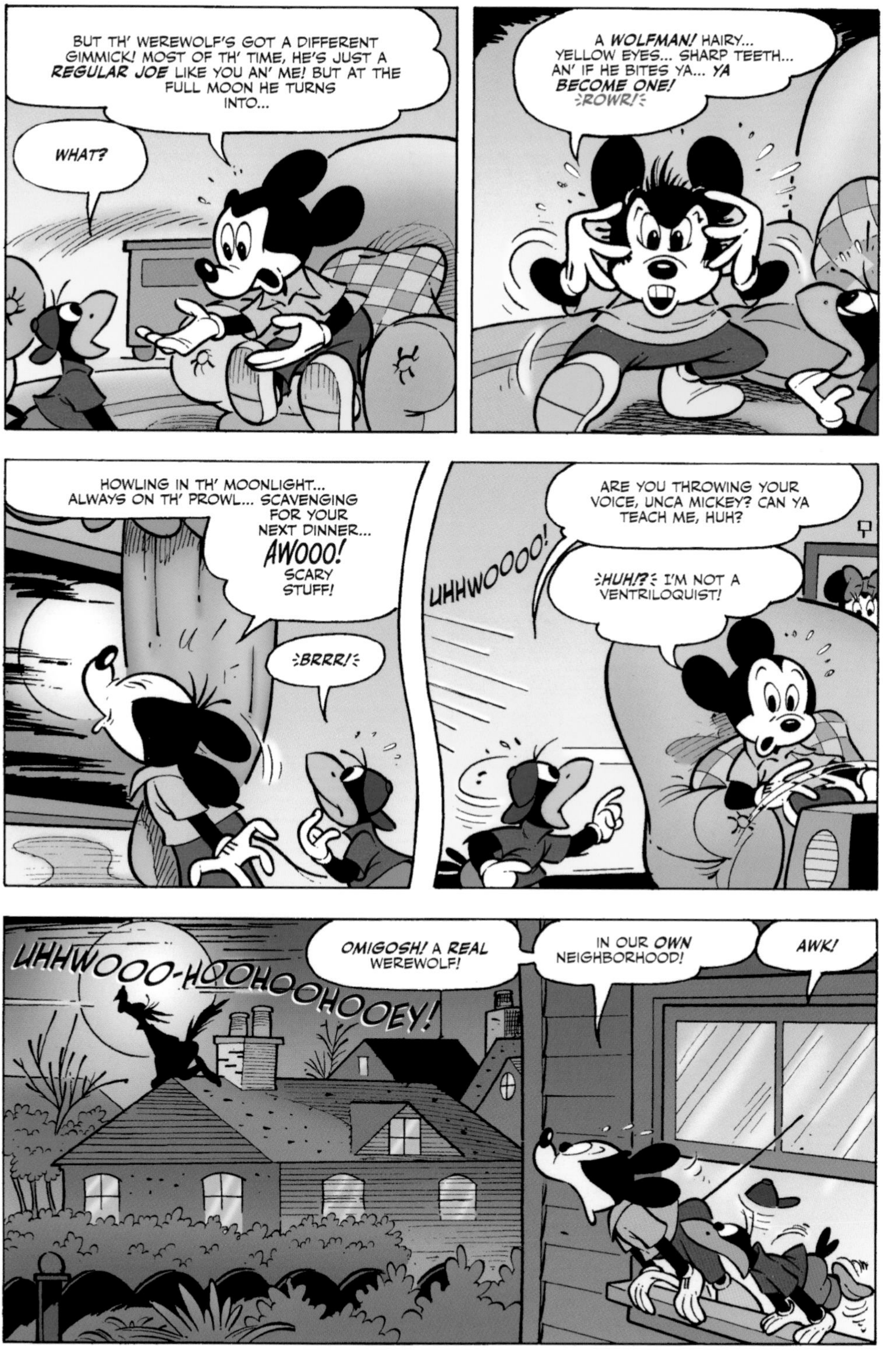
BUT TH' WEREWOLF'S GOT A DIFFERENT GIMMICK! MOST OF TH' TIME, HE'S JUST A ***REGULAR JOE*** LIKE YOU AN' ME! BUT AT THE FULL MOON HE TURNS INTO...
***WHAT?***
A ***WOLFMAN!*** HAIRY... YELLOW EYES... SHARP TEETH... AN' IF HE BITES YA... ***YA BECOME ONE!***
***ROWR!***
HOWLING IN TH' MOONLIGHT... ALWAYS ON TH' PROWL... SCAVENGING FOR YOUR NEXT DINNER... AWOOO! SCARY STUFF!
***BRRR!***
UHHWOOOO!
ARE YOU THROWING YOUR VOICE, UNCA MICKEY? CAN YA TEACH ME, HUH?
***HUH!?*** I'M NOT A VENTRILOQUIST!
UHHWOOO-HOOHOOHOOEY!
***OMIGOSH!*** A ***REAL*** WEREWOLF!
IN OUR ***OWN*** NEIGHBORHOOD!
***AWK!***

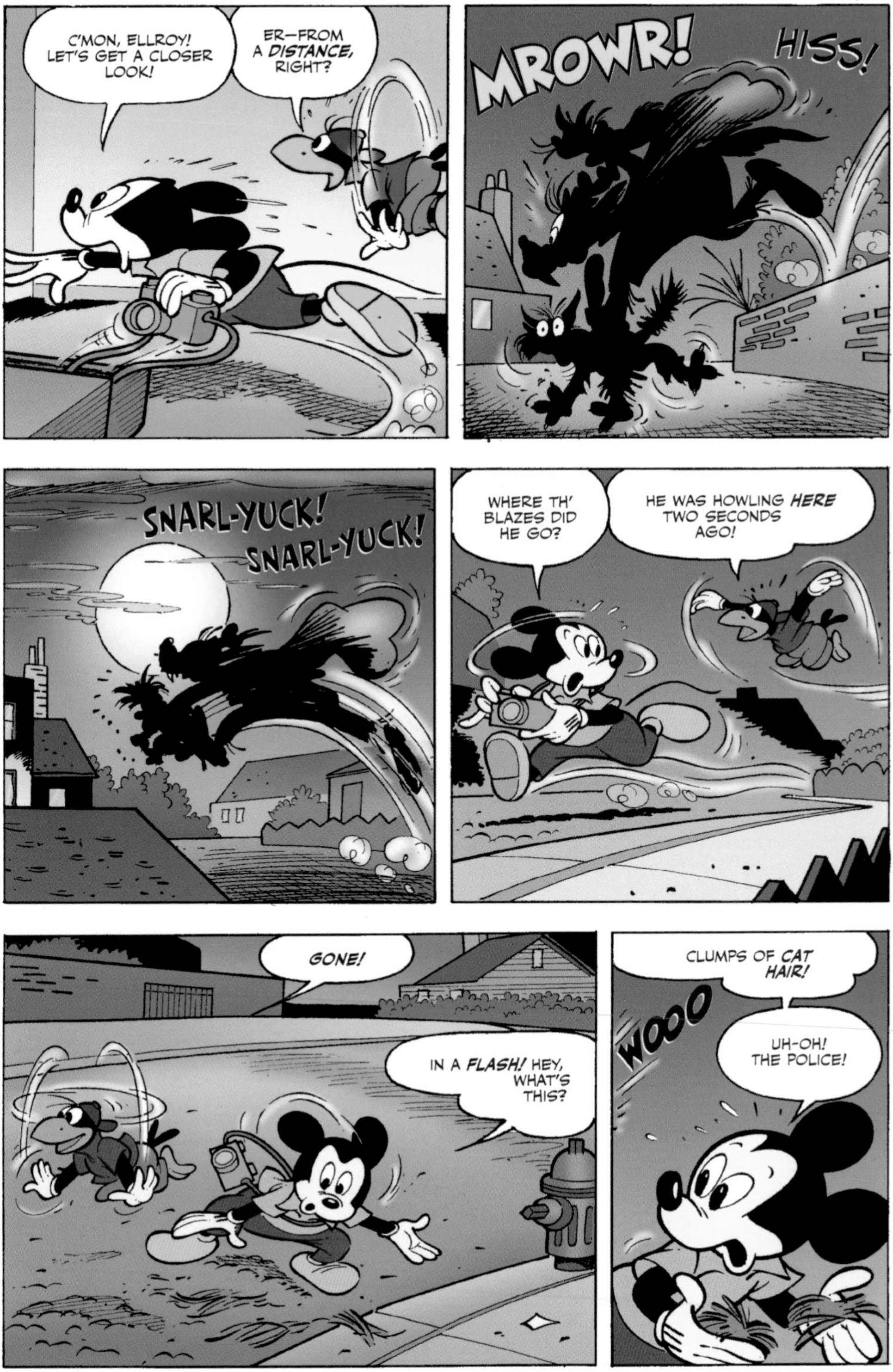
C'MON, ELLROY! LET'S GET A CLOSER LOOK!
ER—FROM A DISTANCE, RIGHT?
MROWR!
HISS!
SNARL-YUCK!
SNARL-YUCK!
WHERE TH' BLAZES DID HE GO?
HE WAS HOWLING HERE TWO SECONDS AGO!
GONE!
IN A FLASH! HEY, WHAT'S THIS?
CLUMPS OF CAT HAIR!
WOOO
UH-OH! THE POLICE!

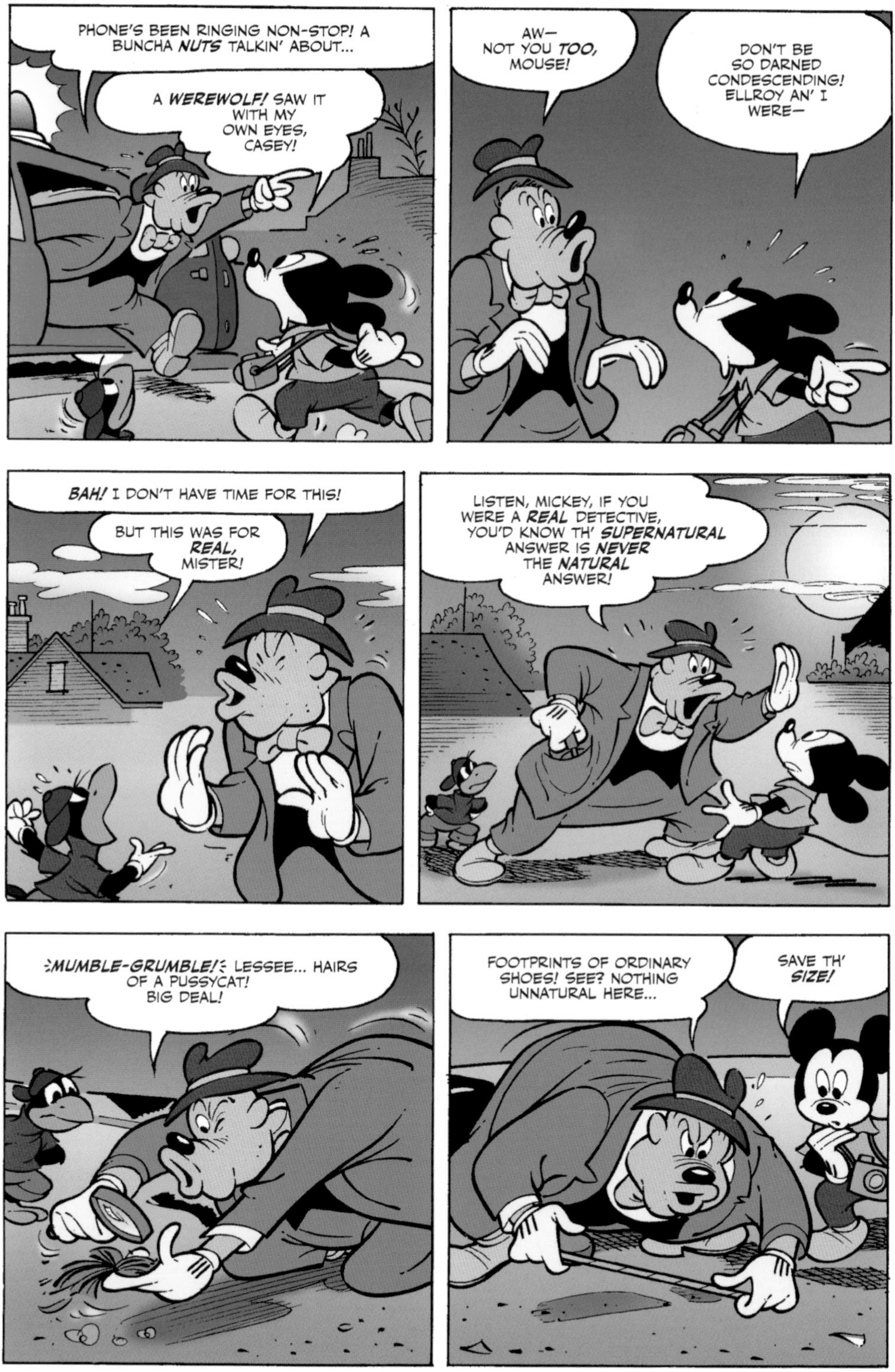
PHONE'S BEEN RINGING NON-STOP! A BUNCHA NUTS TALKIN' ABOUT...
A WEREWOLF! SAW IT WITH MY OWN EYES, CASEY!
AW— NOT YOU TOO, MOUSE!
DON'T BE SO DARNED CONDESCENDING! ELLROY AN' I WERE—
BAH! I DON'T HAVE TIME FOR THIS!
BUT THIS WAS FOR REAL, MISTER!
LISTEN, MICKEY, IF YOU WERE A REAL DETECTIVE, YOU'D KNOW TH' SUPERNATURAL ANSWER IS NEVER THE NATURAL ANSWER!
MUMBLE-GRUMBLE! LESSEE... HAIRS OF A PUSSYCAT! BIG DEAL!
FOOTPRINTS OF ORDINARY SHOES! SEE? NOTHING UNNATURAL HERE...
SAVE TH' SIZE!

WELL! SINCE IT'S MY DUTY, I *HAFTA* MAKE OUT A REPORT OF WHAT YOU *AMATEURS* ALLEGEDLY SAW.

YOU'D BE *SURPRISED*, CASEY! I'VE PROVEN YA WRONG *BEFORE*—

SO *THIS'LL* EVEN THINGS *OUT*, WON'T IT? SEND ME THE "WEREWOLF'S" *MUGSHOT* SO WE CAN PUT IT UP AT THE STATION! ≟*HARDY-HAR-HAR!*≟

STUBBORN OL' SOURPUSS... AS USUAL!

GEE!

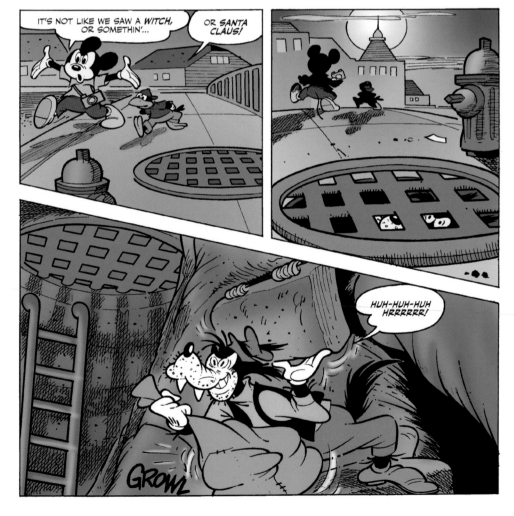

IT'S NOT LIKE WE SAW A *WITCH*, OR SOMETHIN'...

OR *SANTA CLAUS!*

HUH-HUH-HUH HRRRRRR!

GROWL

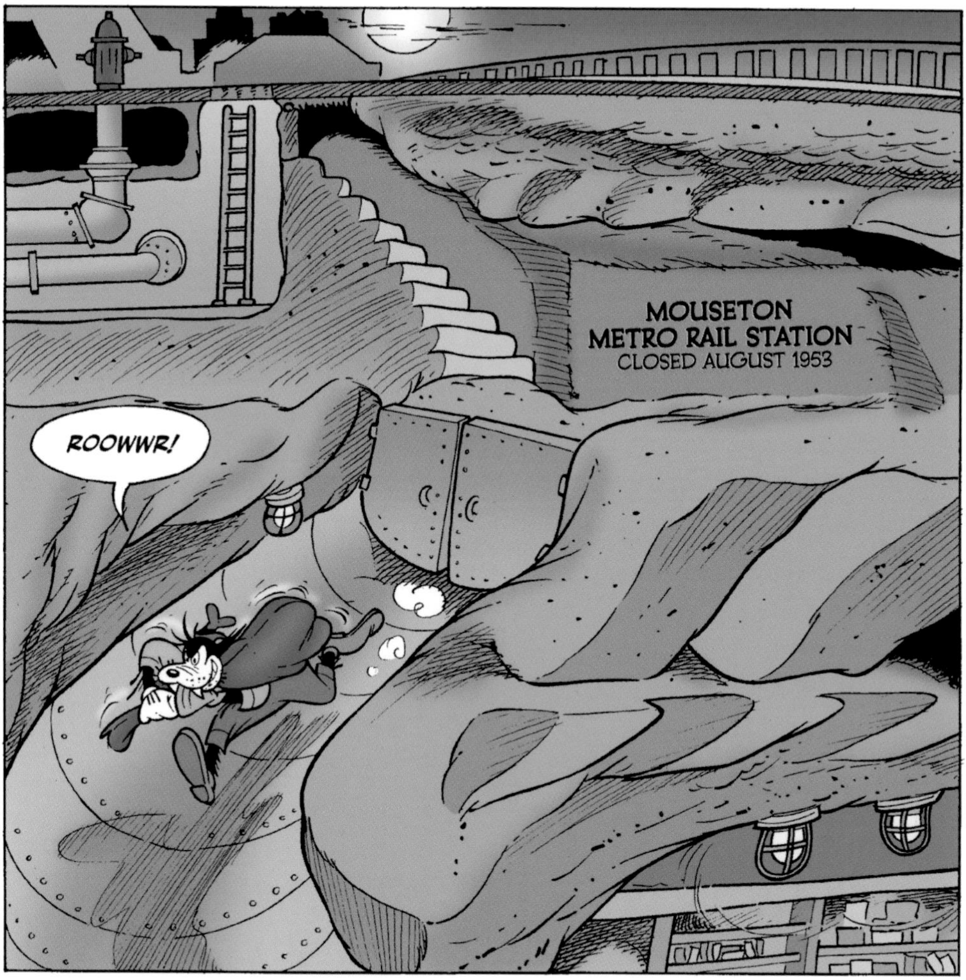
MOUSETON
METRO RAIL STATION
CLOSED AUGUST 1953
ROOWWR!

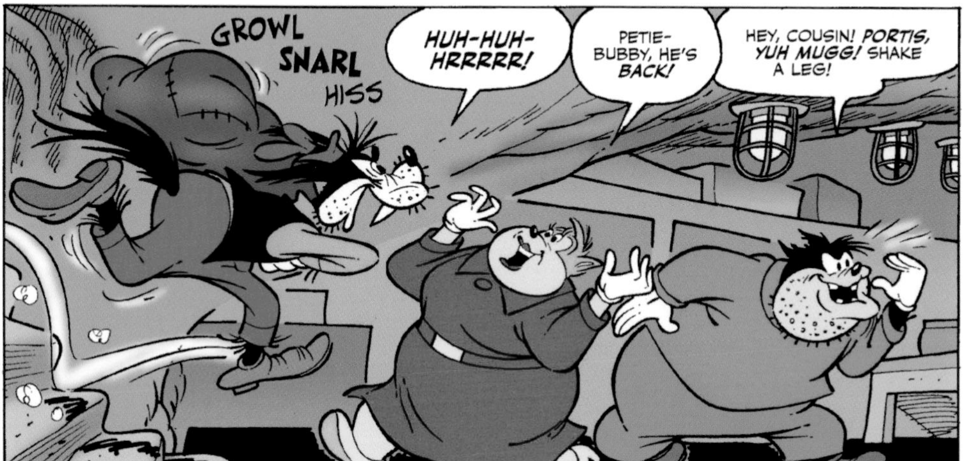
GROWL
SNARL
HISS
HUH-HUH-HRRRRR!
PETIE-BUBBY, HE'S BACK!
HEY, COUSIN! PORTIS, YUH MUGG! SHAKE A LEG!

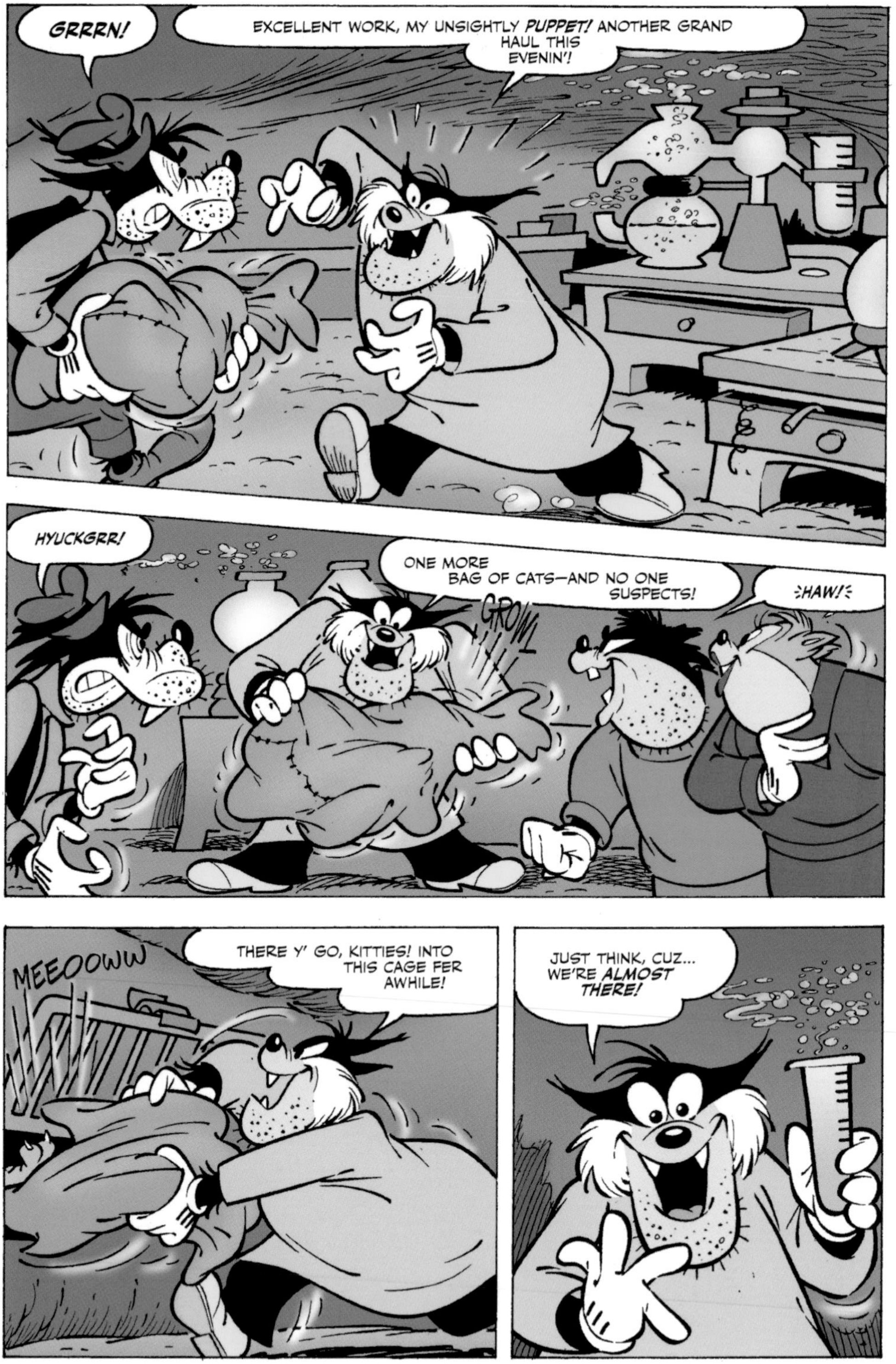
GRRRN!
EXCELLENT WORK, MY UNSIGHTLY PUPPET! ANOTHER GRAND HAUL THIS EVENIN'!
HYUCKGRR!
ONE MORE BAG OF CATS—AND NO ONE SUSPECTS!
GROWL
HAW!
MEEOOWW
THERE Y' GO, KITTIES! INTO THIS CAGE FER AWHILE!
JUST THINK, CUZ... WE'RE ALMOST THERE!

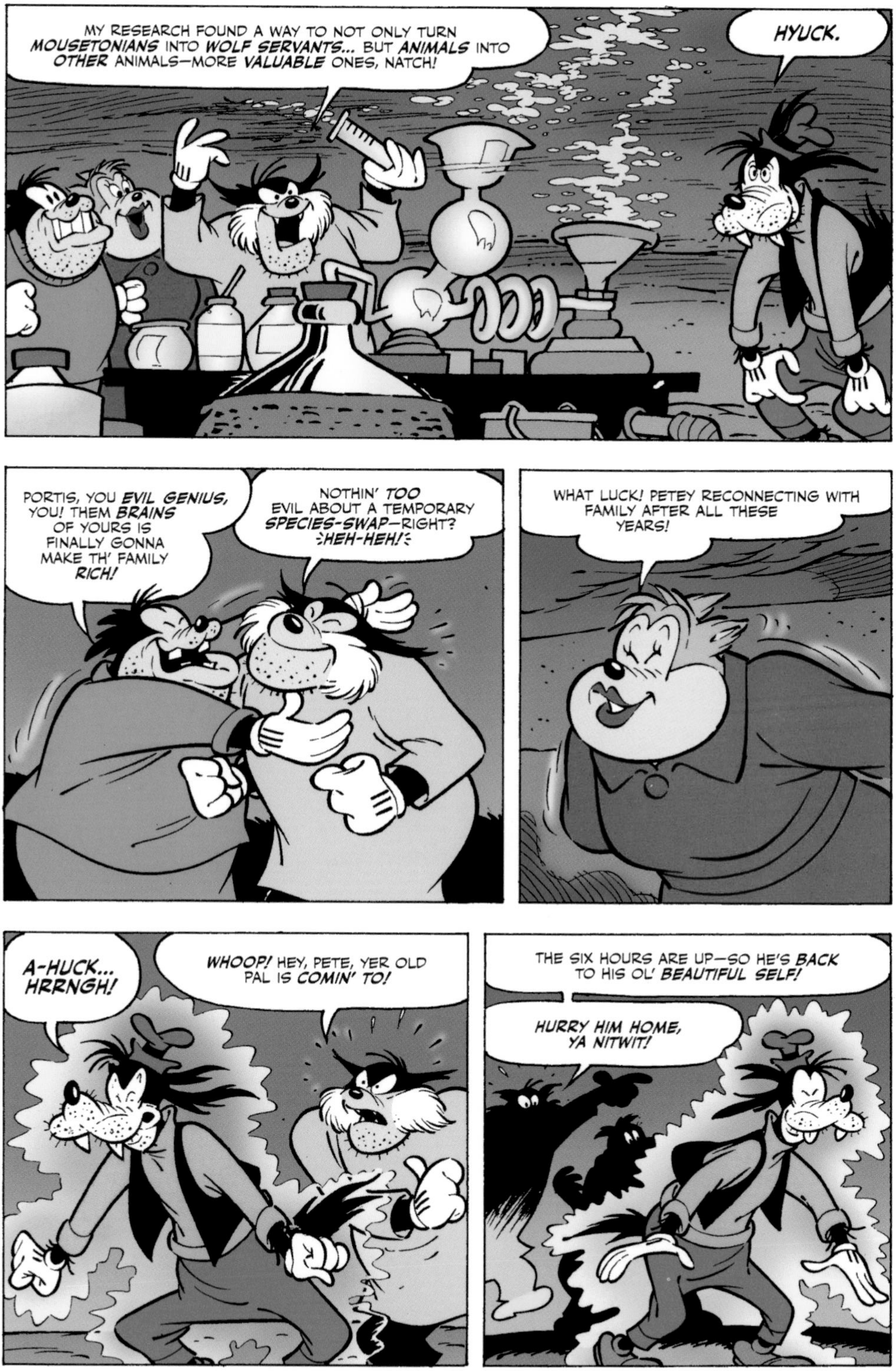
MY RESEARCH FOUND A WAY TO NOT ONLY TURN MOUSETONIANS INTO WOLF SERVANTS... BUT ANIMALS INTO OTHER ANIMALS—MORE VALUABLE ONES, NATCH!
HYUCK.
PORTIS, YOU EVIL GENIUS, YOU! THEM BRAINS OF YOURS IS FINALLY GONNA MAKE TH' FAMILY RICH!
NOTHIN' TOO EVIL ABOUT A TEMPORARY SPECIES-SWAP—RIGHT? HEH-HEH!
WHAT LUCK! PETEY RECONNECTING WITH FAMILY AFTER ALL THESE YEARS!
A-HUCK... HRRNGH!
WHOOP! HEY, PETE, YER OLD PAL IS COMIN' TO!
THE SIX HOURS ARE UP—SO HE'S BACK TO HIS OL' BEAUTIFUL SELF!
HURRY HIM HOME, YA NITWIT!

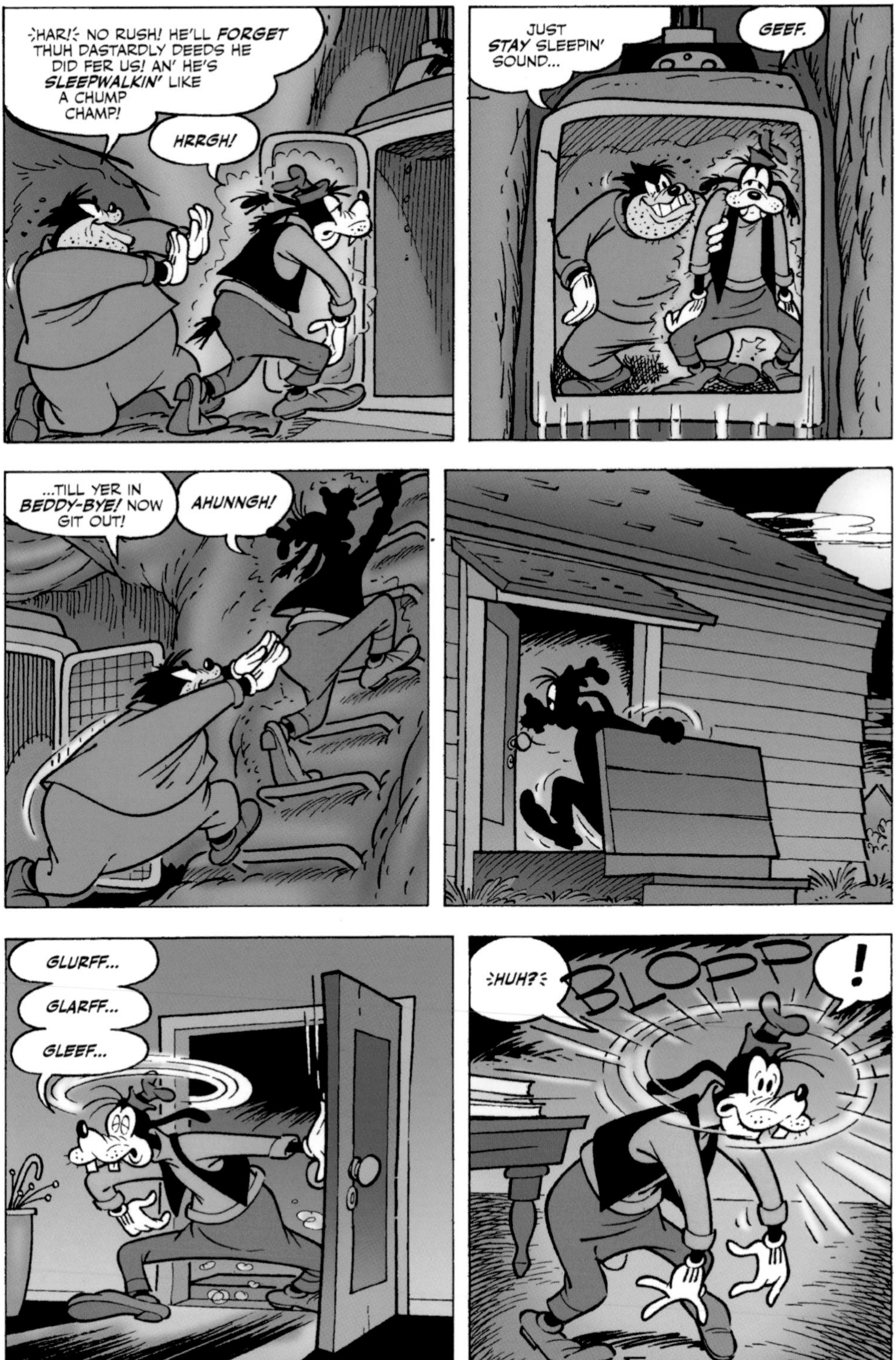

HAR! NO RUSH! HE'LL FORGET THUH DASTARDLY DEEDS HE DID FER US! AN' HE'S SLEEPWALKIN' LIKE A CHUMP CHAMP!
HRRGH!
JUST STAY SLEEPIN' SOUND...
GEEF.
...TILL YER IN BEDDY-BYE! NOW GIT OUT!
AHUNNGH!
GLURFF...
GLARFF...
GLEEF...
HUH?
BLOPP
!

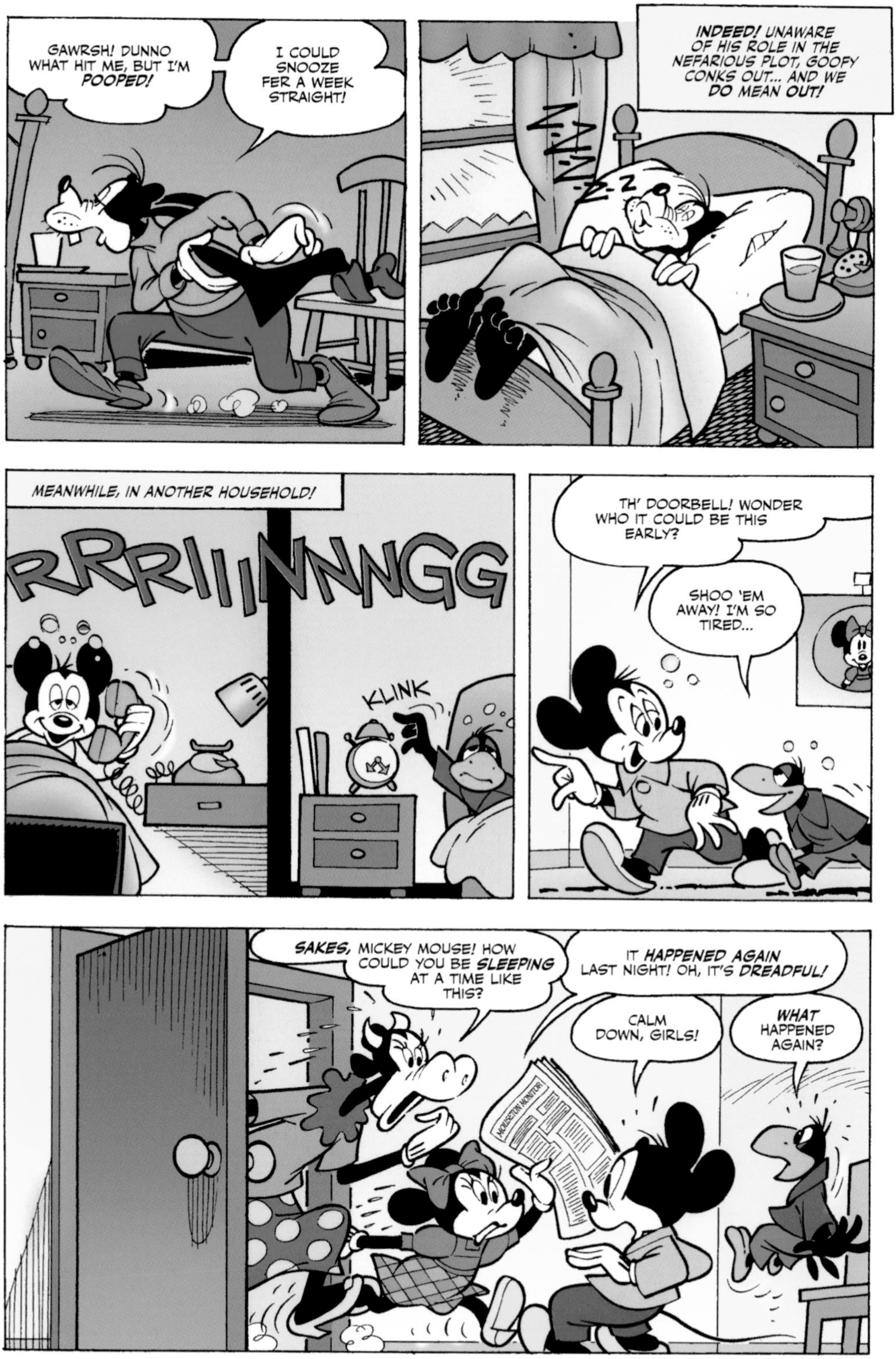

GAWRSH! DUNNO WHAT HIT ME, BUT I'M ***POOPED!***
I COULD SNOOZE FER A WEEK STRAIGHT!
***INDEED!*** *UNAWARE OF HIS ROLE IN THE NEFARIOUS PLOT, GOOFY CONKS OUT... AND WE* ***DO MEAN OUT!***
Z-Z Z-Z
*MEANWHILE, IN ANOTHER HOUSEHOLD!*
RRRIIINNNGG
KLINK
TH' DOORBELL! WONDER WHO IT COULD BE THIS EARLY?
SHOO 'EM AWAY! I'M SO TIRED...
***SAKES,*** MICKEY MOUSE! HOW COULD YOU BE ***SLEEPING*** AT A TIME LIKE THIS?
IT ***HAPPENED AGAIN*** LAST NIGHT! OH, IT'S ***DREADFUL!***
MOUSETON MONITOR
CALM DOWN, GIRLS!
***WHAT*** HAPPENED AGAIN?

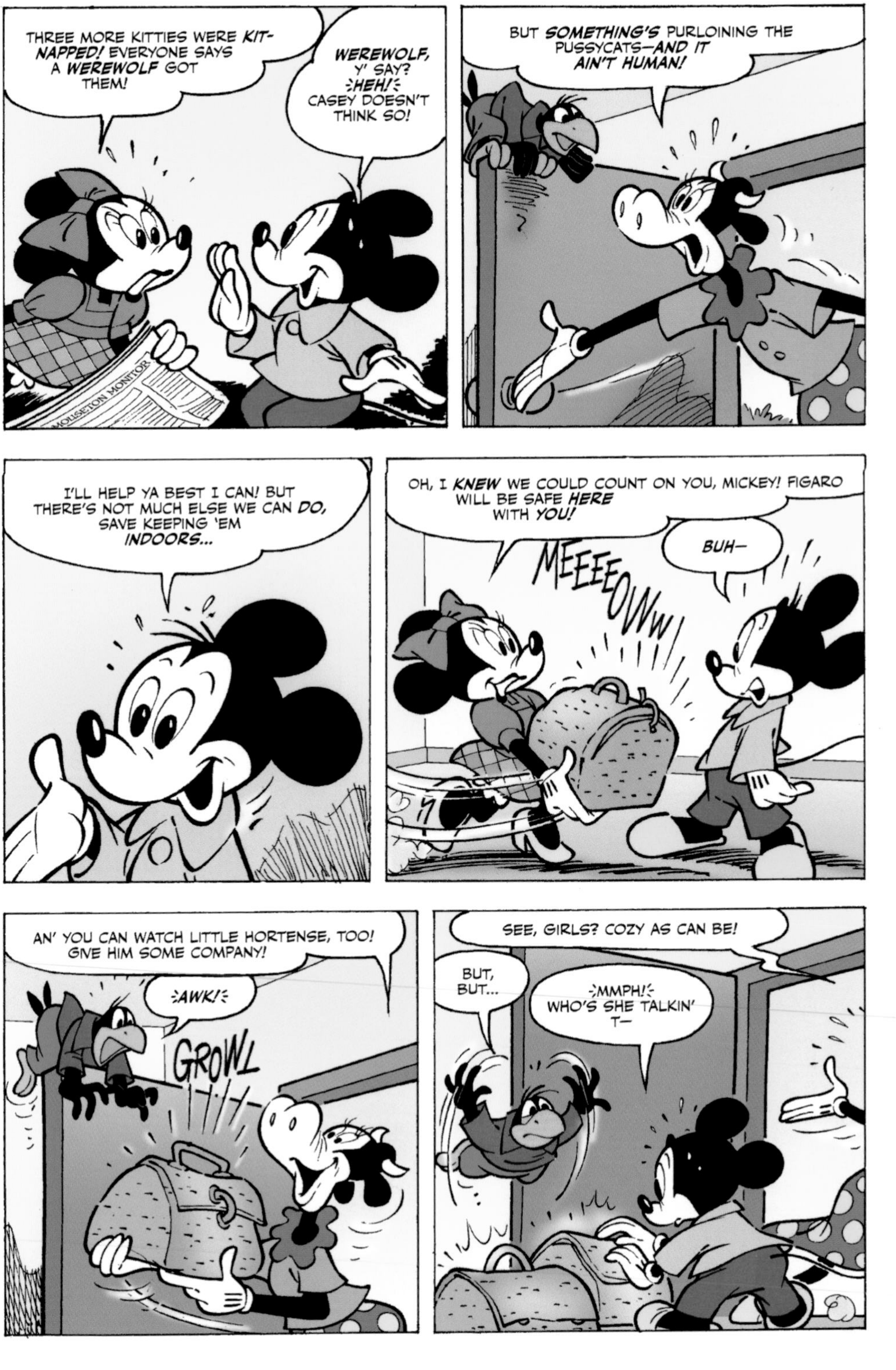
THREE MORE KITTIES WERE KIT-NAPPED! EVERYONE SAYS A WEREWOLF GOT THEM!
WEREWOLF, Y' SAY? HEH! CASEY DOESN'T THINK SO!
MOUSETON MONITOR
BUT SOMETHING'S PURLOINING THE PUSSYCATS—AND IT AIN'T HUMAN!
I'LL HELP YA BEST I CAN! BUT THERE'S NOT MUCH ELSE WE CAN DO, SAVE KEEPING 'EM INDOORS...
OH, I KNEW WE COULD COUNT ON YOU, MICKEY! FIGARO WILL BE SAFE HERE WITH YOU!
MEEEEOWW!
BUH—
AN' YOU CAN WATCH LITTLE HORTENSE, TOO! GIVE HIM SOME COMPANY!
AWK!
GROWL
SEE, GIRLS? COZY AS CAN BE!
BUT, BUT...
MMPH! WHO'S SHE TALKIN' T—

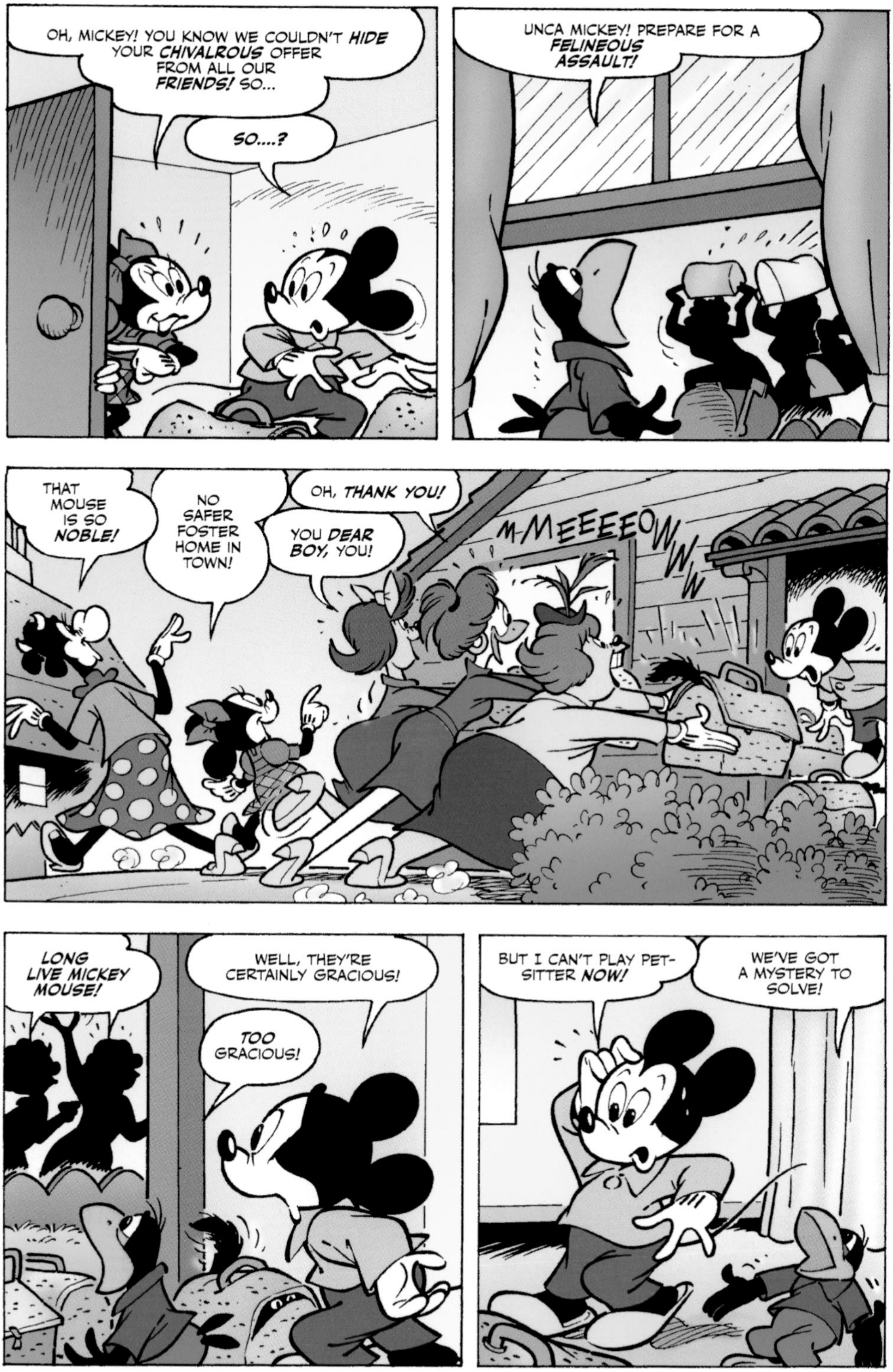
OH, MICKEY! YOU KNOW WE COULDN'T HIDE YOUR CHIVALROUS OFFER FROM ALL OUR FRIENDS! SO...
SO....?
UNCA MICKEY! PREPARE FOR A FELINEOUS ASSAULT!
THAT MOUSE IS SO NOBLE!
NO SAFER FOSTER HOME IN TOWN!
OH, THANK YOU!
YOU DEAR BOY, YOU!
M-MEEEEOWWW
LONG LIVE MICKEY MOUSE!
WELL, THEY'RE CERTAINLY GRACIOUS!
TOO GRACIOUS!
BUT I CAN'T PLAY PET-SITTER NOW!
WE'VE GOT A MYSTERY TO SOLVE!

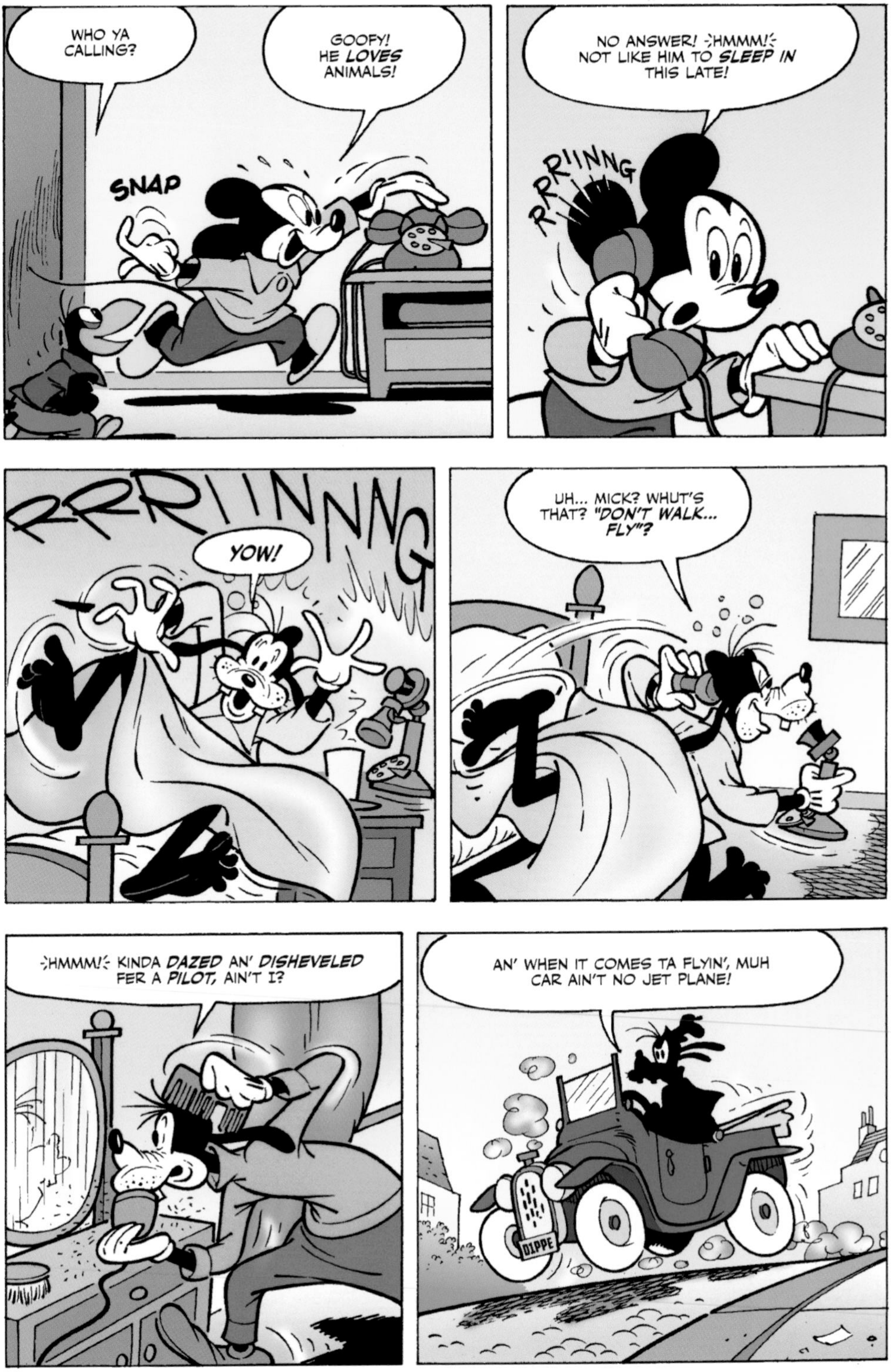
WHO YA CALLING?
GOOFY! HE LOVES ANIMALS!
SNAP
NO ANSWER! HMMM! NOT LIKE HIM TO SLEEP IN THIS LATE!
RRRIINNG
RRRIINNNG
YOW!
UH... MICK? WHUT'S THAT? "DON'T WALK... FLY"?
HMMM! KINDA DAZED AN' DISHEVELED FER A PILOT, AIN'T I?
AN' WHEN IT COMES TA FLYIN', MUH CAR AIN'T NO JET PLANE!
D1PPE

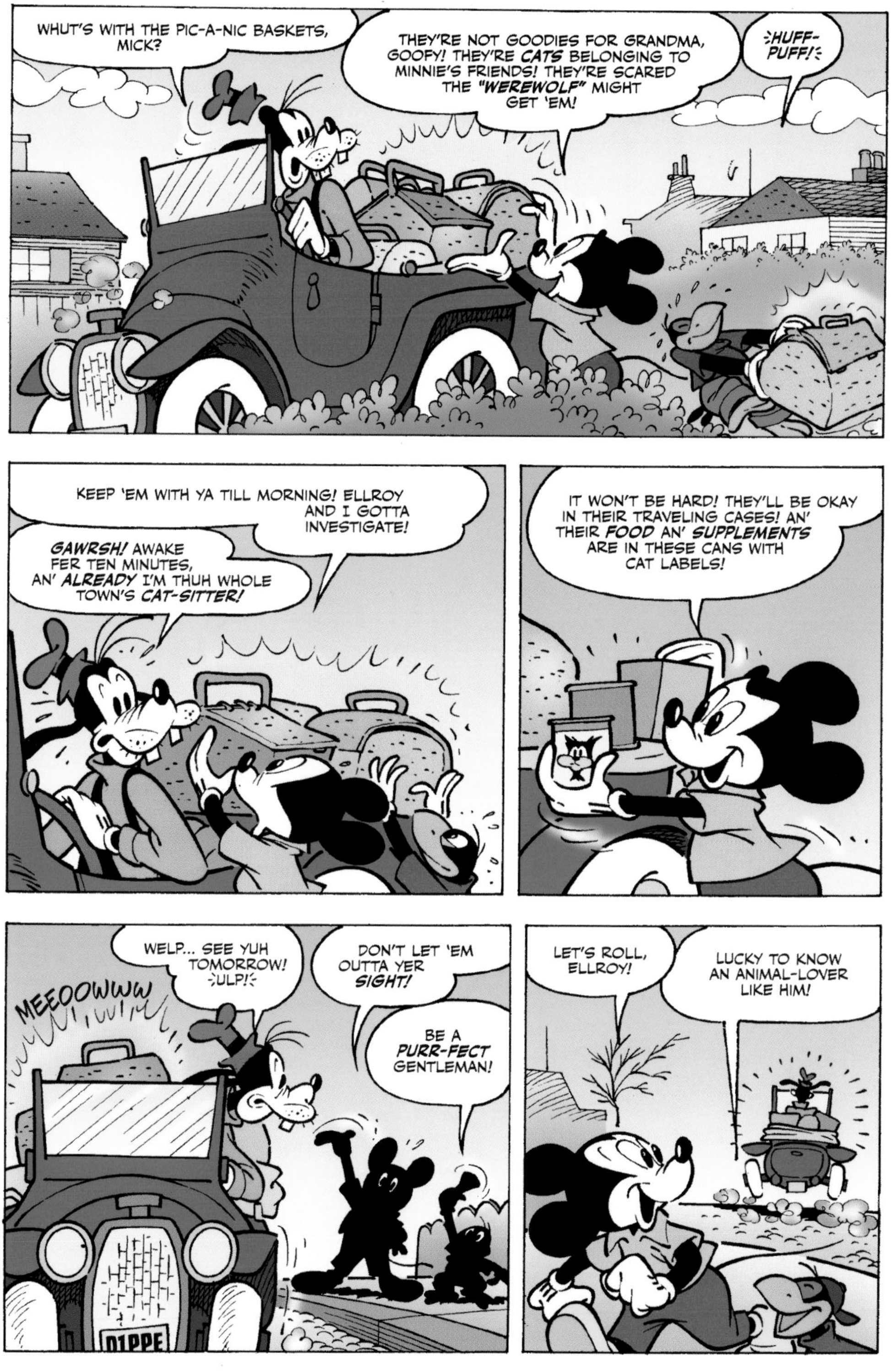
WHUT'S WITH THE PIC-A-NIC BASKETS, MICK?
THEY'RE NOT GOODIES FOR GRANDMA, GOOFY! THEY'RE *CATS* BELONGING TO MINNIE'S FRIENDS! THEY'RE SCARED THE *"WEREWOLF"* MIGHT GET 'EM!
*HUFF-PUFF!*
KEEP 'EM WITH YA TILL MORNING! ELLROY AND I GOTTA INVESTIGATE!
*GAWRSH!* AWAKE FER TEN MINUTES, AN' *ALREADY* I'M THUH WHOLE TOWN'S *CAT-SITTER!*
IT WON'T BE HARD! THEY'LL BE OKAY IN THEIR TRAVELING CASES! AN' THEIR *FOOD* AN' *SUPPLEMENTS* ARE IN THESE CANS WITH CAT LABELS!
MEEOOWWW
WELP... SEE YUH TOMORROW! *ULP!*
DON'T LET 'EM OUTTA YER *SIGHT!*
BE A *PURR-FECT* GENTLEMAN!
D1PPE
LET'S ROLL, ELLROY!
LUCKY TO KNOW AN ANIMAL-LOVER LIKE HIM!

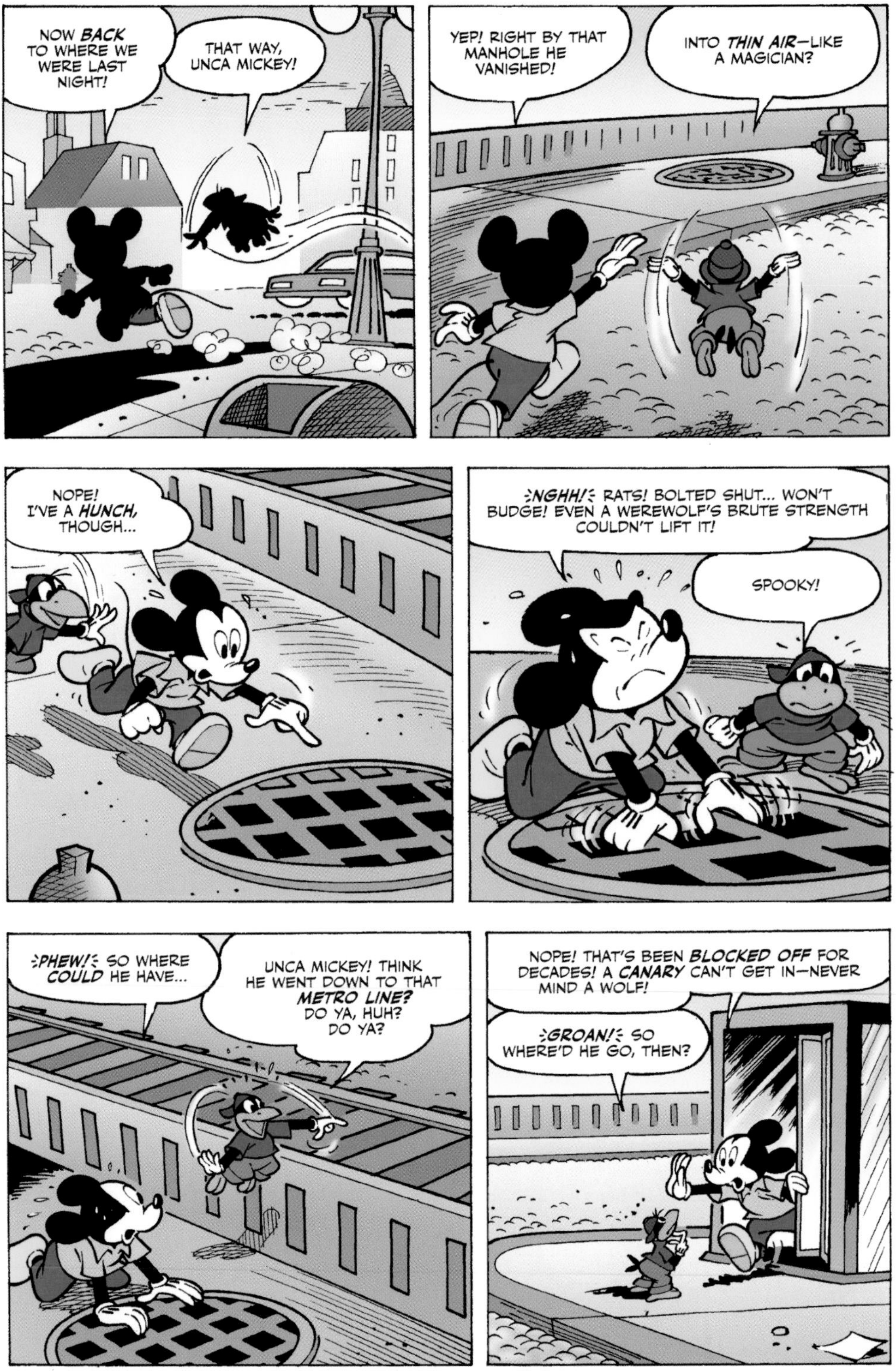
NOW BACK TO WHERE WE WERE LAST NIGHT!
THAT WAY, UNCA MICKEY!
YEP! RIGHT BY THAT MANHOLE HE VANISHED!
INTO THIN AIR—LIKE A MAGICIAN?
NOPE! I'VE A HUNCH, THOUGH...
NGHH! RATS! BOLTED SHUT... WON'T BUDGE! EVEN A WEREWOLF'S BRUTE STRENGTH COULDN'T LIFT IT!
SPOOKY!
PHEW! SO WHERE COULD HE HAVE...
UNCA MICKEY! THINK HE WENT DOWN TO THAT METRO LINE? DO YA, HUH? DO YA?
NOPE! THAT'S BEEN BLOCKED OFF FOR DECADES! A CANARY CAN'T GET IN—NEVER MIND A WOLF!
GROAN! SO WHERE'D HE GO, THEN?

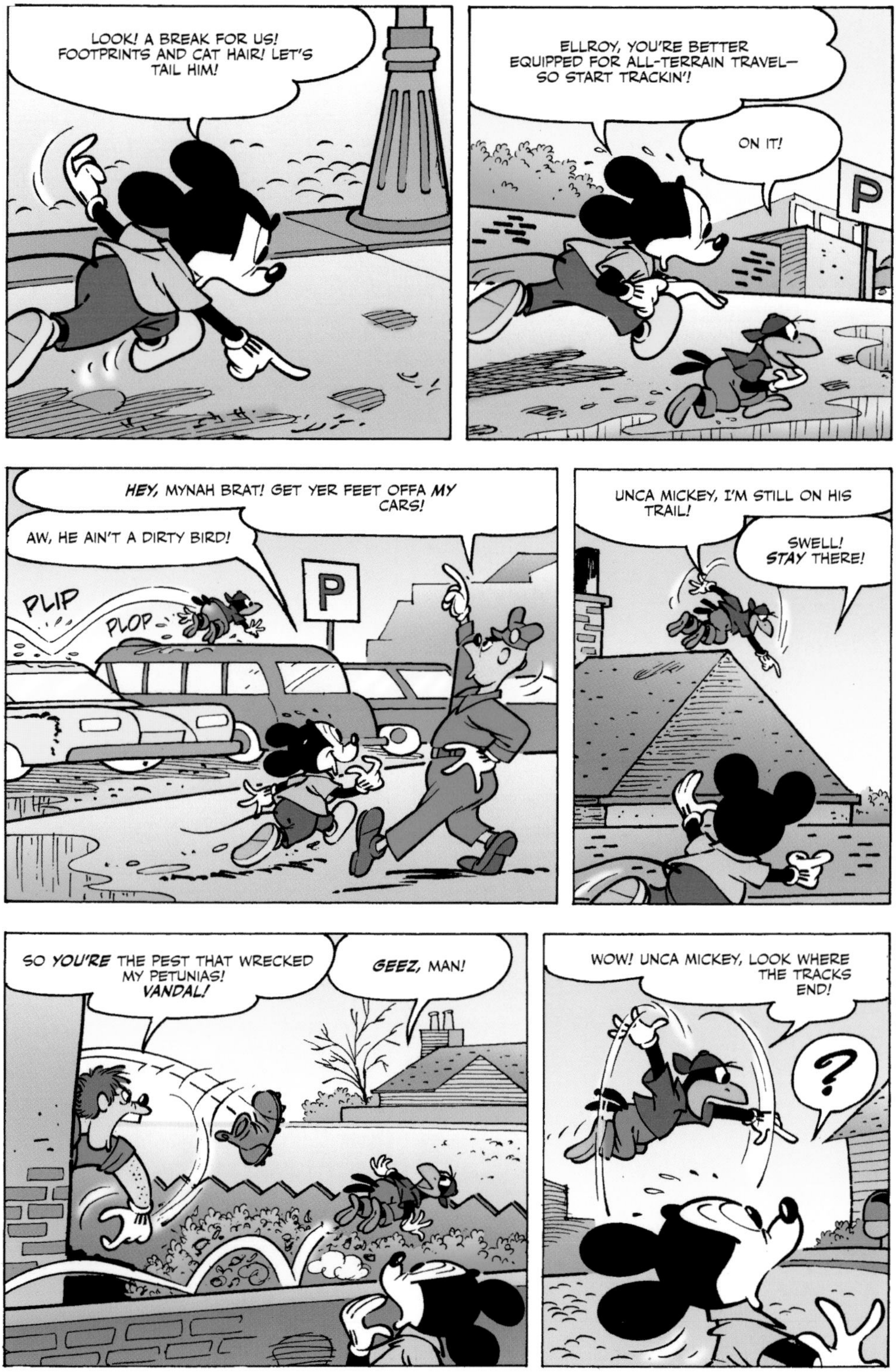
LOOK! A BREAK FOR US! FOOTPRINTS AND CAT HAIR! LET'S TAIL HIM!
ELLROY, YOU'RE BETTER EQUIPPED FOR ALL-TERRAIN TRAVEL— SO START TRACKIN'!
ON IT!
P
HEY, MYNAH BRAT! GET YER FEET OFFA MY CARS!
AW, HE AIN'T A DIRTY BIRD!
PLIP
PLOP
P
UNCA MICKEY, I'M STILL ON HIS TRAIL!
SWELL! STAY THERE!
SO YOU'RE THE PEST THAT WRECKED MY PETUNIAS! VANDAL!
GEEZ, MAN!
WOW! UNCA MICKEY, LOOK WHERE THE TRACKS END!
?

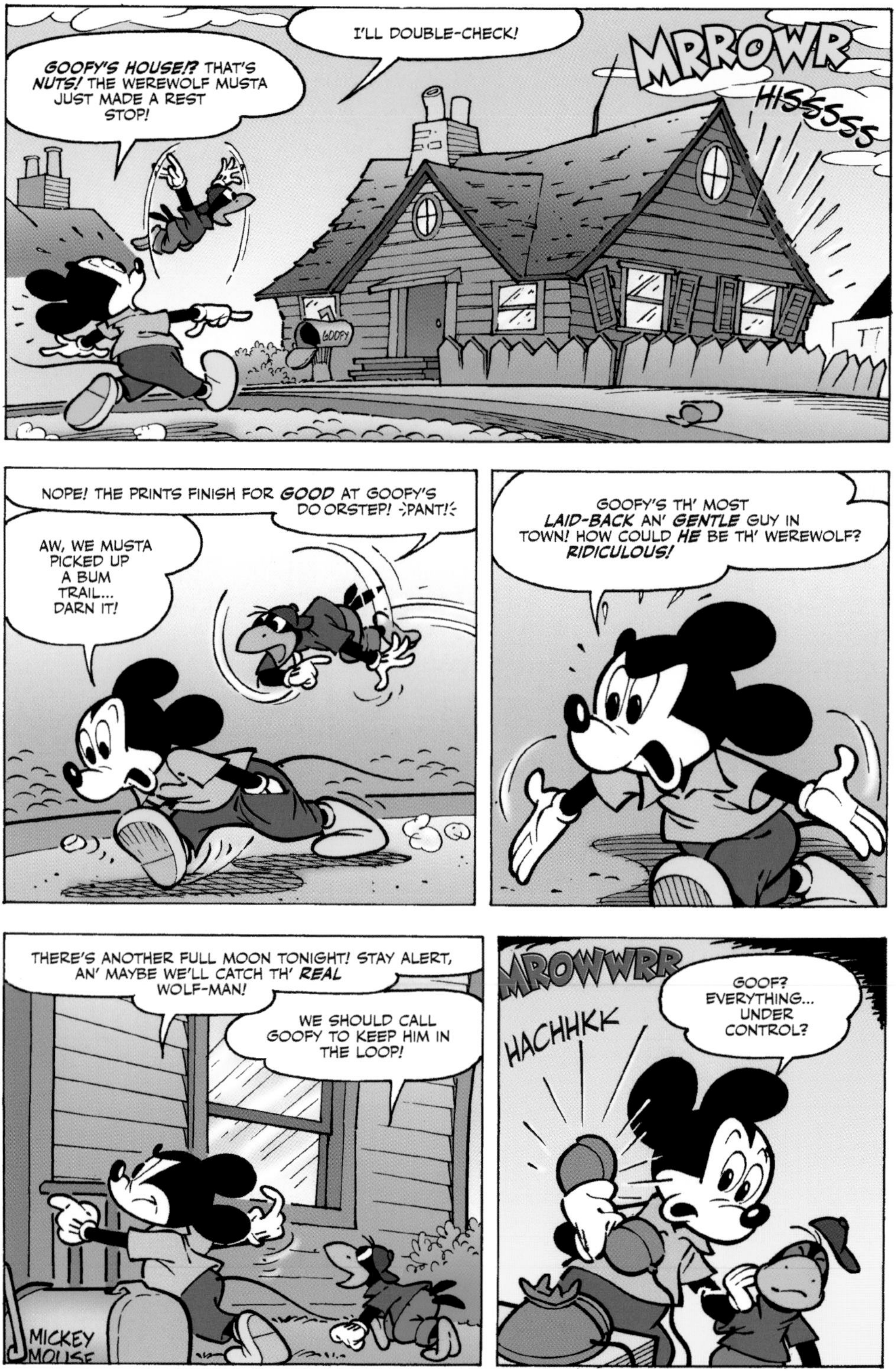
GOOFY'S HOUSE!? THAT'S NUTS! THE WEREWOLF MUSTA JUST MADE A REST STOP!
I'LL DOUBLE-CHECK!
MRROWR
HISSSSS
GOOFY
NOPE! THE PRINTS FINISH FOR GOOD AT GOOFY'S DOORSTEP! PANT!
AW, WE MUSTA PICKED UP A BUM TRAIL... DARN IT!
GOOFY'S TH' MOST LAID-BACK AN' GENTLE GUY IN TOWN! HOW COULD HE BE TH' WEREWOLF? RIDICULOUS!
THERE'S ANOTHER FULL MOON TONIGHT! STAY ALERT, AN' MAYBE WE'LL CATCH TH' REAL WOLF-MAN!
WE SHOULD CALL GOOFY TO KEEP HIM IN THE LOOP!
MICKEY MOUSE
MROWWRR
HACHHKK
GOOF? EVERYTHING... UNDER CONTROL?

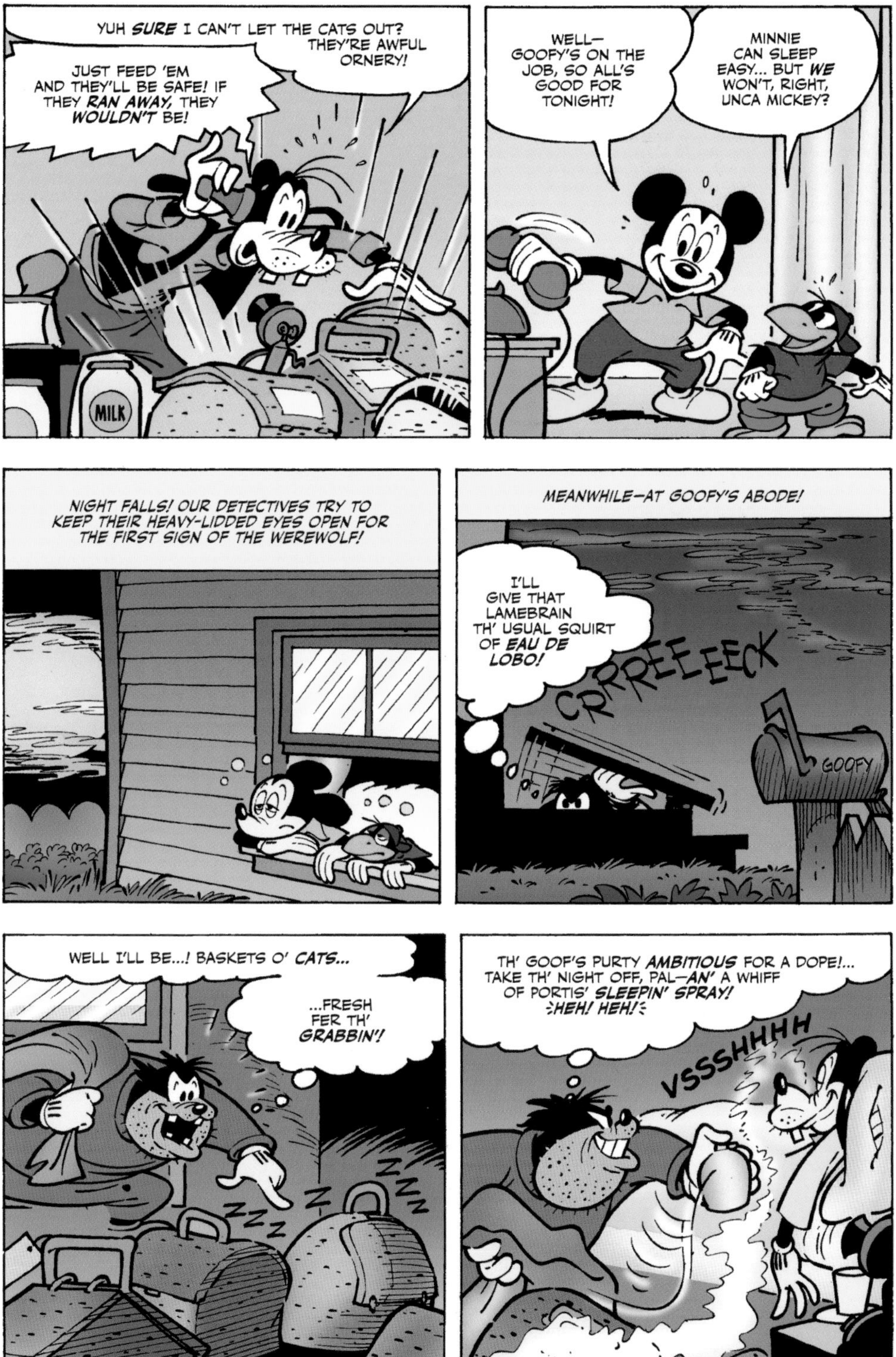
YUH SURE I CAN'T LET THE CATS OUT? THEY'RE AWFUL ORNERY!
JUST FEED 'EM AND THEY'LL BE SAFE! IF THEY RAN AWAY, THEY WOULDN'T BE!
MILK
WELL— GOOFY'S ON THE JOB, SO ALL'S GOOD FOR TONIGHT!
MINNIE CAN SLEEP EASY... BUT WE WON'T, RIGHT, UNCA MICKEY?
NIGHT FALLS! OUR DETECTIVES TRY TO KEEP THEIR HEAVY-LIDDED EYES OPEN FOR THE FIRST SIGN OF THE WEREWOLF!
MEANWHILE—AT GOOFY'S ABODE!
I'LL GIVE THAT LAMEBRAIN TH' USUAL SQUIRT OF EAU DE LOBO!
CRRREEEECK
GOOFY
WELL I'LL BE...! BASKETS O' CATS...
...FRESH FER TH' GRABBIN'!
ZZZ
ZZZ
TH' GOOF'S PURTY AMBITIOUS FOR A DOPE!... TAKE TH' NIGHT OFF, PAL—AN' A WHIFF OF PORTIS' SLEEPIN' SPRAY! HEH! HEH!
VSSSHHHH

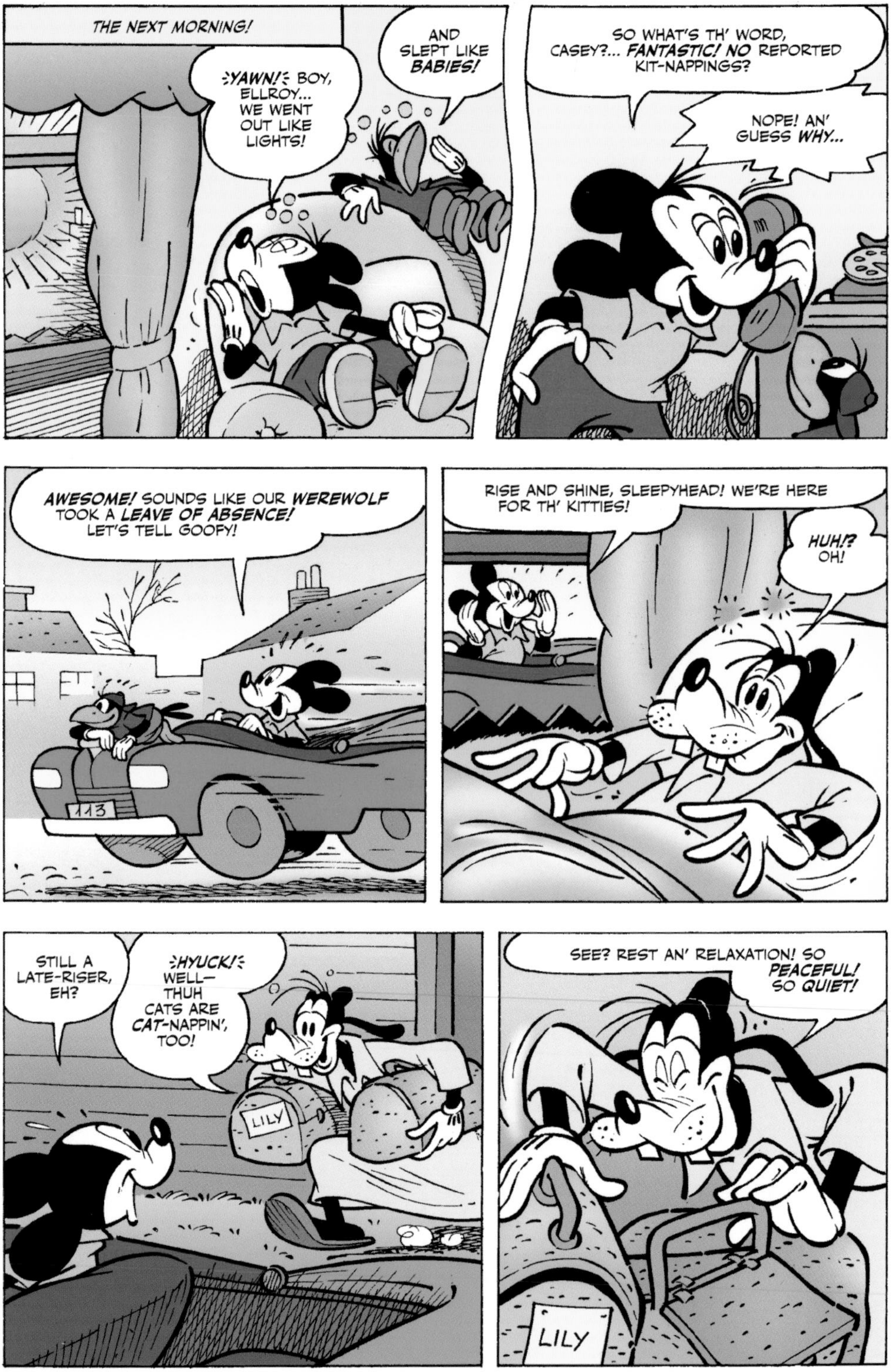
THE NEXT MORNING!
:YAWN!: BOY, ELLROY... WE WENT OUT LIKE LIGHTS!
AND SLEPT LIKE BABIES!
SO WHAT'S TH' WORD, CASEY?... FANTASTIC! NO REPORTED KIT-NAPPINGS?
NOPE! AN' GUESS WHY...
AWESOME! SOUNDS LIKE OUR WEREWOLF TOOK A LEAVE OF ABSENCE! LET'S TELL GOOFY!
113
RISE AND SHINE, SLEEPYHEAD! WE'RE HERE FOR TH' KITTIES!
HUH!? OH!
STILL A LATE-RISER, EH?
:HYUCK!: WELL— THUH CATS ARE CAT-NAPPIN', TOO!
LILY
SEE? REST AN' RELAXATION! SO PEACEFUL! SO QUIET!
LILY

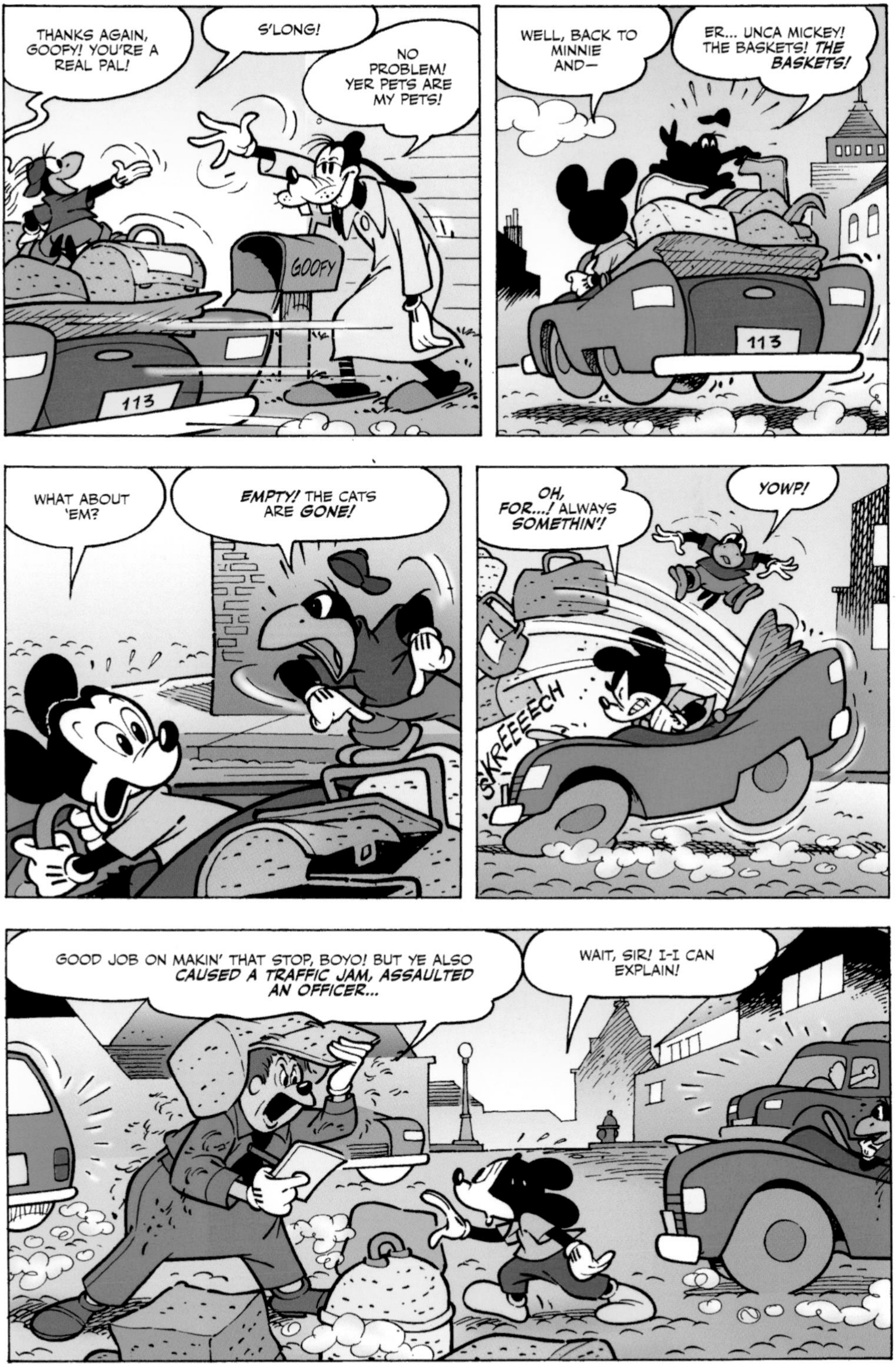
THANKS AGAIN, GOOFY! YOU'RE A REAL PAL!
S'LONG!
NO PROBLEM! YER PETS ARE MY PETS!
GOOFY
113
WELL, BACK TO MINNIE AND—
ER... UNCA MICKEY! THE BASKETS! THE BASKETS!
113
WHAT ABOUT 'EM?
EMPTY! THE CATS ARE GONE!
OH, FOR...! ALWAYS SOMETHIN'!
YOWP!
SKREEEEECH
GOOD JOB ON MAKIN' THAT STOP, BOYO! BUT YE ALSO CAUSED A TRAFFIC JAM, ASSAULTED AN OFFICER...
WAIT, SIR! I-I CAN EXPLAIN!

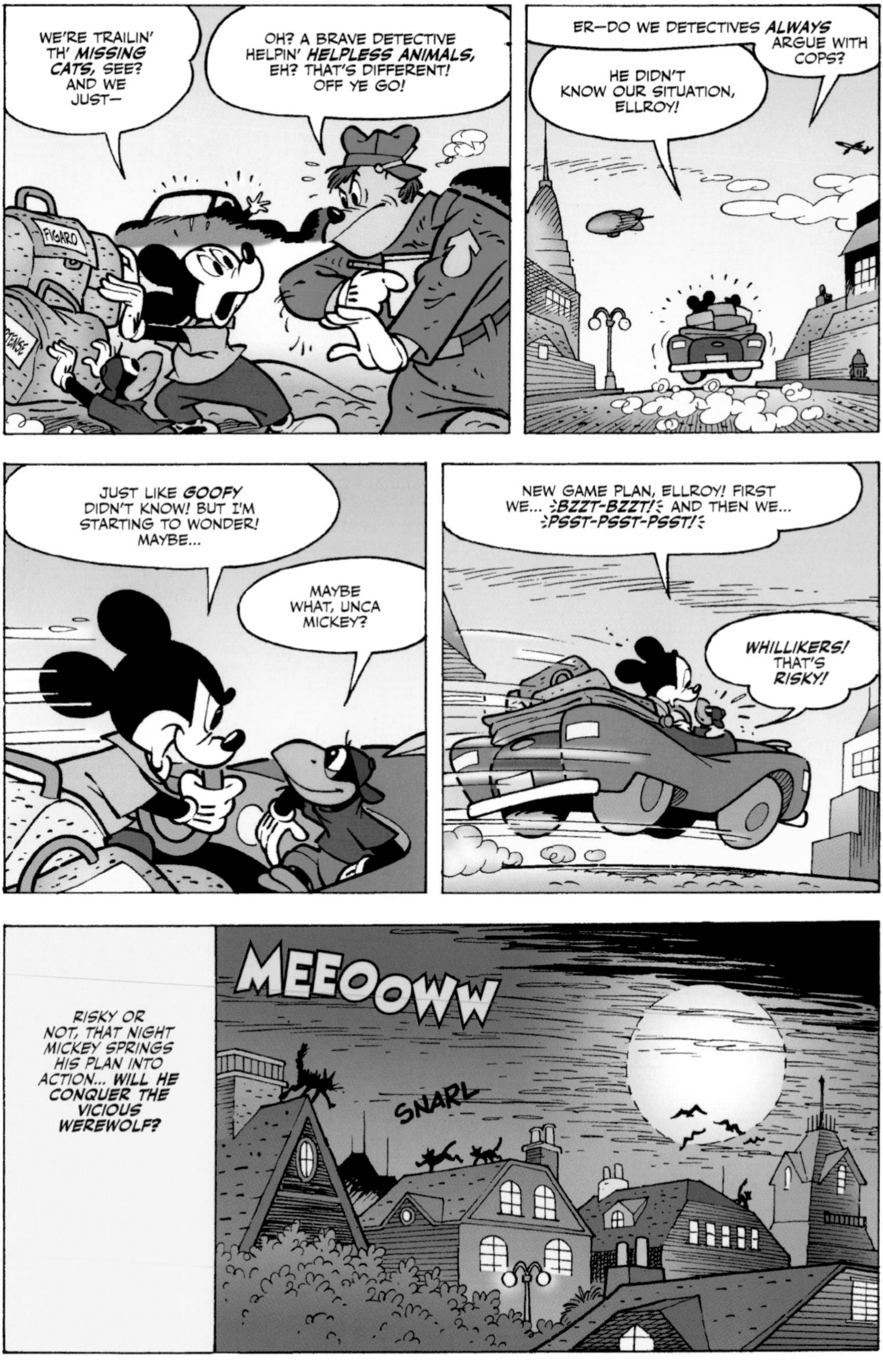
WE'RE TRAILIN' TH' MISSING CATS, SEE? AND WE JUST—
OH? A BRAVE DETECTIVE HELPIN' HELPLESS ANIMALS, EH? THAT'S DIFFERENT! OFF YE GO!
FIGARO
ER—DO WE DETECTIVES ALWAYS ARGUE WITH COPS?
HE DIDN'T KNOW OUR SITUATION, ELLROY!
JUST LIKE GOOFY DIDN'T KNOW! BUT I'M STARTING TO WONDER! MAYBE...
MAYBE WHAT, UNCA MICKEY?
NEW GAME PLAN, ELLROY! FIRST WE... BZZT-BZZT! AND THEN WE... PSST-PSST-PSST!
WHILLIKERS! THAT'S RISKY!
RISKY OR NOT, THAT NIGHT MICKEY SPRINGS HIS PLAN INTO ACTION... WILL HE CONQUER THE VICIOUS WEREWOLF?
MEEOOWW
SNARL

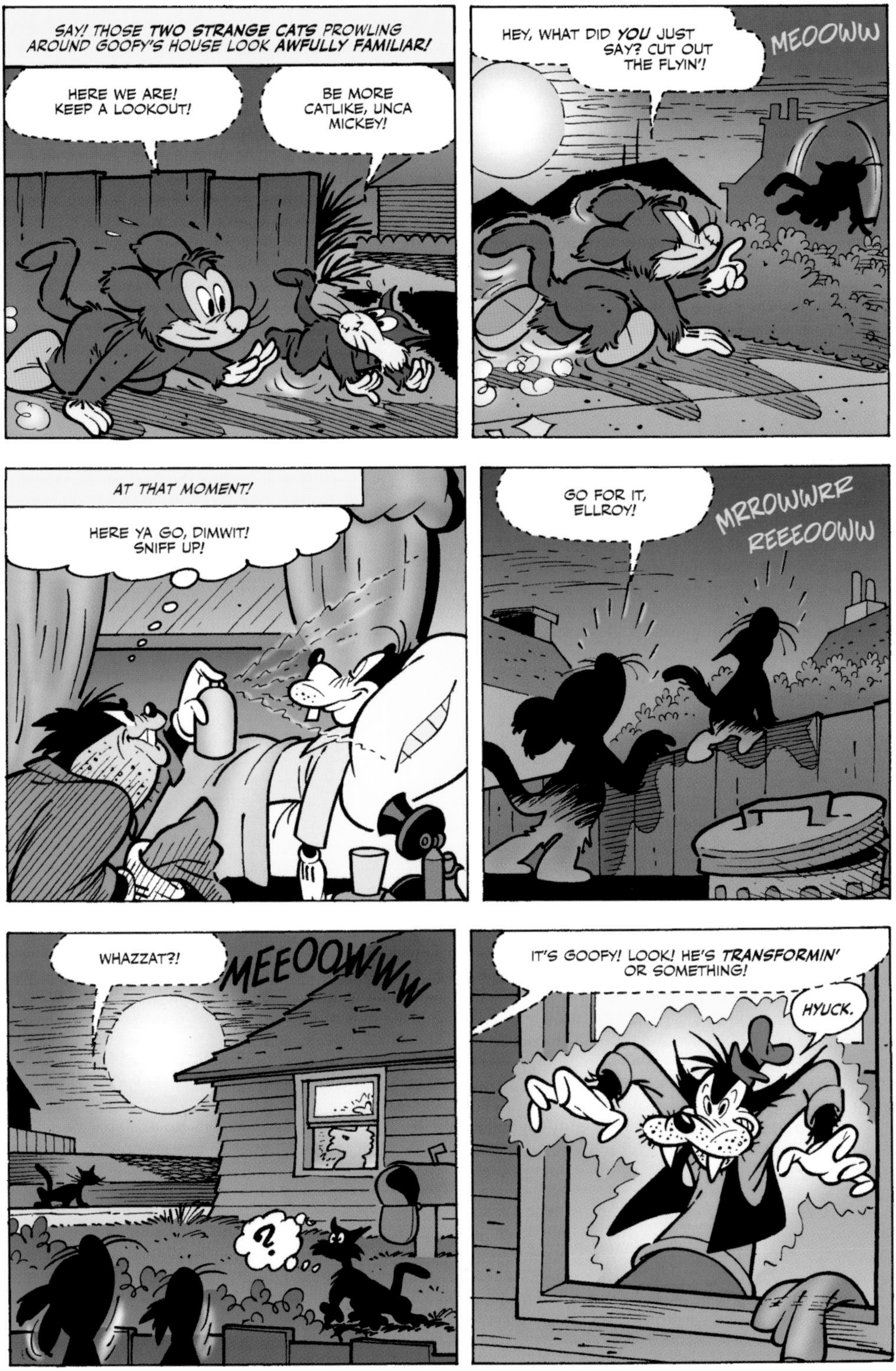
SAY! THOSE **TWO STRANGE CATS** PROWLING AROUND GOOFY'S HOUSE LOOK **AWFULLY FAMILIAR!**
HERE WE ARE! KEEP A LOOKOUT!
BE MORE CATLIKE, UNCA MICKEY!
HEY, WHAT DID **YOU** JUST SAY? CUT OUT THE FLYIN'!
MEOOWW
AT THAT MOMENT!
HERE YA GO, DIMWIT! SNIFF UP!
GO FOR IT, ELLROY!
MRROWWRR
REEEOOWW
WHAZZAT?!
MEEOOWWW
?
IT'S GOOFY! LOOK! HE'S **TRANSFORMIN'** OR SOMETHING!
HYUCK.

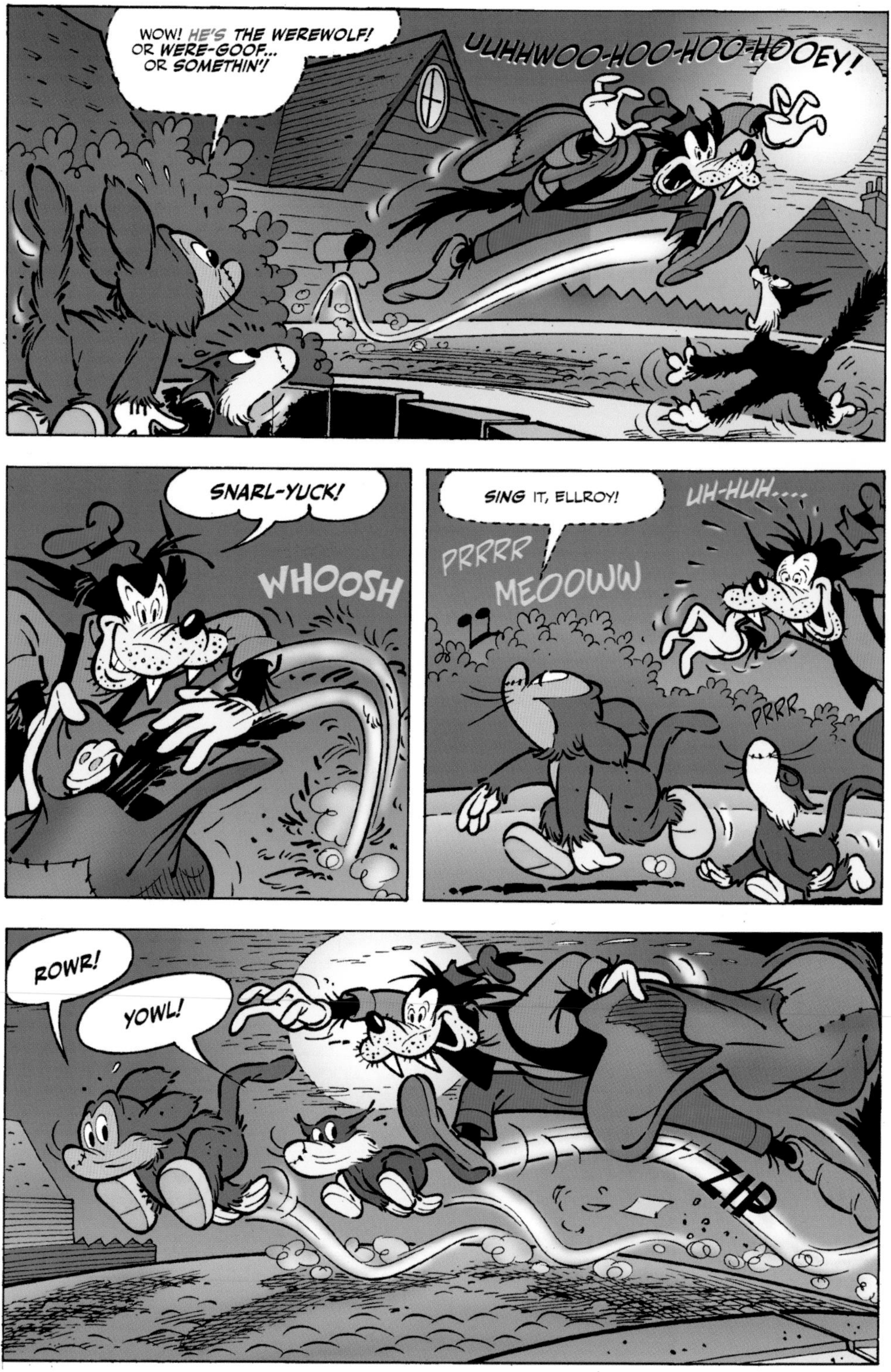
WOW! HE'S THE WEREWOLF! OR WERE-GOOF... OR SOMETHIN'!
UUHHWOO-HOO-HOO-HOOEY!
SNARL-YUCK!
WHOOSH
SING IT, ELLROY!
UH-HUH....
PRRRR
MEOOWW
PRRR
ROWR!
YOWL!
ZIP

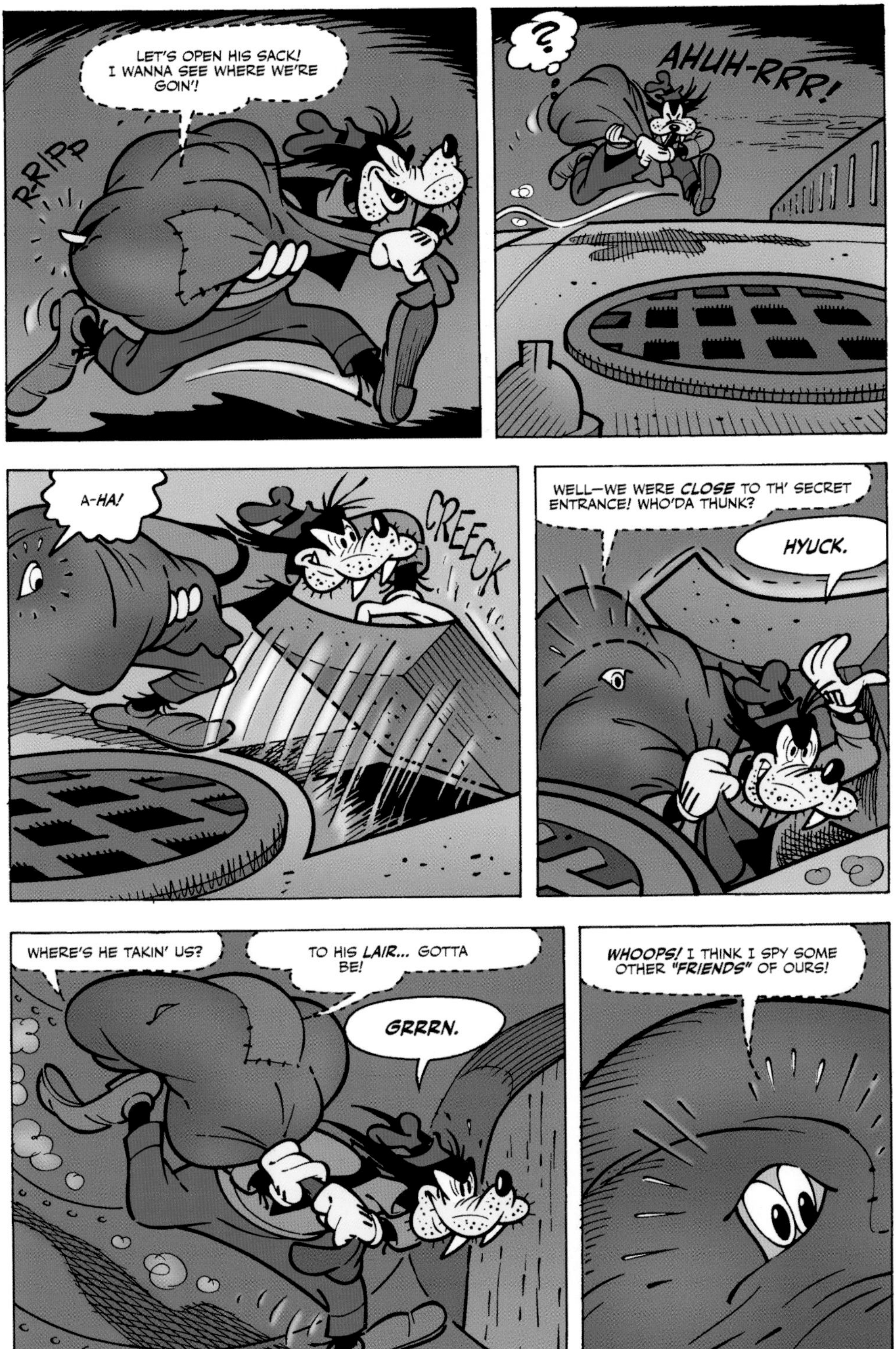
LET'S OPEN HIS SACK! I WANNA SEE WHERE WE'RE GOIN'!
R-RIPP
?
AHUH-RRR!
A-HA!
CREECK
WELL—WE WERE CLOSE TO TH' SECRET ENTRANCE! WHO'DA THUNK?
HYUCK.
WHERE'S HE TAKIN' US?
TO HIS LAIR... GOTTA BE!
GRRRN.
WHOOPS! I THINK I SPY SOME OTHER "FRIENDS" OF OURS!

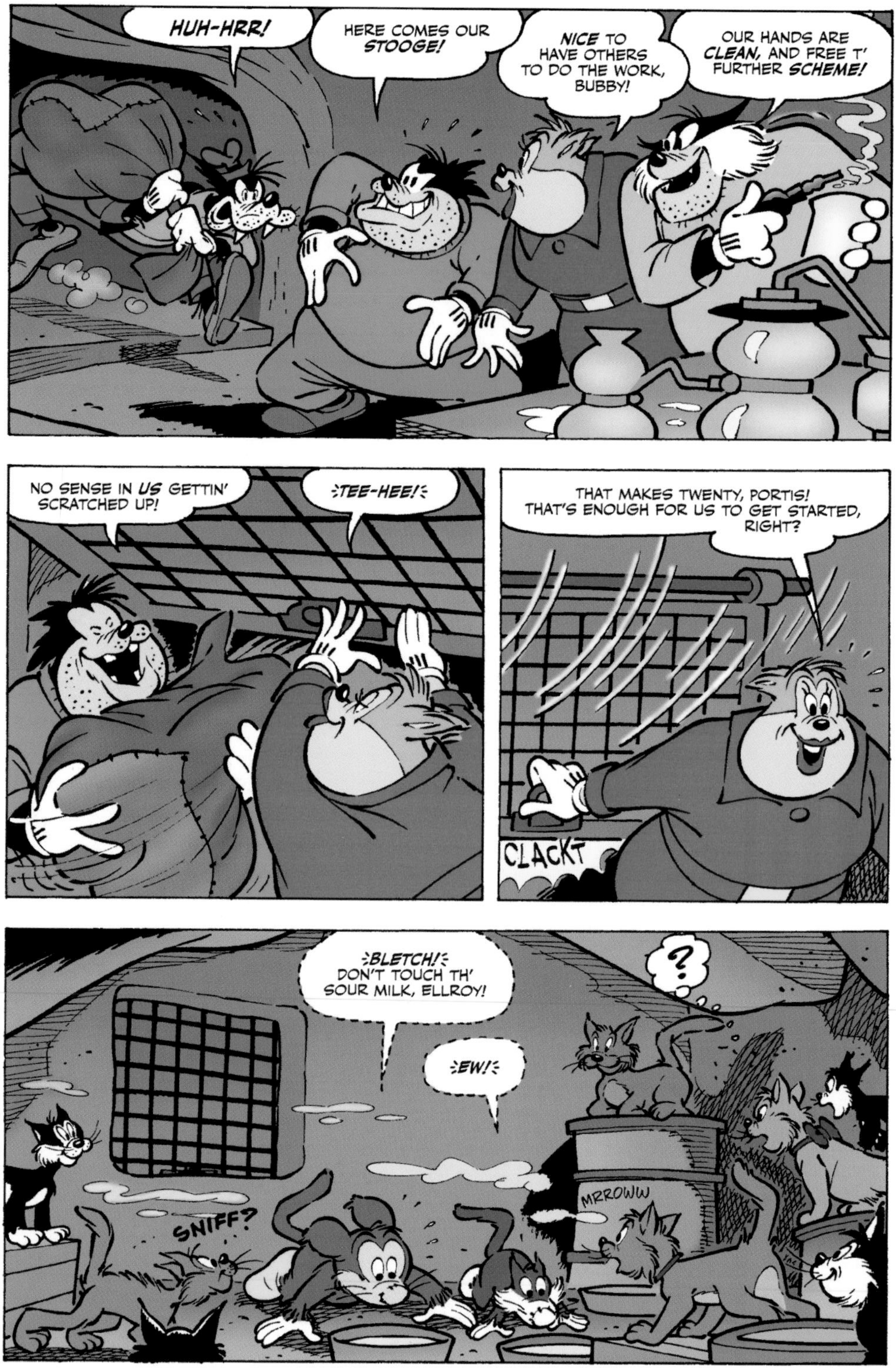
HUH-HRR!
HERE COMES OUR STOOGE!
NICE TO HAVE OTHERS TO DO THE WORK, BUBBY!
OUR HANDS ARE CLEAN, AND FREE T' FURTHER SCHEME!
NO SENSE IN US GETTIN' SCRATCHED UP!
TEE-HEE!
THAT MAKES TWENTY, PORTIS! THAT'S ENOUGH FOR US TO GET STARTED, RIGHT?
CLACKT
BLETCH! DON'T TOUCH TH' SOUR MILK, ELLROY!
?
EW!
SNIFF?
MRROWW

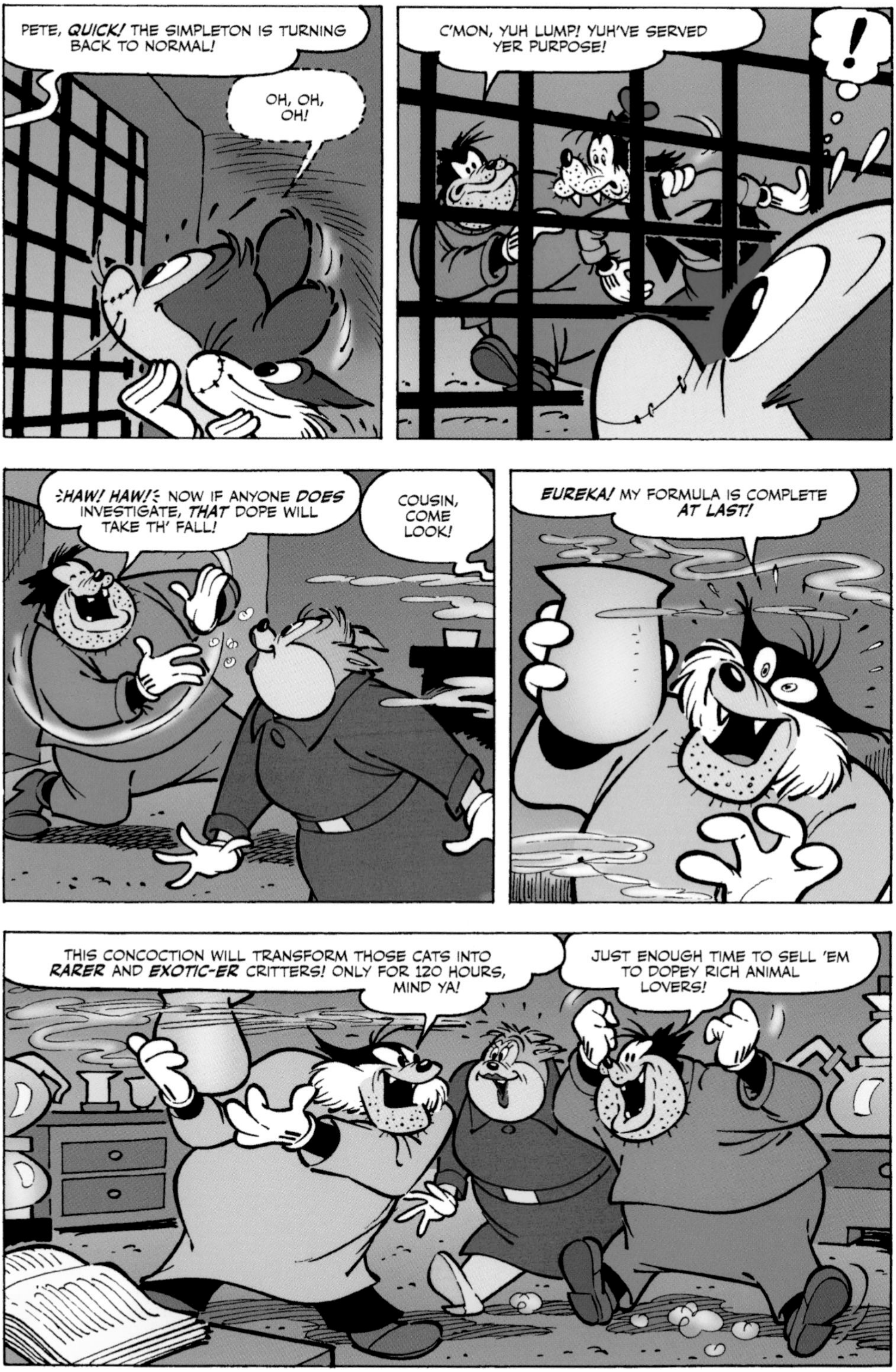
PETE, QUICK! THE SIMPLETON IS TURNING BACK TO NORMAL!
OH, OH, OH!
C'MON, YUH LUMP! YUH'VE SERVED YER PURPOSE!
!
HAW! HAW! NOW IF ANYONE DOES INVESTIGATE, THAT DOPE WILL TAKE TH' FALL!
COUSIN, COME LOOK!
EUREKA! MY FORMULA IS COMPLETE AT LAST!
THIS CONCOCTION WILL TRANSFORM THOSE CATS INTO RARER AND EXOTIC-ER CRITTERS! ONLY FOR 120 HOURS, MIND YA!
JUST ENOUGH TIME TO SELL 'EM TO DOPEY RICH ANIMAL LOVERS!

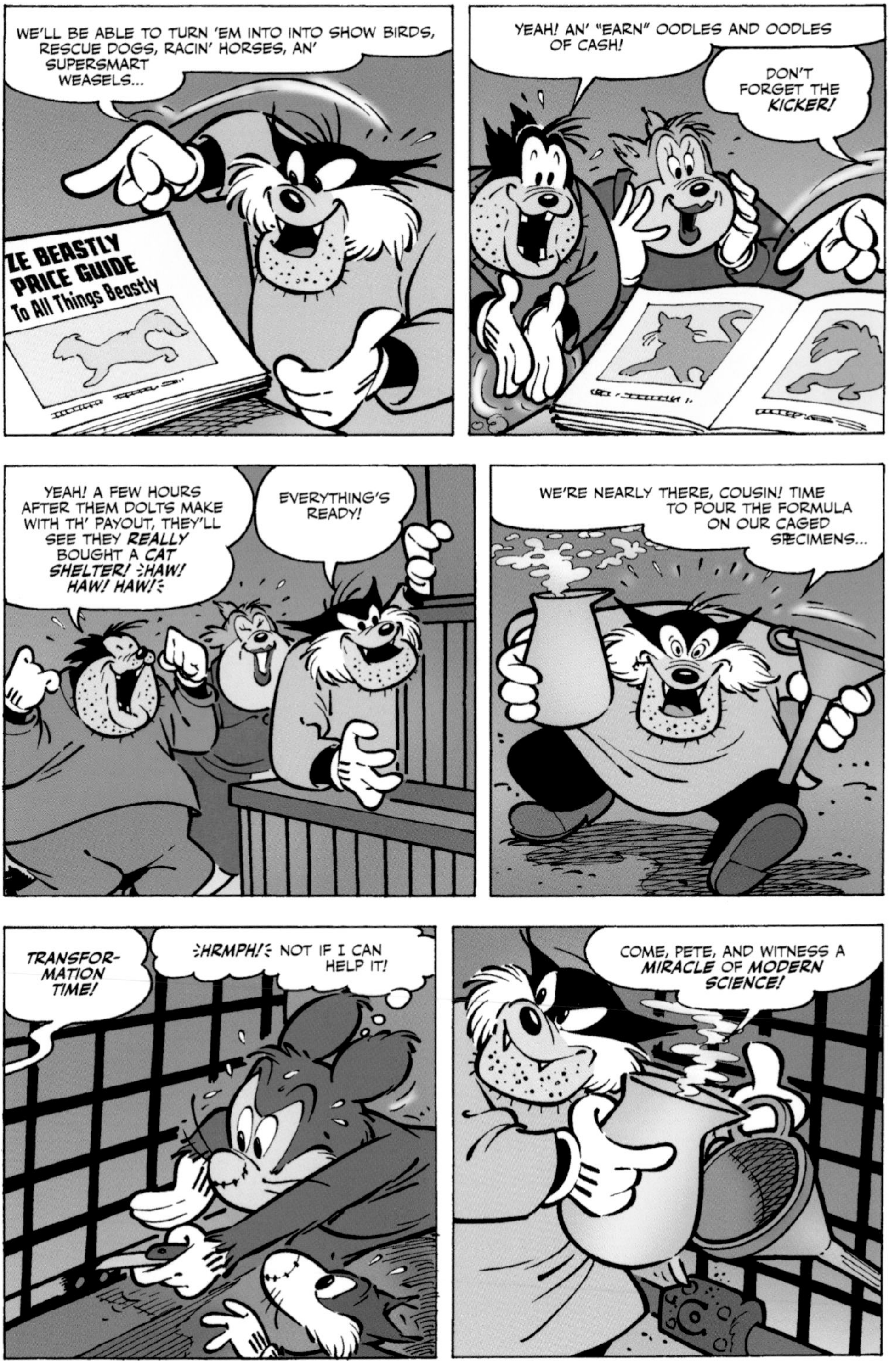
WE'LL BE ABLE TO TURN 'EM INTO INTO SHOW BIRDS, RESCUE DOGS, RACIN' HORSES, AN' SUPERSMART WEASELS...
ZE BEASTLY PRICE GUIDE To All Things Beastly
YEAH! AN' "EARN" OODLES AND OODLES OF CASH!
DON'T FORGET THE KICKER!
YEAH! A FEW HOURS AFTER THEM DOLTS MAKE WITH TH' PAYOUT, THEY'LL SEE THEY REALLY BOUGHT A CAT SHELTER! HAW! HAW! HAW!
EVERYTHING'S READY!
WE'RE NEARLY THERE, COUSIN! TIME TO POUR THE FORMULA ON OUR CAGED SPECIMENS...
TRANSFORMATION TIME!
HRMPH! NOT IF I CAN HELP IT!
COME, PETE, AND WITNESS A MIRACLE OF MODERN SCIENCE!

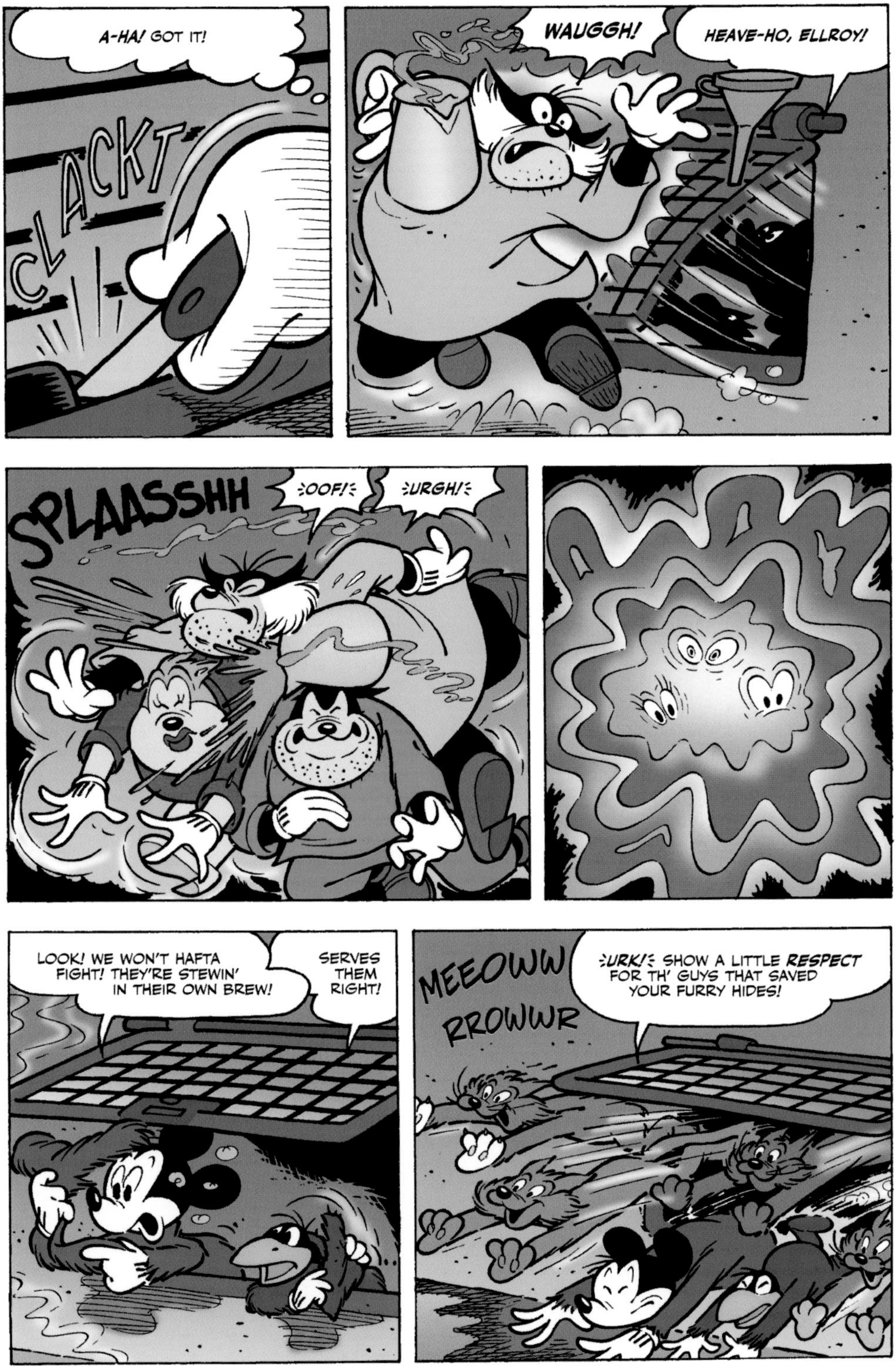
A-HA! GOT IT!
CLACKT
WAUGGH!
HEAVE-HO, ELLROY!
SPLAASSHH
OOF!
URGH!
LOOK! WE WON'T HAFTA FIGHT! THEY'RE STEWIN' IN THEIR OWN BREW!
SERVES THEM RIGHT!
MEEOWW
RROWWR
URK! SHOW A LITTLE RESPECT FOR TH' GUYS THAT SAVED YOUR FURRY HIDES!

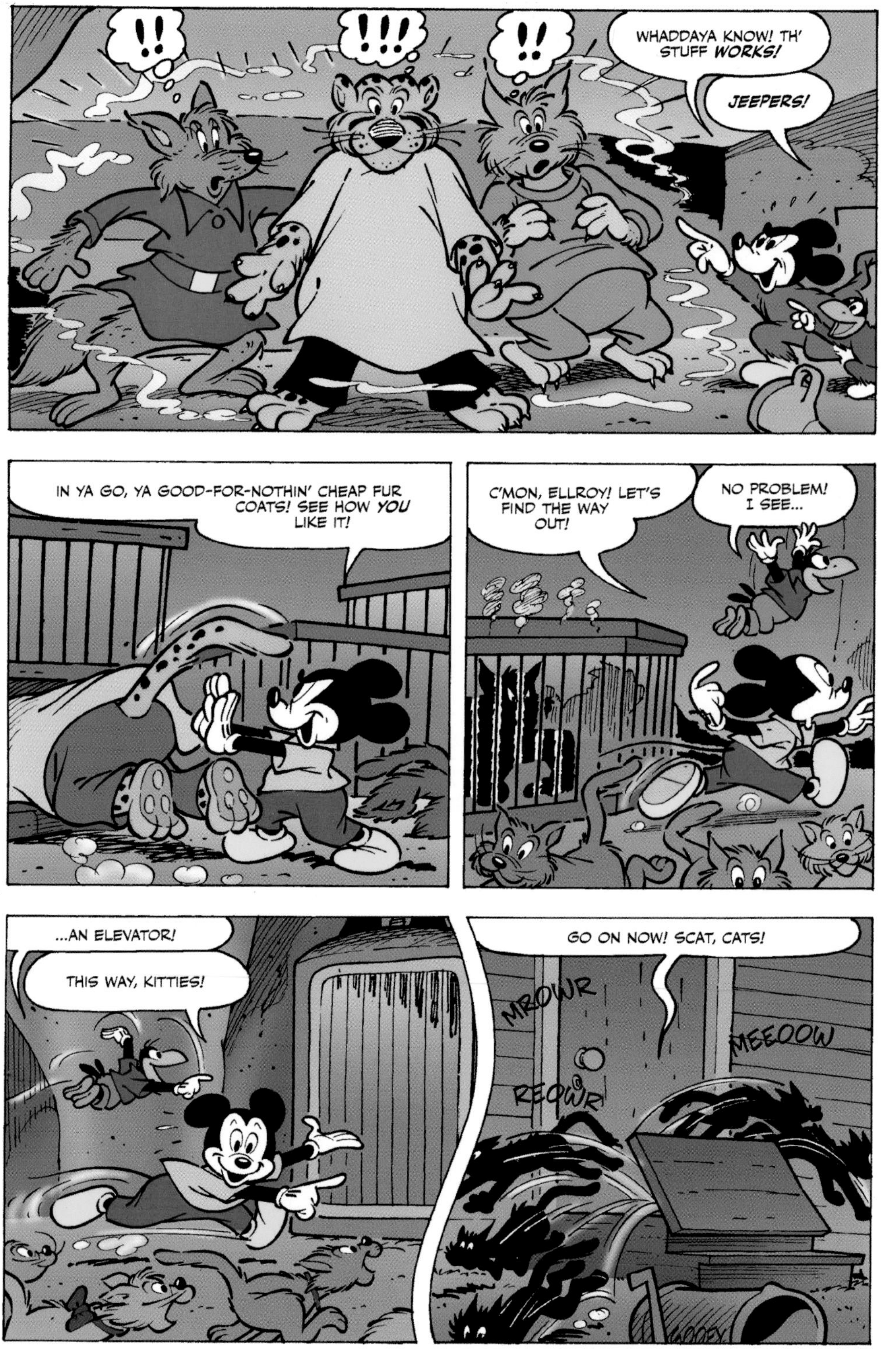
!!
!!!
!!
WHADDAYA KNOW! TH' STUFF WORKS!
JEEPERS!
IN YA GO, YA GOOD-FOR-NOTHIN' CHEAP FUR COATS! SEE HOW YOU LIKE IT!
C'MON, ELLROY! LET'S FIND THE WAY OUT!
NO PROBLEM! I SEE...
...AN ELEVATOR!
THIS WAY, KITTIES!
GO ON NOW! SCAT, CATS!
MROWR
MEEOOW
REOWR

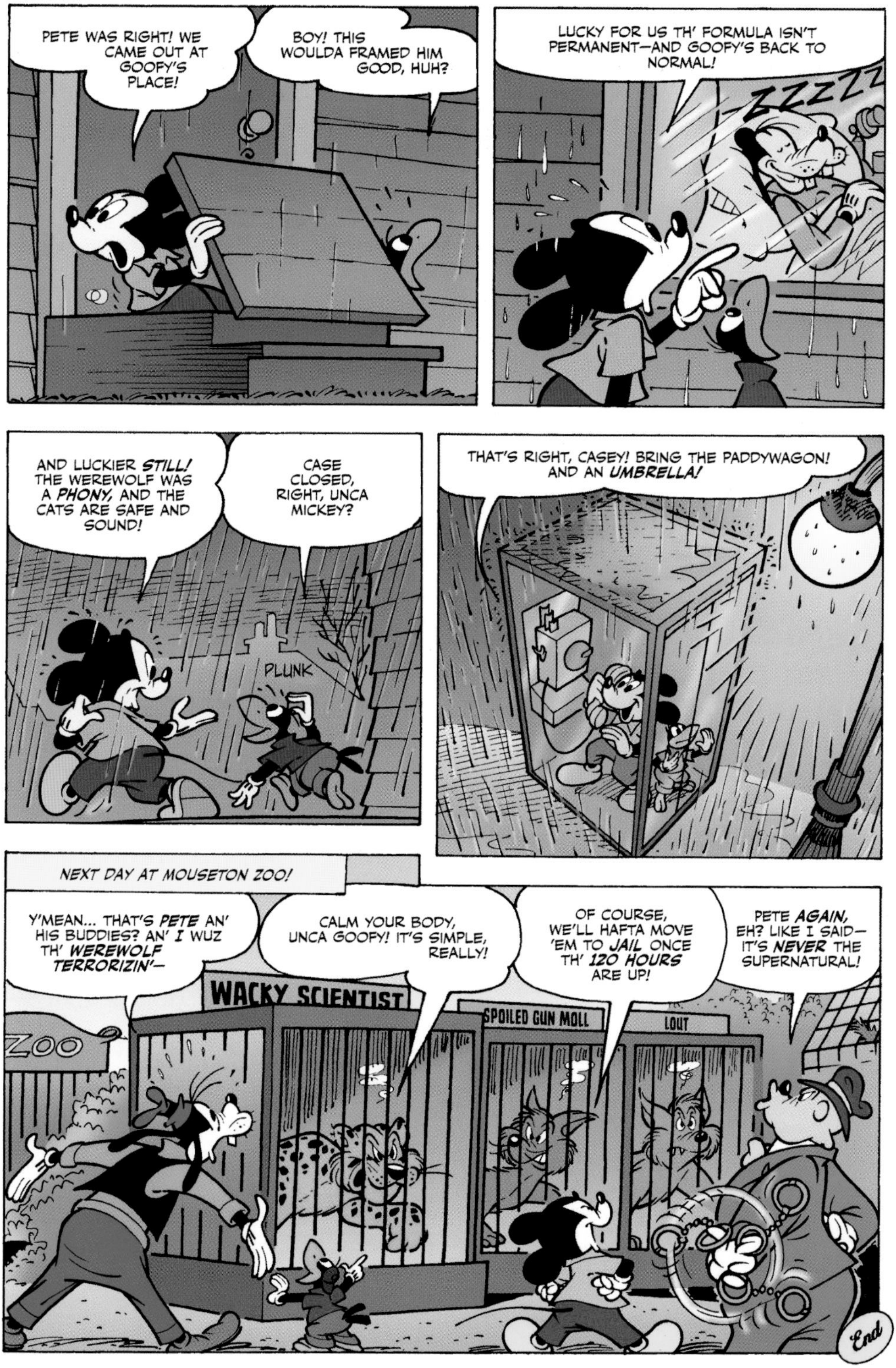
PETE WAS RIGHT! WE CAME OUT AT GOOFY'S PLACE!
BOY! THIS WOULDA FRAMED HIM GOOD, HUH?
LUCKY FOR US TH' FORMULA ISN'T PERMANENT—AND GOOFY'S BACK TO NORMAL!
ZZZZZ
AND LUCKIER *STILL!* THE WEREWOLF WAS A *PHONY,* AND THE CATS ARE SAFE AND SOUND!
CASE CLOSED, RIGHT, UNCA MICKEY?
PLUNK
THAT'S RIGHT, CASEY! BRING THE PADDYWAGON! AND AN *UMBRELLA!*
NEXT DAY AT MOUSETON ZOO!
Y'MEAN... THAT'S *PETE* AN' HIS BUDDIES? AN' *I* WUZ TH' *WEREWOLF TERRORIZIN'*—
CALM YOUR BODY, UNCA GOOFY! IT'S SIMPLE, REALLY!
OF COURSE, WE'LL HAFTA MOVE 'EM TO *JAIL* ONCE TH' *120 HOURS* ARE UP!
PETE *AGAIN,* EH? LIKE I SAID—IT'S *NEVER* THE SUPERNATURAL!
WACKY SCIENTIST
SPOILED GUN MOLL
LOUT
ZOO
End

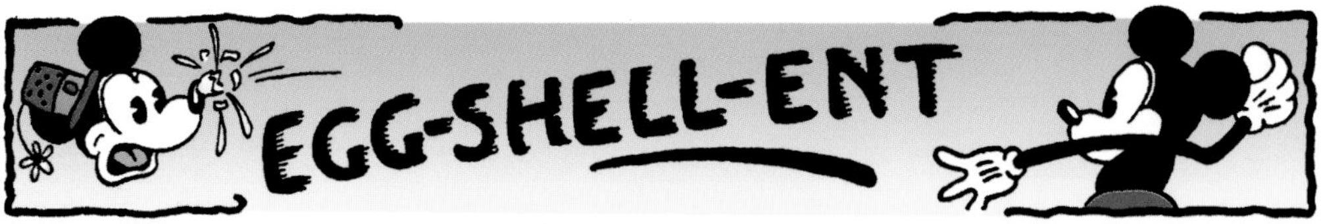
EGG-SHELL-ENT

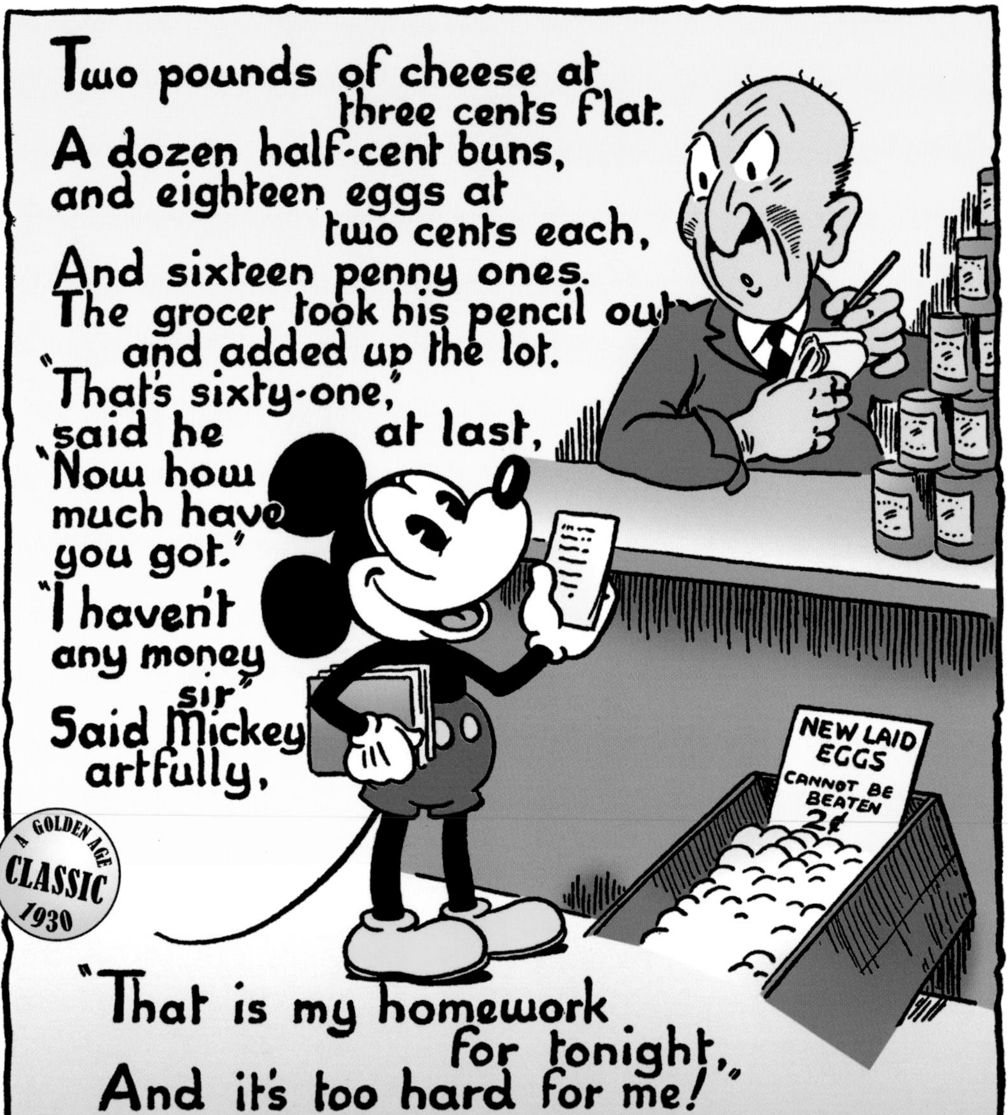
Two pounds of cheese at three cents flat.
A dozen half-cent buns, and eighteen eggs at two cents each,
And sixteen penny ones.
The grocer took his pencil out and added up the lot.
"That's sixty-one," said he at last,
"Now how much have you got."
"I haven't any money sir," Said Mickey artfully,
NEW LAID EGGS CANNOT BE BEATEN 2¢
A GOLDEN AGE CLASSIC 1930
"That is my homework for tonight,, And it's too hard for me!"
U MMA 1B16

Originally published in *Mickey Mouse Annual* #1 (United Kingdom, 1930)

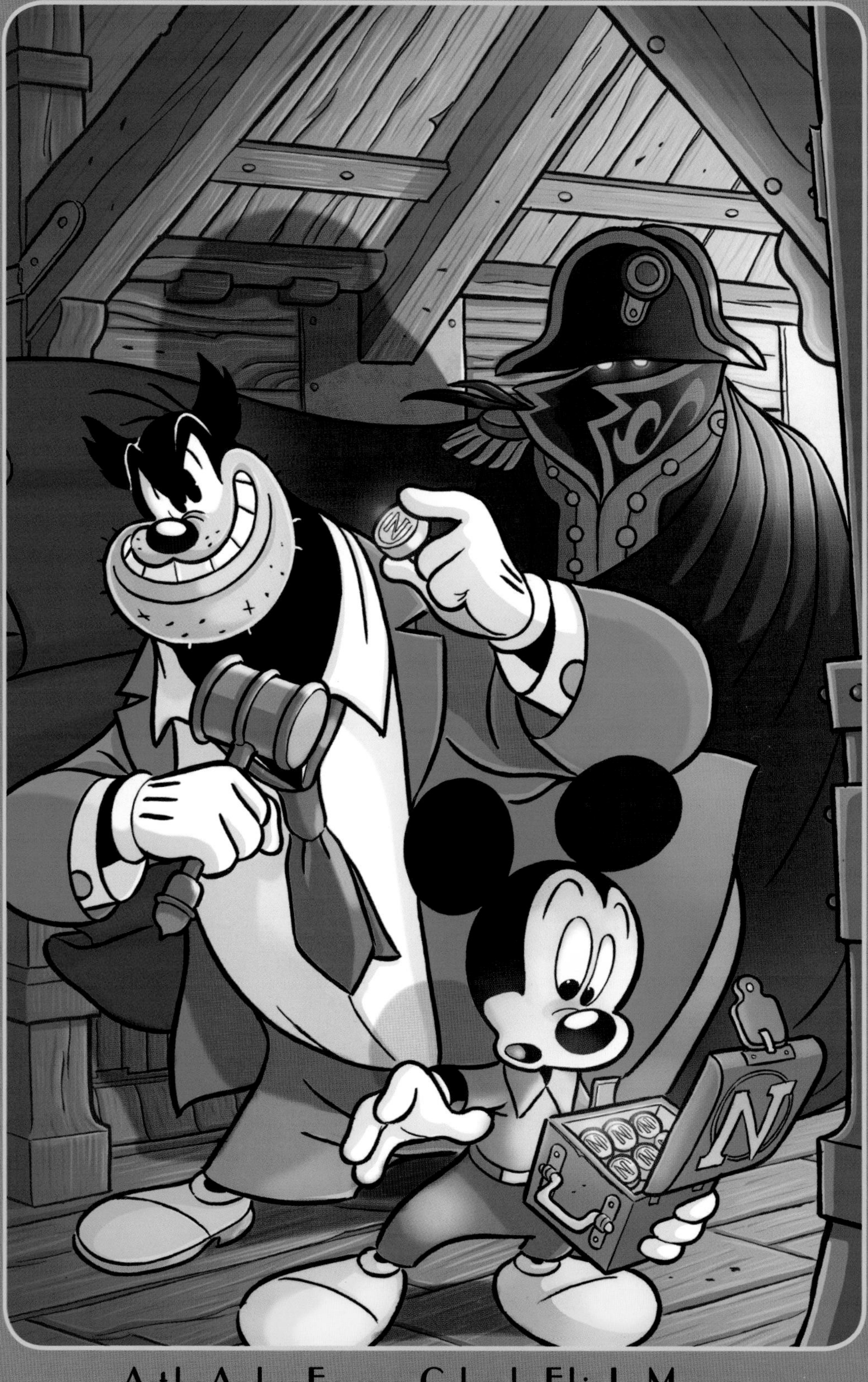

Art by Andrea Freccero, Colors by Fabio Lo Monaco

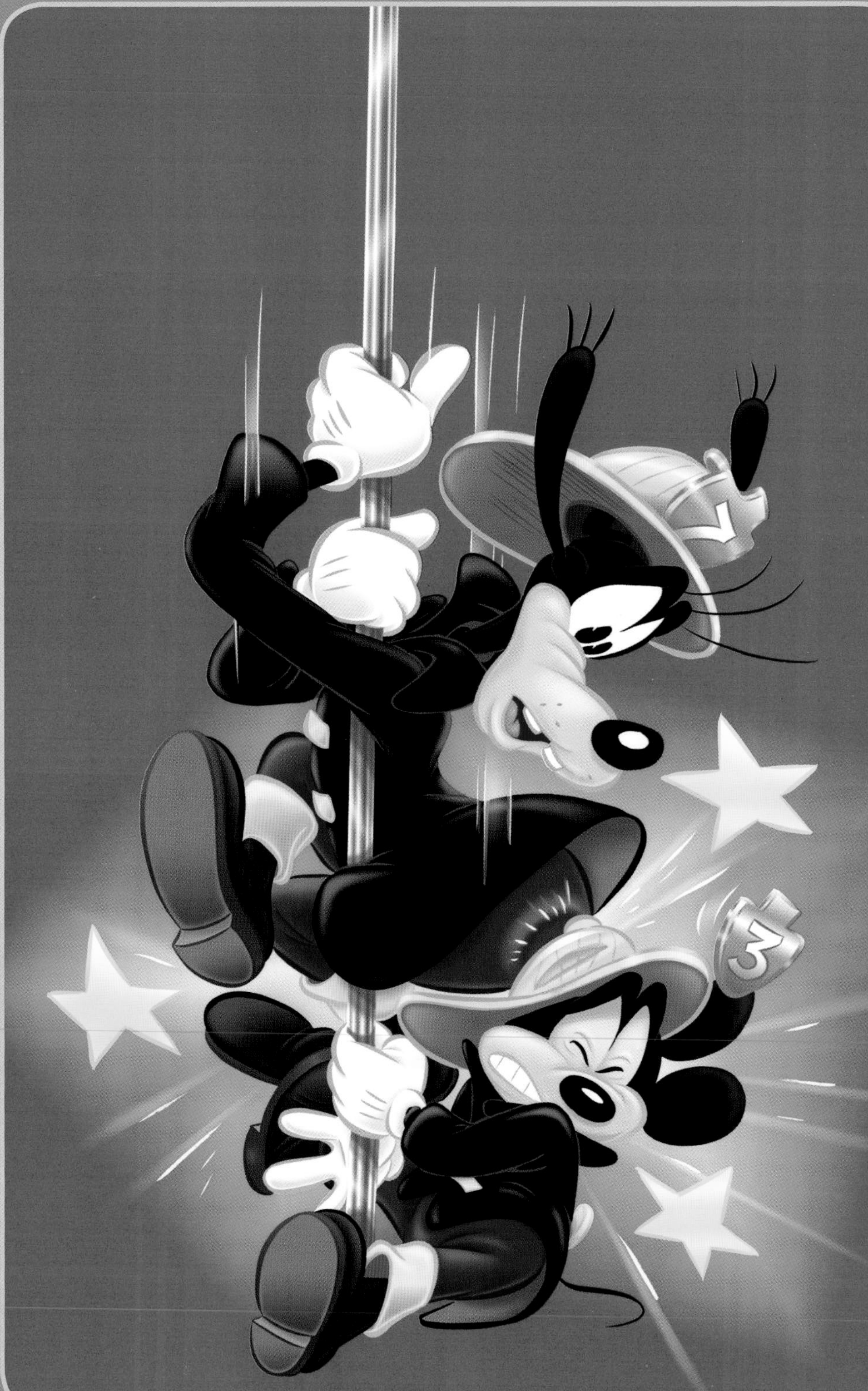

Art by Ulrich Schroeder and Daan Jippes, Colors by Hachette

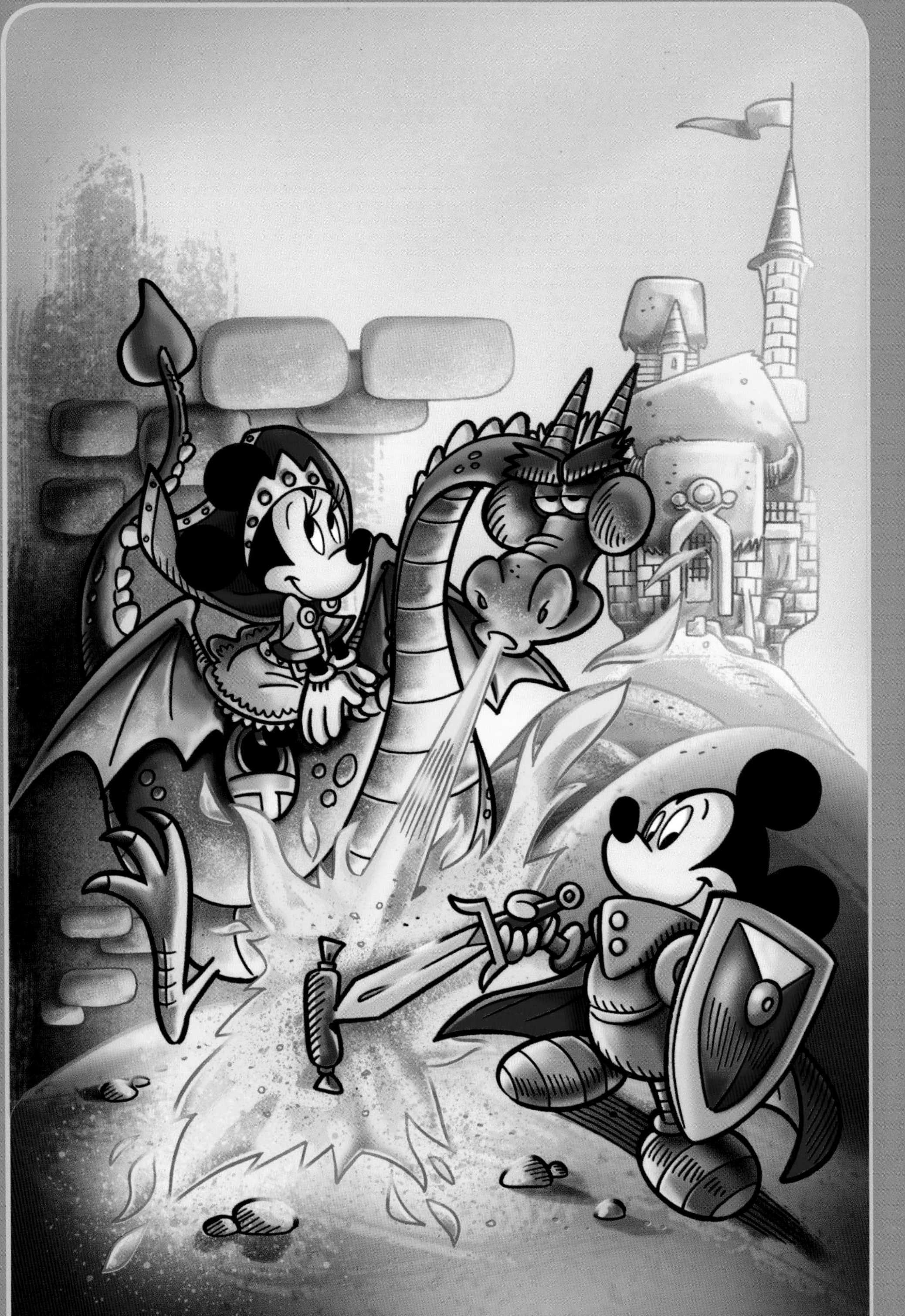

Art by Marco Gervasio, Colors by Marco Colletti

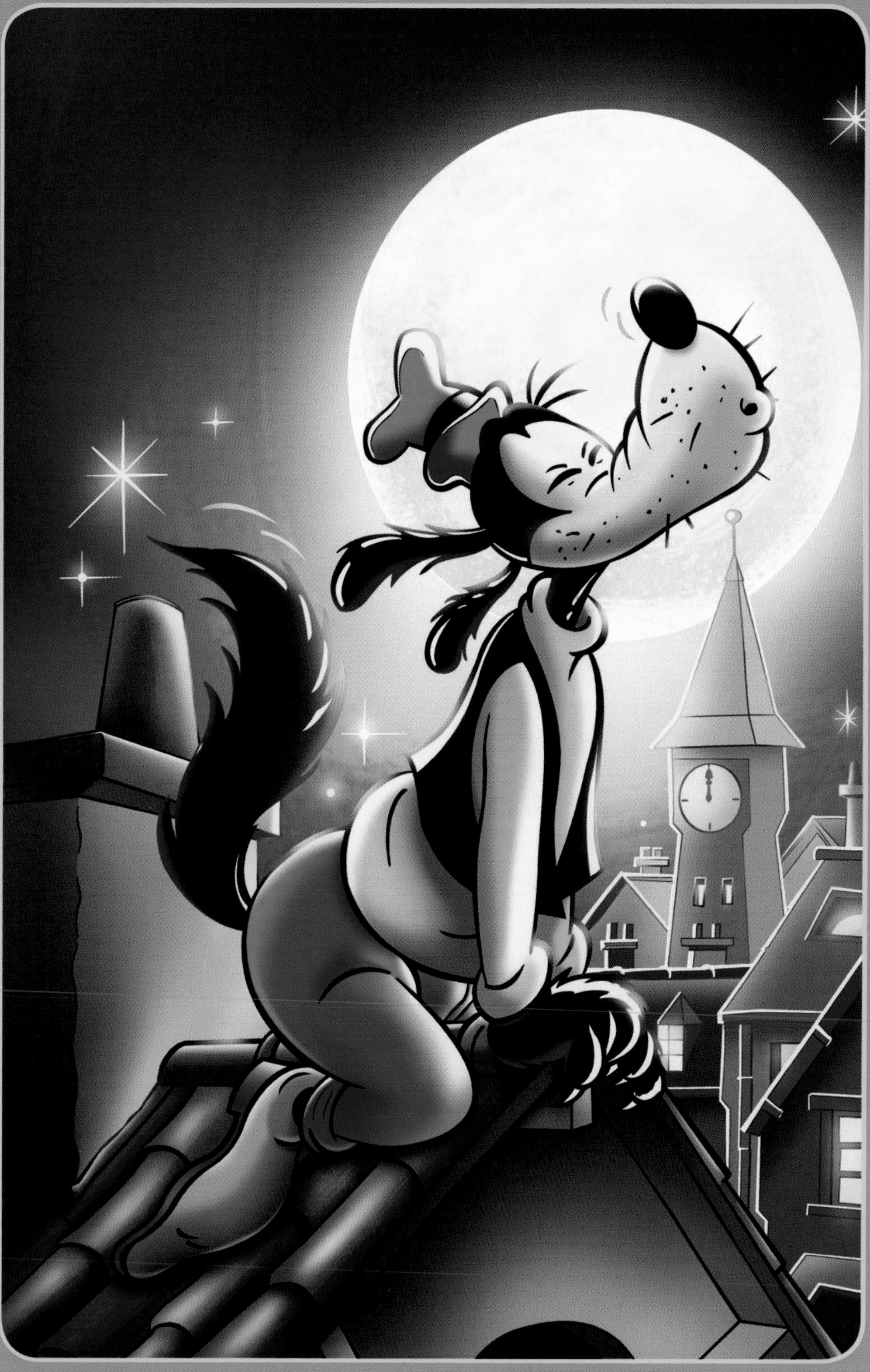

Art by Patrice Croci, Colors by Marco Colletti

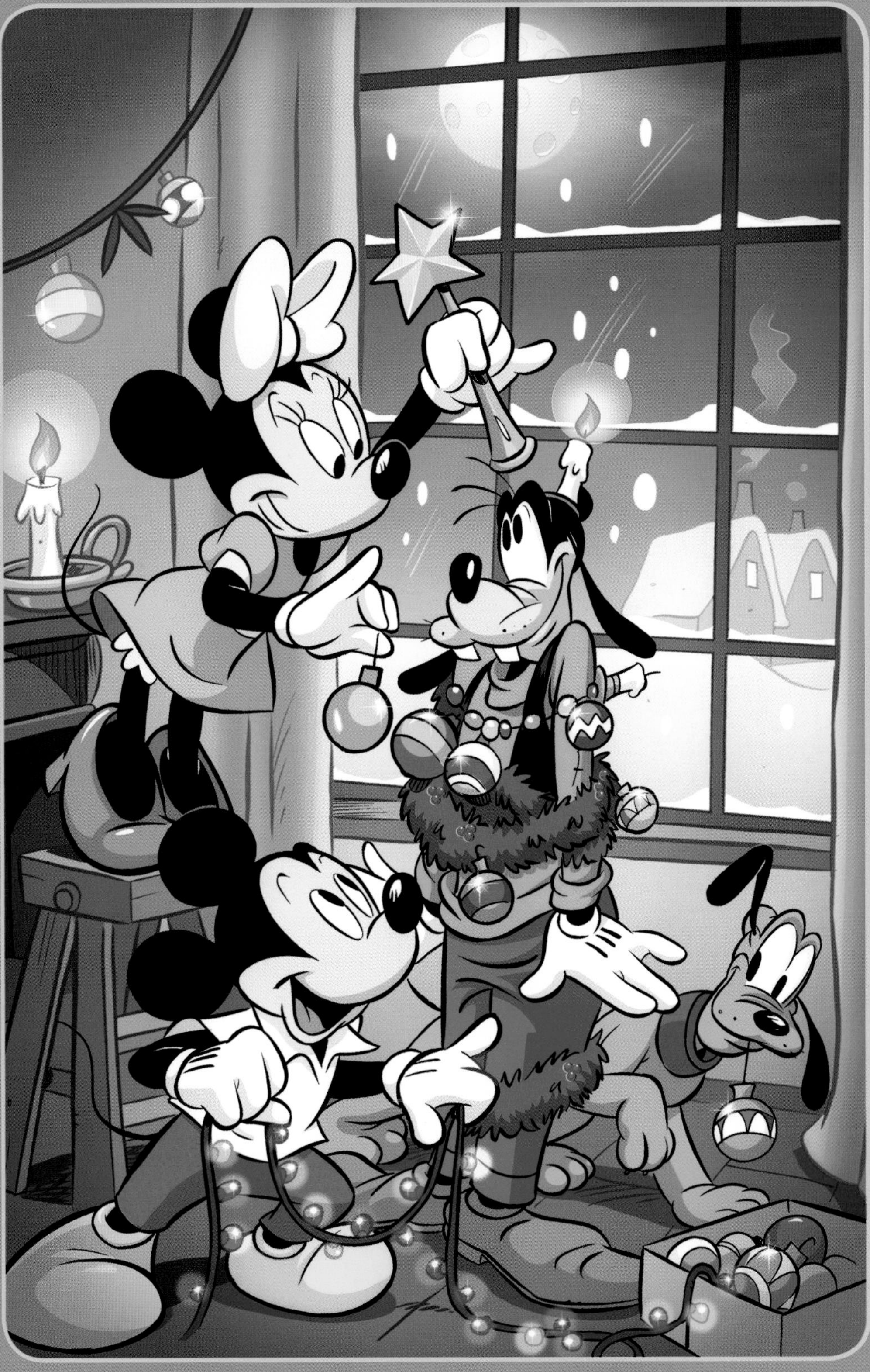

Art by Fabrizio Petrossi, Colors by Ronda Pattison

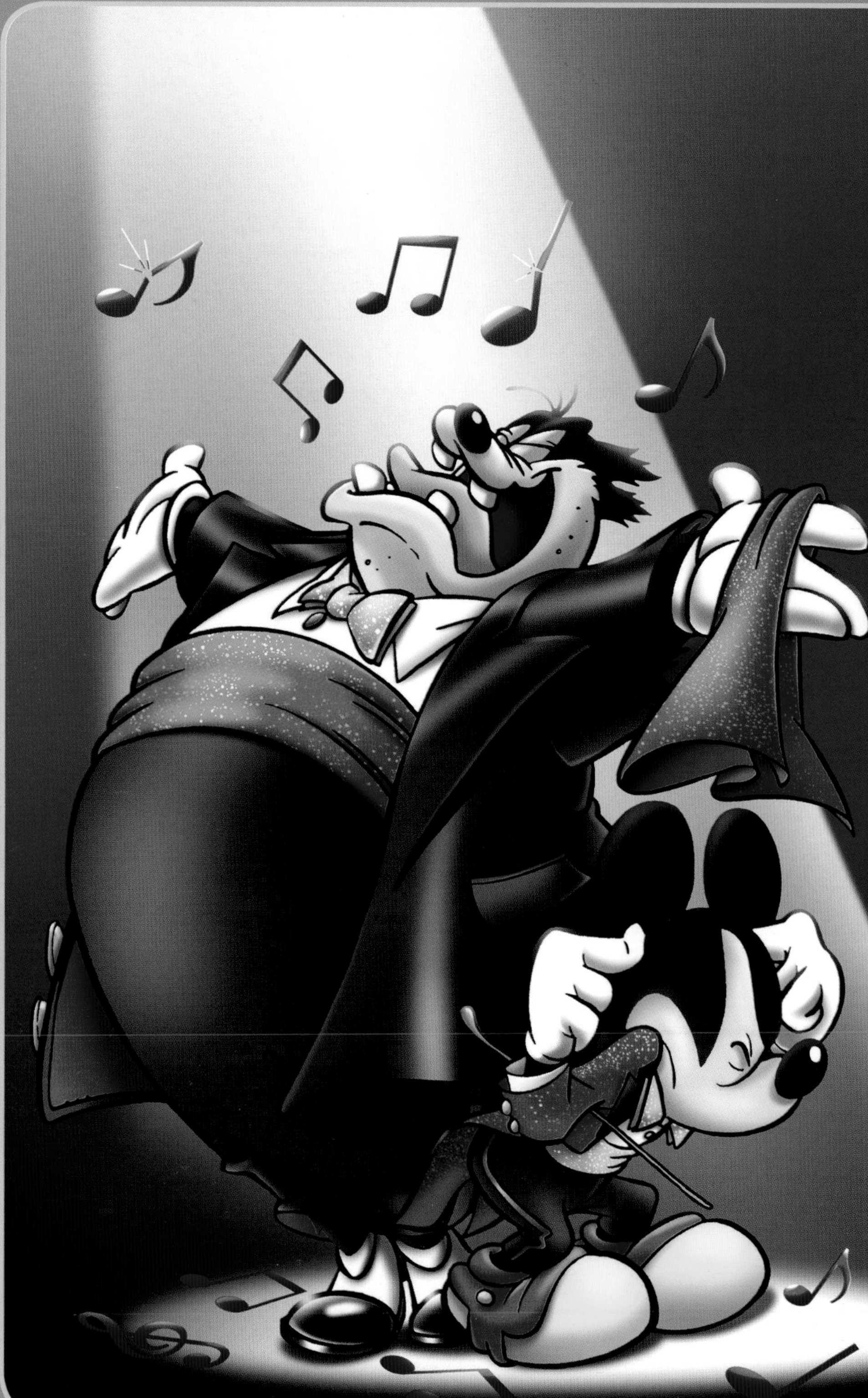

Art by Marco Ghiglione, Colors by Marco Colletti